Corporate Escapades

T.K. AMBERS

STAR SPIRIT ADVENTURES

Edited by Kate Seger

Cover design by Getcovers

Printed in the United States of America in EB Garamond.

Published by Star Spirit Adventures

First edition 2025

Paperback ISBN: 979-8-9878663-9-9

Books by T.K. Ambers

<u>The Runway Dreams Mystery Series:</u>

Runway Dreams: A Pricey Affair

Runway Dreams: A Fox in the Fold

Runway Dreams: Prideful Vengeance

<u>Contemporary Romance:</u>

Corporate Escapades

Dedication

In the middle of writing this novel, I experienced not one, but multiple heart-wrenching losses. The kind of loss that sucks the air out of the room and makes you feel as if you may never know how to breathe again. Am I forever changed? In many ways, yes, but I'm a survivor and as a survivor, I dedicate this story to those who left my life beginning in 2021, and to those of you who loved them, too. I send *Huggles* your way, as I understand how it feels. Though they have left us, their memory will live on.

Corporate Escapades

T.K. AMBERS

Chapter One

Without a cloud in the sky, the sun beat down, unforgivingly, on Flores, Nevada, scorching the already cracked desert floor. Thirty minutes away, in Las Vegas, the heavens opened up, dumping an unceremonious amount of water on the streets, carrying away a year's worth of grime, and anything else that got in its way. On any other day, Paris DeMarcé would have gladly taken the heat over the rain, but today wasn't any other day. It was the first anniversary of the worst day of Paris's life.

Paris brushed a bead of sweat from her forehead and pushed back her long wavy black hair. Glancing around the Sense of Adventure boardroom, she reached for her purse under the table and pulled a bottle of Percocet from its cluttered depths. Keeping her gaze on the client, her hands shook as she fumbled with the safety cap. Her eyes swept the room once more before popping a pill into her mouth.

Brothers Vic and Jack Alarie sat next to Paris at the table. Their clients sat across from them as they discussed the ins and outs of their upcoming nuptials. Jack's brown eyes widened as he tried to keep up with the conversation. The entire scenario was too much for the tall, gangly teenager, who'd rather be playing video games than spending a day shadowing his older brother.

"That's the bulk of it, right, Paris?" asked Vic, his piercing blue eyes locking onto hers. "Did I miss anything?"

Paris's teeth dug into her bottom lip. Taking a deep breath, she slowly let it out. She hadn't heard a word of their conversation. "Yeah. I think you covered everything," she lied.

Like a robot, Paris nodded her head to Vic's closing statements. Her heart pounded in her chest. Reaching up, she wiped her brow and began fanning herself with a file folder. Looking around, she again went for the bottle. Her clammy hands slid on the plastic as she wrestled with the cap and nearly dropped it. Waiting for the clients to turn their attention away, she popped another pill into her mouth. Jack watched her out of the corner of his eye.

"Okay, then. We'll see you next week," said Vic, as the couple exited the room.

Paris pushed herself up from her seat and wobbled toward the exit. She wanted to put as much distance between herself and work as possible. She shoved her way past Vic and Jack and fast-walked toward her condo. Entering the elevator, she wiped her eyes and brow. Her chest tightened as her heart thumped out an irregular beat. She jammed her hand into her purse and grabbed the bottle again. This time, the cap flipped into the air and bounced across the floor. Several pills fell into her hand and she tossed them back into her mouth. The bottle was empty. She didn't bother to retrieve the cap. She couldn't breathe, and if she hadn't known better, she would have thought she was drowning in one of the Las Vegas culverts.

When the elevator stopped on her floor, the rampant flood waters floated her out the door and toward her condo. Reaching for her door handle, it seemed to be just beyond her grasp. She didn't care. Letting herself fall backward into a cloud, she felt safe and warm. Best of all, there were no tears, no anger, and no pain. A smile spread across her lips.

"Paris!" she heard an urgent voice in the distance. "Paris!" and then everything turned white.

Jack was there. She could hear him. Thump, thump, thump. Paris could feel something on her chest, but what, she wasn't sure? "Call an ambulance!" she heard him yell. "She's not breathing! You better not die on me!" his voice was shrill. Paris didn't know what all the fuss was for. She felt perfectly fine. She again heard Jack yelling. "Vic, I think I need you to—" he began, and then everything went quiet for a second as a chill crept over her.

"Damn it, Jack!" she heard Vic shout, followed by more thump, thump, thumping. She didn't care. The warm fuzzy feeling had come back and she could see someone waving at her in the distance.

• • • • • • • • • •

Paris, though unconscious, could still hear voices. They were worried she might not wake. Someone mentioned *before the accident*, and Paris's thoughts drifted back in time.

It was the Alarie DeMarcé Group's first Touch a Heart Fest, and Paris was sitting in the dunk tank as her sister, Alli De-Marcé, wound up to throw. She watched the release. The ball whizzed toward her, hitting the front of the tank. "Is that all you've got?" she yelled to her sister. "I've seen toddlers throw better!" Paris laughed. It was all in good fun. The money went to a charity to help children in need of life-saving surgeries.

"I've got two more throws!" Alli yelled back. "I'm gonna get you on one of them." Pausing, Alli pulled her shoulder-length black hair into a ponytail and fastened it in place. "Time to get serious." She smiled radiantly as she wound up for her second throw. This one barely missed the bullseye.

"Nice, but that's not gonna do it!" yelled Paris. "Maybe you should let one of the boys throw for you!"

"No, no," said Alli. "I've got this!" Wrinkling her nose, she wound up for her third throw. On the release, she exhaled and her perfectly straight bangs puffed into the air.

Paris took a deep breath as she prepared for the bench to give way. She plunged into the water and instantly had the air knocked out of her. It was colder than expected. Her entire body prickled with goosebumps. Resurfacing, she choked and sputtered as she pushed her black hair out of her eyes.

"Ha! I gotcha!" yelled Alli as she danced around.

"Laugh it up!" coughed Paris. "You're in here next!"

In the distance, Paris heard a siren, and the cold was again setting in. Someone was squeezing her hand. She heard Vic's muffled voice say, "Don't you dare leave. You get back here and fight, damn it! Do you hear me? You don't get to take the easy way out." His voice went quiet and Paris's brain took her back to another moment in time.

"Next up, we have the lovely Paris DeMarcé. She's the daughter of Mikel and Nicola DeMarcé. Sister to Alli DeMarcé. And, yes, men, she's single. Who wants to start the bidding? Can I get one hundred dollars?"

"One hundred!" yelled a man in a black pin-striped suit.

"Two hundred!" countered Paris's sister.

"Now, can I get three hundred?" asked the auctioneer.

Paris was thrilled to be a part of the date auction, but she'd recently gone through a terrible breakup. She had no desire to date anyone, but the money was for a noble cause, so she swallowed her sadness and did it for the kids.

"Seventeen thousand dollars," said the auctioneer, "to the man in the green fedora."

"Seventy-five thousand," called a voice she recognized all too well.

"Can I get eighty?" called the auctioneer. "Seventy-five thousand, going once. Seventy-five thousand, going twice. Sold! To Mr. Vic Alarie!"

"Paris was shocked. Vic was a giver. There was no doubt about it, but outside of work, they were not friends. Stepping down from

the stage, she met him at the cashier's cage. "Why'd you do that?" she asked quietly.

"I know you're hurting. I don't want you to suffer through some stuffy date. Besides. I planned to make a high bid on the auction either way. We can go to dinner and discuss work or say nothing for all I care. You get a free meal and some peace of mind, knowing your date isn't trying to take you home with them." He looked at her with sincerity in his eyes.

"Thanks," she replied. "You're too kind." Paris's mind faded to black.

"When will she wake up?" asked a muffled voice.

Staring into the light, a figure came into view. Paris's heart swelled with happiness as she recognized the smiling face. "You're here!"

"Paris. You need to wake up. You can't be here. Not yet."

"I don't want to go back," said Paris. "I'm tired and every-thing hurts. I can't do this anymore. I miss you."

"If you don't go back, you'll create the same pain you're feeling for those who love you. You have a lot more work to do. You have other lives to save. Your purpose isn't fulfilled."

The light faded and Paris was again in the dark. She could feel water trickling down her face as her sorrow seeped out.

• • • • • • • • • •

Two days had gone by and Paris had not awoken. Her mother, father, and ex-friend, Mya, sat by her side, waiting. In the early hours of the morning, she mumbled something barely audible.

"What's that, honey?" asked Paris's mother. Her father moved closer and waited.

Mya exhaled, and a tear floated down her cheek. "I think she said Touch a Heart Fest."

Chapter Two

One Year Earlier

"Paris! Open up! Today's the day! Setup for Touch a Heart Fest is about to begin!" Not even the devil himself could wipe the grin from Mya Jones's face. Mya couldn't sit still. The idea of helping others exhilarated her. It was one huge thing she and her best friend, Paris, had in common. She and Paris's sister, Alli, stood in the hallway of the condos where Paris lived. Mya swayed as she waited for her bestie to answer the door. She held a bouquet of balloons in one hand and a carrier of coffee in the other. She nudged Alli, who hit the door buzzer again.

Alli frowned. "You think she's still in bed?" Tapping her foot, she pressed the buzzer two more times.

"She'd better be in there," replied Mya. "She took Mr. Radke and his family out to dinner last night to celebrate their son's engagement."

"Why'd she do that?" Alli asked, her brow furrowed.

"The Radke's have been with us for years. Taking them out for dinner is Paris's way of saying thanks, and a way to gain their son's future business. His wedding will bring in boat-loads of money for the company."

"Does she do things like that often?"

"Yeah," replied Mya. "She loves to schmooze her clients. She genuinely cares about them. While you were away during your freshman year of college, she helped find a bone marrow donor for the Makenzie's daughter, Jenny. Your sister always goes the extra mile."

"It sounds like it. Hopefully, one day, I'll be as big of an asset to our family company as she is."

"I'm sure you will," said Mya. "I mean, you've been away for four years. Writing and hosting sommelier events are not the same as modeling and working in the mailroom. It'll take some time to acclimate yourself, but Paris and I both know you'll do well," she smiled.

"Thanks," said Alli. "It means a lot, knowing you're backing me."

"Always." Turning back to the door, Mya blew her red chin-length hair away from her face. The balloons she held bobbed around, magnetizing her hair. "That girl's too busy taking care of everyone else to take care of herself. You have the key, right? Should we go in?"

Alli nodded and pulled a key from her pocket. Bending toward the door, her shoulder-length black hair swung forward as she pushed it into the lock. She was about to turn the knob when the elevator dinged behind them. The girls turned to see who was approaching.

"Hey!" yelled Paris as she bounced out of the elevator. "What's up?" She wore her wavy black hair in a high ponytail that cascaded down between her shoulder blades. Her well-toned body glistened with perspiration from the run she'd returned from, causing damp spots to show through on her black athletic top.

"Paris! You were supposed to sleep in," said Mya. "You're not getting enough sleep. You'll end up rundown again." She shook her head, recalling the many times through high school and college in which Paris tried to coerce her into joining in on her early morning run.

"I couldn't sleep," Paris said with a frown. "I'm too keyed up about today's festival. Alli, open the door." Alli swung the door open, and they proceeded inside.

"Here," said Mya, who shoved the balloons toward Paris. "These are for you."

Paris grabbed the balloons from her friend and smiled. "Thanks, Mya. You're always so thoughtful. I heart you," she said while making a heart with her hands. She placed the balloon bouquet on the breakfast bar and looked up at them. "*Good luck*. I'll say. We need to raise a lot of money today."

"But first," said Mya, "some coffee." She held a cup out to Paris, who snatched it from her hand and inhaled deeply.

"Heavenly." Closing her eyes, she exhaled. "There's nothing like coffee from Java Dough to start the day off right." Opening her eyes, she looked at Mya and Allie. "Ready to set up?" Paris turned toward her refrigerator and grabbed a paper from underneath a large magnetic picture of the three of them standing over a grill. The photo was from the first Touch a Heart Fest the previous year. They were now on the third event of its kind, and the attendance had more than tripled.

Letting out a yawn, Alli ambled over to the breakfast bar and grabbed a cup from the carrier. Reaching up, she bumped her glass to the side of her sister's. "Ready as I'll ever be."

"I don't feel like we're ever ready for these events," said Mya. "We barely finish one, and we're on to planning the next. Don't get me wrong, I love every moment," she said. There was an amazing feeling that accompanied their work. They raised a lot of money for sick children, helping them get necessary surgeries. They also put together funds to fulfill the wishes of terminal patients.

Touch a Heart Fest was born after Paris helped the Makenzie's daughter get her transplant and Paris realized how great it felt to help a family in need. Mya pushed Paris to run with her idea and Paris immediately pulled Mya and Vic aside to brainstorm ideas for the festival and what they'd do with the money they raised. When they brought it to the ADG board, they were thrilled to add a new charity event to their annual schedule. Paris and Vic always pitched in some of their own money to help, as did each of their parents and Vic's uncle Cristo. It felt good to give back. The first festival was such a success that they decided to host it twice per year.

Paris looked down at the paper in her hand. "I'm ready, but you, my friend, are a perfectionist, so I imagine nothing ever feels quite finished," she said pointedly. Perusing the sheet, she looked over the list of activities they needed to accomplish before the event opened that afternoon. "It's ten minutes to nine right now. Vic assured me he, Brody, and Jack would meet us on the grounds at nine-thirty. Did you eat breakfast, Alli?" She and Mya were always looking out for her little sister. At twenty-two, Alli was five years younger than Paris and didn't always think practically. Most often, her head was lost somewhere in the clouds, fantasizing about what her life would be like in the future. She loved life and didn't have a care in the world. Paris wished she could be so free, but she also loved the structure and hard work she put into raising money for children in need.

Alli nodded. "Mya grabbed me a cinnamon raisin bagel."

"Mya, you're the best," praised Paris. "Let's go." Turning on her heel, she headed back out the door with her sister and friend following closely behind.

• • • • • • • • • • •

At twelve-thirty, the festival grounds were in working order and ready for guests' arrival. Paris and Vic were sure to include plenty of rides and games for the kids to take part in. They also hired several upscale food trucks to pull in some of the area's local foodies. There was a tent for playing Bingo and a tent where a silent auction would take place. For those who enjoy a more formal meal, there would be a five-course meal in the park beneath the stars with a dance to follow. The event had something for everyone.

"What do you think?" Vic asked Paris. He and his cousin Breanna had finished hanging lights in the dance hall and were relaxing at one of the decorated tables.

"I think we did a great job," said Breanna. She ran her fingers through her spiky blonde hair, now damp from the afternoon sun.

Paris nodded. "It looks gorgeous. I'm impressed with how quickly you got the job done." As she scanned the area, Mya, Alli, Jack, and Breanna's twin brother, Brody, approached the table.

"We made one last round, and I think everything's in order. All vendors are accounted for. The auction's ready to go. The rides have been tested and are in working order. We have garbage cans spaced appropriately throughout the grounds. The last of the porta-potties have been set up, and all the delivery trucks have left. Is there anything else you can think of that we may have missed?" asked Mya.

Paris checked over her list, and a frantic look crossed her face. "Did we disperse the ticket rolls to the ticket booths?"

"Done," chimed Jack. He gave her a double thumbs-up.

Paris relaxed her tensed shoulders. "Thank you. For some reason, it's not checked off my list."

"No worries," said Jack. "I saw the rolls sitting on the table in the auction tent, so I took care of them myself. I meant to tell you."

"Nice work." Paris had to stop herself from reaching out to muss his hair. He was still a child in her eyes. He was the youngest of the Alaries, and as such, he worked hard to prove his manliness and worth.

"I think we're set," said Vic, who had snagged a beer from one of the beverage booths. He cracked it open, took a long cool drink, then handed it to his little brother.

"Don't give him that," scolded Mya. "He's not old enough." She retrieved the beer from Jack's hand and took a drink. "But it does taste good on such a hot day." She handed it back to Vic.

"No more alcohol until this evening," stated Paris. "We still have a lot to do. Now, let's discuss work assignments. Your helpers will meet you at their assigned locations in fifteen minutes. Breanna, you and Jack will be running the bar by the dance hall. Brody, you're, of course, in charge of photographing the event. Mya, you keep the entertainment stage on track. Alli, you're hosting the wine bar and tasting from two until six in the dance hall. Vic and I will greet guests and make sure they donate to the cause. Here are your walkie-talkies in case you need anything. This is how we'll maintain contact this evening. Our parents will come in and alternate with us on and off for breaks as the night goes on. Let's all put our hands in," Paris requested with excitement. "Vic, you do the honors."

The group placed their hands on top of each other, and Vic grinned. "Here's to success! Now, let's go make some money!" The group broke away, and he turned to Paris. "How do you feel?" he asked. He stood at an even six feet tall. He was muscular and had a rugged charm about him. His wavy brown hair hung in his piercing blue eyes as he took her in.

"Good," she replied, then off-handedly, "You should have cut your hair. It's weird seeing it this long."

Vic pinched his chin. Nodding, he pushed his hair back.

Paris stifled a laugh as she watched him. "I think this'll be the best Touch a Heart Fest yet."

"You've done an awesome job."

"You too. When it comes to charity, we work well together, don't we?"

"Charity does that," he said with a smile. "I'm sure we'll be back to our regular selves tomorrow."

"That's too bad," said Paris. "I kind of like this side of you."

"Don't get used to it," he teased. He handed the remainder of the beer to Paris and then reached out his other hand and pulled her to her feet. "Shall we?"

Paris took a swig of the celebratory beer, and linking her arm with Vic's, she allowed him to lead her out of the dance hall. It was time to change into their evening attire and move on to phase two.

· · · ● · ● · ● · · ·

Several hours later, the party was in full swing. Paris looked out over the crowded dance hall and watched as her little sister and her helper, Val, poured wine for twenty people. Alli was an amazing sommelier. Her food and wine pairings came together as if by magic. At only twenty-two, she was truly gifted, and people from all over came to her wine events at ADG.

Paris walked across the room toward the wine bar, her flowing lavender Chanel dress swishing in the cool evening breeze, the scent of roses from the nearby gardens tickling her nose. She was in her element.

"Paris, lovely to see you this evening," said a middle-aged gentleman with dark-rimmed glasses. "Have you come to taste some wine with us?"

"No, Devon, not tonight." She winked at the poker celebrity and his new wife. "I have to keep my head about myself, as there's still a good portion of the evening to go. Is Alli taking excellent care of you?"

He nodded in return. "She always does."

Paris turned toward Alli. Her sister joyfully interacted with her guests as she poured the tasting glasses for one of their newest dessert wines, which she was serving with a cinnamon truffle. As she finished the final pour, she turned away from the group. Paris moved toward her. "Are you okay?" she whispered.

"Not really," said Alli. Her face took on a green hue as she grasped her stomach. "I think I might be sick." Turning away, she made a mad dash for the condo.

Val's eyes widened, and she motioned for Paris to follow. The group was so busy discussing the wine and truffle pairing that they hadn't noticed Alli's spontaneous disappearance from the tent. Paris hurried after her sister. She marched through the door to the condo and headed for the common bathroom in the entryway. Pushing the door open, she could hear the agonizing sound of her sister's retching.

"Alli, are you okay? What's going on?"

Alli let out a groan. "Just give me a minute. I'll be fine."

"Are you drunk?" demanded Paris. "I told you not to drink at these events. It makes you look bad. You need to be professional at all times," she scolded.

"I'm not drunk," replied Alli. "Please stop."

Paris frowned. "You're not drunk? Really? You're bent over the toilet doing what then? This is just like last year at the Food and Wine Festival, when you couldn't hold your liquor, and I had to take over the tasting for you. How can you be so careless?" she demanded. As she waited for an answer, Brody strutted into the bathroom, as if he belonged there.

Alli and Brody had been dating for three years and were nearly inseparable. He was a kind sweetheart who was madly in love with Paris's sister. He looked like a surfer, with his pierced ears and sun-bleached hair fastened behind his head. He was fit and well-tanned and stood nearly three inches taller than his cousin Vic. Everyone loved Brody for his great sense of humor and gentle demeanor. He was one of the good guys, sweeping in to rescue Alli as usual.

"What are you doing here?" asked Paris.

"Alli, I'm here. What do you need? Are you okay?" asked Brody. Squinting his deep brown eyes, he leaned his head against the stall door as if to hear better.

"She's definitely not okay," replied Paris. "I think she's intoxicated."

"Alli, you haven't been drinking, have you?" he asked.

"No! I haven't. Tell my sister to butt out!"

"What's going on?" asked Paris.

"I radioed and asked him to meet me," said Alli. "Just go away, Paris."

Brody turned to look at Paris, his smile flatlined. "She's pregnant," he whispered.

"Don't tell her that! Why'd you tell her, Brody?"

"What?" Paris's face paled and her stomach gurgled. "How?"

"Well, I'm assuming it happened like it usually does. Boy meets girl, boy and girl sleep together, baby comes out nine months later," Brody replied evenly.

Turning away from Brody, Paris addressed Alli. "Mom and Dad are going to flip. Why didn't you tell anyone?"

"I did tell someone. I told Brody last night."

"Last night? You only found out LAST night?" she asked. "Alli, you're so irresponsible. Think of what this will do to your career. You're a wine savant. You taste wines as part of your job. How can you do that if you're pregnant?"

"Well, Paris, I guess I'm now useless to you," she said as she shoved open the door and emerged from the stall. Turning to

Brody, she said, "Let's go. I need some food, and clearly, my sister's not in a supportive mood." Turning, she pulled Brody toward the door.

"Alli, wait!" called Paris. "We'll figure this out. Please come back."

Frowning, Brody looked at Paris and shook his head as he allowed Alli to lead him away. "We can discuss this more later," he said. "I'm sure she'll calm down once she's eaten."

"Please, Alli, don't go. I'm concerned, and I'm sorry. I didn't mean to upset you!" yelled Paris.

Pausing in the doorway, Alli pointed an angry finger at her sister. "Go deal with your event, Paris. My life decisions are no longer of any concern to you."

· · • • · • • · · ·

Fifteen minutes had passed since the blowout with Paris. Brody and Alli were cruising down the highway with the top down in Brody's black Miata.

"I love this time of year," said Alli. Flores in the spring is perfect. Eighty during the day, sixty at night. I wish it could stay like this always," she said.

"Are you okay?" he asked. "I hate that you and Paris are fighting. You know she's just worried about you and the news caught her off guard. She tends to overreact when she's stressed. This event isn't exactly stress free."

"I know, but she needs to take a chill pill," replied Alli. "It's not like I can take this situation back. We're having a baby either way, right?"

"Yeah, we are." He replied contentedly. "Do you still want to move to Las Vegas?"

"Not anymore. Flores is much safer and less criminal."

"Criminal?" asked Brody.

"Well, you know, Sin City." She laughed.

"True. I always thought Flores was a great town to raise children in. Besides, all of our family's here. Maybe down the road, we can revisit the concept of living in Lake Meade or Henderson, but right now, the commute doesn't sound too great, with a little one on the way."

"Totally agree with you," she replied as the car began to shake.

"Hold on," said Brody, his face wrinkling in concentration. "I think we may have blown a tire." He slowly eased the car onto the shoulder for inspection. Hopping out, he ran around to the passenger side to take a look. "Yep, back tire's f'd. We'll have to call for assistance. This car doesn't come with a spare."

Alli sat in the passenger seat, humming to herself as she watched the traffic go by.

Hanging up the phone, Brody climbed back into the car and sat down. "It'll be at least half an hour. This isn't how I pictured the night going." Shifting his body so that he was looking at her, he grabbed her hands in his. "I love you, Alli.

Everything will be okay. You'll see. Paris will come around, and your parents will be excited to meet their first grandchild."

"You're amazing," she said, looking into his eyes. "You always know just what to say. How do you do that?"

"It's a gift." He looked at her adoringly.

"You make every day feel special. As long as we're together, and our baby is born healthy, what more could I want?" she asked.

"How about a little heat and passion?" He flashed her his most charming smile.

"Well, that goes without saying," she replied as she gently touched his face.

Unable to contain their excitement as they waited for roadside assistance, they held each other close, kissing and basking in the warmth of their blossoming future.

Coming up for air, Alli noticed a buzzing sound emitting from her purse. "Hold on a second," she told Brody. Pulling the phone out, she saw it was Mya. "Hello?"

· · · · ● · ● · · · ·

"Hi. Paris told me what happened. Are you okay?"

"Yeah. I'll be fine," she said.

"I don't think she meant to hurt you," said Mya. "You know Paris."

"Yeah. I know Paris. I love her, but she can be so maddening at times." She hated fighting with her sister. Why couldn't they get along?

"She's going to call you later. Please talk to her. You're the only sister she's got. You need to work through this and forgive her for her dramatic reaction," said Mya.

"I tell you what. If Paris calls, I promise to apologize and forgive her. I know in the end she means well. By the way, Mya, what do you think about our news?"

"Oh, Alli, congratulations. I'm happy for you both," said Mya. "You'll be a wonderful—"

"Hold on, Mya. We blew a tire and are waiting for roadside assistance. I think they might be here. Give me a sec?" she requested, pulling away from the receiver. "Brody, is that them?" she pointed toward a set of bright headlights heading toward the shoulder.

Brody, turning, saw the lights and realized they were coming way too fast. "Oh, my God!" he yelled as he laid on the Miata's horn.

Alli could hear Mya screaming through the receiver, but she was frozen in place. Brody fumbled for his keys as he continued to slam on the horn. Awakening, the driver jammed on his brakes, causing the metal beast to emit an angry groan. The smell of burning rubber filled the air. Alli knew it was too late. Everything was moving in slow motion. As the truck collided with the Miata, Alli's phone was ejected from her hand, and the sensation of being airborne took over.

· · · · ● · ● · ● · · ·

On the line, Mya could hear a horn and then high-pitched screaming that sounded like her friend, followed by crunching metal and the loud screeching of brakes. The screaming stopped, and there was a brief crackling sound. Panicking, Mya yelled Alli's name, but there was no answer. Dizziness flooded her head as she fought to slow her breathing. Hanging up, she dialed 9-1-1.

Chapter Three

Present Day

I t was the event of the year. Everyone who was anyone within the food and wine community was accounted for. Sommeliers, chefs, bakers, club owners, brewers, caterers, writers, critics, and celebrities, flocked to Flores each year to take part in the Festival of Food and Wine.

The creators of the three-day festival were none other than Paris's parents, Mikel and Nicola DeMarcé. The DeMarcés were known for throwing lavish parties, but this party gave its guests cake and let them eat it too, and the best part was that a large portion of the proceeds went to Feeding America.

Paris could only assume from the turnout that attendees would pay virtually any cost to be there. The most expensive tickets were set aside for celebrities who wanted privacy along with all the amenities. The festival, despite being named for food and wine, encompassed so much more. It was cultural and artistic—a glamour for all the senses. Attendees could take in multiple shows, competitions, and live musical performances on three different stages. There were artistic displays, tropical flowers, and a plethora of exotic and tasty foods and beverages from around the world.

Lucky souls who worked for ADG take part in everything free of charge as a thank you from Mikel and Nicola for their hard work throughout the year.

To some, being an employee at ADG was the 'cat's meow,' but for Paris, it had simply become a cage to contain her. Everything had gone south one year and two months earlier. She couldn't seem to pull herself out of the Hell she was currently living in, but to those outside of ADG, she had it all.

"Hey, Paris!" called her angry father as he let himself in and stomped through her luxury condo. He was dressed in a specially tailored Armani tuxedo. Sighing heavily, he said, "I've been looking everywhere for you." Realizing she was on her balcony, he asked, "Are you decent?"

Paris didn't answer. "I'm coming out there, so you'd better be decent," he stated. Stepping out onto the balcony, he assessed his daughter and her surroundings. Thankfully, she was covered by numerous bubbles. Unthankfully, they were overflowing to the patio below. With any luck, the downstairs tenants were at the festival and wouldn't notice his daughter's carelessness.

A large rain cloud had rolled in, threatening to downpour on the festival below. In reality, the possibility of rain was low, and the sun would soon be back in play. Tiny fairy lights wrapped around the railings and, hanging from the pergola, lit up the cloudy sky with a relaxing glow. He glared at his daughter, who was zoning out as she stared into the distance.

"Hello? Are you going to say something?" Mikel demanded.

"You've found me, haven't you?" Paris grabbed her black bubble-soaked mane and gently rang it out.

It was day two of the festival, and she had no desire to go. All she wanted was to be left alone to drink wine and soak her cares away in her tub. As if exiting a dream, she squawked, "Dad, seriously, you can't just barge in here. I'm in the tub!"

"If you did as was expected of you, I wouldn't have to barge in here like a madman. You can soak later tonight, but right now, I need you downstairs," he replied curtly. "You have an obligation to your family and the Alaries, to be present."

In the past, her father would have never shown up in her condo unannounced, but all of that had changed two months earlier when Paris had overdosed. After that, he acquired a key to her residence and revoked her privacy privileges.

Paris tipped her head back and squinted up at him. "Isn't Vic there? I should think his presence is enough. Perhaps I'm away on business elsewhere?" She knew this wouldn't fly with him. He was old school. Family had to be present, and all accounted for. Too bad one of them was missing. She wished it was her. She wished so badly that she had ended her miserable life the night Alli and Brody died, or the night she took too many Percocet.

Despite her family's beliefs, she wasn't addicted. She rarely took the pills, but now and then, she threw her cares aside and toyed dangerously with the idea of death. Each day had turned into one brain-splitting headache after another and she had minimal desire to live. Her love for her family was the only thing that kept her present on most days.

Reaching down, her father grabbed her towel in one hand and then, averting his eyes, held his other hand out to his daughter. "Let's go. You know you have to do this. You and Vic are hosting several events. We laid out a plan, and you agreed to follow through. This will be good for you," he said.

Paris very much doubted it. The festival had been thrown upon her without a choice. After Alli's death, she had given up organizing charity events. It was one thing to plan and follow through with her own job, but this was above and beyond, and it forced her to interact with hundreds of people she had no desire to be around. Since the accident, she hid away as much as possible. She knew everyone was talking. Let them talk. She didn't care.

She reached up and took her father's hand, letting him gently pull her out of the spa. Looking past her father, she noticed Mya was standing behind him. Stepping forward, Mya grabbed the towel from Mikel and wrapped it around Paris.

Mikel looked back at his daughter as he stopped to adjust his purple paisley tie. "Mya will help you get ready. I have to head back downstairs. Several events are starting shortly. Be sure you kick it into high gear. I don't want to send your mother up. She doesn't need any more stress today." Turning, he walked out of the condo, leaving Mya to deal with Paris.

"You want to tell me what's going on?" asked Mya. Moving into the living room, she picked up a nearly empty bottle of tequila and shook it gently to make a point. "You can't drown the pain in alcohol and drugs," she said softly. "It's been over a year since Alli and Brody died. When will you start living your life again?"

Paris stared at her old friend and watched as a tear ran down Mya's face. She couldn't speak. There were no words. There had been no words since the accident. She simply shook her head.

"Fine," Mya replied sadly. Wiping the tear, she moved on to the master bedroom and into the closet. Rifling through dress after dress, she located an emerald green silk A-line piece. It was perfect for the occasion.

Glancing down, Mya moved on to shoes. She grabbed a pair of black lace-up stilettos and walked over to Paris's jewelry armoire. Opening the second drawer from the top, she retrieved a pair of dangling black diamond earrings and a matching black diamond necklace. She knew Paris hated it when people dressed her, but they were short on time. Her ex-friend would look stunning in black and green with her beautiful silky hair.

Stepping out of the closet, she noticed her charge had moved on to showering. She crept over to the door and opened it a crack. "I set your outfit on the bed. Do you want me to help you with your hair, or can I trust you'll continue getting ready if I wait in the living room?" Mya knew she was treating Paris like a child, but it seemed necessary at this point in Paris's life.

She had been Mikel's assistant, but in the months following Alli's death, she was constantly sent to deal with Paris. After a while, Mikel made Mya Paris's assistant. He thought it would help ease the tension, but in reality, it had only made it worse.

It was quiet for a moment, then Paris said, "Have a seat. Help yourself to some wine or bubbly, if you like."

Mya sat on the white leather settee sipping a glass of water, when Paris finally emerged from her bedroom. She'd helped Paris pick the settee three years earlier. It was a Christopher Guy Lafite and Paris's favorite piece of furniture.

"This thing is still quite comfortable," commented Mya. "As always, you have great taste."

"I know, but honestly, you're the one who found it for me, so you should compliment yourself," she replied, waving her off.

Mya wondered if Paris knew how cold she acted. It had been that way ever since Alli's death. She didn't have the heart to leave Paris, even though she knew she didn't deserve to be treated so harshly. Paris had been her best friend. They were like sisters once. She hoped and prayed daily that Paris would snap out of it and be her friend again, but now that an entire year had gone by, Mya was losing hope.

"Do you need anything from your place before we head down?" Paris asked.

"No, let's get this over with." There was a time when Mya would have been ecstatic to attend the festival, but when she was expected to watch over Paris all night, fun was no longer in the equation. She drained her water glass and hopped off the settee. Depositing the cup in the dishwasher, she paused for a moment. "Hold on. I need to use your lavatory before we go." Mya acted like a proper lady and rarely said words such as toilet or john. Words which Paris wouldn't think twice about using, as of late.

Ducking into the bathroom, Mya looked into the mirror to be sure her makeup was acceptable. Grabbing Paris's brush, she swiped it through her straight, shiny red hair, which hung at her jawline. Looking over her attire, Mya made certain that her black slip dress was wrinkle-free. She had to be flawless because the media would be snapping photos of her and Paris all night long. She hated it, but photos were part of the life she had chosen. Paris had once loved the limelight, but these days, Mya was lucky if the girl got dressed and left the condo.

Emerging from the bathroom, she headed for the door. "Let's go." Paris followed as she exited the condo. The look on her old friend's face was pure disgust. *This day will be pleasant indeed*, thought Mya, but at least she had gotten Paris dressed and out the door, which was half the battle.

• • • • • • • • • •

Hour by hour, the day faded away. Paris emceed the ice sculpture contest and took part as a judge in the exotic baked goods competition. She and Vic hosted a wine and tapas pairing event, which was packed to capacity. Mya followed everywhere

Paris went, making sure she stayed on schedule. Paris hated it but loved not having to worry about what time it was because she knew Mya would remind her.

At seven that evening, Paris was on her own. Mya found herself preoccupied with Cristo Alarie, Vic's uncle, and one of her parents' business partners. He was going through some sort of midlife crisis where he seemed to feel the need to express how young he felt by dating women half his age. So far, Mya hadn't taken the bait, which pleased Paris, despite how irritating she found her to be.

Wandering through the crowds, she headed for the ballroom, grabbing a glass of Prosecco as it bounced by on one of the festival penguin's trays. She had to hand it to her mother. The place looked amazing. A canopy of fairy lights, navy blue tulle, and magnolias hung down from the ballroom ceiling. The scent alone could make you fall in love with the first person you saw. Paris, luckily, wasn't the type to worry about finding romance. She had her eye on one particular man and only one, but so far that evening, he hadn't appeared.

Stopping to lean against a large pillar, she took a deep breath in and slowly let it out. Reaching into her purse, she pulled out a Percocet and popped it into her mouth. It was the first one she'd taken since her overdose. Everywhere she looked, she half expected to see her sister.

Continuing to lean against the pillar, she sipped her Prosecco and glanced around the tent. The tables along the perimeter were covered in navy blue cloths with lit-up bowls, each containing a single floating magnolia. On the far end of the large tent sat the orchestra belting out classical ballroom music.

"Do my eyes deceive me?" sang a familiar voice. "Paris De-Marcé, what a wonderful surprise!"

Paris jumped at the sound of the voice. She hadn't noticed anyone approaching. "Breanna! I didn't realize you were coming home for the festival. How've you been?" Paris forced a smile at Brody's twin. "How's Juilliard?" Breanna was one of the newest teachers at the school of dance. "They let you sneak away for this crazy event?"

"Well, if by sneak you mean take a break for a few days, then yes," she replied. "How about you? What's new? This color is fabulous, by the way," she said, motioning to Paris's dress.

"Thanks. You look pretty great yourself. Red has always been a pleasant color with your tanned skin," she replied. Breanna wore a curve-hugging red slip dress with a large slit down the right side. It was no surprise it looked good. She could pull off a dirty paper bag if she had to. Her friend the chameleon. She frequently grew her hair long and then chopped it all off. No matter the length, she always looked superstar-beautiful. "I see you've grown your hair out since I last saw you. How long has it been, thirteen months?" Her blonde hair had been short and spikey the last time she visited. Breanna furrowed her brow, staring back at Paris, waiting. "Don't look at me like that. I'm fine," said Paris.

"To your first comment, yes, it's been thirteen months." Rolling her eyes, she said, "You know my hair grows fast. To your second comment, that's not what the grapevine is saying, but that smile looks wonderful on you."

"Tell that grapevine to shove it." Paris shrugged. Breanna had only just arrived, and she was already prying. Paris loved her, but she didn't need any lectures from someone who had escaped the pain of everyday life after Brody and Alli by moving away and choosing a career path outside the family business.

"Vic tells me you go to work and party in your flat, and that's it. You rarely join the family for anything. You barely speak to Mya. You know, when Brody died, I went to grief counseling. It really helped," she said gently.

"I'm fine. Vic should mind his own business." Paris knew Breanna cared, but she also felt abandoned by her, which, like many other things in her painful life, brought out further anger.

"He's worried about you, Paris. The whole family, including my family, are all worried. They're discussing committing you." She gave Paris an evil grin.

"Oh, girl, now you're reaching," she said. "The whole family seems to get off on telling me what I can and can't do. Vic hates me. You know that." The last time she and Vic had spoken outside of work was at the hospital the night of the accident. Mya had told him about the fight she and Alli had. It was none of Mya's business to tell Vic about the baby or the argument. He'd accused her of being insensitive, which, honestly, she was in complete agreement with. She also believed he blamed her for their deaths.

"Okay, you got me," replied Breanna. "Jack is the only person I've spoken to, and his concern has me feeling concerned. I haven't discussed you with the rest of the family, but Jack tells me they're worried about you."

"Stop worrying. I told you, I'm fine." She wished Breanna would drop it and let her be.

"Paris, you and I both know you're walking a fine line, and it's only a matter of time before you fall again."

"Whatever. Can we please move on?" The subject flared her anger, and Breanna was the last person she wanted to be mad at. Of all the people in her life, Breanna was the only person who could say she understood how Paris was feeling. She, too, had lost a sibling that night. "How long are you here?"

"I leave tomorrow night." Breanna looked apologetic. Julliard waited for no one.

"That's not even two days," said Paris. "Why can't you stay longer?"

"You know the answer to that, but I promise I'll try to come back more often."

Paris reached out and poked at Breanna's nose ring. "That's new, huh? It looks good on you." Paris thought Brody would have loved the nose ring. After all, he had pierced both of his ears.

"I never thought I'd sport a nose ring, but I really love the look. The only downside is that I can't wear it to work. Oh," she said as she turned away briefly, "don't look now, but there's my cousin."

"Yeah, look who he's with," said Paris.

"My goodness. Is that Devon Heathrow's wife?" Breanna looked surprised. Vic had a way of charming all types of women. She should have known marital status or fame wouldn't be an issue. Vic chased every pretty thing that came through the door, no matter if they were wearing a danger sign. If he couldn't have them, he appeared to want them even more.

"Yeah, Devon's been playing in the World Series of Poker Tournament all day at the MGM Grand in Las Vegas. He sent her here because he didn't want any distractions. I wonder if he knows what she does when they're apart?"

"I doubt it," said Breanna. "He doesn't seem the type to put up with such nonsense."

Paris considered Meagan. She wore Louis Vuitton from head to toe. She even carried a black Louis Vuitton clutch, but the most impressive part of her outfit had to be her shoes. They were exquisite. Beautiful brown Louis Vuitton Star Trail ankle boots, and Paris bet they were just her size.

"We should go over there," said Breanna as she removed a small bottle of perfume from her black and red Prada and spritzed herself. The purse matched her dress perfectly.

"I don't mind moving closer, but I don't care to socialize with Vic," replied Paris.

Breanna furrowed her eyebrows and stared back at her friend for a moment. "Don't you two have to speak regularly? You work together still, correct?"

"He's a jerk. Everyone at work's afraid of him because of his temper. I avoid him as much as possible."

"That's not the Vic I know," she said as she looked over at him and Megan. "He always acted considerate of his coworkers. He's the guy most people wanted to work for because he loved handing out promotions and bonuses.

"People change," said Paris. "It's different for you. You're his family. He treats you like his sister. I'm not the only person with a different attitude since the accident."

Breanna winced at Paris's statement. "I think we're all one enormous family. Don't you agree?"

"I don't have a family anymore."

Breanna shook her head. "That's cold, Paris. I've always looked at you like a sister. We grew up together and have a history. We did all the things sisters do."

"We aren't children anymore. We're adults. Why don't you go talk to Vic? I need another Prosecco," she said as she turned away and left Breanna gawking after her. Retrieving a glass from another passing tray, she decided to take a seat near the orchestra where she could listen to the music and keep an eye on Vic, Breanna, and the naughty Mrs. Heathrow.

She watched as Vic and Breanna chatted for nearly an hour. Then Mya appeared. Grabbing Breanna by the arm, she guided her away. Most likely to schmooze it up with some up-and-coming actors. Paris continued to watch Vic and Meagan. They seemed awfully close. She watched as he brushed what must have been stray strands of blonde hair, behind her ear. She placed a hand on his wrist. Leaning in, she whispered something in his ear and lightly bit his earlobe as she pulled away. Vic reached down and cupped her bottom while she reached back and grabbed his free hand to lead him out of the tent.

Paris waited until Vic and Meagan exited, and then, scooting off her chair, followed safely behind them. She watched as they practically skipped out of the festival. Paris thought perhaps they were headed for one of the gardens, but no, Vic was leading her back to his place. *Predictable,* she thought. Everything with Vic led to sex.

Paris continued to follow. She knew this location well. He was in the condo at the opposite end of the hall from her. She hadn't been inside his place in years. As she continued on, an idea came to her.

She waited for the elevator door to close behind Meagan before she got into the second car. Pressing twelve, she followed them up. They were halfway down the hall when she exited. She watched from a distance as Meagan jumped up and wrapped her legs around Vic, devouring his mouth with her ferocious pink lips. They slammed into the wall outside the condo, knocking a print askew. Meagan squealed with excitement. Paris worried they might not make it inside before stripping naked. Thankfully, he only paused for a moment before refocusing his attention on opening the door and carrying her out of sight.

After the door slammed shut behind them, Paris slunk further down the hall until she stood directly in front of Vic's door. She couldn't hear anything. Slowly, she reached out and turned the handle. It was unlocked. Pushing the door open a crack, she paused to listen. The noises she heard were coming from the bedroom. Pushing her way inside, she quietly closed the door behind her. She was shocked to see that his condo had been completely updated. She didn't recall any furniture being hauled in or out. How had she missed it?

Wandering around, she looked at the art and tested out the furniture. He appeared to have decent taste. She wondered if Mya had helped him decorate. The colors were shades of blue, which matched his Van Gogh replicas. He had a cushy coffee black couch with some beautiful grey and brown distressed wooden coffee tables. His area rug was in colors that mimicked *Starry Night*. The place felt clean and comfortable. Not the bachelor pad she recalled from earlier years.

Creeping toward the hall, she could see light emitting from the bedroom. She scanned the room, but didn't see Meagan's boots anywhere. Paris felt disappointed. She must have made it into the bedroom, still wearing them. She decided then and there that she would go after them. She marched down the hall past a pedestal holding a decorative vase until she stood in front of the bedroom door. Getting down on her hands and knees, she gently nudged the door open enough to see inside. Sure enough, Meagan had removed the shoes and tossed them to the floor at the foot of the bed. She cringed at the thought of going into the room, but Meagan's back was to her, and they were making so much noise she doubted they'd notice.

Inching the door open halfway, she crept toward the bed until she was close enough to snag her prize. Reaching out, she grabbed them by the laces and maneuvered her way backward. Her heart pounded in her chest as she closed the door and continued to back away from the room. She couldn't recall the last time she'd felt so alive. In her excitement, she completely forgot about the pedestal. Knocking into it, the vase tipped and crashed to the tile floor, breaking into several large pieces.

"What was that?" she heard Meagan chirp.

"Stay here," said Vic as he barreled through the door and nearly tripped over Paris, who was still crouched on the ground. "What are you doing here?" he demanded, his face turning crimson. "Oh. My. God. Are those her boots? Paris! What the hell?"

At the mention of *her boots*, Meagan, wrapped in the sheet, came bounding into the hall. "You know this woman? Is she seriously trying to steal my boots? I'm calling the police!"

"Now, hold on," said Vic. "Do we really need to bring the police into this?"

"She's trying to make off with my thirteen-hundred-dollar boots!" shrieked Meagan. "It took me forever to talk my husband into buying them!"

Paris couldn't find her words. Her mouth hung open as she stared at Vic, who was completely naked, and only two feet away from where she sat on his floor. She had to admit, the guy had it going on. He donned a six-pack and a solid five inches flaccid. She couldn't tear her eyes away.

Realizing she was staring at him; Vic walked back into his bedroom and pulled on a pair of sweatpants. "Better?" he asked. "I think this," he said, motioning to his body, "is the least of your worries."

"Yes, I need an officer sent over immediately," Meagan said into her phone. "What's your address?" she asked Vic.

"2100 Primrose Garden Place, Building A, Unit 1201," he said. Continuing to scowl at Paris, he motioned for her to stand.

Meagan hung up the phone and looked at Paris. "The police are coming for you. You're so screwed. What kind of idiot tries to steal another woman's shoes while she's in the room? I don't know who you think you are, but you'd better get yourself a damned good lawyer. Thief!"

Not knowing how to respond, Paris said, "Yeah, well, at least I'm not a slut!"

Meagan let out a growl and lunged at Paris. Pulling away, Paris hauled back and punched her smack dab in the center of the nose, which made Meagan yelp and hit the ground with a loud thud.

"You, bitch!" Then, gasping for air, she said, "Oh, my God. I think you broke my nose! What will I tell my husband?"

Trying to calm her, Vic picked Meagan up and led her into the living room, leaving Paris standing in the hall once again, with her mouth agape. She'd never hit anyone before. This was not good. *Why'd I hit her?* Paris groaned. Backing up, she leaned against the wall. She didn't know what to do. She could go to her place, but most likely, the police would simply follow her there. Paris didn't want to cause any further trouble, so she stayed put.

Five minutes passed, and two officers arrived at the condo. Visiting Meagan first, they got her side of the story and then came back to ask Paris for her version.

"Mrs. Heathrow is accusing me of stealing her boots," she said. "I didn't steal them."

"Um, miss, are those the boots in question?" asked the officer closest to her. He was sporting an impressive handlebar mustache.

Looking down, she realized she was still holding the boots in her left hand. *Great.*

"Yes, but I haven't left the apartment with them. I'm not planning to leave the apartment with them, so technically, I haven't stolen anything," replied Paris.

"Did you attack Mrs. Heathrow? She says you broke her nose," chimed the second officer, who was none-to-happy about her response. His face looked as if it were stuck in a permanent scowl.

"She attacked me, and I defended myself," said Paris. "I hit her out of reflex."

"I don't see any marks on you," said handlebar-mustache.

"No, because I defended myself before she could hurt me," said Paris through gritted teeth.

"Have you been drinking?" asked the scowling officer.

"Seriously! If you're planning to arrest me, just do it already!" yelled Paris.

"Our pleasure," replied the scowling officer. "Read her, her rights," he told handlebar-mustache while he proceeded to place the handcuffs on Paris's wrists.

Vic reappeared in the hallway and, taking in the situation, said, "Whoa, is this necessary? I mean, she really didn't mean to hurt Meagan."

"Oh, really?" spouted Meagan. "They should arrest you too, you jerk!"

"Now, now, Mrs. Heathrow. Let's calm down," replied handlebar-mustache. "Vic, we have to take her in. We have her on attempted theft, breaking and entering, and assault and battery. If you want to bail her out, you'll have to come down to the station."

"This is my home; don't I get a say? She didn't really break in," said Vic. "The door wasn't exactly locked, and she lives next door."

"Sorry, kid, we still have her on assault and theft," replied handlebar-mustache as he led Paris toward the door.

Sighing, Vic said, "Fine. Paris, I'll be right behind you." She could hear the irritation in his voice, but was thankful he planned to come after her.

"You're bailing her out?" screeched Meagan. "Why?"

"For more reasons than I care to admit," he replied sharply. "I think you'd best be going. Don't you have a husband to get back to?" he asked, pointing her toward the door.

"Vic Alarie, you're a real jerk!" she hissed as he slammed the door in her face.

"That's what they all say," he said quietly.

Walking over to his fridge, Vic grabbed a beer and proceeded to flop down on his couch. What the heck just happened? Had Paris lost her mind? Despite his general distaste for her, he had to attempt to make things right. The last thing he needed was the press to find out about his affair with Meagan and Paris trying to steal her shoes, then decking her in the nose. It was a bad situation.

Finishing his beer, he retreated to the bedroom to find more suitable clothing. Once dressed, he called for his driver and began the jaunt down to the main floor.

It only took fifteen minutes to arrive at the station. When the car came to a stop, he lowered the window separating him from the driver. Leaning forward, he said, "Ricky, if I'm not back in thirty minutes, come check on me, please."

"Sure thing, Mr. Alarie."

Opening the door, he stepped out of the limo and adjusted his suit coat and tie. *No need to look like a vagrant walking through the doors*, he thought. Pausing for a moment, he took in the station's exterior. Built of brick, it looked cold and un-feeling. He couldn't help but think he and the building had something in common. Pulling his wallet out, he checked to see how much cash he had. More than enough. "Let's do this," he said out loud.

••••••••••

It was eleven in the evening, and the festival was still in full swing. Paris's parents, Nicola and Mikel, and Vic's parents, Dom and Jessamine, were relaxing in a tent listening to a jazz group and enjoying the fruits of their labor. They were deep in conversation about the success of the festival when Dom's phone vibrated. Glancing down, he saw it was the local police department. "Excuse me a moment," he requested of his friends.

Walking away from the crowd, he picked up the call. "Dom speaking."

"Hey, Mr. Alarie, it's Brett. We've got a minor problem. I've got your son down here at the station."

"Super," replied Dom. "I didn't even realize he'd left. What's the damage?"

"Yeah, you might want to sit down for this."

Twenty-minutes passed before Dom returned to the table, his bald head looking as red as a tomato. The others stared back at him, waiting for him to speak.

Cracking his knuckles, he said, "Vic and Paris are in jail."

"What?" asked Nicola.

"Not again," said Mikel, shaking his head.

Jessamine narrowed her eyes. "Again? What do you mean again?"

Dom, looking at Nicola and Jessamine, said, "Paris entered Vic's apartment while he was with Meagan Heathrow and attempted to steal Meagan's boots. When Meagan confronted her, Paris punched her in the nose."

"She hit her?" Nicola asked, her green eyes widening.

"That girl has a problem with stealing, and now she's becoming abusive. It's shocking that she hasn't been arrested more times. How'd Vic end up in the cell with her?" asked Mikel.

"Oh, you're gonna love this," said Dom. "He bribed a cop."

Jessamine's head dropped into her hands as she let out a groan. "Why didn't he call us?"

"He just did," replied Dom. "Apparently, I need to better teach him how to handle these types of situations. Anyway, I told Brett to leave 'em in there tonight to think about what they've done. We can deal with them tomorrow after the festival has ended. Brett will keep things quiet for now. No use causing a commotion in the middle of our largest event of the year."

"What about the media?" asked Jessamine. "Won't Meagan talk?"

"Nah, unlike our son, I know how to deal with these situations properly. I called our lawyer. It'll probably cost us a little, but tonight's episode won't reach the media. Little Mrs. Heathrow has enough to lose. She dropped the charges for fear that her husband might find out the truth. Spending one night in county won't kill Vic or Paris. If anything, it'll make them think twice before acting out next time."

"Tomorrow, we need to sit down and have a real discussion about how to handle our children," said Mikel.

"What do you mean, our children?" questioned Jessamine.

"Jessamine, come on," said Dom. "Our son isn't much better. He's constantly losing his temper at work. He sleeps with a different woman every other night. They're both on a destructive course. If we aren't careful, something much worse than a night in jail could happen. The papers have picked up on his demeanor and Paris's. They know about the overdose and that she's accused of theft. Anyone who isn't blind can see she's been separating herself from the family as much as possible. Mikel and I have had to talk her out of trouble more times than we care to admit. Our children have been a growing disaster ever since—" stopping, he let out a deep sigh and shook his head. "You know what I'm saying."

"Yeah," replied Mikel. Reaching out, he patted Dom on the shoulder. "We all hoped they'd snap out of this destructive behavior, but they haven't. It's time to do something before we lose them too. Tomorrow, we meet early to discuss a plan of action. We've all enjoyed too much drink tonight to launch any serious plans. Let's try to salvage what's left of this evening. The kids are safe, for now."

Raising his glass, Mikel looked at his partners. "A toast to change, my friends. Tomorrow's a new day." The wheels within his mind had already begun to spin.

CHAPTER FOUR

S hape up. The words echoed in Mikel's head as he walked into the boardroom. He was the first to arrive, which was not unforeseeable since he'd been an hour early. He felt the need to write out some notes regarding the plan he'd mentally formulated the previous night.

He called Cristo earlier that morning to invite him to the session. It was only appropriate that the company's five creators should be there to hash out the details together. Cristo wasn't overly excited since his child wasn't the problem, but he agreed that action was long overdue.

Looking back, it had been 32 years since the four friends had begun the company. They started out with a spark of an idea, and it took off like wildfire. After two years, they'd become so big that they brought on Dom's younger brother Cristo as a partner in ownership. Mikel was acting CEO, Dom the COO, Jessamine CFO, Nicola the Marketing Manager, and Cristo the Production Manager. They owned five magazines, four high-end restaurants, two hotel chains, and the adventure and event planning agency, Sense of Adventure. It was Sense of

Adventure that had breathed life into all the other business avenues. Together, they ran a smooth operating company. There was no room for out-of-control offspring.

Pressing a button, Mikel requested a fresh batch of pastries and coffee from Java Dough, their very own bakery and coffee shop. The business was located inside the ADG building right next to Sense of Adventure.

Over the past year, Mikel watched Paris alienate herself from her friends, family, and colleagues. She'd lost her zeal for life and for helping others. He feared the consequences that might follow if his daughter didn't learn to grieve more appropriately. While he appeared to be tough, Paris's destructive behavior hurt him to the core. In some ways, he lost both girls on the same day.

Dom fought a similar battle with Vic. More than one client threatened to file suits against ADG when they found out Vic had slept with their wives. Try as he might, Dom couldn't control him. Vic marched to the beat of his own drum. Luckily, his brother Jack was a kind-hearted soul who stayed out of trouble.

Jack's strength surprised Mikel. Dom admitted the same on more than one occasion. Jack fell hard for Alli and had been quite upset when Brody won her heart, but he conceded like a gentleman. When Alli passed, he shut down for two weeks, and then, as if nothing had happened, he came back to work and moved on. He laughed, he interacted, and he moved his infatuation over to Paris, much to Paris's dismay. While separated in age by five years, Alli and Paris looked like twins, though they had unique personalities and different hairstyles. The shadow of Alli that he saw in Paris, drew Jack in.

Lord, how he missed Alli. A tear rolled out of his eye and caught on the scar on his cheek as he thought about his daughter. She was happy and lived her life fully. He'd give anything for one more day with both of his daughters. Raising his hand, he brushed the tear from his cheek, recalling the day Dom had given him the scar. Sure. They'd fought over a girl once, but it had been nothing like the situation surrounding Vic and Paris.

Without the strength of family and friends, ADG might have perished, along with Brody and Alli. Somehow, the business survived. Today was a new day, and for the sake of them all, Paris and Vic were about to learn a hard lesson about tough love.

"Your pastries and coffee, sir," said Mandy, as she set the boxes on the boardroom table. "Have a nice day," she said as she exited the room. She nodded to Nicola as they passed each other.

Walking up to Mikel, Nicola leaned in, wrapping her arms around his neck, and kissed him. "You were up quite early this morning."

Mikel sighed. "I couldn't sleep. Too much on my mind."

"Me either. After you got up, I went for a walk in the park. It was nice to enjoy the crisp morning air." Grabbing two cups, Nicola poured them each some coffee. "Here, you look like you could use this." Opening the pastry box, she grabbed herself a bear claw. "Do you want one?"

"Nah, thanks, hon. I can't eat right now."

"I understand. Let me start the meeting, okay?"

"Be my guest," he replied. He was glad he didn't have to.

"Welcome, strangers," said Nicola as Jessamine, Dom, and Cristo straggled in. "How'd you sleep?"

"Sleep," snorted Cristo. "What's that?"

"So, no sleep then?" asked Dom. "I guess I slept as well as possible, considering the current state of things. I sent Byron to pick up the kids this morning. I figured sending the lawyer instead of one of us would give them an idea of the seriousness of their situation. They're back at their condos, sleeping things off. Byron told them to be here at three for a mandatory meeting. They both agreed to be present."

"Great," said Nicola. "We should have everything ironed out by then. I'm letting you all know right now that I expect us to stay in this room, except for bathroom breaks, until we nail down a plan to deal with their behavior."

"I agree, and I think it's more than fair," replied Dom. "We have to protect them as well as our company."

"Yeah, too bad we weren't able to do that sooner," commented Cristo. He was no stranger to loss. Before the loss of his son, he'd also lost his wife six years earlier to cancer.

Jessamine walked up behind his chair and placed her hand on his shoulder. "I know, Cristo. I wish that too. Losing Brody and Alli has been a tough blow for us all."

"Cristo," said Dom, "while we're discussing taking care of family and the business, I feel I need to get something off my chest. I'm quite concerned about you as well. Your conduct at some parties has been questionable. You're making some of the staff uncomfortable. I need you to tone down the drinking when you're at work events. If you're not careful, I fear we'll have a sexual harassment suit on our hands."

Cristo leaned in, narrowing his eyes at his brother. "What? Are you kidding me, Dom?"

"No, he's not," backed Mikel. "I've seen it too. You grabbed Mya's butt right in front of a couple of reporters yesterday. As far as I know, you two aren't in a relationship, and she's turned you down before."

"She's just playing games. She has feelings for me, too."

"Has she told you that?" asked Nicola.

"Well, not in so many words, but I know she does. We have something special. She enjoys flirting with me."

"I haven't seen her flirt with you," replied Mikel. "It doesn't matter. You need to use discretion. Either drink less or don't drink at these events if you can't control yourself. That's all there is to it."

"Geez, Mikel, you know I'd never intentionally hurt anyone."

"Sweetie," said Nicola, "we know you don't want to make anyone uncomfortable, but when you allow your pain to take over and you start drinking heavily, you're no longer yourself."

"I guess I've been hitting it kind of hard since the anniversary," he replied sheepishly.

"Do you need help?" asked Mikel.

"Let me ask this," replied Cristo. "Do you feel I need help?"

Dom considered him for a moment. "Not necessarily. One can hardly fault you for falling off the wagon when the anniversary comes around. If anything, you could use some counseling, which I know you don't want, but maybe it would help you obtain closure? We've all gone through it, and while I can't speak for everyone else, I know it helped me immensely."

"I found it helpful as well," replied Mikel, "and I've never been the type to go to counseling."

"Okay," replied Cristo. His voice hesitant. "If you think it'll help, send me some recommendations for decent people, and I'll think it over. No promises, though."

"Good," replied Jessamine. "It's a small step forward," she said with a smile, even though she knew Cristo most likely wouldn't think it over. He'd never been one to share. That aside, she knew he was a good guy.

"Now," said Mikel, "on to more pressing issues."

Nicola straightened her willowy frame in the chair, her black jaw-length hair falling forward as she moved. Reaching up, she pushed her sweeping bangs aside and narrowed her green eyes in concentration. "We've got a pretty big problem at the moment. Cristo, I don't know if Mikel gave you all the details, but last night, Paris and Vic were arrested."

"Oh, shit," he replied. "I knew something happened, but you didn't give me that information." He looked at Mikel with questioning eyes.

Mikel nodded. "I know. I kept my mouth shut because I needed to process. This is a sensitive situation, and I didn't want to let my anger take control."

"What did they do now?" Cristo asked with concern.

"First, I want to address something that affects us all," said Nicola, pursing her maroon lips. Vic and Paris are creating an abundance of negative publicity. The most recent headline said, *Careless Heiress Tarnishes Family Name.* Another said, *Vic Alarie Sleeps with Local Judge's Wife.* Obviously, headlines like that are damaging to our company."

Mikel shook his head. "Dom and I keep running interference, and they keep messing up. How are we supposed to protect them, and our company, from these types of mistakes?"

"Are they really mistakes?" asked Cristo. "I mean, if you slept with a judge's wife, wouldn't you know?"

"I'm sure he did," replied Dom. "That's the problem. He doesn't care. There are no consequences. "Perhaps mistake isn't the right word, but you get what I'm saying. It's a problem, and it affects us all."

Cristo looked at Dom and Mikel with empathetic eyes. "What are we gonna do?"

"That's why we're here," said Nicola.

"To discuss what we should do," added Dom.

"We could give them a warning, and if they end up in the papers again, they're fired," said Cristo. "No more trust fund. No more company."

Jessamine pounded her fist on the table. "That's not an option. I don't want to punish our children when they're obviously hurting. I might be a softy, but there has to be a better way."

"Let's not get ahead of ourselves, dear. Not everything can be fixed with a hug," replied Dom. Jessamine rolled her eyes at him.

Biting his bottom lip, Mikel nodded as he further processed what Cristo had said. "Cristo may be onto something. I'll admit, I had a similar thought. What if we can achieve the best of both scenarios?"

• • • • • • • • • • •

It was two-thirty in the afternoon when Paris pried herself from bed to answer the loud banging on her condo door. Whoever it was, was quite persistent. Prying open the peephole, she saw Mya on the other side. She rolled her eyes.

"Paris!" yelled Mya. "Are you awake?"

Groaning, Paris closed the door to the peephole.

"I can hear you," Mya snapped.

"Good then read between the lines," she said as she turned away from the door. Mya immediately began banging on it once again. "What do you want?" asked Paris.

"Let me in!" she yelled.

Not wanting to argue, because of the pounding headache she was experiencing, Paris walked back to the door and opened it. Mya shoved a glass of orange juice and three generic painkillers into her hands. "Super," said Paris. She tossed the painkillers in her mouth and downed the juice. It felt refreshing as it rolled down her throat. Turning away, she went back to the settee and flopped down on her back.

"Get ready. Your father didn't send me over. He doesn't want me to do you any favors, but your mother asked me to be sure you made it to your meeting on time. May I ask? What exactly did you do last night? No one would tell me. Just that Chase Lansell and I are to be at the meeting, too."

"None of your damn business," said Paris. "I can't imagine why they'd need you there."

"Don't snap at me. I didn't do any of this to you," she said as a tear rolled down her face. "We've been best friends since we were in middle school."

"Not anymore," replied Paris. Her voice came off colder than even she had expected. "I can't stand to look at you. I'm going to my room to get dressed." She left Mya standing in the living room with tears silently flowing.

Mya thought back to earlier days when she and Paris were still in college. They would plan weekend trips home from school because they hated being away from one another. They spent their summers volunteering at the same camp for under-privileged children, because they wanted to make a difference together. She and Paris were strong, kind, and caring women who could previously rely on each other to be present. Now, Mya couldn't even get Paris to utter one kind word to her.

Mya walked to the bathroom, shut the door, and turned on the faucet to splash cold water on her face. She gazed at her pale, shaky reflection. She didn't understand why it had to be like this. Grabbing the hand towel, she dried her face and continued to stare back at herself. She looked awful. Her hair was matted with tears, and her blue eyes were red and puffy. She rarely slept anymore. Nightmares plagued her sleeping mind, and when she woke, they didn't go away. The sound of the crash and Alli's screaming played on constant repeat. Paris's anger was a recurring trigger.

"Mya," said Paris as she pounded on the door, "I'm ready. Let's go."

Taking a deep breath, she smoothed her hair and shook out her arms. "You can do this," she said quietly to her reflection. Turning, she opened the door and was met by Paris's owly stare.

"You gonna pull it together?" asked Paris. The coldness was still present in her voice, though she was speaking with more control.

Without a word, Mya pushed past her and headed out the door. Calling over her shoulder, she said, "Chase's meeting us in the lobby. Your mom sent him to get Vic." Paris didn't acknowledge her. Mya turned to see what she was doing. "Damnit, Paris!" she yelled. Paris had opened a bottle of pills and was about to pop one in her mouth when Mya snatched the bottle away.

"Hey, give it back!" she shrieked.

"Percocet again?" Marching past her, Mya went back into the condo.

"Don't you dare!"

"I'm doing this because I care about you!" Paris launched herself at Mya, but not before Mya had dumped the contents into the disposal and flipped the switch on. The disposal clanged and gnashed as it ate up every last pill.

"You dirty little bitch!" screamed Paris.

The words stung, but Mya refused to give Paris the satisfaction of showing it. "You need to be sober for this," she replied confidently. "I'm not sorry for what I've done. Alli wouldn't want to see you like this. She would have done the same."

Paris raised her hand and slapped Mya across the face. "Don't you dare bring her into this!"

Mya, covering her cheek from the sting, said nothing. She walked out the door and headed for the elevator. She couldn't let Paris see her cry again. Inside the elevator, she hit the button to close the door before Paris had a chance to get in. She could take her own car down. When the doors opened on the main floor, Vic and his assistant Chase were patiently waiting and immediately recognized that something was off.

"Whoa," said Chase, "what happened to your face?" Reaching out, he gently touched the redness. Mya looked like she might cry, so he wrapped his muscular arms around her and pulled her into a protective hug.

"Paris happened," she sniffed as the second elevator door opened and Paris stepped out.

"What did you do to her face?" asked Vic.

"Come over here, and I'll show you," said Paris. Vic looked like he wanted to strangle her. She loved egging him on. She watched as he took an angry step toward her, his muscles twitching. Chase immediately put his five-foot-seven frame between them, holding up his arms. Paris stuck her chin out at him, then turning on her heel, she scurried away.

Mya looked up at Vic. His jaw set and muscles tensed. "It's not worth it. What would you do, anyway?"

"I should lay her out," he said through gritted teeth. "She deserves it."

Raising an eyebrow and pursing his lips, Chase shook his head. "Just—no, dude."

Reaching out, Mya placed her hand on Vic's chest. "Don't stoop to her level. Ever. Even if you broke her jaw, you'd do more harm to yourself than you ever could to her."

"You know I'd never hit her," he said more calmly. "I'm just shocked that she'd hit her closest friend. It's bad enough she hit Meagan the other night. She's becoming abusive."

"I know. According to Paris, we're no longer friends." Mya smiled sheepishly. "We'd better get moving. We'll be late." Paris had already exited the building.

"Are you sure you're okay?" asked Chase as he looked her over. "Do you need another hug?"

Mya smiled at the handsome, toned Native man standing before her. They would have been perfect for one another, had it not turned out he preferred men. Over the years, as they got to know one another, Chase became her honorary big brother. He had a big heart and took it upon himself to watch out for her when Paris ended their friendship.

"You know I always need another hug—but we don't have time for that right now. Raincheck?"

"Always," said Chase.

"I still can't believe she hit you, of all people," said Vic.

"Me either," replied Mya. Her face was swollen, and it still hurt, but she didn't regret destroying the few pills left in the bottle.

"If she ever does that again—"

"She won't," said Mya. "I threw her pills down the disposal. We have to get her off that junk."

"Dang!" said Chase. "You're a badass, sister!"

"Yeah, you'd think she would've learned after landing herself in the hospital," said Vic.

"She has to want to quit," replied Mya. "I'm not really sure how serious the pill issue is. I know she overdosed, but I don't know if the pills are actually an addiction or her thinking she wants to end her life?"

"What's the difference?" asked Chase.

Mya looked at him with confidence. "The difference is, if she isn't taking them regularly, she can stop if she wants to. If she's popping them regularly, then it's an addiction and will require serious help from a rehab center. My gut says it's the former. I honestly think she felt so low she wanted to see how far she could take it. She wanted to die. Not that this scenario improves the situation. She still needs help."

Vic shook his head. "How does one get her to stop flirting with death?"

"That's the million-dollar question, isn't it?" asked Mya.

Upon arriving at the boardroom, the trio stepped inside. Paris had already taken a seat at the table.

"I'm glad to see you all made it on time," acknowledged Nicola. "I trust everyone got enough sleep after the party?" her words were directed at Mya and Chase. "What happened to your face, dear?" she asked.

Before Mya had a chance to answer, Paris chimed in. "I slapped her."

"You did what?" her father used his angry parent voice.

Paris, becoming defensive, said, "She was talking about Alli and—"

"Paris," said Mikel, "I don't care what she said. You don't hit people. Ever. I thought maybe you would have learned your lesson after last night."

"Where did we go wrong?" asked her mother, shaking her head. She ran her fingers through her long, sweeping black bangs. "I just don't know what to do with you?"

"Don't let her fool you," said Mya. "She hit me because I dumped her Percocet into the garbage disposal." She wouldn't let Paris off that easily. She needed to take responsibility, and that meant Mya couldn't cover for her anymore.

Paris turned bright red. "I should slap you again!"

"ENOUGH!" boomed Mikel. "You'll shut your mouth and listen. You're done with pills. If I catch you popping another pill or hitting anyone, you'll be ejected from this family so fast your head will spin. Do I make myself clear?"

Paris's mouth dropped open and her eyes widened, but she nodded her understanding.

Vic let out a snort as he tried to stifle his amusement. Jessamine shot him a warning look.

"Things are changing here and now," said Nicola, tapping the table with her pointer finger. "You're creating bad blood within the company and bad headlines outside. No more bad headlines. No more firing people for no reason. No more sleeping with other men's wives. No more stealing. Mark my words, if you do not turn things around, you will lose everything. We're done letting your bad behavior slide. We all suffered great loss. You will no longer tarnish Alli and Brody's memory."

"Do you understand what's expected of you?" asked Dom. Neither Vic nor Paris said a word. "This is serious. We've worked hard to build this company, and we're not letting you destroy it or this family. So, do you understand?"

"Yes," Vic replied solemnly.

"Sure," said Paris.

"Okay," replied Nicola. The look on her face said she wasn't buying it. "If you mess up again, you'll have a rude awakening."

"We get it," said Vic.

"Now, one more matter of business," said Mikel. "Mya, you too are on our radar."

Mya's look turned to panic. "What do you mean?" she asked.

"We're all concerned," said Mikel as he motioned his hand to include his partners. "You've suffered greatly with these losses. Not only did a friend of yours die, but your best friend has turned her back on you."

"Are you kidding me?" asked Paris. "She isn't suffering."

"Zip it," said Mikel. "With your permission, we'd like to pay for you to go to grief counseling. We can't make you go, but we hope you will. If you refuse, we may need to discuss moving you to a different part of the company because we cannot sit back and watch Paris continue to take her anger out on you." His eyes shone with sincerity.

"That's a load o—"

"Paris, so help me," said Nicola. "If you don't stop now, I'll personally take your trust fund away."

Paris closed her mouth instantly.

Continuing, Mikel said, "Think it over. You don't have to answer right now."

"If you'd like to discuss things further, dear, we can talk more after everyone else leaves," said Jessamine.

"Okay," replied Mya. She didn't know what to think, but perhaps further discussion would ease her mind. "I have some questions for after the meeting."

"Perfect. I'm certain I have some answers," said Jessamine.

"Now," said Mikel, "if there's nothing further, this meeting is adjourned with the exception of Mya."

Paris and Vic got to their feet and exited the boardroom, followed by Dom. Vic scowled at Paris, and she scowled back. "You're an awful person," he said. "If it weren't for you, we wouldn't be in this mess."

"Knock it off," scolded Dom. "You did this to yourselves. I honestly don't want to see either of you until the gala next weekend. I'm putting you on an involuntary leave of absence to think about your actions. Now get out of my sight before I come up with a worse punishment."

Both Vic and Paris veered toward the nearest door to escape Dom's angry glare. Neither spoke a word as they hoofed it back to their respective condos.

Chapter Five

It was the night of the Gala and Mya stood outside Paris's door waiting for an answer. The week had been quiet. She hadn't yet agreed to go to counseling. Mikel and Nicola gave her a week to consider, but informed her of the options if she decided not to go. She didn't want to admit defeat. She knew Paris was angry and hurting, but she believed her friend was still in there somewhere.

Growing impatient, she knocked a second time. Paris didn't answer. As she turned to walk away, Vic exited his condo.

"Hey, Mya, I think Paris left already. I heard her talking to someone by the elevators."

"Well, that answers my first question. Apparently, she is avoiding me. Thanks for letting me know. How was your week?"

"It was weird. I don't recall the last time I missed work. That job's pretty much my life," he said with a sigh.

"Do you agree with the things they said?" she asked, waiting for his reaction.

Vic's face wrinkled as he considered the question. "I don't know. I don't think it's as bad as they're making it out to be. Maybe I'm a little hard on my employees from time to time."

Mya could tell he was in denial. He did not know how cold he had become. She once watched him fire an intern for spilling coffee on herself. The intern was mortified, and Vic's anger only added to the humiliation. Dom later called the intern and offered her a spot at one of the magazines to make up for his son's extreme reaction and to get her out of the way before they had a lawsuit on their hands.

"Not just a little, Vic. A lot. You even scare me at times, and I've known you most of my life."

Vic straightened his tie and pushed the elevator button. He didn't speak the entire ride down. Mya continued to watch his face, which seemed to agonize over something. Maybe her comment?

"Hey," he said as the elevator doors popped open, and they began walking again. "I never meant to scare you, and I hope I never do again. It bothers me to know you've felt that way."

"I'm not scared right now," she said with a half-smile.

"That's good." Pausing, he turned to her and said, "You look beautiful, Mya. I hope you enjoy tonight. You deserve to have some fun. Anyway, I need to run an errand over at the main office. If you will, please tell my parents that I've called for a ride, and I'll be along shortly."

"Sure thing," she said. Continuing on, she headed for the limo waiting curbside. The partners, along with Paris and Jack, were already seated. Cristo planned to follow separately in his own car to ensure he didn't drink too much.

"Nice tux, Mr. DeMarcé," said Mya as she climbed into the limo. Mikel wore a blue Vince Camuto slim-fit tuxedo, which he pulled off magnificently. He believed in dressing well, but he shopped all different brands despite the billions he had in the bank. Price did not dictate what he bought, whereas Paris seemed to be of the mindset that the pricier the item, the better it would be.

"Thank you, my dear." Mikel flashed a debonaire smile.

"Good evening, Mya," said Dom. "Have you seen Vic?"

"Yes. He'll follow us. He needed to stop off at the office."

"That boy's mind is always on work," said Jessamine. "We should have forced him to take time off to grieve last year. Maybe we're to blame for his emotional stagnation?" Jessamine let out a sniffle.

"Let's not point any fingers," replied Dom, squeezing her hand. "Grief is a tricky thing. We'll get through this."

"I agree," said Mikel. "Pointing fingers won't fix it. Let's enjoy ourselves tonight." Turning to Paris, he gave her a wink. "I think Paris and Vic understand our concerns, and they will put in the work to make improvements."

Paris nodded stoically at her father.

Sitting across from Paris, Mya looked her over cautiously. She wore a short red satin dress with metallic silver stilettos, probably Versace, though Mya refused to stare and give Paris a reason to bite her head off as she attempted to place the brand. Paris was a huge fan of Versace, as well as Louis Vuitton and Prada. She wore her long wavy hair twisted neatly atop her head with slightly poofed bangs. Dangling silver earrings adorned her ears and a matching necklace hung just above her cleavage. The jewelry most likely came from Tiffany, another of Paris's favorite brands. Only the best for Princess Paris.

"Paris," said Mya, "How are you this evening?" Mya wanted to show Mikel and Nicola that she and Paris could have a polite conversation. She hoped she was right.

Paris looked up at Mya and immediately frowned. "I'm fine. How are you?"

"Well enough. You look nice," added Mya.

"Thanks," replied Paris. "You look decent too."

Mya knew the poor compliment was the best Paris would do. She didn't need Paris to tell her she looked good. She knew she did. She wore a black and navy long lacy dress with black heels and black stud earrings. The dress, unlike Paris's, was not expensive, but it fit her well, and it made her feel beautiful. She wore her hair clipped into place with a black barrette.

"Where'd you find those heels?" asked Paris. "They look pretty cheap."

"Wow, Paris, totally uncalled for," scolded her mother. "I think you look gorgeous. The heels are great with that dress."

"Thanks, Nicola," replied Mya. *So much for making nice in front of the parents*, she thought.

•••••••••••

The second the limo stopped, Paris bolted. She needed to distance herself as far as possible from Mya and the rest of ADG. She waltzed into the ballroom like she owned the place and instantly put on her fake smile for all to see. Assessing the room, she headed straight for the bar. Without a drink, she didn't know if she could make it through the evening.

"Good evening, Ms. DeMarcé," said a voice that Paris could only describe as chocolate decadence for her ears. She spun around to face him and her heart fluttered.

"Mr. Tom Mariano, how are you this fine evening?" she replied in her silkiest voice. Paris had harbored feelings for him since the day they'd first met seven years earlier. Never had she made an advance on her handsome coworker. His blue eyes sparkled back at her. She wanted to reach out and run her fingers through his luscious black locks. Or, even better, roll around in a set of satin sheets while her body entangled with his long, lean, and muscular one. Her lips longed to taste his perfect olive skin. He had a certain charm and confidence that pulled women in. When he laughed, the sound was rich, and she wanted to be its cause.

"I'm well. Would you care for a drink?" Tom held out a glass of wine. "I hoped I'd find you here," he confessed.

"Really?" asked Paris as she grabbed the glass. While she held her poker face, she grinned wildly on the inside. They worked together at Sense of Adventure, and at times he seemed to flirt with her, but this was the first time he had gone out of his way to get her attention.

"Really," he replied. "Why don't we find a table?"

"Okay," she said. Grabbing her free hand, Tom led her to the opposite side of the ballroom. She took a seat as he situated himself across from her.

Smiling, he took a sip of wine, then said, "You look lovely this evening."

"Thank you," she said, blushing.

"I want to talk to you about the Prescotts."

Paris's smile flatlined. "What about the Prescotts?" The Prescott family had come to Sense of Adventure to plan the perfect sweet sixteen for their daughter Sophia. She wanted the party to be themed, and money was of no concern. Paris was excited to take their family on as clients. She had planned many birthday events and was a natural when it came to satisfying young women's imaginations. She knew what girls wanted, especially when the budget had no cap.

"I'd really like to work their account," he replied. "I golf with Mr. Prescott, and he's become an excellent friend. He requested me for the job. I'm coming to you as a courtesy to let you know that I'm merely doing as requested. I hope you understand."

In one fluid motion, Paris rose from the table and flicked her wine glass forward as she stepped back, sending white wine droplets into the air. "Oops," she said. "I'm so clumsy some-times." The fire had instantly gone out. Tom was known as a shark, but this was the first glimpse Paris had been given of his predatorial maneuvering. "Thank you for the heads up. Now, if you'll excuse me, I need to find myself a different drink."

"Paris," said Tom, as he wiped wine from his jacket, "don't be like that. I really did want to spend some time with you this evening."

"Well then," she replied curtly, "I guess you shouldn't have stolen my client." Turning on her heel, she left him gaping after her. He had hurt her pride, and she'd be damned if she would give him the pleasure of her company after he took away the only client she'd been excited about in months.

Stopping off at the bathroom, Paris looked at herself in the mirror. Her dress had survived the wine shower. Her makeup was intact. She looked good, but she felt terrible on the inside. *Someone should put me out of my misery*, she thought. As she continued to stare into the mirror, she heard the click of approaching heels.

"How's it going?" asked Mya.

"God, you again? What? Are you my shadow? Why are you constantly following me around?"

"I'm sorry," said Mya. "I'll find a different bathroom, I guess." Turning away, she headed for the door.

Calling after her, Paris said, "Do whatever you want. It's a free country."

Mya paused and let out a deep sigh. "Is it? Most of the time, I feel like I'm more trapped than the animals at the zoo."

Paris watched her leave. There had been a time when she would have told Mya everything. She would have laughed and cried with her. They would have had each other's backs. That time was over. Paris had made sure of it. The loss of Mya hurt, but Paris, like a car whose brakes had gone out, couldn't seem to slow down or stop herself from certain destruction.

Exiting the powder room, Paris noticed the band had begun to play. People would begin flocking to the dance floor. It was the perfect time to check out the silent auction. She had high hopes that there would be some expensive couture items to bid on. Maybe some shoes. She loved shoes more than anything.

Walking into the auction room, her heart sank. There, on the opposite side of the room perusing the goods, was none other than Meagan Heathrow. She let out an unladylike growl as she added the unfortunate situation to her list of things that were ruining her night.

"Yeah, you might not want to go in there right now," Vic whispered in her ear. "I plan to avoid that situation like the plague it is, and I suggest we move out of sight immediately."

Paris followed him back to the ballroom. "This is where we part." She waved him off as she headed for the bar.

"Yeah, it's probably best you stay away from the silent auction. I wouldn't want you to get in trouble for stealing anything." Vic laughed.

Without so much as a glance, she shot back, "Try not to bribe any cops tonight."

"Hey, if you weren't such a psychopath, I wouldn't have had to bribe anyone. Who sneaks into someone else's condo and tries to steal their date's shoes? Ya lunatic!"

Paris spun around and glared at him. "Who leaves a major media event with someone else's wife and then takes her up to his own condo? Idiot! You deserved much worse than you got!"

"What I do is none of your business!" he growled.

Without realizing it, they had each taken several steps toward one another and were now screaming in each other's faces. Those around them had stopped to stare. Their angry banter had drowned out the band and all other sounds within the room.

Mya, noticing the confrontation, rushed over to Paris and Vic to diffuse the argument. Jack, who had been talking with Mya, ran after her to help.

"Stop! You're making a scene," she hissed as she tried to pull Paris away from Vic.

"You're so awful, Paris. No one likes you!" boomed Vic.

"Yeah, well, everyone thinks you're a cold-hearted man-whore!" lashed Paris. "A first-class dick."

"Vic, man, let's go," said Jack. Grabbing his brother's arm, he pulled him toward the doors. "This is not the place for an angry outburst," he stated as his eyes scanned the room.

Vic shook his head in anger. "You're not worth it!" he called over his shoulder as he followed Jack.

"Hey!" said an angry voice. Both Paris and Vic stopped and turned to see their red-faced fathers staring them down. "Both of you, get out," hissed Mikel.

"Dad, he—" protested Paris.

"I don't want to hear it!" snapped Mikel.

"The limo is waiting outside. You are to leave immediately," instructed Dom. "What you've done here tonight carries serious consequences. I hope you're prepared to face them."

"Dad—" pleaded Vic.

"Don't," replied Dom. "You were warned. It's over. Now go, or I'll have you removed. Mya, I want you and Jack to escort them to the limo." Without another word, he and Mikel headed back to their friends, who were all whispering amongst themselves. Dom knew the scene the kids had caused would be a public relations nightmare, but part of him thought maybe it would be best to let it ride. Force them to deal with the consequences of their actions. *No protection this time around,* he thought.

Mya and Jack walked Vic and Paris to the limo and watched as they silently climbed inside. No one spoke a word. Tears ran down Paris's face and her body shook with humiliation.

Vic glared at Paris the entire ride. He blamed her for the outburst and for provoking his anger. She had ruined his entire night. Paris was absolutely the worst human being he knew.

· · · ● · ● · · · ·

The following workday began like any other. Vic checked into all of his accounts, met with three of his current clients to sort the details of their upcoming travel adventures, and looked over some new client matches to debate who was best suited for whom. With a stroke of luck, he never once ran into Paris, which had him wondering if she'd even bothered coming in to work?

Entering their condo at the end of the workday, Vic's luck ran out. Paris stood in front of the elevator, tapping her foot as she waited. "Great, it's you," he said with disdain. He felt as if his temperature had risen at the sight of her. He peeled off his grey suit coat and folded it over his arm.

"I hope you realize you don't have to talk to me," remarked Paris. "I mean, it seems simple enough, but you never seem to keep your mouth shut, which is exactly why everything went to hell last night."

As the elevator doors opened, they both stepped inside. Clenching his teeth, Vic reached out and pressed their floor number. When the doors reopened, they both exited and went in opposite directions. Vic reached his door first. Inserting his key, the lock didn't budge. From down the hall, he heard Paris say, "What the heck?" Her key didn't work either. Clearly, not a coincidence.

"What do you know about this?" yelled Vic.

"Nothing, you?"

"No. Obviously, I don't know what's going on," he replied angrily, "but I'm sure it's all your fault!"

"My fault, whatever!" Paris shot back. "You're the one with the boiling hot temper!"

"Oh, good, you're both here," said Mya, her voice catching slightly as she and Chase exited the elevator.

"Your presence is requested in the boardroom," added Chase.

"Mya, what's going on?" Vic demanded.

"We know as much as you do. Sorry, man," said Chase. He hated confrontation, but he always stood up for what he believed was right. As Vic's assistant, Chase knew how volatile Vic could be. Things needed to change, and he was secretly happy the day had finally arrived. He didn't hate Vic, but he didn't particularly like him either.

Mya motioned for them to follow her into the elevator. "Let's go." Vic and Paris traipsed back down the hall and into the elevator.

"They're punishing us, aren't they?" asked Paris.

"Gotta be," replied Vic. "What else would this be? Your behavior the other night really torqued them off."

"You're both equally to blame," stated Chase with too much enthusiasm. "It might be best if you don't speak. We just want to get you to the boardroom and be done with it."

"Be done with what?" asked Paris. "What exactly is there to be done with?"

"If it were me, I'd fire you," replied Chase.

"Chase, hush!" demanded Mya. "We don't know what's happening. We were told to retrieve you for the meeting. That's all."

The walk over to the ADG building felt agonizingly long to Paris. She was anxious and did not know what to expect. She hoped Chase was wrong. Would their parents really fire them?

Why had they waited until now? She and Vic had been at work all day.

Entering the boardroom, they found all the key players seated and waiting. Nicola stood in greeting and asked them all, including Chase and Mya, to take a seat. Walking over to the door, she shut it behind them. Normally, they kept the door open, but today was different. Paris could feel her palms beginning to sweat.

"Have you seen this?" roared Dom, tossing a paper over to Vic and Paris. The headline read: *Alarie & DeMarcé Battle Verbally at Fundraising Gala.* "I don't think I need to tell you how bad this is."

"It's never okay to lose your cool in public," said Mikel. "Consider the camel's back broken."

Jessamine raked her fingers through her long, curly auburn hair, her blue eyes brimming with tears. "You have no idea what you've done, and I'm afraid I can't stop what's coming. The board is in agreement."

Nicola nodded. "I hoped after last week's conversation that you'd figure things out and do better, but you wasted no time reverting to bad behavior."

"We feel you've left us no choice," said Cristo. "Actions such as yours require a firm response from the company."

Standing, Mikel looked at them both. "You may have noticed we've changed the locks on your apartments."

"Yes," replied Vic. "Hard not to."

"Here's what happens next," said Mikel. "We'll lay things out for you, and you'll keep your mouths shut until we ask if there are questions, okay?"

Paris had never seen such an angry and piercing look from her father. Both she and Vic nodded their understanding.

Nicola stood. "As of right now, you no longer live in the condos, and you won't be in the family building either," she added. "You'll move to employee housing across campus."

"Effective immediately, you've been demoted," stated Dom. "As your family, we hold you to higher standards. That said, we also recognize where this mess stems from. It's time to heal and move forward with your lives."

"You no longer own company cars," said Jessamine. "You don't have access to the company limos either. If you need to go anywhere, you'll do so by foot, public transportation, or nicely asking your assistants for a ride." Looking at Mya and Chase, she added, "You two have every right to say no to their requests. This is not an obligation; I want to make that clear." She watched Mya and Chase nod their understanding.

Moving on, Cristo said, "Your belongings are no longer yours. Kiss them goodbye because they'll stay locked up in your old condos until further notice. If you fail to turn your behavior around, those belongings, as well as your condos, will be given away, and you'll have to start over on your own."

"Your assistants will now become your babysitters," added Mikel. "Chase and Mya, you're each getting a raise because babysitting children is more daunting than your normal daily tasks. If you two want to act like kids, we'll treat you as such. If either of you gets physical with Mya or Chase, it'll result in your immediate discharge from ADG and the family. This shouldn't be an issue, but apparently, Paris has a violent streak in her as of late. It pains us to make these decisions, but we've enabled your poor behavior for much too long."

Nicola looked at Vic and Paris to be sure they were paying close attention. "There are several guidelines we expect you to follow. First, your trust funds and company expense funds are now closed off from use. You'll be allotted a new account with a debit card. Each account will have $1,500 to get you started in your new lifestyle. This is all the money we're going to give you, so you best use it wisely. Second, we expect you to keep up with and maintain all of your bills and living expenses, including your rent, utilities, and proper work attire. Aside from your bank card, you will not be allowed any credit cards, and again, there will be no stealing tolerated," she said, looking at Paris. "You will also abstain from drug use. If we find out that you used drugs, stole, or manipulated anyone into letting you use their credit card, you will be let go from the company immediately."

"You'll begin your new jobs in the mailroom tomorrow," said Dom. Both Vic's and Paris's mouths fell open, though they didn't utter a sound. "You will behave when you're at work. That means no fights and no yelling. Anything that isn't proper etiquette for work is grounds for punitive action.

Believe me when I say we can always further demote you. Is that clear?"

"Yes, sir," replied Vic.

"Yes," acknowledged Paris.

"Your babysitters are here to help you," stated Mikel. "They'll work with you to put your lives back together. They are your business confidants, and they'll call you on your bullshit."

"Now," said Jessamine, "We did discuss forcing you into therapy to deal with your issues, but all of us agree that forcing someone into therapy does not mean they'll work at improving, so we've decided against it. If you'd like to see a therapist to help you sort out your feelings regarding loss as well as your new situation within the company, we'll gladly pay for it. Mya, if you're not up to handling this situation with Paris, please see me after the meeting, and we can have you temporarily switch places with Dom's assistant, Molly." Despite her statement, everyone knew Mya would never back down from the challenge of dealing with Paris. It wasn't in her nature.

"In the meantime, I hope you'll consider talking to each other," said Mikel as he looked at each of them in turn. "You will work together to get through this. If you're upset about your current situation, you have no one to blame but yourselves. You will not complain to your babysitters about how you got here, but you may complain to one another as much as you like, though I hope you won't. Hopefully, it's sinking in that neither of you is innocent under the current circumstances."

"Furthermore," added Nicola. "We'll reward you if you succeed. However, you're both responsible if one of you cannot live up to an expectation."

"We will check in with you every week," said Cristo. "During our Monday morning check-ins, you'll find out how you're doing and whether we're promoting you. You should also know that we may have others report to us regularly on your behavior at work."

"If you manage to get it together and work your way back up the corporate ladder, we'll welcome you with open arms. If you don't straighten yourselves out, we'll reserve the right to sever ties between you and the company. Do you understand?" asked Dom.

"Yes," replied Paris and Vic in unison.

Dom nodded his head. "You're our children, but strict action is necessary in order to preserve the reputation of this company. Believe me when I say we take no pride in having to move forward in such a manner. Act like the adults you're meant to be, and we'll treat you as such. If there are no further questions, we'll give you the keys to your new apartments and have Mya and Chase take you to them."

Paris and Vic had no questions. Both were too shocked to speak. Mya grabbed the keys from Mikel, and she and Chase hustled them across campus to the employee housing where they too lived. The building was newly remodeled, except for the top floor.

Looking at the numbers and locations of the new apartments, Mya surmised that her place was much larger and nicer than what Vic and Paris were receiving. Both apartments were on the twelfth floor. Arriving at the first door, Mya handed Paris the key. Paris inserted her key into the lock and swung the door open. Mya cringed when she saw the inside.

"Holy crap!" screeched Paris. "Are we in hell?"

"My, oh my," said Vic, with a whistle. "I didn't know ADG owned such small and rundown-looking apartments."

Mya followed Paris inside. It was a fully furnished studio. The only room inside the apartment was the bathroom, which had a dingy shower stall, pedestal sink, and toilet. Outside the bathroom was a closet with a built-in dresser and clothes hanging bar, as well as a small stacked washer and dryer that looked as if they'd seen better days. The place had to be roughly six-hundred square feet. A bed was next to a small discolored orange and brown paisley loveseat in the living room, which had a small entertainment center across from it. The television was a twenty-four-inch but appeared to have a slight crack in the upper right corner of the screen. Mya speculated it was probably because someone accidentally threw a gaming controller at it. A coffee table stood in front of the loveseat, and at the opposite end sat the kitchen, which held a small fridge, sink, microwave, and range. There were a few cabinets and shelves and a small pantry, but even then, there was barely room for the coffeemaker and toaster.

"I've been in larger and cleaner hotel rooms," said Paris. "This place is a dump. Look at that ugly furniture."

"Yep, me too," commented Vic. "Here's hoping my place doesn't look as ugly as yours."

Mya felt claustrophobic just looking at it, and it wasn't even her place.

"This blows my mind," said Chase. "I had no idea apartments could be this small."

"Super," said Paris. "How much does this place cost?"

Mya picked up a paper from the coffee table and looked it over. "It says your rent is eight-hundred-and-fifty per month. That includes utilities."

"So, we have six-hundred-and-fifty dollars left to buy food and clothes?" replied Paris.

"Yup, that's about right," said Vic. "However, will you get by?"

"Vic, your apartment is directly next door," said Chase.

Vic shook his head. "Of course, it is."

"Here," said Mya, handing him the key.

Chase followed Vic next door. Upon opening the door, they found that the only difference between Vic's apartment and Paris's was that they were flip-flopped regarding the location of each item, and they were different colors. Paris's was orange, brown, and white, and his was navy, tan, and brown. A much better color palette. Walking to the window, he found he had a view of the park, which wasn't half bad.

"It's not terrible," said Chase. "I mean, it could be worse. They could have cut you off completely and fired you without a chance at redemption." Which, let's be honest, he had truly hoped for after the year Vic had put him through.

"Dude, spare me," he said. "If you really want to help, go get a bottle of Jack and let's drink until I forget I live here."

"Will do," replied Chase. "I'll order a pizza too." Anything for a chance to witness his boss's further agony.

"Good man," said Vic. "Be sure to see if the girls need anything, won't you?" He knew Chase disliked him, but he'd play his game if it meant getting his hands on some liquid happiness.

"Already on it," he said as he left the room. Vic's thoughtful request surprised Chase. He felt bad for Paris. Despite knowing Vic and she deserved what was coming to them, it would be a hard fall for anyone of their power and background. The pair had grown up in luxury, and tragedy had sent them spiraling out of control. Chase felt a twinge of sadness for them both.

· · · · ● · ● · · · ·

That evening, Vic and Paris called a temporary truce. They sat with Chase and Mya, drinking Jack and Coke and sharing a Margherita pizza from their favorite Italian restaurant up the street. Chase brought chips and a deck of cards, and they played poker around the little coffee table in Vic's apartment until eleven that night. Paris didn't want to admit it, but that first night in their new apartments had been entertaining, until two in the morning.

At two that morning, Vic woke from a dead sleep to the sound of Paris screaming. Hurrying toward the sound, he pounded on her apartment door. "What's wrong?"

"There's a bat!" she cried as she swung open the door. "It buzzed my head and woke me up."

"I don't see it," he said. "Where is it?"

"I think it's in the bathroom," she replied as she crawled under the kitchen table.

"Okay, I'll check it out," said Vic. Flipping on the light, he agitated the bat, and it flew directly at him, which caused him to shriek like a little girl.

"Did you get it?" asked Paris, her voice quivering. She was terrified of all vermin.

"No, I didn't get it! It flew back into the living room. Open the doors and windows!" he demanded. Walking back through the living room, he went to the kitchen to see what he could find. Grabbing a frying pan, he felt prepared to fight the winged demon.

"There it is," said Paris, pointing toward a cabinet in the kitchen.

Vic approached the bat carefully. As he went to hit it with the frying pan, it took flight and flew out the window. Paris bounced into action, slamming it shut behind the winged menace. "Thank you!" she said, exhaling. "I didn't know what to do."

"Glad I could help. Have a delightful night. I'm going back to bed," he said with a yawn. Vic did not know what the next day would bring, but he knew if he didn't get to sleep soon, the next day would be more agonizing than dealing with an entire army of bats.

At six in the morning, Paris awoke to the sound of drilling and hammering. "What in God's name is going on?" she demanded as she stomped across the room. Opening her door, she saw Vic already standing in the hall.

"Lord have mercy!" he bellowed. "They put us on a floor that's being remodeled!"

Chapter Six

Much to his chagrin, Vic could not fall back to sleep and was pulled out of his bleary-eyed gaze at the ceiling by the sound of loud knocking. Rolling over, he noted it was now seven in the morning. Throwing back the covers, he dragged himself out of bed. His head was pounding. All he wanted to do was sleep, but he pulled on the clothes he had arrived in the day before and headed for the door. The knocking continued.

"Hold on," he barked. "I'll be right there." Throwing open the door, he saw Chase standing outside looking fresh as ever, holding a tray of coffee and grinning. He noticed Mya was next door waiting for Paris to answer. She held a paper bag in one hand. He hoped the paper bag would join the coffee shortly.

"Morning, boss. How'd you sleep?" asked Chase.

It was obvious from his disheveled appearance that it had not been well. "What sleep?" he replied. "Paris had an unexpected visitor last night, which jolted me awake, and then this damned drilling and pounding began at six this morning, which gave me a total of three hours of shut-eye."

Forcing a frown, Chase said, "Here, enjoy some coffee on me. I should have warned you. You're the only two people on this floor. It's the last level of the building to be remodeled."

"That's just swell," replied Vic in defeat. He bet Chase was laughing on the inside as he divulged this tasty bit of information. The little pissant was enjoying his misery. Swallowing his pride, he said, "Thanks for the coffee. I need it." Turning away from the door, he motioned for Chase to come inside and have a seat. He was probably getting what he deserved, considering how he'd treated Chase in the past. Kharma had caught up.

"I told Mya we'd come over to Paris's apartment," said Chase. "I figured you'd be ready to go before she would."

"Yes. Indubitably," replied Vic as he succumbed to following Chase next door. "What are you wearing?" he asked. "Is that pink and purple?"

"Oh, this? Yeah. You like it?" asked Chase, as he did a spin so Vic could see his button-down shirt better. It was purple with pink flamingos.

"I'm really not sure," Vic replied, feeling perplexed. He felt just the sight of the shirt might be threatening his manhood, but he kept it to himself.

"Oh, well, it's all good," he said with a smile. "It'll grow on you."

"Doubtful," replied Vic. "Are all of your clothes that vibrant?" Chase had been his assistant for months, but Vic had not bothered to pay attention to his appearance.

"Yes, they are," commented Mya. "He's the most colorful person at ADG."

Beaming from the compliment, Chase tossed back his dark hair and replied, "Thanks, dear, I try."

"Have a seat, Vic," said Mya. "Enjoy a muffin. I have chocolate chip, blueberry, strawberry cream cheese, and pumpkin. Which would you prefer?"

Pulling out one of the chairs at the tiny kitchen table, Vic obliged. "I'll go with strawberry cream cheese."

"Great choice," she replied as she handed him the muffin.

"So glad you didn't take pumpkin, 'cause it's my fav," said Chase. If Vic had taken the pumpkin muffin, he would have secretly disliked him even more.

"Okay, that leaves chocolate chip for me since Paris always goes with blueberry. I would have chosen that or the strawberry anyway."

Having a seat, the threesome munched on their breakfast while waiting for Paris. Thirty minutes later, she finally joined them at the table.

"I don't know how I'm supposed to look presentable in the same clothes I wore yesterday. I took a shower, but I don't have a curling iron or actual hairspray. Luckily, there was a blow-dryer and some trial-size toiletries. This is maddening," she complained. "I don't even have my full makeup kit anymore. Thankfully, I keep an extra eye shadow, lipstick, and mascara in my purse. The rest of my face looks ghostly, though."

"Girl, you look radiant with or without makeup," complimented Chase.

"Thanks," she replied with a small smile.

Chase flashed his pearly teeth at Paris and Vic. "Anyway," he said, "don't you worry your pretty little head. We're going out shopping just as soon as you finish your breakfast. Mikel was happy to allow you to come to work in the same clothes as yesterday, but your mother, bless her lovely little soul, said absolutely not and allotted time for shopping this morning."

"Oh, thank goodness," said Paris. Grabbing the last muffin, she set to work polishing it off. "Where are we going shopping?" she asked between bites.

"Andretti's," said Mya. Before Paris protested, Mya stopped her. "You have limited funds, and Andretti's has everything you could need at an affordable price. You'll be fine." Paris looked as if she was about to choke on her muffin, so Mya again cut in. "Please, trust me. This is temporary. I know you're miserable right now, and you feel out of your element, but you'll make it through to the other side. I'll help you find things that are inexpensive but still make you look good. Once you have more money coming in, you can then decide to upgrade your belongings. Focus on one hour at a time. You've got this."

"She's right, Paris," interjected Vic. "You don't need all that fancy stuff. You'll look great no matter what. And remember, no stealing," he added with a mischievous grin.

"Really, Vic? You just need to rub salt in my wounds, don't you?" griped Paris. "Why are you so mean to me? In retrospect,

I should be the one who's picking on you, since our issues began in college when you caused us to miss our spring break flight to Cozumel."

"Let's not dig up old wounds," said Chase. "It won't help the current situation."

"I agree with Chase," said Mya. "It doesn't matter who did what back when. We need to focus on the here and now."

Paris didn't have any further strength to argue with Mya. She hadn't slept at all since arriving at her new place. She'd be thankful if she made it through the humiliation of her first day in the mailroom, as she was certain several people would be laughing at her situation. Finishing her last bite of muffin, she pushed away from the table and said, "Let's get this horror show started."

"Yes," replied Vic. "What a suitable statement." He joined Paris at the door, and they all shuffled outside. Looking at Chase and Mya, he asked, "Whose car are we taking?"

"We, my friend, are taking the bus," replied Chase. "Them's be the rules your mom provided. She wants you to try it out."

"I've never taken the bus before," mewled Paris.

Vic, rolling his eyes at her, said, "Well then, this'll be a treat."

Marching up the block, they headed for the nearest bus stop. The bus appeared on time and arrived in less than fifteen minutes. The ride, however, seemed to take forever. People were packing themselves in to every seat. The bus smelled like tuna fish, and it made Paris feel ill. She wasn't a fan of tuna under regular circumstances.

The second the bus stopped, Paris hopped up and led the group off. She wasn't excited about shopping at Andretti's, but she enjoyed buying new things. It was a struggle for her to accept that she'd lost everything. She didn't think she could feel any lower, which made her want to spend money. It was how she comforted herself.

"Paris," said Mya, "let's go. You can't stand here and stare at the store all day. We have to go inside, get what you need, and get home so we can unpack and get you to the office."

Cringing, Paris said, "I don't even want to think about work." Mya reached out and grabbed her hand. Paris tried to pull it away, but Mya didn't let go. She yanked Paris along as she moved toward the entrance to the store.

The inside of the big box store was nothing like the stores Paris was accustomed to. The lights were garish, and there were people everywhere. The store was half-grocery, which was convenient, to say the least. Luckily, it included a liquor section.

"Here we are," said Mya.

"Vic and I will pick up the food for both of you since it'll most likely take you longer to find toiletries and clothing," said Chase.

"Okay. Make sure you get an assortment of fruit, some yogurt, granola, almond milk, salad, and veggies," requested Paris

"Yes, Mya gave me a list of items already," replied Chase. "We've got you covered." Turning to Vic, he said, "I gave Mya your toiletry list. If you think of anything else, shoot her a text."

Paris watched Vic nod his understanding. He didn't look too happy either. It had been a long time since Mya had shopped with her, but she had always known what Paris liked. Apparently, their babysitters knew what they were doing. She cringed at the thought. They were adults who had been assigned babysitters.

"Okay," said Mya, "you two hit grocery and clothing, and we'll hit clothing and toiletries. See you in an hour." Grabbing two carts, she headed them toward the women's clothing department. "Paris, I'm leaving you to find clothing while I pick up your makeup and other toiletries. Be sure to get all the essentials, plus business attire and leisure. Oh, and for heaven's sake, be sure to buy practical shoes. You'll be walking a lot."

"Wait, I don't know how I feel about you picking up my hair and makeup items without me," she protested. "I want to know what I'm getting."

"If you come with me to makeup, you won't get the rest of the items you need in time. We have one hour. Besides, I used to do your hair and makeup all the time, or have you forgotten? I know this store, and I know what you need. Trust me."

"I don't trust you. I don't even like you," Paris replied.

Mya shook her head. "For the life of me, I don't know how you can be so cold." Walking away, she left Paris to fend for herself.

As Mya disappeared, Paris felt a slight panic coming on. She didn't even know where the women's clothing was located within the massive store. Reaching out, she fingered the cart handle, leery about the germs.

"It won't bite you, princess," said Vic. Snickering, as he wandered off with his own cart.

Paris sighed. She thought he'd already left. Reaching out, she rested her open hands on the edge of the handle and pushed ahead. Noticing the jewelry counter, she headed in that direction first.

As she perused the jewelry cases, the price tags provided her with a nagging reminder she was on a very strict budget. She had been wearing her diamond stud earrings and diamond heart necklace yesterday when everything changed. They would have to make up most of her jewelry collection for the time being, but perhaps a couple of inexpensive costume pieces wouldn't be so bad.

As Paris looked, she saw something she felt she needed. A string of white pearls. She didn't own pearls. Looking at the different options, she found a small set for sixty-five dollars. It even came with a pair of stud earrings. "I'll take those," she said to the clerk. The woman wrapped the items up for her and put a tag on the package so that the checkout clerk would know what to ring up.

Moving on, she put her emotions aside and grabbed each item on her list as if it were normal for her to be shopping in such a generic store. She knew the situation was temporary, so she went for comfort and versatility rather than a statement. She looked at the items as if they were her favorite brands, which sent a thrill of adrenaline through her body as she shopped.

Finishing in the clothing department, Paris wandered over to liquor. She chose a bottle of tequila and two bottles of wine. She had barely placed the bottles in her cart when Mya reappeared.

"Looks like you've found everything."

"I did okay," she replied. It was a tad difficult working within the allotted monetary guidelines."

"I'm sure," said Mya. "How much are you spending?"

"Four-hundred-and-five," she replied.

"Okay, just so you know, I went bare minimum with your makeup and bathroom items. I found an inexpensive curling iron and the razor you prefer. I spent eighty dollars, but I think you'll find I've covered most of the bases. Hopefully, the items will be sufficient for now. If you find you're missing anything, I'd be happy to lend what you need."

"Thanks," said Paris. Mya gave her a small smile.

"We should head for the checkout; we're cutting it close on time. The boys will be waiting."

Paris followed her to the checkout, where the clerk totaled everything up. Chase added one-hundred-and-ten dollars to her total with food items, which put Paris at five-hundred-and-ninety-five dollars, leaving her with fifty-five until she got paid the following Friday.

"Looks like great minds think alike," said Vic. He, too, had visited the liquor department. "I'll share if you will," Paris replied, looking over the six bottles of wine, case of beer,

and cheap bottle of Scotch in his cart.

Vic's shopping experience had been easier than Paris's, taking him half the time she had taken. His clothing purchases came to three-hundred-and-two dollars. With groceries, liquor, and clothing added in, he spent a grand total of four-hundred-and-seventy-two dollars.

Upon checking out and bagging all the items, the group realized they had to carry a lot of bags onto the bus. Chase decided that, to make things a little easier on them, he would call a taxi. Paris and Vic were both grateful to avoid the bus with their parcels.

Back at the apartments, they hurried to unpack their groceries and choose outfits to wear to work. Paris opted for a white ruffle dress with a brown belt and brown ruffle mule sandals. She kept her diamonds in place. She then applied her new cosmetics and was ready to go.

Vic chose to wear grey pants with a blue button-down shirt, brown belt, and brown loafers. He haphazardly adjusted his hair and added some gel, shaved, and headed for the door. He stopped momentarily and tossed a condom in his pocket for good measure. One never knew when they might come in handy, and for Vic, they frequently did.

Forty minutes later, the group found themselves walking toward the ADG building. A nauseating feeling rose up inside

Vic's stomach. He hadn't been below a managerial position in years. The mailroom seemed beneath him, considering the responsibilities he had previously held as an event planner. Two weeks ago, he'd commanded his team as if they were in a relay race to the finish with planning a last-minute wedding. Two of his charges transferred groups because they couldn't handle his volatile personality. In one year's time, he had developed a reputation as the fiercest manager at ADG, though ADG was generally known for employee empathy and kindness. If his style got the job done, what did it matter?

Paris looked over at Vic, a scowl creasing his brow. She couldn't blame him. She felt their parents had lost their minds. None of her business friend's families would have ever done such a thing. She wondered what the media would say if they found out about their situation. It wouldn't look good for anyone, including their parents. She figured it would only be a matter of time before they came to their senses and dropped the silly game they were playing.

"Okay, guys, we've arrived. This shouldn't be too difficult. You've both been here before, right?" asked Chase.

"I've been here, but never worked here," replied Vic. "I worked in the restaurants and then interned at Sense of Adventure. I moved up from there."

"I've never done this," replied Paris. "I haven't even stepped a foot inside this part of the building. I was a model when I started out, and then I moved on to work as a sommelier and writer."

Raising a brow and shaking his head, Chase said, "Super. This will be fun. Check-in with us anytime if you need advice or moral support."

"If you need to find us, we're helping to cover your positions while you're in the mailroom," added Mya.

Paris's face reddened. "No! How's that possible?" It was bad enough she had to put up with Mya as a babysitter, but a superior? No way.

"Relax. It's not that big of a deal. I'm returning calls to your clients and letting them know they'll be meeting with either Tom or Angela temporarily."

"That doesn't make me feel better," replied Paris. "We'll lose our regular clients." Tom and Angela occupied the other two spots as senior adventure planners, and they were both cut-throats in snagging new clients.

"Need I remind you that you've basically been fired," replied Mya. "The job should be of no concern to you at this time. You have to focus on the task at hand and prove to your parents and the rest of the board that you're of value to ADG and Sense of Adventure. Anyway, we need to go."

Pointing, Chase said, "Walk through that door, and Tonya will meet you on the other side to give you your duties."

"Later, kids," called Mya as she and Chase walked away.

"I don't want to go in there," said Vic. "Everyone will know who we are. We're without a doubt the laughing stocks of the company."

"My thoughts exactly. If we don't go in, things will undoubtedly get worse, right? I don't think we have a choice, do we? I mean, honestly, do we have any choices in this situation other than to do what we've been told?"

"I mean, technically, we could walk away from it all, but that would require money, which neither of us has. You're not exactly a typical working woman. You were raised as an heiress. To make it on your own, you'd probably need a financial advisor and help with your future goals."

She considered his statement. "Maybe you're right? It's not like I've been making goals or living up to my potential as of late." *Could she make it on her own?*

"Do you really want to walk away? I mean, think about it for a minute. Money has never been a problem for you. What would you do if you had none? You have a decent resume, but you're kidding yourself if you think you can leave and easily climb to a position such as the one you held at Sense of Adventure. The media headlines alone might stop you. Not to mention, you make what? A cool mil each year, plus your trust fund? No. Leaving the company is career suicide."

Paris stared at the ground. "Sometimes it's worth the risk of finding happiness. I'm not feeling at all fulfilled. It's a struggle to get out of bed each day. I'm not even certain I want to live this life anymore. That's why I took the pills."

Vic reached out and gently placed his hands on her shoulders. "Listen to me. There's help if you need it. You can go to rehab or counseling. Whatever you need. You can feel better.

No matter where you are, though, you'll have to deal with your pain. I can't see you walking away. To be fair, I can't see it for myself either." He watched as her eyes welled up. "Just hang in there. You can turn all of this around. I'll be right here beside you," he added with an empathetic smile.

"It feels like I'm at the bottom of a pit, and it's slowly caving in."

"I know, but please don't give up yet. You heard our parents. We have to do this together."

"Fine," she sniffed. "I'll give it a shot, but I'm not making any promises."

"Hello?" interjected a voice from behind them. A woman had popped her head out the door to see what they were doing.

"Um, hi," replied Paris. "Can we help you?"

"Well, if you plan on coming to work today, you sure can. My name is Tonya. You were supposed to meet me five minutes ago. You're not off to a proper start," she stated disapprovingly.

"Oh, Tonya, so sorry," replied Vic. "We were having a bit of an emotional moment, but I think we're all good now."

"Well, come on in. We best get you started, unless you plan on quitting before you begin?" Tonya asked, eyeing Paris.

"I'm coming," replied Paris. "I don't have anywhere else to be."

Paris and Vic followed Tonya inside, and she showed them the ropes. It took a couple of hours to relay all the information to do the job, but they were already taking on delivery assignments by that afternoon. Paris was a natural, but Vic was less than enthused to be delivering the company mail.

The day progressed rapidly. Before they realized it, it was four-thirty, and Tonya had sent them on their way. Mya and Chase came to meet them at the door to the mailroom.

"How'd your first day go?" asked Chase. "Did you learn a lot?" He couldn't stop grinning.

"Why are you always so chipper?" asked Paris. "I feel like my feet might fall off. All I did was walk from point A to point B the whole day long."

"Great exercise," said Mya. "You won't have to work out tonight."

Paris shook her head in disagreement. "I'd rather workout. As a matter-of-fact, I think that's what I'll do when we get back to the apartment." Bending over, she pried off her shoes and resolved to walk barefoot the rest of the way home. *Home,* thought Paris. "I can't believe I live in a shitty apartment at the employee end of campus." Mya ignored her comment.

"It's not great, but it could be worse," replied Vic. "We could be off-campus completely."

Chase nodded. "That's very true. The board discussed sending you to live off-campus. Your mother, Vic, said no. You're lucky she has so much empathy for you. She's helped your situation more than you realize."

"No car and off-campus. That would have sucked big time," said Paris, then changing the subject, "I think I'll go for a swim. We do have access to a pool still, don't we?"

"Yeah, you do, as well as the hot tubs," answered Chase.

Mya looked at Paris. "Do you mind if I join you?"

"I can't exactly say no. You live here too," replied Paris.

"Why don't we all go down to the pool for a bit? We can relax in the hot tub and discuss the day," suggested Chase. "If you have anything you need to work through, we can discuss that as well."

"What are you, our counselors?" asked Vic.

"Kind of," replied Mya. "We have strict instructions to help you in any way we can, as long as it coincides with the rules the board gave you."

"Fine," said Paris. "We'll eat dinner and then meet at the pool. Maybe it'll be a relaxing end to the day."

After dinner, the foursome met at the pool. The group conversed very little. They swam some laps and then soaked quietly in the hot tub. Paris could not bring herself to talk about the workday. Vic didn't seem to have much desire to discuss it either. Mya and Chase chattered with each other and paused now and then to include Paris and Vic, with little luck. After Paris finished in the hot tub, she pulled a bottle of tequila out of her beach bag and took a big swig. She noted Vic was watching her every move. "Want some?" she asked.

"Please," he replied as he approached her. Sitting down, he grabbed the bottle. They sat together quietly, watching Mya and Chase. They each thought about the things they'd done to end up where they were at that moment, slogging down tequila and feeling numb to the world.

The next morning, they met at the office at 7:30. Paris planned to do the job and keep her mouth shut. If she could do that, perhaps the board would promote her the following week. She had high hopes of returning to her previous lifestyle. She made it through her second day, as well as the rest of the week, without so much as a hiccup. Tonya told her she was doing great. She felt pleased with herself.

Vic was another story. Day two went well, but by day three, he was bored. He began slacking and pawning his duties off on other mailroom clerks. He disappeared during the day, and no one knew where he was. His lunch breaks lasted more than an hour. Paris ignored Vic's actions, or rather inaction, and went about her job like it was the best job in the world. By the end of the week, Tonya was none too happy with Vic. Paris was certain that he would be in trouble come Monday.

Friday night Paris left work with a sense of accomplishment. She knew she had performed her job to the utmost of her ability. She had been praised by several of her coworkers, which made her feel good. It had been a long time since she'd been praised by anyone. She felt oddly successful.

"What are you doing the rest of the evening?" Paris asked Vic as they, along with Mya and Chase, trudged back to their apartments.

"I have a date," he beamed. "I'm seeing Janel Maren."

"Your ex?" asked Mya. "Why? I thought you two were through months ago?" The look on her face was pure disgust. Mya had never cared for Janel, which was saying something.

"Well, I guess she couldn't stay away." And then, with a grin, he added, "She likes what I'm giving her."

"Ew, gross," ejected Paris. "I don't want to think about that."

"Be careful," cautioned Mya. "I don't trust her."

Vic glared back at Mya. "What could she do?" he asked.

"Trust me, she's a woman. She'll find something to do," said Paris.

"Um, Vic, doesn't she work for the Flores Press?" asked Chase.

"Oh, yeah, I think she started there last month, if I recall correctly?" he replied.

"There's your something," Chase said with concern. "You don't want her writing about your current situation, do you?"

Brushing him aside, Vic said, "She would never do that. I know her well. We dated for a year and a half. She'd never try to hurt me on purpose."

"Well, if you're sure," said Mya. "Still, be careful."

"Didn't you cheat on her?" asked Paris.

"That was a misunderstanding," replied Vic, "and none of your business."

"Does she know you cheated on her?" asked Chase.

"I didn't cheat on her. We unknowingly had different views about our relationship status," said Vic. "Anyway, enough of this. I'm changing clothes and heading out." He exited the elevator and headed for his place.

"Paris," asked Mya, "what are you doing this evening?"

"I think I'll curl up with the book I've been carrying around in my purse," she replied.

"That sounds nice. Call me if you want to hang out," said Mya with sincerity.

"I doubt it. My current situation changes nothing," she commented.

"Okay, then," said Chase with a look of disgust, "I guess we'll see you Monday."

Paris went into her apartment and closed the door behind her. She was tired of the people surrounding her. She would eat a salad, grab a glass of wine, and curl up on the couch with her book. The perfect Friday night. Well, almost perfect. She no longer had her own personal whirlpool, so she couldn't properly soak the week's stressors away unless she wanted to sit down by the pool with the other residents staring at her and wondering what went wrong. *No, thank you very much,* she thought.

Chapter Seven

The weekend came and went, and Paris and Vic both managed to stay out of trouble, or so they thought. On Monday, at six in the morning, the God-forsaken racket of drilling, pounding, and grinding once again jolted the pair awake. It was impossible to ignore the clank, clank, clank, emitting from the apartment across the hall.

Vic rolled over and covered his head with his pillow, hoping he could ignore the sounds and get another hour of sleep, but it was no use. He rolled out of bed and headed for the shower. If he couldn't ignore it, he would take a nice long shower to relax some before heading back to the boardroom.

Paris found herself wishing she had some earplugs when the ruckus began. She ducked under the covers and pressed her hands to her ears, but she could still hear and feel the sound and vibrations of the pounding. Sitting up, she threw back the blankets and let out a frustrated growl. This was not how she wanted to start her Monday. She threw her pillow in contempt.

Clenching her teeth, she sprung out of bed and headed for her bathroom. Turning on the water, she stepped away for a moment to locate a playlist on her phone while the temperature warmed. Finding what she was looking for, she pressed play and stepped into the shower. The needles of hot spray felt great as they massaged into her tired body.

In his own shower, Vic was enjoying his own playlist. The Celtic sound of the *Dropkick Murphy's* filled the room as Vic sang along loudly. No one would have guessed that Vic Alarie was into the concept of singing in the shower, and he preferred to keep it that way, despite how great his voice actually sounded. He had barely finished rinsing when the water cut out. As his playlist began shuffling to the next song, he heard Paris screaming in anger next door. He hopped out of the shower and wrapped a towel around himself.

Banging on Paris's door, he waited a moment and received no answer, so he tried the handle. It was unlocked, so, he let himself in. "Paris? Hello? Are you okay?" he called out.

Paris presented herself in a pair of sweatpants and a tank, with a towel atop her head. "My water has stopped working mid-shower!" she cried. "I'm covered in suds. I can't go to work like this. My hair's a mess! Why are you wearing nothing but a towel?"

"Oh, yeah, sorry. I was in the shower as well and heard your screams. I wanted to make sure you didn't get hurt or something," he replied carefully.

"Don't make any sudden moves!" she blurted. "I don't want that towel coming undone."

"Why not? You seemed to have trouble looking away that night at my condo." He laughed.

Removing the towel from her head, she threw it at him. "I doubt that very much!" she snapped.

"Dang, you weren't kidding. Your hair is full of suds," said Vic. "Why don't we go over to Mya's, and you can finish showering?"

"We need to find out why the water is off and how long it's going to be. This is ridiculous," she whined.

"Calm down, princess, I'll look into it. Get your phone and call Mya. Tell her you'll be over shortly. I'm sure she'll let you use her shower."

Paris picked up her phone and dialed Mya. She hated having to ask for a favor, but she was desperate.

"Hello?" answered Mya.

"Hi. It's Paris. While I was showering, someone turned off the water. I'm covered in soap and desperate. Do you still have water?"

"As far as I know. Let me check." Mya set the phone down and went to the faucet. Flipping it on, she watched as water flowed into the sink. Turning back to her phone, she said, "Yep. My water's still running."

"May I please come over and finish showering at your place?" she begged.

"Yeah, sure," replied Mya. "I'll see you in a few."

Paris hung up the phone and gathered her work clothes. When she exited her apartment, Vic was already dressed and waiting by the elevator. "I tried to talk to one of the workers, but he couldn't hear me. I called and asked Chase to bring coffee. Lord knows I need it this morning. I wonder how long the remodel is scheduled to continue for?" Paris followed Vic into the elevator.

"I don't know, but this is driving me mad," she said. "I feel like I've time-warped to some other dimension."

"Woman, you don't have to tell me how it feels. I'm right here with you."

Stepping off the elevator, Paris fast-walked to Mya's apartment, hoping no one else would be in the hall. Once inside, Mya gave her a new towel, and she headed off to the bathroom to finish cleaning up.

Mya looked to Vic, "How are things? Are you ready for the meeting today?"

"Yes and no," he replied. "I'm already tired of this charade and wanting it to be over."

"You can want, all you desire, but it won't be over until you actually make some changes," she said.

A knock sounded at the door. Vic opened it to find Chase standing in the hallway with four cups of coffee in a cardboard carrier. "Morning," he said happily as he handed Mya and Vic each a cup. "Did everyone sleep well?"

"Not particularly," replied Vic. "This morning, we were once again awoken by the construction at six-o-clock and then while we were showering, the water to our apartments was turned off."

"Oh, that's too bad. Drink your coffee. It'll make you feel a little more human," he instructed.

"You're enjoying this a bit too much," replied Vic. Chase nodded in return and Vic rolled his eyes.

Once Paris had finished her morning routine, the party set out for the main ADG building. Their group was the first to arrive at the meeting. They grabbed more coffee and pastries and took their seats all on one side of the table. The seniors came in and took their seats across from them. Vic felt as if he was at an interview. Little did he know, it was much like an interview.

"Good morning," said Jessamine. "How are you all doing today? Paris, you look a little tired, sweetie."

"I am," she replied. "I couldn't sleep last night, and this morning, while I was in the shower, the workers shut off the water to our apartment."

"Oh, that's terrible! We'll inform the work crew they must notify you from now on if there will be any shut-offs," replied her mother. Paris let out an audible sigh when she realized her family knew the complete extent of their current living situation.

"How about the rest of you?" asked Jessamine.

"I'm good, Mom," replied Vic. "I made it out of the shower before the water stopped." Turning away, he smirked at Paris, who shook her head angrily.

"You look good, Vic. I see you found some clothes to wear. Considering where you had to go, I think you all did fairly well," said Dom.

"Mya, Chase, how about you? How are things going? Are they behaving themselves?"

Chase nodded his head to the affirmative. "I can't speak for how things are when they're at work, but outside of the office, they seem to be behaving themselves."

"Oh, really?" asked Cristo. "Then what's this?" he asked as he produced the morning's paper and slid it across the table to Chase. "Feel free to read the headline out loud."

"Oh, damn," said Chase. "*ADG Heirs Cut Off From Trust Funds And Demoted.* Vic! I told you to be careful. I warned you about Janel. How could you be so careless?"

Vic choked on his coffee, sputtering droplets across the table. He neither suspected Janel would try to hurt him, nor that Chase had an angry bone in his body. The headline humiliated him. One thing was for certain. He and Janel were through for good this time.

"Thanks a lot," said Paris. She had nothing more to say to him. She couldn't believe he'd been so stupid as to tell his ex about their current situation. Now everyone would know, and it was beyond embarrassing.

"Definitely not what we expected to see in the papers this morning," said Nicola. "I would have thought you two would have kept this situation to yourselves," she said, shaking her head in disapproval.

"Moving on to the next order of business," said Mikel. "How do you think you did with your new positions?" he asked.

"I busted my butt," said Paris. "I think I followed directions well, and I got things done. I'm quite proud of the week I had."

"Yes, you did very well," agreed her father.

"Vic, what about you?" asked Jessamine. "How'd you do?"

"I learned the job. It was easy. The week flew by," he replied.

"Uh-huh," said Dom. "What about the part where you quit working halfway through?"

"Dad, I didn't stop working. I just didn't complete as many assignments. The job was simple, but it got boring fast. It's not like the work didn't get done."

"The problem, Vic, is that the person who was supposed to be doing it, did not complete the work. Tell me, what would you do if you hired someone and halfway through the week, they simply stopped doing the job you had trained them on?" asked Dom.

"I'd discuss their performance with them and get them back on track. If they didn't take it seriously, I'd find someone to retrain them," he replied.

"You'd retrain them?" asked Mikel.

"Yes, sir," replied Vic.

"No, sir," replied his father. "You, my son, have fired people for much less."

"He's right," backed Chase. "You've fired people for much less and on their first day of work, even. You've shown no mercy."

"So," said Mikel, "this is what we're going to do. You, my young friend, are fired."

"Seriously?" asked Vic. "You already demoted me to nothing."

"Oh, trust me, there's always somewhere else for us to put you," replied Dom.

"Paris, you did a great job, but unfortunately, you're going with him," stated her mother.

"What?!" shrieked Paris. "Why am I being punished for his mistake?"

"If one of you fails, both of you fail, remember? You had better get that in your heads, or this will be an ugly process," added her father.

"You'll have to take this up with each other," replied Dom. "You're either best friends or worst enemies. It's your choice.

"Now, if you two will excuse yourselves from the boardroom, we must discuss a couple of things with Chase and Mya. You may wait in the lobby," said Cristo as he waved them toward the door.

Paris and Vic got up and left the room. Paris wanted to strangle Vic, but she knew that would only make her situation worse. For now, she planned to ignore him. She would tell him later just how much she hated him, but he could stew in it for the time being.

Vic knew Paris was angry, and he honestly couldn't blame her. He would have been pissed, too, if she had gotten him fired from the lowest job he could have imagined. Apparently, his imagination wasn't so great if other places were waiting for him below the mailroom. He was shocked at how serious the situation had become.

In the boardroom, Mya didn't know what was coming next. She hadn't suspected a further demotion, and in allowing such a thing to happen, she worried that she and Chase would be punished as well. She waited anxiously for the seniors to speak.

"Listen," said Nicola, "we know you're working hard. We expected that there could be hiccups before any genuine changes take place. You're not to blame for these mistakes. We recognize you're doing everything we've asked of you, and that's all we can expect."

"Don't beat yourself up about the article, Chase," said Cristo. "I suspect it would have gotten out one way or another."

"We've resolved to work with the media to put a spin on the situation. We'll let them know that this is a strong and progressive tactic that we've put into place to teach Paris and Vic a lesson and help restore them to their prior selves. The people they were before we lost Alli and Brody," said Dom. "We'll force them to sign a document stating that they may release none of this information until after the situation has resolved itself. Our lawyers are already at work."

"We're placing Vic and Paris in Janitorial. We suspect this will give them a stronger appreciation for those who clean up after them regularly. The job isn't easy, and some people think it's below them, but it deserves respect, and it takes a lot of effort to be successful," said Nicola. "My father, Burt, will be there to look after them and guide them as well. He's good at getting people back on track, and he loves his job, which should help them take their situation a little more seriously."

Nodding, Mikel added, "You'll take them to their new jobs, and you'll continue to encourage and help them in any way you can. Be sure to report to us if there are any issues or positive happenings."

"We will," replied Chase.

"Okay then, you may be on your way. I hope that next week we'll be promoting instead of demoting," said Jessamine.

"Thank you," replied Mya. "We'll do everything we can to help them be successful." Chase nodded in agreement, and then they both retreated.

Once they were out of earshot, Chase said, "That turned out better than I thought it would."

"Yeah, I agree. When Cristo took out that paper, I thought for sure we were in hot water." She was thankful that the board members were giving credit where credit was due, but she also felt sorry for Paris. Paris was actually trying to do a good job, and now Mya and Chase had to tell her she was about to be a janitor. Paris was a complete germaphobe, so this would be a nightmare for her.

Mya and Chase found Paris and Vic waiting in the lobby, as instructed. Paris stood with her body facing away from Vic, who was staring blankly out the window.

"Hey," said Chase. Both Paris and Vic turned to look at him. "We're to take you over to Janitorial."

Paris's jaw dropped. "You've got to be joking. I refuse to scrub toilets. I did nothing wrong," she whined.

"Damn," said Vic. "I was wrong. It can get worse."

"Listen," requested Mya. "I know you don't want to do this. I feel for you. Neither of you even knows how to clean your own homes, let alone a business, but you have to do this if you ever want your regular lives back. Please, think of it as temporary, so you can do the best job possible and move on to the next thing."

Chase nodded to back her statement. "She's right. With any luck, it'll only be for a week."

"I don't want to," Paris whispered. She looked as if she might cry.

Mya waved for them to follow her. They got on the elevator and she pressed the button for the basement. Exiting the elevator, Chase led them to Building Maintenance, which housed the janitorial staff.

Stepping inside, the smell of grease and cleaning supplies assaulted their noses. Burt, who was acting head of maintenance and janitorial, met them. He did not need to work, as he'd hit it big in the stock market at an early age. Burt knew how to invest and he had built himself a multi-million-dollar nest egg, but given his love for fixing things and his inability to sit still, he helped his daughter and son-in-law by running the department.

"Hey, kids," he greeted them. "I see you're working for me starting today." Burt, grinning, handed them their uniforms, consisting of a grey zippered jumpsuit. "Now I know you aren't used to this sort of work," he noted, "but we'll go easy on you starting out."

"Thanks," Paris replied hesitantly.

Burt wrapped his arm around his granddaughter and gave her a squeeze. "Buck up, kid. Things aren't as bad as they seem. Chase and Mya, you may go," said Burt. "They'll be released from my service at four-thirty."

"Bye," said Chase. "Hang in there. You'll do fine."

Paris didn't feel like his encouragement was helpful. She wanted to crawl into a hole and hide until the nightmare ended. She also wanted to bludgeon Vic with a mop for getting her into this mess.

When they were young, the DeMarcé and Alarie children would play hide and seek throughout the Building Maintenance Department. Burt and his crew would play along. There had been a day when Vic and Paris had felt as if Building Maintenance was a magic kingdom that belonged to them. Those days had long since disappeared.

"Your first task," said Burt, "will be to empty the trash and recycling throughout the building. We won't do any training on hazardous materials yet."

"Oh, well, that's a relief," said Paris, as she rolled her eyes.

Burt paused and stared her down for a moment. "You may think this is a joke or a job that's beneath you, but let me tell you something, missy, it's people like me that keep your world clean and moving along. If we don't do our jobs, others can't do theirs. Your streets would be littered with trash, and your restrooms smeared with poop and heaven knows what else. Think of the nastiest gas station bathroom you've ever had to use, and then imagine if it was worse. You're welcome," he snapped. "And, Paris, honey, don't look at me as grandpa during this. See me as your boss," he requested.

"I'm sorry," she said, averting her eyes. "I didn't mean to offend you. You know I've never had to clean before. This is outside my wheelhouse."

"Well, sweetheart, don't you think it's time you learned to be a proper adult?" asked her grandfather. "This is work. Real life lessons. Now, follow me," he ordered.

Vic had kept his mouth shut the entire time Burt spoke. He wasn't thrilled to be a janitor, and he realized he couldn't complain since he was the one who dragged Paris down with him. He worried about what would come next. What if she couldn't do it? They could be trapped at this job for months. He'd have to apologize and get on her good side.

They followed Burt quietly to the supply closet, where he explained what was expected of them.

Paris left janitorial with a large cart that held two bins. One bin for trash, the other for recycling. When the bins filled, she was shown the designated locations for emptying. The job was pretty straightforward, but she wasn't stoked. She didn't want the ADG staff to see her traipsing around as a janitor. What would they think? How would they ever take her seriously in the future?

In actuality, no one seemed to pay any attention to Paris or Vic as they went about their jobs. Both had on their required work attire, which seemed to act like an invisibility cloak. Even when they passed by people they knew, no one noticed who they were or even acknowledged their presence. In emotional defense of her grandfather and his work, Paris became irritated that none of the other staff took notice of the people who were keeping their world clean. In the future, she would have to make a point of saying thank you more often to the maintenance and janitorial staff.

The first day was monotonous, but went by quickly. Day two seemed to last forever as they learned about safety and hazardous chemicals. Burt was long-winded in his explanations, and, as per usual, he thought he was pretty funny. Vic struggled to listen because he neither cared for long explanations nor Burt's sense of humor. On day three, things took a serious turn for the worse.

Burt instructed Paris and Vic to clean the bathrooms on floor twelve. Little did Paris know, there was a clogged toilet on twelve, and it was her job to fix it. She went at it with her trusty plunger, but nothing seemed to budge. Putting some extra strength into it, she heaved the plunger down and was immediately sprayed with fecal matter, and heaven only knew what else. Shrieking, she jumped backward and stepped on the mop handle, which was lying on the floor. Losing her balance from the loose footing, she fell backward and cracked her head on one of the sinks, rendering herself unconscious.

Vic heard the scream as he was cleaning the men's bathroom next door. Rushing into the women's, he found Paris lying on the floor, still unconscious. Shaking her did nothing to bring her around, so he turned on the closest faucet and splashed cold water on her face, which immediately brought her to. Sputtering, she brushed water and dark matter away from her eyes.

"What happened?" she asked with confusion.

"Well, judging by the look of things, I'd say you got sprayed by the toilet and then tripped and hit your head on the sink. Here," said Vic, handing her a dampened towel.

Grabbing the towel, she attempted to clean herself off. "Great. Now I'll smell like a toilet all day."

"Are you okay?" he asked. "You hit your head pretty hard." Reaching out, he ran his fingers over the back of her head. "You have a pretty good bump back there. I think we should get you checked out."

Pushing Vic away, she said with a sigh, "Just leave me alone. You've done enough."

"Paris, I'm sorry. If it's any consolation, I'm miserable too."

"It really isn't. This just goes to prove what an incredibly inconsiderate and self-centered jerk you are."

"Well, it takes one to know one," he spat back. "At least we get to work with your grandfather. That's kind of a plus." He smiled sheepishly. "Would an inconsiderate and self-centered jerk think you should see a doctor about the bump on your head?" Turning away from her, he went back to the men's room. He wasn't about to force her to get help, though he honestly was worried. When he was younger, one of his friends lost a parent to a ski injury in which they hit their head and refused to be looked over by a doctor. *Freak accident*, he thought.

At four-thirty, Vic headed back to Building Maintenance and the Janitorial wing. Paris was nowhere to be seen. "Hey, Burt, is Paris still here?" he asked.

"No, sir. Girl hit her head on a sink. It's a crying shame how clumsy that one is. I made her go to medical. I even offered to stay with her, but she threw a fit, so I left her there and asked her to check in once she finished. She has a mild concussion, and seeing as she was covered in dark matter, and as she put it, traumatized, I sent her home for the remainder of the day. She'll be fine, but check in on her."

"Wow, okay," replied Vic. "I'm calling it a day if that's alright with you?"

"Sure thing, kid," replied Burt.

"Thanks." Peeling off his jumpsuit, he tossed it into the laundry bin. "See you tomorrow."

Back at home, the shower was once again working, and Paris stood in the hot water, allowing the goo of the day's miseries to run down her body and into the drain. She shuddered to think that she had managed to knock herself unconscious. Her grandfather told her she "really needed to be more careful," which was obvious. Doctor Schuh couldn't seem to understand the scenario in which she went from plunging a toilet to unconscious on the ground. Chase met her at medical, and upon finding out she would be okay, couldn't stop laughing about what had happened. He did apologize profusely in-between laughs, and he took the initiative to report back to her grandfather for her.

Rinsing the deep conditioner from her hair, she let the rest of her misery go. Two more days and the week would be over. With any luck, she would be back in the mailroom the following Monday. Feeling low, she wished she still had her pills. "Damn that Mya," she said out loud. Dropping her head into her hands, she grumbled, "I hate my life."

Unfortunately for Paris, the next day wasn't much better. She arrived at work by seven-thirty, and she and Vic were put on light bulb duty. They were to go through each office and replace any light that was burnt out. It seemed simple enough, though she refused to work alongside Vic, as she blamed him for her current employment situation.

At midday, Paris balanced precariously on a ladder as she attempted to change one of the boardroom lights. The maneuver was awkward and her feet and hands wobbled as she tried to remove the old bulb.

"Hey Paris!" yelled Jack.

Paris jumped at the sound of his voice. The large light-tube flew into the air as she fell backward off the ladder. The bulb shattered on the floor, and Paris bounced off the boardroom table, knocking into a chair on her way down, causing it to somersault into the air.

"Are you okay?" screeched Jack, as he scrambled to her side.

She wheezed as she tried to catch her breath. Glass sparkled in her hair, and the chair balanced awkwardly on top of her.

Jack tossed the chair aside. "Don't move," he said. "You're cut, and you may have broken ribs." Pressing the intercom, he called for help. Medical arrived within minutes and hauled her off to see Dr. Schuh once again.

Vic stood in front of his locker, removing his jumpsuit, when Burt walked in. "That granddaughter of mine. Sheesh. She has got to stop with the acrobatics."

"What do you mean?" asked Vic.

Shaking his head, he said, "Day two and I had to send her home again. Today, she fell off a ladder and ended up back in medical. She was much tougher as a child. I don't understand what happened, but I don't think she's cut out for this job. I should have pushed her parents to give her more chores as a child."

"Yeah. Maybe that would've helped," Vic replied with a frown. "Is she okay?"

"She cut her head and her ego and body are both bruised, but she'll be okay, they assured me."

Paris was not okay. Mentally, she felt like she might be suffering a psychotic break. She couldn't believe how lousy her luck had been. Jack stayed with her until Dr. Schuh said it was okay for her to go home. Doctor Schuh told her, "You have got to be more careful. You could have broken your neck." If she had broken her neck, she wouldn't have to deal with the insanity any longer. It shocked Chase and Mya that her day had ended in medical two days in a row.

• • • • • • • • • •

"Hey," said Jack, "let's buy something. That always makes you feel better." He sat in her

living room, smiling back at her from behind a frosty beer. He made it his job to know what Paris liked in the event that she ever took him up on his requests to take her out on a proper date.

Paris stared back at the handsome young man in front of her. He had deep brown puppy

dog eyes, and messy blonde hair that was longer on top and shorn on the sides. She'd never go for him, despite how sweet he could be. He was Vic's little brother, and she couldn't cross that line.

"Or," he said, "we can grab dinner at the café up the street."

"Jack, don't," she replied. He looked incredibly young with his hair pulled back in a ponytail. He wore jeans and a Nirvana t-shirt. *Oh, to be his age again.* "I'll take that beer away from you." He was, after all, not of drinking age, but she knew he drank with his family on a regular basis, and he was nineteen, so when he pulled the beer out of his bag, she let him be.

"What? Can't a guy buy a traumatized girl some dinner?"

"Your brother would flip if I ever were to date you," she replied matter-of-factly. "I liked your first idea, though I'm short on money these days," she said with disappointment.

"It doesn't hurt to browse," said Jack.

"True," she replied happily. Giving in, she sat down on the couch next to Jack, and he handed her his work laptop.

"I think I'll grab some food from *Burritos to Taco Bout*. You want something?" he asked.

"Sure, get me a Supreme, please."

"'Kay, I'll be back shortly."

In the twenty-five minutes that Jack was gone, and before she had a chance to realize what she'd done, Paris managed to spend all of her leftover money. Like a crack addict, she couldn't seem to help herself. When Jack returned with the food, she was sitting on the couch staring at the wall, tears running silently down her face.

"What happened?" he asked.

"I spent it all!" she wailed.

"What? Explain," he requested.

"I spent all of my leftover money. It's completely gone."

"Well, return something," he demanded.

"I can't," she replied. "Non-returnable."

"Paris, what sort of store are you shopping at that you can't return items to?"

"Not a store," she sighed. "An auction."

"Oh, man," he said as he dropped the food on the coffee table. "When I said buy something, I thought maybe a cute shirt, or a new purse, not a bunch of random auction items. Where's your restraint?"

"I have none!" she cried. "I didn't think I'd actually win the bids."

"I can't bail you out," stated Jack. "Our parents made it clear that no one, except Vic, is allowed to give you money. I also have to tell Mya and Chase about this."

"What? No! You can't!"

"I have to. I don't have a choice," he replied. "I've been instructed and threatened basically that if I don't report to them, I'll end up in the same situation as you and Vic."

"This would have been helpful information before you followed me home!" hollered Paris as she threw her unopened burrito at him.

"Hey, watch it," he replied. "I know you're feeling vulnerable, so I'll let it slide this once, but if you ever throw anything at me again, I'll report that as well." Grabbing his bag of food along with the burrito Paris had thrown at him, he stormed out of her apartment. Rushing after him, Paris slammed the door in his wake.

Vic had only been home for fifteen minutes. Long enough to tear off his clothing down to his generic boxers and pour himself some Scotch, when he heard the commotion from next door. He really didn't want to deal with it, but the noises and the voices had piqued his curiosity. It sounded like his younger brother and Paris arguing.

With resolve, he pulled on his sweatpants and proceeded to drag himself over to Paris's. She answered the door, but only after he yelled for her to, "Open up!"

"What do you want?" she hissed through her tears.

"I heard yelling, as well as about your incident today, and I thought I'd check to see if you were okay."

"I'm fine," she replied. She wasn't fine, but she didn't want to deal with Vic.

"Did I hear Jack?" he asked. "There's a beer bottle on your table, and he's the only person I know that drinks that crappy brand."

Paris turned to look at the telltale bottle she'd left sitting out. "Yes, Jack was here, but only because he's the reason I fell off the ladder. He demanded I allow him to accompany me home and stay with me until he felt I would be okay. I tried to say no, but he's very persistent," she complained.

"You aren't dating him, are you?" asked Vic as he eyed her suspiciously.

"Why are you so paranoid?" asked Paris. "No, I'm not dating him, but what if I wanted to? Is that so wrong?"

"Yes. He's my innocent little brother," replied Vic through gritted teeth. "And you're a hungry harpy who tears men apart."

"A harpy? Really, Vic? That's what you liken me to?" Paris's chest ached at his comment. He could be so mean, and she couldn't believe he thought so low of her. She rarely dated, and she didn't sleep around. "How can you say that?"

"I've seen how you work. I just know it's true. Besides, you're into things I don't want my little brother to be a part of," he added.

"Like what?" she demanded.

"Drugs, for starters. Oh, and stealing," he said as he pointed a finger at her.

"Don't point your finger at me, buddy," her voice had raised an octave. "And for the record, I may have tried a couple of things, but I'm done with that."

"Stealing, or drugs?" he asked.

"Obviously, I'm referring to the drugs. I haven't touched a single pill since Mya ground them in my disposal."

"Oh, so you're not done with stealing?" he asked.

"Well," she said, sticking out her chin. "Now that I have no money, I may not have a choice."

Vic shook his head. He was floored at how ridiculous Paris acted. She'd been handed everything in life, yet she chose to steal things simply because she could. It was maddening to think about. "You'll be fine. We'll get our jobs and money back, you'll see."

"No, you don't understand," she said, tears threatening to fall. *Pull it together, Paris,* she thought to herself. The last person she needed to see her cry was Vic. "I've spent all my current money," she added sheepishly.

"What?" demanded Vic. "How?"

"I was upset, and Jack suggested I buy myself something."

"You listened to him? He's a baby, Paris. He barely knows his left hand from his right. Whatever would possess you to take his advice?"

"It sounded like a good idea at the time."

"You need to cancel that order," he said.

"I can't." Her bottom lip began to quiver.

"Yes, you can," he replied. "It's simple. You go to your account and hit cancel."

"No, I can't," she said shakily. "It was an auction. Your little brother has run off to tell Mya and Chase about my epic failure, as we speak."

"Lord, have mercy," said Vic as he stared up at the ceiling. He didn't know what to say. The woman was maddening and seemed to be hell-bent on making his life miserable. He had to admit, though, aside from her clumsiness, she really had put forth some effort into their current situation. At least until now. He would make a mental note to give Jack a sound tongue lashing when he saw him next. That boy always thought he knew what was best, but rarely did he have a good idea outside of his writing. He lived in a fantasy world most of the time. It was all roses and damsels in distress.

Breaking into Vic's thoughts, Paris asked, "What am I going to do?"

"Woman, this better not push us further down the rabbit hole," replied Vic. "I can't even imagine what worse job could be waiting for us if this doesn't pan out."

"You know what," replied Paris, "you're the reason we ended up janitors. I was doing just fine in the mailroom. You're the one who can't keep it in your pants. Slacking off to chase tail is not okay, especially at your age. I would have moved up from there if I hadn't been tethered to your ungrateful butt."

"Ungrateful? Don't make me laugh. You're the queen of ungratefulness, Paris. I don't know what you're going to do about your money problem. It's not my issue. Good luck," he said, slamming the door as he left.

· · · ● · ● · · · ·

Saturday morning, Vic set out to meet his family for a game of tennis. Normally, he and his brother would team up against their parents. The game had become a fun family ritual that took place at least twice per month. Whenever his cousin Breanna was in town, she and Cristo would form a team and play as well. Today his brother and Cristo had some business to attend to, so Breanna had swapped in as his partner.

"You ready for this?" asked Breanna. She was bouncing from one foot to the other, her blonde ponytail whipping back and forth. Her energy was off the charts. He'd be lying if he said he'd never wondered if the girl was on speed, but she'd exhibited such behavior as far back as childhood.

"Give me some of what you're having," he said, "and I think I'll manage."

"Nah, you can't bottle this," she laughed. "We have thirty minutes until game time. You still have a couple of miles in you?"

"You want to run before the match?" asked Vic.

"Come on, Vic, for old time's sake? I miss those high school days when we ran cross country together."

"I usually take Saturday off and play tennis instead. It's easier on the knees."

"Seriously? You must be getting old," she said with a snort. "Do it for me. Please?"

"Fine," he conceded. They stopped to drop their bags in lockers and then were on their way after a brief stretch.

Without wasting any time, Breanna said, "I heard about your situation."

"What situation?" asked Vic. He'd play dumb and see how much she truly knew.

"For starters, it sounds like you lost your job and were asked to move out of your condo because of something that happened the night of the festival. Did you find another job yet?"

Vic stopped running, and Breanna faltered only briefly as she came to a halt in front of him. Lowering his voice, he asked, "Who told you that?"

"Word gets around," she replied, "but I actually heard it from Jack. He said things are a bit of a mess right now because you're no longer a Senior Planner. It's true then?"

"Yeah. It's true," he replied huffily. "This isn't something I care to discuss. I just want to forget about it for a while."

"I'm surprised you're still willing to stick to your weekend ritual, all things considered."

"You don't know the whole story," said Vic. "They're making us jump through some hoops to try to win back their approval and our previous lives. This is some big game to them."

Breanna's face wrinkled in confusion. "Us?"

Vic scowled at her. "So, let me get this straight, Jack told you about my situation, but he failed to mention Paris is in the same boat?"

"What? No. He didn't tell me that."

"Figures. He's always trying to play the protector. He has Paris placed on top of some pedestal. One of these days, she'll fall." He was angry at his brother for being so forthcoming with information relating to his fragile state. Where was the family loyalty? It hurt knowing that Jack could throw him under the bus and raise Paris up all in one slick motion.

"Vic, don't blame Jack. He's basically a child still. He hasn't lived through half of what we have."

"I don't care. He needs to learn that some things should be kept to himself, and if he is going to divulge information to another family member, then he'd better tell the whole damn story and not just the parts he likes."

"Why don't you tell me in your own words what happened?" she requested.

Shaking his head, he said, "It's too embarrassing. I'm still shocked that our own family is putting us out like they are."

"Putting you out? There must be a lot more to this situation than what Jack told me." Her usual smile had turned to a frown as she waited for his response.

"Not surprising," he replied, breaking into a jog. Breanna stepped off after him.

"Tell me, please. Maybe I can help."

"Fine, I guess it's better you hear it from me than from the media. They already have a whiff of this story."

"Oh, geez, that makes things even worse."

"Yeah, tell me about it." Vic took a deep breath, then expelled the entire story of the past few weeks. When he finished, Breanna's eyes went wide, and she stopped jogging. Vic watched as her face contorted and a small laugh escaped her lips. "Oh, you think this is funny?" At that moment, Breanna lost control, doubling over and laughing hysterically. "Come on. Get it all out of your system," he replied with a scowl.

"I'm sorry," she said between gasps for air. "I really am."

Raising an eyebrow, he frowned, slowly nodding his head. "Yeah, it genuinely seems you are."

Managing to get a hold of herself, she paused and took a deep breath. "Our parents are brilliant. Don't you get what's happening?"

"Yeah, we're being punished."

"That's only half of it," she said in a more serious tone. "They're testing you."

"What do you mean?"

"You really don't know how lucky you are. I swear to you, this is much more than a simple punishment. They're looking for something, or you'd already be out on your own. Consider this a blessing because you still have a shot." She grinned as she took off at a full-on run. "Let's go. We're cutting it close if we plan to play tennis today."

Vic ran after her, his mind reeling at the discovery she'd made. Were they being tested? If so, why? He knew they'd made mistakes, but what was the point of this whole situation other than to punish them? He'd bring the conversation to Paris at a later point in time. Perhaps she'd have some insight.

Chapter Eight

It was week three and Vic and Paris found themselves sitting at the boardroom table. The room was quiet as everyone poured a cup of coffee and passed around bagels and tubs of cream cheese. Paris had a knot in her stomach and couldn't bring herself to eat. Instead, she stared at the blue-gray walls and the many art prints the board had chosen as decoration. Each image was of some exotic place with blue-green waters, palm trees, or caverns. All strategically placed to promote a calm and relaxing feel. Much to her chagrin, she found herself wishing she could crawl into one of the images and disappear.

Never had she felt so out of place in her own life. This time, it was she who had messed up, and the knot grew as she thought about the possible punishment awaiting her. The sooner the meeting began, the sooner she could deal with the next obstacle.

"Paris," said her mother, "how are things going for you?"

Paris's stomach flipped and acid rose up in her throat. Swallowing, she slowly looked up. She didn't want to answer the question, but she knew she had no choice. "Not well," she replied. "I had a complete emotional breakdown and spent my remaining money on an online auction." Her eyes dropped to the table as she swallowed, trying to maintain her composure.

Nicola let out a short sigh. "I'm sorry to hear that, my dear. Even during times of stress, we must learn to be in control of our actions."

"That's disappointing to hear," noted her father. "How does this situation make you feel?" he asked Paris.

"I'm embarrassed," she said, raising her eyes to look at her father.

"That's a fitting response," said Nicola.

"Vic, what do you think about Paris's situation?" asked Jessamine.

"I think it's unfortunate," he replied, scowling in Paris's direction.

"Don't you think it's partially your failure, too?" asked Dom.

Vic's head whipped around to look at his father. "What? Why is it my failure?" asked Vic. "She did this on her own time. How can I possibly control her when we don't live together?"

"He makes a grand point," replied Jessamine. "Which gives me an idea. We'll come back to that in a moment. First, I want to check in with Mya and Chase. What insights do you have into last week?"

Mya chimed in and said, "I believe Paris has had a rough week. Some of it's not her fault. She did her best and ran into some unforeseen situations, which caused a couple of accidents at work. We filed the necessary paperwork, but the week took an emotional toll on her, which is why she had a breakdown and spent all of her money. While I know she made a mistake, I'm asking that you take her week into consideration and cut her some slack this one time."

It shocked Paris to hear Mya sticking up for her. She didn't know why the girl bothered, but she was thankful for the undue kindness.

Jessamine's face grew stern. "Let's for a moment consider Paris's prior position as a Senior Planner. Regularly, Paris handled sizeable sums of her client's money. What if she had a bad day and spent her client's money on an auction? Is that okay?"

"Well, no," replied Mya. "She spent her own money in this scenario."

"Did she?" asked Jessamine. "Consider that her success and failures are linked to Vic's. Would that not mean the money is both of theirs? How is that unlike her client?"

Mya's mouth dropped open as her understanding set in. "You're right. It's inexcusable in either case."

"Indeed. Her actions were selfish, and she did not act like a rational adult," replied Jessamine.

"Chase, what about Vic?" asked Cristo.

"He's doing great. His money's in order. He worked hard this week and completed all tasks assigned to him." Chase clasped his hands together with satisfaction.

"That's wonderful," replied Cristo. "We've received the same information from Burt."

"If you'll excuse us," said Nicola, "we need to have a brief discussion, and then we'll let you know what happens next. Mya and Chase, you may stay, but I ask that Paris and Vic step out into the hall at this time."

Vic and Paris exited the room. Once the door was closed behind them, Vic turned to Paris, who had tears in her eyes. "Don't do that," he said. "There's no reason to cry at this time."

"You don't know that," she replied. "We could be further demoted."

"I really hope that doesn't happen," said Vic. The idea made him uncomfortable. "By the way, I spoke to Breanna. She thinks we're being tested."

Paris arched an eyebrow. "Tested on what?"

"I'm unsure, which is why I'm telling you. Do you have any thoughts?"

She shook her head. "Believe me, if I think of anything, I'll let you know, but right now, I'm emotionally and physically drained. I have no idea what I'm going to do about my money situation. Frankly, I'm a little scared, which is a rare feeling for me."

"I still can't believe you spent all that money on an auction. My mom's right. That's selfish."

"I shop when I'm stressed," she admitted. "Your brother was of no help."

"Yeah, trust me, I'm none too happy with him."

"I won't be able to pay my rent or even buy food," stated Paris. She once again looked as though she may cry at any moment. She tried to pull it together, but her lip began to quiver uncontrollably.

Vic debated hugging her but decided against it. He didn't like Paris, and a hug would most likely be misconstrued. "Seriously," he said, "you have to pull it together. Someone will be coming for us any moment. Do you really want them to see you cry?"

Paris looked at him, and the tears overflowed and ran down her cheeks. True to traditional Vic style, he was acting cold as ever. On cue, the door to the boardroom opened. Paris turned away, wiping the tears from her face. Luckily, the person retrieving them was Chase and not one of their family members.

"You may come back in," said Chase as he motioned them toward the entrance.

Paris and Vic took their original seats and waited anxiously to hear what fate would hold in store for them.

"We've reviewed the week and made some decisions," said Dom, as he ran his hand over his bald head. "You'll be staying in Janitorial. Paris, we wish you a better week than last. It sounds like you're lucky to be intact after the mishaps you suffered. Unfortunately, because of your financial indiscretions, we've decided that you and Vic will be moving to different housing."

"We feel," noted Jessamine, "that you'll be more inclined to help one another succeed if you live in the same apartment."

"No!" blurted Vic. "I can't live with her!"

"Vic," barked Dom, "you don't have a choice. You're to help each other succeed. That's part of the deal. Right now, Paris is in trouble, and this is the best solution we could find. Contrary to your belief, we don't enjoy treating you like children. Now show us what you're made of so we can restore you to your rightful positions within the company."

"Mya, Chase, please take the morning to help them move into their new places. We'll call Janitorial to let them know their shifts will begin in the afternoon and extend into the evening."

Paris winced at having to move in with Vic. While she knew living with him was a recipe for disaster, she kept her mouth shut because she also knew Jessamine was right. It was the only option at this point. She had thrown her rights away for a Chanel clutch and a new pair of Jimmy Choo stilettos. She had no one but herself to blame.

· · · · ● · ● · · · ·

It only took an hour to gather their things from their current apartments and scoot on down the hall to their new combined home. It had been too much to hope that they'd escape the noise of the morning renovations. Vic assumed this was all part of their punishment, either that, or their parents were trying to hide them from the other residents.

The new place was larger, which was a relief to Paris. It had a large balcony with a table and chairs, as well as two reclining sun chairs. Decorated in shades of blue and green, it felt more tranquil than the last place. They each had their own bedroom, with closets incorporated. They would share a bathroom, but at least it was slightly larger and had built-in closet storage, a full-size shower, and a vanity with his and hers sinks.

The living room held a couch, loveseat, and one cozy over-stuffed chair, all a cream-colored microfiber. They had a fireplace and a built-in bookcase with several books from all different genres. The television, mounted above the fireplace, appeared to be roughly forty inches. Not huge, but decent enough.

They even had a large kitchen with a breakfast bar and bistro table with chairs. This apartment had already been remodeled, which came as a surprise to both Paris and Vic.

"Not bad," said Vic.

"This is an upgrade compared to the places we've lived previously," commented Paris.

"Yeah, but we traded in our privacy," he pointed out.

"You two need to look at it as a positive change," stated Chase. "This doesn't have to be a negative experience. Truthfully, I'm shocked they gave you one of the upgraded two-bedrooms since I know for a fact there are other apartments of the same size that have not been redone yet. They must have felt sorry for Paris and the week she'd had."

"Honestly," said Mya, "you're lucky you weren't further demoted in your jobs. Jessamine talked Mikel into moving you into this apartment together, over his intentions of forcing you to do community service and to request a loan to pay your rent at your previous apartments."

"I'd choose this situation hands-down," replied Vic. "Forced community service with a work-group would be highly embarrassing for the company. I'm certain people would recognize us, which means it would only be a matter of time before it hit the newsstands."

Paris said nothing. She was thankful that Jessamine had such a soft and kind heart. Her own mother, while loving, held no qualms about taking strict action.

"The only catch is that this apartment is slightly more expensive," said Chase. "You now owe eleven hundred per month for rent, and as you know, Paris has no money to pay."

"Yeah, I'm painfully aware of that. Paris, as a trade, you'll do all the housework until you're able to pay your portion of the rent and grocery bill. Sound like a deal?"

Paris sighed. "It would appear I have no choice."

"No, you really don't have a choice," said Vic. "You're not my wife or my girlfriend, so you've got to pay." He added smugly. "As it is, I might have to see if Jack will spot me for the remainder of the month."

The week progressed onward, and Paris and Vic tried to stay out of each other's hair as much as possible, but Vic's patience were wearing thin with Paris's morning routine, and Paris was becoming quickly agitated with Vic's evening routine. On top of it all, the remodeling noise continued at six in the morning, despite their requests to have it begin at a later time.

Each morning, it took Paris two hours to get ready. Vic would knock at the door and beg her to hurry up for fear they'd be late to work. She would refuse to let him in while she was doing her makeup and hair. In the evening, Vic would watch television until eleven-thirty each night, cutting into Paris's ten o'clock bedtime. She frequently asked him to turn down the volume, tossing and turning as she tried to ignore the noise coming through from the other room. She tried earplugs, but they hurt her ears and only led to further discomfort and frustration. With little sleep, she'd be abruptly jolted awake at six o'clock by the hammering and clanking up the hall.

On Tuesday, Paris discovered a leaking pipe in the eighth-floor ladies' room. She was instructed to oversee the job and assist in any way necessary, which seemed easy enough. The plumber was fairly new and failed to recognize the compromised state of the pipe he was working on. As he tightened things up, the pipe broke loose, which caused water to spray out everywhere, soaking him and Paris. Screaming, Paris tried to escape the spray, but she tripped over the plumber's tools and once again was propelled backward. She launched straight into an open stall and cracked her head on the rim of the toilet, which caused her to see stars.

"My goodness, you again?" asked Dr. Schuh. "What happened this time?"

She told the doctor what had happened and then requested to go home, but Dr. Schuh insisted on a CT scan to be sure she was okay after the previous week's incidents. The scan checked out, and she was sent on her way, with the familiar feeling of embarrassment. Dr. Schuh had been surprised that, in all of Paris's follies, she had only acquired one concussion. He proclaimed she must be one of the unluckiest or luckiest people he had ever treated. Paris was inclined to think it was the former, but was thankful she hadn't suffered worse.

When Vic arrived home, Paris was on the couch icing her neck and head.

"I hear you had another accident. This has got to be a record of some kind, don't you think?" he asked.

"Most definitely. I really hate this job," she replied. "If it weren't for my grandfather, I don't think I'd be able to tolerate it."

"Maybe you need to be more careful," replied Vic.

"Maybe you need to keep your mouth shut. You think I don't already feel crummy enough?" she snapped. "For the life of me, I cannot figure out how I end up in these predicaments."

"Maybe you just suck at life," Vic responded angrily.

The conversation escalated until they were both yelling and throwing jabs at one another. The evening concluded when Vic and Paris each marched to their own bedrooms, slamming the doors behind them.

Paris cried herself to sleep. She was miserable, and she wished she could talk to her sister or a friend, but in reality, she had no one. She alienated all of her friends, and there was no one left in her corner. Not even Vic, who was in the same crummy situation as her. She wished she could fall asleep and never wake up.

Vic laid awake most of the night thinking about how he could improve his situation and get Paris out of his home, but there was no viable answer. He was stuck. He couldn't kick her out. How was he supposed to have an intimate relationship with anyone when Paris was always home? He fell asleep thinking about how he could remedy his intimacy issues.

As the week progressed, Paris had several minor mishaps, but nothing that sent her back to medical. Despite hating the job, she continued to work hard. She rarely worked alongside Vic anymore. Burt realized the two didn't get along and sent them to different sections of the building to avoid any conflict.

Vic did his job with ease, despite disliking it intensely. His only motivation was to do well so he could move to a better job in the near future. Paris felt a similar motivation but hoped her clumsiness didn't stand in the way. They were both thankful for the distance between them.

Before they knew it, Friday evening had arrived. The pair waltzed into their apartment, ready to relax. Opening the fridge, Vic grabbed two beers and handed one to Paris as a peace treaty. Trudging into the living room, he flopped down on the couch and she on the loveseat. Neither spoke a word for over an hour. Vic got up once and replaced their empty beers with full ones.

"Are you hungry?" asked Paris.

"Starved. The weekend's here. Why don't we order a pizza?"

"Sure, if that's what you want," she replied.

"It's easy, and I don't feel like going anywhere or cooking. Lord knows you're a terrible cook," he said.

"Hey, I resent that," replied Paris. "I'm not a bad cook. You're just highly critical."

"Well, I am a food critic," he replied matter-of-factly. "I also have a chef's background, so there's that."

"Exactly, so how could I possibly live up to your high standards?"

"Come now," he said, "burnt toast is well below most human standards."

"That was one time!" she protested.

"Let's not fight," he said with a sigh. "It's time to relax. We've had a long week. Let's order our food and enjoy our beers. Why don't you pick out a movie while I call and order?"

Two hours later, Vic and Paris were relaxed from the alcohol and contented by their full bellies as the movie came to a close.

Turning off the television, Vic turned toward Paris. "Tell me something," he requested. "Why do you steal? What's the purpose behind it?"

"Direct, huh? I don't know. I guess stealing makes me feel alive. Why do you have such a bad temper and sleep with anything that moves?" she countered.

"I don't sleep with anything that moves," he shot back. "I haven't slept with anyone in over a week."

"Oh, wow, a week," replied Paris. "I can't imagine how you're able to survive."

"Funny."

Shaking her head at him, she asked, "But honestly, why?"

"Probably for the same reasons you steal and previously popped pills."

"Tell me, since you seem to have everything figured out, why do *you* think we do these things?"

This time Vic shook his head at her as he gave in to the truth. "Loss. Right? We do it because of the pain we feel from the loss."

"You're still hurting?" asked Paris. She never thought he'd admit it. There wasn't a day that went by in which she didn't wish Alli was still alive.

"Yes," he replied. "Brody was my best friend. We kept each other sane. How do you say goodbye and move on from a loss like that?" Tears pooled at the corner of his eyes and he blinked them away, taking on a more serious face.

"I miss my sister so much," replied Paris. "I'd give anything to have her back. I'd sell my soul."

"That's pretty extreme," replied Vic. "I don't think Brody or Alli would want you to sell your soul to bring them back."

"You wouldn't do the same?"

"No. I'm pretty strict on that rule."

"Do you think we'll ever get past this?"

"I think there'll always be a piece that hurts and longs to have them back, but I believe we have to find a way to move on. Don't you think it's time? I, for one, don't want to be arrested ever again."

"Yeah, me neither," replied Paris.

"Then you have to stop stealing things. Stealing will surely land you in jail."

"I'll think about it," she said half-heartedly. He was catching her at a vulnerable time when she actually had no money to buy even the small things she wanted, but she knew he was right.

"And stop with the pills. You'll kill yourself if you keep on with that. I don't think your parents deserve to lose both of their children."

Paris's expression went dark. "I told you, I haven't tried to take any pills since the first day in the boardroom. Mya ground up the last of them in my disposal."

Vic cocked his head as he looked at her. "That's good. Smart girl, that Mya."

"Whatever," replied Paris. "I wasn't taking them enough to become addicted."

"That's what an addict would say," noted Vic. "Just don't. I won't tolerate living with an addict or a thief."

Paris jumped up from the loveseat. "Okay, womanizer."

"I'm not a womanizer," Vic barked.

"Yeah, you keep telling yourself that. Anyway, I'm going to bed," she said and disappeared into her room.

Vic thought about her words. He knew he had a voracious sexual appetite, but did that make him a womanizer? It wasn't as if he was incapable of meaningful relationships. He wanted something real, but the last girl he'd given his heart to had pulverized it and divulged his private life to the press. How could a man trust any woman after an incident like that? Pushing himself up, he turned off the living room light and headed for bed. He was tired and didn't want to think about his conversation with Paris any further, but her words had cut deep enough to haunt him while he slept.

········

It was one in the morning when a loud banging sound woke Paris from her sleep. At first, it didn't register that the sound was someone pounding on her door, but then she heard Vic asking if she was awake.

"Paris, wake up!" he hollered.

"I'm awake," she replied groggily. "What do you want?"

"There's been an accident," said Vic. His voice came out with a shakiness that was uncharacteristic of him.

"What?" squeaked Paris. "What kind of accident?" Fear flooded her body turning her legs to jelly. She found herself propelled back in time to the night when Alli and Brody were killed. What if it was her parents or her grandfather?

Vic could hear the fear in her voice. He didn't know how to proceed, so he was as direct as possible. "Mya and Chase," he said. "They were out with some friends this evening, and their car was hit by a drunk driver on the way home. Chase called and said they were in an ambulance and being transported to the hospital. I told him we'd meet him there."

Paris's mind felt numb, but the adrenaline coursing through her veins gave her the strength to jump out of bed. Trying not to panic, she pulled on her sweats and a pair of socks. "I'll be out in a minute," she called to him as she searched for her tennis shoes.

When Paris emerged from the bedroom, she realized they had a problem. "How will we get to them when we don't have a vehicle?"

"I called Jack. I'm sure he's already outside waiting for us."

They hurried from the apartment without another word. When they arrived in the lobby, Jack was indeed waiting for them. Paris crawled into the backseat as Vic took the spot in front. Feeling as if the blood had drained from her head, she gasped, "I can't breathe."

"Don't think about what's going on," replied Vic. "Focus on positive thoughts and try to relax. Take a deep breath in and let it out slowly."

Paris tried to do as he said, but it was of no use. She began to hyperventilate, and before she knew it, she could feel herself slipping into unconsciousness.

Vic, realizing he had lost her, unfastened his belt and crawled into the back seat. "Jack, do you have anything to drink?" he asked.

"Yeah, here," he said, handing him his water bottle.

Vic pulled Paris over and placed her head in his lap. Grabbing her wrist, he assessed her pulse, which seemed okay. Lightly tapping her cheek, her eyes began to flutter open. "Hey," he said. "Come on back to me. You're okay."

"What happened?" she asked.

"You hyperventilated and fainted," he replied. Paris tried to push herself up, but Vic stopped her. "I think you should rest for a moment."

"I'm okay, I think." Paris looked into his intense blue eyes. She was shocked that he could be so kind and caring.

"I'm sure you're fine, but I still think taking it easy with moving isn't a bad idea."

She took his advice and was oddly enjoying the sensation of lying in his lap, but then she wondered what was wrong with her? Had she hit her head when she fainted? Deciding to fight the feeling, she gently pushed away from him, and despite his disdain, he helped her back into a seated position and handed her the water.

"Drink it," he said softly. "It's Jack's. As far as we know, he doesn't have any major diseases yet."

"Gee, thanks," replied Jack from the driver's seat. Vic slugged his shoulder. "Jerk," replied Jack.

"You know I love you, little brother," said Vic. You could hear the fondness in his voice.

"I know," said Jack.

"How long until we're at the hospital?" asked Paris.

"We're nearly there," said Jack.

"Do we know anything about Mya or what kind of shape either of them is in?" asked Paris. A knot had formed in her stomach. It seemed to be a trend as of late.

"Chase said Mya was driving and that they were hit from the driver's side. Her car's pretty messed up. He was told that she's stable, but he doesn't know much beyond that."

"What about him?" asked Jack. "Is he okay?"

"They weren't completely sure. He said they wanted to check him over more to be on the safe side. I guess he hit his head pretty hard against the window," replied Vic.

At the hospital, Chase met them in the waiting room.

"They'll be retrieving me any moment," said Chase. "I need to have my head scanned. The doctor said they're admitting Mya. She didn't respond well when they checked her over. She's pretty banged up, and they want to monitor her overnight. They said it would take about an hour to get her situated, but then we can see her. I tried to call her family, but apparently, they're on vacation in Madrid. If anything changes, we'll need to track them down."

Paris looked at Chase, and she could no longer hold back her emotion. Tears flooded her cheeks as she tried to stifle her sobs.

"Paris," said Chase, "it's gonna be okay."

"We could have lost her," wailed Paris. "We could have lost both of you."

"Trust me, it was scary, but we're going to be okay," replied Chase.

"Come here," demanded Vic. Paris didn't move. She was afraid to move, especially

toward him.

Stepping forward, he pulled her into his arms and held her tight as she sobbed into his t-shirt. Despite her conflicting feelings, his arms felt safe and warm, and she preferred the woodsy scent of his cologne to that of the sterile waiting room.

"I think this is a wake-up call," he whispered to her. "We need to move forward with our

lives. Brody and Alli would be heartbroken by how we've been acting."

Paris pulled back and looked up at him. His eyes were glossy and she could see a year's worth of sadness in them. She knew he was right.

"We've pushed enough people away, don't you think?"

"Yeah. I don't want to lose Mya like I lost Alli," she replied honestly.

"No, and I'm growing quite fond of Chase, so losing him would be a pity as well," he said quietly so only she could hear.

"He's a pretty great guy." Wiggling out of his arms, Paris took a step back and dried her eyes. A nurse came into the room and called Chase's name.

"I'll see you two in a bit," he said as he headed toward the nurse.

"Should we take a seat?" asked Jack. "We still have about forty-five minutes until we can see Mya."

Vic nodded. "Let's. I'm tired, and I don't feel like standing around while we wait."

Jack led them over to some reclining chairs and a couch where they made themselves comfortable. Vic looked over at Paris. She was already reclined back in her chair and, from the looks of it, nearly asleep. He didn't know what had come over him. Holding her in his arms had felt too good. Was he developing a soft spot for her? Or even worse, feelings? Shaking his head, he brushed the idea aside and settled in on the couch for a nap. The feeling would pass. No need to make something out of nothing. It had, after all, been a high-stress evening.

Chapter Nine

The hospital released Mya on Saturday afternoon. Paris borrowed Jack's car and saw to her retrieval. The look on Mya's face was pure shock when the nurse wheeled her out, and she saw not Jack but Paris in the driver's seat.

"Hi," said Paris. "How are you feeling?"

"Awful," she moaned. My whole body hurts. My left arm looks like it has a baseball in it, it's so bruised. I can't even turn my wrist. I have to keep it in a sling for a week or two. My nose was also broken, but I won't be needing surgery. It hurt like a mother when they set it. I also have two bruised ribs. I'm gonna be sore for a while, but on the plus side, I'm alive."

Paris's lip quivered, though she managed not to cry. "Thank God you're okay."

"I'm surprised to see you," admitted Mya. "I thought for sure Jack was picking me up." She could see the fear in her friend's eyes. She wondered what was going through her head?

"Jack had an assignment to deal with, and besides, I wanted to do it," she replied with an awkward smile.

The majority of the ride was quiet. Paris had a determined look on her face as she drove through downtown and back to the ADG complex. Mya let her concentrate since she knew Paris had barely driven in the past few years. She wondered what her motivation was in coming to her aid? Perhaps she wanted something? She sat quietly and pondered.

As their drive ended, Mya turned to Paris. "Why'd you decide to pick me up?" She watched Paris as she maneuvered Jack's green Volkswagen into its designated parking space.

Unbuckling her belt, Paris turned her body to face Mya. "I owe you an apology," she said, her voice trembling. "When I heard you'd been in an accident, it took me back to the night of Alli's death. I couldn't breathe. I know I've been terrible to you, and not just recently, but for an entire year. You never deserved that. It's my fault that I never made-up with Alli before she went out that night. It was never your fault. I want us to be friends again if you accept my apology. I need you, Mya. I know we don't share blood, but you're my other sister."

"Paris, you need to know. I spoke to Alli earlier that day after she left the festival. She was upset, but she knew the two of you would work it out. She would have forgiven you. You have to let it go. You girls had many arguments over the years, but you always made amends. That day would have been no different than any other. You would have made-up, and things would have been fine."

"You don't know that for certain," she replied sadly.

"Yes, I do. She told me that she knew you meant well. She said she would forgive you."

Paris once again could feel tears welling in her eyes.

"If it helps, I forgive you for Alli." Leaning forward, she wrapped Paris in a hug, and Paris hugged her back. "I've always been here. Even when things were tough, and you pushed me away. I knew you'd pull through the pain at some point."

"I wish it had been sooner," she replied. Pulling away, she looked at Mya and said, "Thank you for never giving up on me."

"No, thank you," replied Mya. "All I care about is that I have my friend back. Now," she said, "can we please order some food? I'm famished. And we need to have a girl's night. It's long overdue."

"The food or the girl's night?" asked Paris. This time her smile was more natural.

"Both," laughed Mya.

"Do you mind if I stay at your place? I'd feel better knowing you're not alone."

"Girl, I'm going to be fine, but you can definitely stay at my place. Let's grab some of your things, order food, and veg out on my couch."

"Okay, let's," she replied, as a warm feeling flooded her chest.

The evening turned out to be exactly what both women needed. The conversation went on straight through the movie they'd chosen to watch. They discussed everything from Paris's vices to Mya's as well as their lack of satisfying love-affairs and their current hopes and dreams.

Paris hadn't realized how much of a void had been left by her rejection of Mya and Mya hadn't realized how much she had held inside due to Paris's emotional unavailability. Their relationship seemed to pick up right where it had left off.

"I think we should meet with Chase and Vic in the morning and put together a genuine game plan for how you'll handle the work and family situation going forward. If you two don't get on the same page, you might do even more damage. I, for one, don't want to see you ousted from the family or the business, especially when you're finally making some progress," said Mya.

"I agree," replied Paris. "I've been so angry."

"You stopped living your life when Alli died. I wanted to help you, but I had no idea how. I was terrified when you overdosed. You have to promise me you won't ever do that again. She lived her life fully, and she would want you to do the same."

Paris looked at Mya and nodded in agreement. "What do you feel needs to happen for me to get my life back on track?"

"The board trusted Chase and I to look after you and guide you through this exercise. They want to see you make serious amends. I honestly think if you do not work with Vic, you'll sink this ship, and there'll be no going back. You have to make all your decisions together in order to succeed. And, when you're ready, you need to show them you've gained back your desire to run charity events."

"Okay. How do you propose we do so?"

"Well, like I said previously, we need to meet up with Chase and Vic and create a game plan. The charity aspect will come with time. Also, I have my suspicions that there's more to this job situation than either of you has been led to believe. I could be wrong, but I think the partners are looking at who their successors will be when they retire. If they can't trust you two, they won't put you in charge of their life's work."

"Wow," replied Paris. "That thought hadn't even occurred to me."

"They're not getting any younger," said Mya with a smile. "You've honestly never thought of the future and saw yourself running ADG one day?"

"No. I don't spend much time thinking about the future."

"Huh," she said. "I don't know why I'm surprised. I guess you've always lived your life one day at a time. Do you, or did you, have dreams about where you wanted to ultimately end up in your career?"

"I dream about traveling like our clients do, but I guess I never bothered to dream much about the future of my career. The company has always been in the background, and I think I've always seen myself as part of it."

"So, basically, you've been doing what you believe is expected of you," stated Mya.

Paris dropped her eyes to the floor. Mya was right. She'd simply gone along with the plan that was put in place. She hadn't dreamt of anything in her future. She was young and naïve. She focused on her charities and getting things done one day at a time. When Alli died, she imploded.

"Look at me," said Mya, her tone compassionate. Paris brought her eyes up to meet Mya's. "You still have time to make a plan. You're only twenty-eight. We can figure this out."

"I'm an idiot!" spouted Paris. "What's wrong with me?"

"There's nothing wrong with you. I think it's possible that your parents were so wrapped up in the business that they forgot to stop and consider whether or not you want to be a permanent part of it. You were born into this, and sometimes there's a certain expectation from family that we will continue their legacy. The question is, do you want to continue with their legacy?"

"I don't even know," she replied quietly.

"Luckily, you don't have to make an immediate decision."

"When do I need to make a decision by?" she asked, panic rising in her voice. "How can I move forward and have no idea what I want for my life?"

"Calm down and breathe," commanded Mya. "Let's first focus on setting things right. Perhaps as we work on the current situation, you'll iron out the unknown."

Paris shook her head, trying to clear her thoughts. "I feel like a coma patient who finally woke up."

"It's really not that bad," said Mya. "What matters is that you're awake now."

"You say that, but right now, everything feels a little like life or death."

Mya held up her hands, "Okay, okay," she fired back. "I'm gonna open a bottle of wine, and we're going to forget about the company's future for the rest of the night. You hear me? Let's focus on our friendship and have some fun for a change."

Paris let out a deep sigh. "Okay." She hoped she'd be able to move beyond her fear of the unknown. Did she want to run ADG? When the partners retired, would there be five new partners to replace them? Who would those partners be? She couldn't see Breanna joining the company full-time. Breanna was a dancer, and her heart lay outside the company. Jack was in love with writing, but was he interested in running the company? She already knew Vic was after the position of CEO. If Vic took her father's position, where would she go? Did she also want to be the CEO? Mya was right. She needed to stop, and forget about the company for the rest of the evening. She could worry about it tomorrow. Right now, she should be celebrating the return of her friendship with Mya.

"Here," said Mya, as she handed Paris a glass of her favorite Pinot Grigio. "To rekindled friendship."

"Amen to that." For the first time in two years, Paris felt as if she could breathe more easily. That night she slept soundly, knowing that she and Mya were again on the same team.

· · ● ● · ● ● · · ·

It was seven in the morning when Paris woke to the sound of her phone buzzing on the coffee table next to her. She'd slept on one end of the large red L-shaped couch in Mya's apartment. Opening her eyes, she yawned and reached for her phone. Mya was still fast asleep at the other end of the couch.

"Hello?" she asked quietly.

"Hey, Paris, it's Vic. You didn't come home last night," he noted. "Are you okay? Why are you speaking in a hushed tone?"

"I'm at Mya's. She's still asleep and I don't want to wake her."

"Really?" he asked with amusement. "Forgive my surprise. I thought you two were over."

"Things change," she replied sharply. "Get to the point. Why are you calling me at this hour?"

"Come on. It's seven in the morning. Many people are up by now or even earlier. It isn't like I'm calling in the middle of the night."

"It's Sunday, Vic. What do you want?" she asked again. Rolling over, she resituated herself and pulled the covers back up over her arms. Mya liked to keep her apartment cool, which always left room for cozying up inside a big fluffy down comforter. Paris thought it was the perfect condition for sleeping, which made her early wake-up call from Vic even more un-wanted.

"We need to talk about some things," he replied.

"Couldn't this call have waited?"

"Fine," he gave in. "We can talk later."

"How about we, including Mya and Chase, meet at our place for lunch?" she suggested.

"Okay. I'll see you at noon," he replied.

Paris hung up the phone and tossed it onto the floor. Since Mya was still asleep, she figured there was no harm in being lazy for a couple more hours.

· · · · ● · ● · · · ·

Paris and Mya arrived at Paris's apartment early, but Vic and Chase were nowhere to be seen. "Come on in," said Paris as she held the door open for her friend.

"This apartment really isn't bad," said Mya.

"It's okay. I wish we had a second bathroom, but considering the lack of belongings I currently have, this suits my needs. Do you want something to drink?"

"Sure," she replied. "I'd love a soda if you have one."

"Diet?" asked Paris as she rifled through the fridge.

"Actually, I drink regular now," replied Mya. "I rarely drink it, so I figured it was healthier."

"Ah, so you listened to my ranting, huh?" She had been trying to get Mya to switch to regular for years. The calories might be missing from the diet, but obviously, they had to replace them with something, and Paris swore that something was giving people cancer.

"Yes, I did," replied Mya. "I also saw an article in *Modern Fit Woman*, which discussed the negative aspects of diet soda. You were right. It's really not better."

Paris handed Mya her beverage. "You still like Cream Soda, right?" Cream soda had been both of their favorites since they were young. Paris only drank regular Cream Soda, while Mya had only drunk diet. She was happy that she no longer needed to keep both in stock.

Mya nodded. "Where do you suppose those men are?"

"Who knows," replied Paris. She flopped down on the sofa next to Mya and was about to turn on the television when Chase and Vic arrived.

"Hey, ladies. I hope you're hungry," said Vic, as he handed Mya and Paris each a lettuce-wrapped burger and sweet potato fries.

"You read my mind," replied Paris. "I've been craving a greasy burger and fries."

Vic plopped himself down on the loveseat while Chase took his place on the overstuffed chair. The group ate in silence, and as soon as the last crumb had been consumed, Chase grabbed all of the meal's refuse and whisked it away to the kitchen garbage. Returning promptly, he said, "Okay, now that everyone has a full tummy, it's time to get down to business. First up on the agenda is Vic and Paris's longstanding distaste for one another."

"Great," groaned Vic. "Is this a necessary discussion?"

Mya stood and joined Chase in front of the coffee table. "We feel that you two need to swallow your pride and behave as though you actually care about, and even like, one another," she said.

Chase nodded. "I don't care if you have to put on an act every single time you leave this apartment. You're now best friends, and you care about everything the other person says or does."

"Why?" asked Vic. "What does this prove?"

Mya arched an eyebrow at his question. "It shows partnership. It provides closure to anyone watching, that you can get along and possibly run a business together."

"Besides," added Chase, "your parents are best friends. Everyone sees you as an extension of that friendship. They want to believe the off-spring of the partners are also best friends. You can hate each other in private if that's what you really want, but in the public eye, you should appear as if you're close and you have each other's backs."

"I know I can do that," replied Paris, "but Vic doesn't exactly exude friendliness."

"What do you believe will happen if we don't agree to do this?" asked Vic.

"We already know your parents have decided you must succeed together or not at all. Not working together means they cannot leave you in charge of their company. Do you want to lose the company?" asked Chase.

"Absolutely not," replied Vic. "You know I want this company more than anything else."

Chase looked to Paris. "What about you?"

Shaking her head, she said, "I don't know what I want."

"Let me ask you this," said Chase, "do you want to fail at proving yourself capable of working as a team with Vic?"

"No, of course not," she said. "I want our parents to trust and believe in us.

Vic looked at Paris. "Do you want to give this a shot?"

"More than anything," she replied. "I'm ready to start living again."

Vic nodded, "Okay, bestie. Let's show 'em what we're made of."

"Great!" said Mya. "That's what I wanted to hear."

"Now that we've agreed upon committing to each other in this situation, let's discuss your income. Paris, you can't make any more 'wild hair' purchases. You don't have the money for it," said Chase. "Vic, you're going to be in charge of the money for the time being."

"Living on such a fixed budget is more stressful than I could have anticipated," said Paris.

Vic nodded in agreement. "That's because you've had everything handed to you."

"You aren't any different," said Paris.

"I'm not saying I am," replied Vic.

"Hold up," said Chase, "you both need to make changes. No more expensive specialty beers, Vic, and no random shopping sprees, Paris. You'll start cooking meals rather than eating out every night. Cooking at home can save a lot of money. Not to mention, Vic, you have mad culinary skills. There are tons of small ways in which you can change your routine and spend more thriftily. You don't need to buy every food staple as a name brand. The store brands are often from bigger name brands you love, anyway. You can continue to share an apartment, which clearly helps."

"I think those are valid points," said Mya. "What do you think? Is that something you can try?"

Paris let out a sigh. "Yeah, I guess so."

"What the heck, sure," said Vic. He knew he didn't want their situation to decline further, so he was willing to do any number of things in an attempt to improve, even if it meant he had to watch Paris's back.

The next morning, Chase and Mya retrieved Paris and Vic from their apartment and escorted them to the boardroom. For once, the news was positive. Paris and Vic were promoted back to the mailroom. Paris was thankful. She didn't know if she could handle any more accidents due to her lack of prowess in the field of Building Maintenance.

The week flew by, and Vic and Paris were seen several times by the board, eating lunch together, walking together, or even sharing a joke with one another. Jessamine and Nicola were excited to see that a change appeared to be taking place. The kids were getting along and staying out of trouble. The future had potential.

Chapter Ten

Monday came with a couple of surprises. Walking into the boardroom, Vic and Paris were greeted with a buffet of tasty breakfast foods and gourmet coffees.

"We're quite pleased with the progress you've made," said Mikel. "I have to admit, I was a little worried that you two wouldn't be able to pull it together, but you appear to have made progress. Nice work."

"Thanks," replied Vic. For once, he felt like he had something to smile about. "I believe I speak for both of us when I say it was not easy, but we're working through our differences, and we've actually become friends."

"It's about time," said Dom. He smiled at his son and patted him on the back. "I'm proud of the work you've put in. Let's keep it up. This is only the first obstacle in a long course."

Nicola looked at Paris and Vic. "Because you've shown such initiative in working together, we're offering you upgraded individual apartments."

Vic had always liked Nicola. She was beautiful and smart. Truly a driven woman. He was pleased to hear about the upgraded apartment offer, but new motivations had him wanting to keep things the same. Turning toward Paris, he said, "Do you want separate apartments or to continue to share a place for the time being?" He waited for her to contemplate his question.

"You know, I never thought I'd say this, but I want to continue living with Vic for the time being. He's holding me accountable for my actions, which I guess I needed. Can we stay together, or is that against the rules?"

"I'm surprised to hear you're willing to share a home with someone else," said Nicola. "I don't see why not. We'll locate a larger three-bedroom unit for you and have your things moved this afternoon while you're at work."

"We don't have to move our own belongings?" asked Vic.

"The perks of success," laughed Dom. "See, son, it doesn't take much to make us happy. Don't make us regret it, okay?"

"We won't," replied Vic.

"Great work," commented Cristo. "Mya, might I have a word with you outside?" he asked as he sidled up beside her.

Paris watched Cristo lead Mya out of the room. Her friend looked a bit uneasy. She knew Cristo was interested in Mya, but this was the first real interaction she'd noticed. She couldn't picture her friend with Cristo. He wasn't her type. Mya was into men with dark skin and six-pack abs. Men who viewed her as a princess and took their lives and work quite seriously. Doctors and lawyers. She was not into scruffy play-boys. Cristo was decent looking, but Paris had heard on more than one occasion that he had a tendency to take things too far when drinking. She didn't know what that meant exactly, but she worried about her friend's safety.

"What do you suppose that's about?" whispered Vic.

Paris jumped. She hadn't realized he was standing so close to her. In a hushed tone, she replied, "I don't know. It's a little concerning, don't you think?"

"More than a little. He's near twice her age," said Vic. "Now that you've rekindled your friendship, I think you should talk to her about it later."

"Yeah, I agree," she replied. "I don't want him to hurt her."

Breaking into their whispered conversation, Jessamine said, "One more bit of news for you. We've decided to promote you to assistant level. Vic, you'll work under Tom Mariano and Paris, you get to work for Angela Martini. Since they're the same level as your previous positions in the company, I trust you'll know what's expected of you."

Paris's smile faded. She was nervous about working under Angela. She'd never cared for her, and Angela seemed to despise her. Looking at Vic, she knew he was feeling something similar. Tom and Vic had a tendency to butt heads. Forcing a smile, Paris said, "That's great news, isn't it, Vic?"

Vic swallowed his pride and nodded begrudgingly. He knew he had to play it cool and take Paris's lead, which was something he never would have pictured himself doing. "Simply spectacular."

"Providing everything goes well this week, you'll be given a bonus next week to be used on buying yourselves some new professional clothing. Keep up the good work," said Mikel. "We hope that we'll be able to promote you back to your rightful positions sooner than later."

"We've got this, Dad," replied Paris.

"Good deal," said Mikel, "I like the enthusiasm. It's a wonderful improvement." Walking over to her, he grabbed her in a side hug. "Remember," he said, "I'm still your father outside of the office. If you need to talk, my door is always open."

"Thanks," she replied. Out of the corner of her eye, she saw Mya scoot back into the room and take her seat.

Looking at Vic, Dom said, "Same goes for you, son."

"I know," replied Vic. He and his father connected regularly on weekends, but most often he dealt with his own issues, since Jack was younger and required more of his parents' time.

"I'm feeling pretty good today," said Dom. "What about you?" he asked Mikel.

Mikel nodded. "I feel great."

"What do you say we give the kids an early out on Friday, providing the week goes well?"

"I say, that sounds like a pretty nice plan," he replied.

Dom looked to Mya and Chase. "Get us a report on Friday morning, and we'll let you know if the week was a success. If it has been successful, they can cut out at noon. In fact, I'm feeling so wonderful today; why don't the four of you take a little trip out of town this weekend and relax at the cabin?"

"That sounds great," said Mya.

"You and Chase have been more than good sports about this situation. It's only fair we include you as well. Now, since breakfast has ended and we've handed out our good news for the week, you may proceed with your day," he said, waving them on.

Paris, Vic, Mya, and Chase exited the room together.

"Wow!" said Vic. "He must be in an exceptional mood. He never offers to allow anyone to stay at the cabin unless he's present."

"Yeah, I heard that," replied Paris. "I think we should do it," she said excitedly. "I could use some time away from the city, couldn't you?"

"Oh, definitely," he replied. "I'd love to get outdoors and do some hiking. It helps clear my mind."

"What about you two?" asked Paris. "Are you game as well?"

"Heck yeah!" replied Chase. Mya nodded her agreement.

"Okay, it's settled," said Vic. "We'll work our butts off this week, so we can go to the cabin and relax." The excitement he was feeling reminded him of going to the cabin as a child. His father would take him hiking and fishing. They'd swim and have bonfires in the evening. He couldn't remember the last time he roasted a marshmallow. It was definitely time for a break. It had been a long time since his last visit.

The group chattered about the weekend as they walked to their more than familiar jobs. They both knew how to do the work, and the territory was a good deal more comfortable than the previous two positions they'd held. There was no way they could mess it up.

Sense of Adventure was located on the first floor of ADG. Paris breathed a sigh of relief as she entered the wing. Each planner had their own office, and there were four different rooms for meeting with clients. Each room had its own theme. The rest of the staff worked in a central open-concept area.

The place was far from typical. The entry had a hallway that split and offered three different routes for clients to choose from. The first took them to an outdoor area that looked like an island oasis with a pool surrounded by sand and a tiki bar that boasted complimentary beverages to all who were of age. The second was called the Library Café, which had all sorts of high-end sweets and treats to choose from, as well as virgin or alcoholic beverages. There were comfy couches and recliners as well as intimate reading nooks built for two. The third hallway led to Fantasy Land, which was sectioned off into various rooms meant for several types of activities. There were thirty rooms, and the themes ranged anywhere from passionate nights to games and tea. These mystical areas were meant for one of two things. Relaxing while contemplating the next big adventure or finding a romantic partner.

Outside of the halls of passion were also standard meeting rooms, but they were reserved for the less exciting parts of the process, such as signing contracts, making payments, and first-time meetings. Clients who came in for these purposes would enter through a different entrance where they would be greeted by one of the front desk attendants, offered a beverage, and then deposited in the room that corresponded with whichever planner they were working with. These particular rooms were painted in grey and held large posters of people experiencing the adventures they had planned.

Paris thought about all the things they offered. There were matchmaking sessions, honeymoons, hiking excursions, parties, once-in-a-lifetime trips, etcetera. You name it, and Sense of Adventure would find a way to make it happen, as long as it was legal. If you wanted to go sit in the mountains of Colorado in a log cabin and smoke marijuana for a weekend, they'd make it happen. Everything from your ride to Colorado to the place you would stay, the activities you'd partake in, and the food you'd consume, would be laid out in the plan.

The clients who came to Sense of Adventure were from all different lifestyles and monetary backgrounds. Paris and Vic both loved a challenge, and it was exciting to plan on a budget or without one. There was no limit to what they could do when they put their minds to it.

Vic would never admit it to his family, but his favorite part of working for Sense of Adventure was playing matchmaker. While he had a hard exterior, he had a soft gooey inside that knew what romance should look like. He could always tell if two people would click, and he excelled at setting up the perfect first date. His first dates ranged from tea in the Library Café to sky-diving or running with the bulls in Pamplona. The extraordinary was always in Vic's game plan, and he hoped one day he could share in some of the amazing adventures he knew existed around the world with his romantic match.

"Good morning," said Angela as she met Mya, Chase, Paris, and Vic in the employee lobby. "I see we'll be working with you this week," she purred. Her attention was directed at Vic.

Paris watched as Vic gave her his most dashing smile. Already, the knot had returned to her stomach. Vic needed to focus. Angela was all legs, with her short black skirt, which accentuated her sexy tight butt. Her long blonde wavy hair fell loosely down her back and framed her face, which held perfect red porn star lips. Her blue-green eyes had the longest thickest black lashes Paris had ever seen, but it was her fake breasts, displayed by a red corset which she wore with a low-buttoned white blouse, that really stole the show. Paris was appalled by the way Vic stared, mesmerized by her every word and the way she reached out and gently touched his shoulder with her masterfully manicured red nails. She was no kitten but a full-grown lioness who could do some serious damage.

Interrupting her thoughts, Tom sauntered up to the group. "Sorry I'm late," he said. He winked at Paris and then turned his attention over to Vic. "Vic, you'll be my assistant this week. I'm sure we'll get along just fine." Getting right to business, he led Vic off to his office, where he could speak more directly about the week's agenda.

Mya and Chase said goodbye to Paris and headed off to do Paris and Vic's rightful jobs, to the best of their abilities. Paris was not particularly happy about working under Angela, but she could see the finish line, and she was not about to give up. She followed Angela into her office.

"Take a seat," said Angela. "You'll be at the desk outside my office, of course. I expect you to answer all calls routed this way and to set up my appointments. You'll bring me coffee each morning along with oatmeal. I prefer it with blueberries and cinnamon. I'll have a coffee break at two in the afternoon as well, and you'll bring me a scone from the café at that time. You will not come into any of my meetings, and you will not speak to any clients other than on the phone. Have I made myself clear?"

"Yes," replied Paris. She was disgusted that Angela was only giving her part of the actual job. It was insulting the way she was being treated, and it was emotionally frustrating that she wasn't allowed to go to any meetings. The meetings were the most exciting part of the job. *This is going to be a long week*, she thought, and she was right.

··•••••••··

Vic watched as Angela went out of her way to speak to him each morning and to bump into him each afternoon. Her sex appeal was distracting, and he found he had to force himself to focus and not search her out when he was sitting at his desk. She was never hard to find, with her high-pitched tinkling laugh. That laugh sent a shockwave to his groin. He kept telling himself that she was off-limits and he would avoid her like the plague, but as each day went by, he felt as if he was fighting a losing battle. Vic held no memory of her dressing so provocatively in the past. He wondered what had changed, as well as what he might find underneath her scant clothing.

Paris was dealing with her own Angela issues. Each morning Angela would angrily demand a change to her coffee order. She'd tell Paris how incompetent she was and that she couldn't believe her parents had ever allowed her to work at ADG. She knew Dom and Cristo were big fans of Angela and that she seemed to have immunity within the company for some reason. Paris didn't care why, but she couldn't wait to be out from under her.

On the other end, Tom was extremely kind to Paris. He greeted her each morning, and frequently offered to take her to lunch. He complimented her clothing, even though Paris knew her clothes were nothing exceptional. His kindness pulled at her heartstrings and made her want even more one-on-one time with him. One morning, he even went out of his way to correct Angela's coffee order for her. Paris had been grateful. She was so tired of Angela's angry and abusive comments. It was as if the power had gone to Angela's head.

Paris decided to keep her head down and do her work. She wouldn't fight back against Angela, and she wouldn't let Tom get in the way. She worked harder and harder to do the job to the best of her abilities. She was slightly jaded that Vic seemed to have gotten the better end of the deal. Tom took Vic nearly everywhere and let him do the job to its fullest. He had a great boss, and the office eye candy, all doting over him and how exceptional he was.

By Friday, Paris felt she'd earned an early release and the cabin weekend. She prayed Dom was in a giving mood. At eleven that morning, they were given the green light. Paris let out a sigh of relief. She couldn't handle one more moment with Angela, for fear that she might snap and do something regrettable.

Packing up her desk, she prepared for the following week with the hope of promotion. She had done her best. If she found herself stuck in this position another week, she didn't know how she'd get through.

"Hey," said Vic as he waltzed up to her desk. "Are you ready to head out?"

Paris glanced at him as she slid the rest of her minor belongings from the week into her bag. "I couldn't be more ready," she replied. Dropping her voice down, she said, "This has been the week from hell."

"Really?" asked Vic, his brow furrowed. "Once we're out of here, you'll have to elaborate."

"Sure." Swinging her bag over her shoulder, she led them out of the building and to the walkway that led to their apartment. "Angela's a demon," she said. "I don't know what I did to piss her off, but it's quite clear that she doesn't like me and that she wants to make me miserable."

"Okay," replied Vic. "How do you figure?"

"Well, for starters, every time I bring her coffee, she tells me the order is wrong. I always write her order down. Tuesday, it was cinnamon and a splash of cream. Wednesday, it was cream with three sugars. Thursday, it was no cream, cinnamon, and two sugars. Today she wanted it black. Whenever I return from getting her request, she tells me a completely different combination, as if it were what she asked for from the beginning, and I KNOW she's messing with me and trying to break me down."

"Really?" asked Vic. He couldn't believe Angela would mess with the owner's daughter like that. "Could you be stressed and misinterpreting what she asked for?"

"No!" snapped Paris. "I'm not crazy." She didn't feel she should have to defend herself to Vic. He had no idea what it had been like working with Angela all week. All he saw was boobs and a short skirt. "It's not just the coffee," she spat back.

"What else?"

"She's mean. She never has anything nice to say. I try to anticipate what she might want next, but it's never the right thing, and she lets me know. Wednesday, she kept me from my lunch break because she wanted a letter retyped for the fourth time!"

"Did you mess it up the first time?" asked Vic.

"I didn't write the first letter. Besides, it wasn't even work-related!" exclaimed Paris. "She had no right to keep me from my break."

"So, why didn't you stand up for yourself?"

"Because she's awful, and I didn't want to hurt us any further," replied Paris. "What would you have done?"

"I would have told her to stick it where the sun doesn't shine," said Vic with a laugh. "If it wasn't work-related, she didn't have a leg to stand on."

"Yes, but she would go out of her way to make it sound as if I was the screwup and that I was being rebellious. The board would probably take her side. I don't think that's a risk I wanted to take, do you?"

"Maybe not," he replied. "I'm sure things are fine. They let us out early, right?"

"True. There's no way I could've done any better, so if they don't promote us, we'll have some serious issues getting out of this hole."

Vic nodded at her. If she was being honest with him and she had done her best, it was now out of their hands. He decided to forget about it for the time being. He'd butted heads with Angela in the past, but only over details for a party. Never had he seen a vicious side to her. "Let's pack so we can get out of here," he said as they entered the elevator. Continuing on toward their apartment, he further pondered the curious situation between Angela and Paris, which brought him directly back to the curves of her body. He had to change his thoughts quickly to avoid an awkward conversation between him and Paris.

• • • • • • • • • • •

It was five in the evening by the time they arrived at Vic's family cabin in Rock Valley. They'd stopped for provisions along the way and were fully prepared to eat well over the coming days.

It had been years since Vic had visited, but the view from the yard was still beautiful. The lake looked like glass, reflecting the trees along the shore. As the leaves rustled in the breeze, he smelled mountain flowers and fresh water, bringing back memories from childhood.

Rock Valley was a small town situated at the foot of the Sheep Rock Falls Mountain Range. The mountains, capped with snow, towered majestically over the small town. While the range was quite small, it still provided an array of outdoor activities, including some impressive waterfall hikes.

As a child, Vic had spent many hours hiking in the SRF Mountains. He loved the smell of the crisp mountain air and the spray of the falls. His cousins would visit and they'd swim in the lake and sit around the bonfire telling stories and cooking campfire pies and marshmallows. He'd never wanted those days to end.

He missed his cousin dearly. They had spent countless hours together working, playing, and getting into mischief. Looking up at the cabin, he could almost see Brody looking back at him from the kitchen window.

"Are you okay?" asked Paris. Vic jumped. She was surprised at how on edge he seemed. "It's been a while, hasn't it?"

"Yeah. Three years, I think. The last trip we'd planned was with you, Brody, Alli, and Mya. As you know, that never happened. I guess I haven't felt much of a need to visit. Especially since my parents and Cristo renovated the inside after Brody passed."

"Who takes care of this place?" asked Chase.

"Cristo usually comes up once or twice a month. My parents visit every few weeks. We have caretakers who regularly tend to the property when they're unable to make the trip," said Vic.

"I love it here," said Mya. "It's so peaceful."

Paris nodded in agreement. "I need a little peace." Looking to Vic, she asked, "Will you be able to do this, or do we need to carry you in?"

"Don't make fun," scolded Chase. "I'm sure this isn't easy."

"I'm not making fun of him. I know this isn't easy. I, of all people, get it."

Vic nodded in acknowledgment. He hadn't taken Paris's comment to be a jab.

"Why don't you give me the key?" requested Mya.

Vic dug into his pocket and gently tossed her the key. Reaching out, Paris grabbed Vic's hand. Once Mya opened the door, she gently led him up the steps and into the cabin. He gripped her hand tightly.

"Which room is yours again?" she asked.

"I don't think the makeup of my room changed, though I know the other rooms were modified some. It should be down the hall. The last door on the left." He felt silly letting the past haunt him. He followed Paris to his room. He watched as she lightly pushed the door open and led him inside. He tossed his duffel on the floor and dropped her hand. "I'm fine," he said, brushing away the feeling of inadequacy.

"You don't look fine," she whispered. "Your hands are clammy. Do you wanna talk about it?"

Vic sat down on the bed and watched as she seated herself next to him. Tucking her legs beneath her, she stared him down. He never spoke about his feelings. He would much rather ignore them. Why bring up the past? "I'll be fine," he replied. She shook her head at him. Reaching out, she placed her hand on his forearm. The touch felt warm, and it sent an unexpected tingle through his body.

"You told me it was time to move on. You can't move on without facing your past."

He nodded. "I guess I thought we were invincible. I never imagined I'd be living my life without Brody. He was more like a brother than a cousin."

"I know," she replied calmly. "So many things remind me of Alli every day. It hurts all the time. Nothing can replace them, but you said yourself, we need to live our lives again, right? Look at how much time I wasted being angry at Mya. I guess we have to make fresh memories, but continue to appreciate what little time we had with them." His eyes were watery, but he held it together, like most stubborn and larger-than-life men. "Just so you know, when we talk about them, you're in a safe place. I'll never judge or tell you your feelings are wrong. I truly understand."

"I know you do." He gave her a kind look. She wore a cherry red tank top and white shorts. She had messily piled her wavy black hair on top of her head, her bangs feathering out around her eyes. At that moment, he felt genuinely understood. Even more, he felt as if he was being drawn toward her. Her bright red lips looked as if they were inviting him in.

He tried to brush the thought aside, but then she placed her hand on his leg, and the feeling drove him further toward madness. Normally, he didn't allow himself to think of her in a sexual way, but there was something to be said about knowing you were in the presence of someone who understood you. Someone you could easily talk to.

Squeezing Vic's leg, she asked, "Do you want to lie down for a bit? I can give you some space to sort your feelings. Or, if you want, I can stay and be supportive. We don't have to talk." Looking into his eyes, she could see a look she'd never seen before. She continued to stare at him, waiting for an answer. Reaching up, he grabbed her wrist and pulled her toward him. She felt her whole body go weak. Placing her hand on his chest, she stopped him from coming any closer. "I'm going to get you some water," she replied as she hopped off the bed and exited the room.

"Paris, wait." The knot returned to his stomach as he watched her leave the room. *Perhaps it was for the better*, he thought as he let his head drop back onto the pillow.

Vic's advance shocked Paris. They rarely acted friendly toward one another. What was he thinking? One thing was for certain: she should not allow him to get any closer.

When she returned to his room, to her relief, he was snoring softly. She placed the glass of water on the nightstand next to him, and, closing the door behind her, she left him to sleep it off, whatever it was. Heading back to the kitchen, she found Chase and Mya had finished unpacking all the food items for the weekend.

"Which rooms should we stay in?" asked Chase.

"I'll stay in Cristo's room," said Mya.

Paris arched an eyebrow and turned to look at her friend. She watched Mya's face turn crimson. Obviously, something was going on. "How do you know which room is Cristo's?" she asked. "You haven't been here since they renovated the floorplan."

"Oh, um, I already looked at all the rooms. It's the middle room on the right, and the only one that makes sense. The décor gave it away." She shrugged.

"Uh-huh," replied Chase. "I'm sure it did, honey. Anyway, I'll stay in the room next to yours. I think it's a guestroom. There's nothing overly exciting about it, but lots of wide-open space. Perfect for my morning yoga."

"Perfect. I'll stay in the master suite," added Paris. "There's a beautiful balcony with a view overlooking the lake and the mountains. I'd love to sit out there with a glass of wine and watch the sunset." Turning, she headed for the door. "I'll be right back. I need to grab my bag out of the car."

Mya ran after Paris as she left the house. "Do you want to go for a walk before dinner?" she asked. "I want to take in as much nature as possible. We so seldom get out of town."

"Sure," said Paris. "Vic's taking a nap, and it sounded like Chase might do some yoga, so we have time." Grabbing her bag, she hauled it into the room across from Vic's and dropped it on the floor in front of the dresser. She was already wearing her tennis shoes, but she threw on some different clothes since she was currently wearing Mya's.

Heading back to the living room, Paris now wore black yoga capris, a white tank, and a black and white straw hat. She was proud of the restraint she'd practiced when Mya took her shopping. So far, everything had come in handy.

"Ready?" Mya sat on the couch eating a red, white, and blue popsicle. "Oh, that looks yummy. Takes me back to child-hood," she commented. Heading for the freezer, she grabbed one for herself.

Outside, the sun still shone brightly enough for beads of sweat to appear on Paris's skin. The breeze coming off the mountains felt refreshing, and kept the town much cooler than the temps back home. Heading out, they wandered down the dirt path behind the oversized cabin.

"Have you been here recently?" asked Paris.

"No," said Mya. "Some of my fondest memories are of the weekends spent at your family's cabin. I wish they hadn't sold the land. I miss it."

"Yeah. Me too. I heard my mom mention that she's trying to talk my dad into buying another cabin. We spent more time with the Alarie's at our cabin than they did here I think."

"Too bad that storm took it out," added Mya.

"Yeah. Totally sucks. Anyway, I've visited this cabin on a few occasions with Alli."

"How does that make you feel?" asked Mya. She paused to assess her friend.

"It makes me miss her. We had a lot of fun. I remember the last time I was here. We hiked up a path to a tire swing and spent the afternoon swimming and lying out in the sun. It was wonderful."

Mya continued on. "Do you think Vic's okay? He seemed awfully upset when we first arrived."

"Yeah, he just needs some time. There are a lot of memories, and with them, a lot of pain resurfacing."

"I wish we could wave a wand and fix it all," said Mya sadly. "I miss Alli and Brody too."

"We all do," said Paris. Reaching out her hand, she squeezed Mya's shoulder. "At least we have each other."

"That we do, and I think Chase has made an excellent addition to our little group."

"I agree. Chase is special. An all-around good guy." Paris paused and gave Mya a slight frown. "So, on a different topic, do you want to tell me what's going on with you and Cristo?"

Mya paused and looked at Paris with suspicion. "Nothing, why?"

"Do you really expect me to believe that? I think anyone can see that you're hiding something."

"It's nothing," she replied forcefully. "I've turned him down many times, but he keeps persisting."

"If it's a problem, Mya, you need to speak up. Persistence is harassment."

"It's under control," she insisted.

"Okay, if you say so. Just remember, you can talk to me about it. I promise to listen and not judge."

"I know, but there's nothing to talk about."

"Fine," she replied, taking a breath. "Do you suppose we should start planning the next Touch a Heart Fest? It's been over a year and I feel like I've let the community down."

"I think that's a great idea. We'll let the seniors know we're planning it, but we'll take it slow, because you have a lot on your plate right now."

"I'm fine with that. Let's at least set a date and get the word out so the community knows. I need to make amends."

"Sounds good. We can discuss it more on Monday."

The girls continued to walk quietly, taking in their surroundings. They followed the path around the lake. When they finally returned to the cabin, it was ten after seven, and

Vic was outside drinking a beer while he grilled chicken and vegetables.

"That smells delicious," said Paris. "How long before it's ready?"

"We'll give 'em another ten minutes. Will you two set the picnic table, please?"

"Sure thing," replied Mya. She and Paris went inside to grab the necessities.

Returning with her hands full of condiments, Paris asked, "Did you sleep at all?"

Vic looked up at her. "Briefly."

"You were snoring a little when I brought the water in, so I let you rest."

"I feel a lot more awake now," he stated. In actuality, what he meant was that he had observed Paris's lack of reaction toward his advancement, and he was now pretending he was over it. He noted that she changed clothing for her walk. Even in yoga attire, the girl looked good.

"Do you need any help?" asked Paris.

"Nah, I've got it." He purposely cut her off. His tone had come out sounding a bit colder than he had intended.

Paris watched him as he meticulously tended to the chicken and veggies. She hadn't mentioned his advance to Mya. Paris was unsure how she felt about the situation. She didn't want to be another one of his one-night stands or a distraction from his feelings of loss.

Ten minutes later, the group found themselves settled in at the picnic table with their favorite beverages and a feast of juicy chicken, potato salad, roasted asparagus, and chocolate brownies for dessert. Dinner was delicious. They drank their beers and told stories about past hiking and camping trips. They also played a couple of drinking card games, and before long, Chase and Mya were both shuffling off to bed, leaving Vic and Paris alone with each other.

"So, tell me the truth," said Vic, "have you ever dated anyone from work or had a thing for a coworker?"

Paris rubbed her eyes with the back of her hand. The drink was definitely getting to her, but she thought, what the heck? "Yes, there's someone I've had a thing for over the past many years, but so far he hasn't noticed and I haven't made any advances."

"Oh, really? Do tell," replied Vic. He was surprised that Paris had a love interest. He never saw her with anyone, but he'd heard rumors about her love life.

"Okay, if you think you can keep it to yourself?"

Vic nodded at her. "I promise."

"Tom Mariano," she replied solemnly.

"Tom? Seriously? What do you like about him?" asked Vic.

"For starters, he's driven. I don't know anyone who lands more clients than he does. It also helps that he's smoldering hot," she admitted with a blush.

"Hm. I'm surprised by that. He seems to be quite vain, doesn't he?"

"How so? I guess I hadn't noticed."

"Trust me, Paris, that man is in love with his own reflection. He knows he's attractive, and he flaunts it."

"He flaunts it?" Paris was appalled by Vic's statement. "How do you mean?"

"I'm not going to delve into this any further with you. Just watch him. You'll see."

Paris wasn't so certain that Vic was right. She hadn't seen Tom's vanity previously.

"Play Poker with me," insisted Vic.

"Isn't that kind of boring when we only have two people?" she asked.

"Nah, we'll make it interesting." He laughed. "If you win, what do you want?"

"I want you to yell, 'Paris is amazing!'" She laughed. "Haven't you ever had feelings for a coworker?"

"Dozens of times," he admitted. "I think we should play Strip Poker. That's more interesting and gives you more reason to try not to lose." He gave a nod for emphasis.

"Okay, fine," she agreed. "Do you sleep with coworkers frequently?"

"No, not really," replied Vic. "I try to stay out of the building with my relations."

"Yes, but do you succeed?"

"A gentleman never tells." He had a mischievous grin on his face as he laid out the cards.

"You're no gentleman!" she shot back.

"Why not?" Vic was slightly hurt by her response.

"I can tell you've done this before," she said pointedly.

"Well, even if I have, how does that equate to not being a gentleman?"

Fanning out her cards, she asked, "Do gentlemen try to swindle women out of their clothing?"

"Touché," he said. The grin never left his face. "But in all seriousness, probably. I think you'd be hard-pressed to find a man who wouldn't try, given the chance."

Paris looked at her cards. "What you're implying is that there are no gentlemen."

"Maybe gentleman is a word not so dissimilar to super-man?"

Looking up at him, she narrowed her eyes. "I don't believe that. There are true gentlemen out there somewhere. My father is a gentleman."

"Really? So, you're telling me that the gallant Mr. DeMarcé did not get the beautiful Mrs. DeMarcé naked, the very first chance he got? He was above that?" Vic knew he had her with that response, but whether she would admit it was the question.

"Yes, I'm saying exactly that," she scoffed as she took a swig from her bottle of beer. She watched as Vic pulled his cell phone out of his pocket. "What are you doing?"

"Looking for some music to play."

"Don't change the subject! I think you're wrong. My father's not the type of man who would try to get a woman naked unless he was making love to her."

"Oh, really?" asked Vic.

"Yes, really!" persisted Paris.

"Sorry to burst your bubble, Paris, but I'm pretty sure you're wrong. He's as hot-blooded as the rest of us when it comes to getting a beautiful woman naked, but if he is as you say, he won't have a problem with me calling and asking him if he's ever been a part of such shenanigans."

At his response, Paris spurt beer from her mouth. "You're not calling him!" she yelled as she grabbed for the phone. He yanked it out of her reach, and she lunged toward him. With his massive free hand, he palmed her forehead and held her at bay. Paris flailed like an angry monkey as she heard the phone ringing over the speaker. Vic set the phone out of the way, grabbed her in a bear hug, and wrestled her to the ground.

"Don't ask him that!" she wailed. "You're such a jerk. It's none of our business!"

"Shh," he said. "Let me do this, and if I'm wrong, I'll give you a hundred bucks."

Looking at him, she shook her head in defeat. After all, she wasn't the idiot asking such a personal question.

"Hello?" answered her father.

"Hey, Mikel, it's Vic."

"Good evening, Vic. What can I do for you?"

"Well, sir, I have a question for you."

"Shoot," he replied, "but make it quick. I'm in over my head playing Strip Poker with a couple of ladies from the office."

"Hey, say no more," replied Vic. "We can talk later."

"If you're sure?" asked Mikel.

"Completely. Have a nice night." Vic turned off his phone and set it on the table. Paris stared at him, her mouth agape.

"Don't look at me like that." He laughed.

"What did you do?" she demanded.

"Excuse me? What do you mean?"

"You know exactly what I mean. What did you do?"

Vic burst out laughing. "You should've seen the look on your face!" he gasped.

Paris frowned.

Pulling himself together, he replied, "I texted him. I told him we had a bet and that I would be calling momentarily and that he was to reply that he was in the middle of a game of Strip Poker with some ladies from the office."

"And he just obliged you? What is this world coming to?" she demanded.

"Come on, Paris, it was a joke. We joke around all the time. Your father is as human as the rest of us, and also a man. We're like family. It isn't far-fetched that we can joke around with each other at times."

"So, in reality, you didn't get the question answered," she pointed out.

"No, but I already know the answer. He's told me a particular story from back in school, and I guarantee it proves my point. Don't be upset," he said. Paris had a bitter look on her face. He hated to see her angry. "Your father is a gentleman, but even gentlemen play games every now and again."

"Maybe," she replied, shaking her head. "You realize you've slain a giant, don't you?"

"Darling, every girl must see the day when they realize their father is human too. It's not like I told you he's a murderer or drug dealer. I simply changed your fairytale."

"I guess," she responded quietly.

"I know what will cheer you up," he said as he jumped up from the floor and headed toward the kitchen. "This will make you feel much better!" he called out. Walking back into the room, he held out a bottle of Spiced Rum and two shot glasses. He knew her well, despite their lack of pleasantries over the years. Setting the glasses on the coffee table, he poured them each a shot. "Let's start out with a different game before getting to cards."

"Which game would you like to play?" she asked hesitantly.

"Truth or Dare," he stated. "You can even pick truth every single time if you want."

"Okay, I'll bite. Why do you want to play Truth or Dare? Isn't it a bit childish?"

"Quite the contrary," he replied. "Truth or Dare is a game that allows two people to learn about one another as well as gain trust. Though I have to admit, children generally use it to embarrass each other. In our version, if you don't want to answer the question or do the dare, you drink. What do you say?"

"Okay," she said, "let's give it a try."

Grabbing his shot glass, he raised it in the air and motioned her to do the same. "Do you promise to maintain safety and honesty throughout the game?"

"I do," said Paris.

Clanking his glass to hers, he said, "Bottoms up."

Paris downed the shot and immediately felt her stomach warm. "Maybe pour me one more before we get started?" she requested.

"Sure thing." Vic poured them each another shot, and they both drank them down. "You can go first."

Climbing up onto the couch, she made herself comfortable and watched as Vic took his place at the opposite end facing her. "Truth or Dare?" she asked.

Vic smiled at her and replied, "Truth."

"Okay," Paris thought for a moment. She wasn't really sure where to start. Vic was staring at her in anticipation. Licking her lips, she asked, "Have you ever paid for sex?"

Vic's eyes went wide in disbelief. "I'm not answering that question."

"Really?" she asked. "The very first question and you won't answer? Wasn't this your idea?"

"Sure, but I didn't think you were going to ask such a ridiculous question."

"If it's so ridiculous, why don't you just answer?"

"Just pass me a shot, and we'll move on," he said.

Paris poured the shot and slid it his way. In one smooth move, he snatched it up and dumped it down his throat. "Ahh, tasty," he replied. "Now, where were we? Oh, yes, Truth or Dare?"

She was appalled that he didn't answer the question and frustrated because she wanted to know if he actually had paid for sex, which meant he was even more despicable than she'd first anticipated. "Truth." She watched as he ran through the possibilities in his mind. She was terrified of the things he might come up with. She knew her first question was very personal, but it was something she and Mya had always wondered.

"Have you ever kissed a woman, and if yes, why?" he inquired slyly.

"Yes," she replied without hesitation. She didn't care if he knew. "It was Mya. We were twenty-one, and we were at a party together. There was this creepy guy following me around, and I wanted him to leave me alone, so Mya and I pretended we were a couple. The kiss was her idea, being into drama and all. She figured it would prove to him that he had no chance."

"Wow, did it work? Did he leave you alone?"

"Yes. He said he could tell we were really into each other, and he apologized for harassing me."

"You know," he replied, "that could have gone the opposite way."

"Oh, believe me, I know. I told her the same thing, but she said to trust her, and that she had a hunch he'd be put off by it. Luckily, she was right. Truth or Dare?" she asked.

"Dare," he replied.

Laughing at him, she said, "I dare you to drink another shot."

"I'm not sure you're very good at this game." he replied as he grabbed the bottle, pouring himself another shot. "Bottoms up!" he slammed the shot glass down on the table. "Truth or Dare?"

"Truth."

"Okay, Paris," he said, scooting a little closer, "why do you hate me?"

Instead of answering right away, Paris poured herself another shot and drank it down.

"That bad?" he asked.

She shook her head at him. "No. I don't hate you. You have no idea what it takes for me to admit that."

He looked at her with concern. "What is it then? Why is it so hard for you to admit you don't hate me?"

"If I'm being honest, I don't like the way you act. You don't have any genuine relationships outside of your brother, Breanna, and your parents. You're angry and short with most of the people you work with. For once, I would like to see you show some real kindness and compassion toward your coworkers, like you used to. When was the last time you actually rewarded someone for hard work?"

Vic looked at her for a moment, taking in what she was saying. This was not the first time he'd heard this. "You know, you aren't always the most personable either."

"True, but I don't fire people for ridiculous reasons. I'm not the one with a fearful nickname."

"Nickname?" he asked. "What nickname?"

Paris's jaw dropped. Did he really not know? "Most of the staff call you Diablo. It's been going on for over a year now." She shrugged. "I really thought you knew."

"Wow. That's cold," he sighed. "Do you know what they call you?" He watched as her eyes got big.

"No, what?" she demanded.

"I don't know." He laughed. "That's why I'm asking."

"You're so funny. Ha, ha, ha. Truth or Dare?"

"Truth," he said loosely. The alcohol was definitely taking effect. He wasn't much for shots. Normally he was more into sipping.

"Do you have a thing for Angela Martini?" she asked.

"You have to admit, she's pretty freakin' hot."

"I certainly do not need to admit that," replied Paris. "She's my boss at the moment. I think she's utterly vile and quite possibly trying to seduce you for no good reason. Also, she dresses like a cheap hooker."

"That's not very nice. You think she's trying to seduce me?"

"Why else did she suddenly start dressing in such skimpy clothing?"

"So, this was a sudden change?" he mused. Paris had noticed too.

"You didn't really notice her before, did you?"

"I guess you have a point there. Pick your poison," he requested.

"Truth."

"Tell me, Paris, do you really have a thing for Tom?"

"We're terrible people," she replied. "It would appear we both like our handlers." She grinned.

"Tom? You're telling me you genuinely like him and that you've never noticed how vain he is?"

"Vic, it's not new. I've had feelings for Tom since the day I met him. He's a stunning male specimen. I'd give anything to taste his lips," she purred, "and I maintain that I don't think he's vain."

"Here," said Vic, handing her another shot. "I don't get what you see in him, but who am I to judge? To scandal," he said as he raised his glass to hers.

Paris drank the shot and then shook her head at him. "Whatever. It's only a scandal if something happens. Even then, I'm not sure it qualifies."

Vic eyed her up and down. She was gorgeous. There was no question about it.

"You like what you see?" she asked.

Realizing he'd been caught, he gave her his most charming smile and reached for her hand. "You're very pretty," he said softly and squeezed her hand ever so slightly. He watched as the corners of her mouth curled upward. "How come we haven't managed to be closer over the years?" he coaxed.

"I think in part we've had other goals for what we wanted," she replied quietly. His touch was doing unspeakable things to her insides. It was unsettling to think that he could make her feel anything so intimate.

Launching himself forward, he pressed his lips to hers. Her eyes went wide, and she instantly pushed him back and moved further away. Turning his head slightly to one side, he squinted at her as he contemplated her body language. She wasn't scowling at him. What he read was shock and, at the same time, desire.

"What was that?" she demanded.

"Here is how I get women," he replied. "I'm very good at reading body language, and I know when precisely to make my move. Tell me you aren't feeling this, and I'll pretend it never happened," he said in a low and even tone. He watched her. She didn't move a muscle, but her breath had quickened. "I can tell you're interested. When was the last time you were with anyone intimately? This doesn't have to be anything more than sex, but you have to tell me no," he stated, "or I'll come over there." She still didn't budge or utter a syllable.

Leaning forward, he stretched out his hand and lightly touched her elbow. Then, moving slowly, he gently dragged the tip of his nail down her arm and paused at her wrist. Her breathing was still quick, and her pupils dilated. She couldn't find the words to tell him no. She didn't want to say no.

Abruptly; he closed his hand around her wrist and squeezed firmly.

Paris lost control. Her whole body tingled with desire. When his hand closed, she could no longer contain the feeling. She pushed off the arm of the couch and lunged toward him. He pulled her into his embrace. Their lips smashed together as they hungrily drank each other in. If she'd been told two hours earlier that this would happen, she wouldn't have believed it.

Vic's fingertips worked their way up underneath her shirt and slid gently along the underside of her breasts, testing the waters further. She moaned lightly and tore open his shirt so she could feel his bare chest. Her hands felt soft and warm against his skin. He felt oddly safe in her presence.

Paris was further drawn in by the firmness of his chest as she ran her fingers over it. He had always been in great shape, but until now, she had never wondered what it would be like to touch him in such a wanton manner. Sliding her fingers down his body, she made her way toward his waist.

Holding tightly, Vic scooped her up and carried her to his room, closing the door behind them. *Consequences be damned,* he thought. She would be his, if only for one night. He would worry about the rest when morning came.

·····•••····

The morning light arrived, and Mya awoke feeling rested and ready to begin the day. She'd slept well and was ready to hike to the waterfall. Heading toward the bathroom, she saw Vic's door open and watched as Paris backed herself out and went into her own room, clearly not realizing she had an audience.

"Morning, Mya," called Chase. He came out of the room behind her and headed toward the kitchen, cup of coffee already in hand. Pausing for a moment, he asked, "Do you want some coffee? I'm about to make a second pot."

Mya lifted her wrist to check the time on her watch. It was barely seven in the morning. "You already drank an entire pot of coffee? What time did you get up?"

"I couldn't sleep. I was up at five. Went for a swim and sat out on the dock watching a couple of fishermen."

She took in his hot pink swim trunks. They had palm trees on them. Indeed, he was still wet from his swim. "No coffee for me. Don't go overboard," she warned. "We're hiking today."

"Oh, I know," he replied as he shooed her away with his free hand and continued back to the kitchen.

Mya hurried into the bathroom to freshen up before anyone else could distract her. Meanwhile, Vic, wearing only his sleep shorts, meandered out of his room and into the kitchen where Chase engaged in a battle with the gas stove.

"Do you know how to work that?" Vic asked.

"Of course, I do!" he snapped.

Vic sat and watched him flick the nob back and forth. He found it amusing since he knew the stove was long past its prime and no longer would light without the use of a kitchen match. As he continued to smirk at Chase, Mya appeared next to him. "Yeah, that's never going to do it."

"Chase," said Mya, "you need a match to light it."

Turning around, Chase gave her a funny look. "Why? It's supposed to ignite when you turn it, right?" He looked at Vic, who was trying not to laugh.

"It's old," replied Vic. "It needs some help. The igniter's broken. Check that drawer on your left. There should be some kitchen matches."

Chase flung the drawer open and snatched up the box of matches. Retrieving one, he struck the side of the box and watched the match ignite. Placing it by the burner, he turned the knob and a larger flame appeared. "There we go," he mused. "Eggs will be ready shortly. Mya, will you please throw some toast in the toaster?"

"Sure thing," she replied.

"Hey guys," said Paris as she walked into the room. She was already dressed for their hike.

"Morning," replied Vic. He was happy to see her but a little annoyed that she'd snuck out without a word. He wondered if she regretted their late-night tryst.

Paris nodded toward Vic and then poured herself a cup of coffee. She felt bad about sneaking out that morning, but she didn't want to make things awkward for everyone else. She wasn't fully aware of her true feelings regarding Vic. He was a handsome and thoughtful lover. She felt safe at the moment, but she wondered in the back of her mind what last night had meant to him?

"I need to tell you two something," said Mya as she climbed onto one of the breakfast stools. "I have some concerns. I received a text from Cristo's secretary, Bryn. She says she overheard a conversation yesterday at lunch. There are rumors that some of your colleagues might be out to sabotage your progress."

"Sabotage us? But why?" asked Paris.

"Not everyone wants to see you successfully restored to your former positions," replied Chase.

Vic shook his head. "Like whom?"

"We don't have actual names, but there are murmurs that whoever holds your positions within the company might one day be next in line to run it. And keep in mind, your prior behavior is a sore subject with quite a few people," noted Mya.

"So, what you're saying is, our coworkers hate us?" asked Paris. "That's wonderful."

"You need to show them you can make amends and be kind and considerate leaders. Act like the bosses you once were," said Chase.

"I know we've both had our heads up our butts for a while," said Vic, "but I think it's safe to say that we're ready to fight for what's ours. I don't want to see anyone else run the company that our family put their friendship, love, time, and hard-earned dollars into building." Paris nodded to back him.

"Good. Start watching your backs, as will we," said Chase.

"It'll be only a matter of time before the saboteurs see you as a threat and realize you're making amends. Once that happens, there's no telling what a desperate person might do," noted Mya.

Paris felt the knot forming in her stomach again. She was prepared to fight for her place within the company, but if people fought dirty, many secrets or rumors might come out, and the press had not been too kind to her over the past six months.

CHAPTER ELEVEN

Monday morning, Vic stood patiently in the entryway to their apartment, waiting for Paris. He watched as she filled her coffee mug and grabbed an apple from the fruit bowl. She walked over to the sink, gave the shiny red fruit a rinse, and took a small dainty bite out of one side. Juice squirted from the apple as her teeth and lips made contact. He watched as she licked the sweet droplets from her upper lip. How could such a harmless action cause such a huge stir within him?

The weekend had been full of fun and relaxation for the foursome, but Vic was a bit surprised that he and Paris hadn't spoken a word to one another about their late-night activities. Normally he wasn't one to dwell, but something about her had hooked him. He could now see the more sensual side of Paris. The hungry carnal energy she brought to the bedroom. Sure, he had taken many one-night lovers, but this was no ordinary feeling following it up. Not even Janel had elicited such a response from him. Their relationship had been casual, or so he believed. Janel had other thoughts on the matter.

While they'd never agreed to be monogamous, she apparently thought they were of the same mind. When he realized they, in fact, were not, he ended the relationship.

"Are we ready?" asked Paris, breaking into Vic's thoughts.

"Yeah. Ready when you are," he replied.

"Let's get this over with. Hopefully, there won't be any negative surprises," she said.

Vic could hear the anxiety in her voice. He wished he could put her at ease, but he knew anxiety didn't always listen to reason. He reached for her hand, but she turned away smoothly as if she hadn't noticed. He watched her hips sway lightly as she marched off toward the elevator. He couldn't help but stare at her tight, round butt. He felt his groin begin to swell and quickly changed his thoughts to Tom Mariano, the lucky bastard who held Paris's interest. The thought instantly deflated him.

"Are you coming?" Paris asked, holding the door.

Vic was standing outside the elevator, in a daze. "Sorry. I got caught up in my thoughts for a moment." He stepped forward into the car. What did Tom have that he didn't? He, after all, was heir to ADG and Tom was merely a dedicated worker.

"You look angry," replied Paris. "Did something happen?"

Vic shook his head. "No, everything's fine. It's no big deal." In reality, it was a big deal, but he wasn't ready to admit it or to succumb fully to his feelings. Especially if Paris was not on the same page.

"You sure you don't want to talk about it?" she asked.

Shutting her down, he said, "I'm good. I'll let you know if I change my mind."

Mya and Chase were chatting in the lobby when the elevator doors opened, and Vic and Paris stepped out.

"Morning!" Chase called out. He seemed happy as usual. "How is everyone?"

"I feel pretty good," replied Paris. "I slept great. The week-end really helped."

"That's super," he replied with a little too much excitement. He wore a yellow button-down shirt with smiling suns, which mirrored his happy persona.

"What about you, Vic? How are you?" asked Mya, following the question with a yawn.

Vic shrugged. "I can't really complain, but you look a little tired."

"Lots on my mind, I guess. Are you both ready for today? Here's hoping we get some positive news about last week."

"I concur," replied Vic.

The group headed off down the block toward the ADG building.

"Now, let's remember what we discussed over the weekend. Keep your eyes peeled. You never know who might be out to hurt you," said Chase.

"Yeah," agreed Mya. "Don't let your guard down. Don't get too close to anyone."

Paris looked at Vic, who gave her a nod of understanding. "We know," replied Paris.

Together they entered the boardroom. Their families were already seated. They stood in greeting and welcomed them back.

"How was the lake?" asked Dom.

"It was peaceful," replied Paris. "We hiked, kayaked, and relaxed by the water. I couldn't have wished for a nicer reprieve."

"Glad to hear," said Dom. "Vic, you're awfully quiet. Did you not enjoy the weekend?"

"On the contrary, I enjoyed it a little too much," he stated.

Dom's expression changed to that of interest. "We can discuss that in more detail later."

Paris blushed and turned away at his comment. Apparently, she wasn't completely immune to the after feelings of the night they shared.

Nicola passed around two trays of sticky buns while Molly, Dom's secretary, poured them each coffee, milk, or water. Paris watched her as she moved around the room. She was young and naïve. Barely nineteen and dressed in what she considered to be professional attire. Her oversized jacket and grey pencil skirt did nothing for her. She often stopped to push up her large round glasses, which kept slipping down her nose. Her dress made her look as if she were middle-aged rather than young and vibrant. Her ashy brown hair looked flat and dull. Paris made a note to pull her aside some time in the future and teach her how to properly dress for success, though she was unsure how much she would be able to help with her clumsy awkwardness. She had already slipped three times and tripped over her hideous black mules, stepping out of one as she tried to regain her composure.

Mya leaned in toward Paris. "Are you watching Molly?" she asked quietly.

"Yeah, she's a mess, isn't she?"

"Poor thing. She could be beautiful, but she consistently chooses the wrong clothing for her body. She needs to at least wear things that fit. This look is sloppy. I'm surprised Jessamine hasn't stepped in," said Mya.

"Totally agreeing with you. She could also use a little depth in her hair. That ashy tone, though natural, does nothing for her eyes. What are your thoughts?"

"I was thinking maybe we could kill two birds with one stone. Invite her over and do a makeover of sorts and also recruit her to keep an eye out for potential enemies. It might be fun," said Mya.

"I don't want her to think she's a charity case and that we're attacking her. How do we go about suggesting such a thing?" asked Paris.

"I suppose we could simply ask her to hang out. See if she's heard the gossip and whether she knows who's gunning for your jobs."

"That's not a bad idea," replied Paris. "If she helps us, in return, we can reward her by teaching her how to better dress to enhance her features. Though, honestly, I want to help her either way."

"When should we do this?"

"How about Thursday night? That way, we can give it a little more time to see if any new information presents itself."

"Sold," she replied. "I think that's a great plan. I'll ask her about meeting on Thursday when we're finished here. That way, we can get her to pay closer attention to what's happening in the next few days."

Hearing the clanking of a glass, Paris turned her attention away from Mya and watched as her slim and willowy mother stood up. Her dark red lips held a warm smile as she looked from Paris to Vic.

"You two have had another wonderful week." She beamed. "I'm happy to announce that we're promoting you once again. Congratulations, you've made it back to your primary positions. We'll be watching to see how well you work with the other employees. You have six more weeks to prove to us you want to be here and that you're team players."

Nicola stepped back and took her seat while Jessamine stood up from hers. "I agree with Nicola. You've both performed well. We're happy to see you getting along and working with those around you. As a bonus, we're giving you each five hundred dollars to buy some new business attire since you'll be meeting with clients and need to look the part." Jessamine paused to brush her long curly auburn hair away from her face, then focused her gaze on Paris. "I know last week was especially straining on you, Paris, but you stuck with it, and we're all especially proud of how you handled the pressure. Angela can be a bit tough at times, but you kept your cool."

Paris grinned triumphantly. "Thanks." She had no idea that the board realized how obnoxious Angela could be.

Nicola, as if she had read her daughter's mind, replied, "We asked her to test you to see how you would respond to changes in direction. We're pleased you didn't make a scene, and that you continued to do your best to complete each task. I'm sure it wasn't easy."

Paris said nothing. She was shocked to find her own mother had asked Angela not to go easy on her, but then she had ended up in the current situation of her own volition.

"We're prepared to end this meeting early, with the knowledge that you know what you need to do next," said Dom. "Have a great week, and remember, we're here if you ever need further guidance."

"Mya and Chase will be your assistants," added Mikel. "Best of luck." He smiled and waved them out of the room, but not before Cristo chimed in.

"Mya, if you'll stay behind for a moment after the others have left, I need a word with you."

Mya nodded hesitantly in his direction. Paris watched her friend's shoulders stiffen in response to his voice. Something wasn't right.

"Do you want me to wait?" she whispered.

"No. I don't want to make you late," replied Mya.

"If you're sure," said Paris hesitantly. Even as she said it, she knew she couldn't leave without her. She had plenty of moments from the previous two years that she needed to make up for. She followed her coworkers out of the room. The board turned to the left while Chase and Vic paused outside the door. Cristo shut the door behind them.

"That was quick," said Chase. "I didn't think they'd be so short on words."

"Shh," hissed Paris. She had her ear pressed to the door. "I need to find out what's going on in there. Something's not right." She strained to hear what they were saying, but everything was muffled. She moved away from the door, feeling defeated.

"What's up?" asked Vic.

"I really don't know, but isn't it strange how your uncle is calling her aside? She's not his assistant, nor does she work with him all that closely."

"Perhaps he's been put in charge of relaying tasks to her?" said Vic.

"No," replied Chase. "I'd be aware of it."

"So, what is it?" asked Vic. Just then, the group heard a loud thud coming from within the

room. Paris jumped. It sounded as if someone had run into the door. "Should we go in there?" she asked.

"No," said Vic. "I don't want to do anything to jeopardize our situation."

"But she might be in trouble," protested Paris. "What if he's hurting her?"

"If he was hurting her, I would think she'd have yelled," replied Chase.

Paris shook her head. She felt helpless. All they could do was wait for Mya to come out, which she did, but a moment later.

Cristo blew past the group, scowling his disapproval toward their loitering, as he retreated. Mya emerged from the room, visibly shaken. Paris stepped toward her. "What happened?"

"I don't care to discuss it," she replied. "We need to go. You shouldn't have waited."

Vic and Chase looked at each other in confusion, then followed Mya down the hall. Paris brought up the rear. She was lost in thought, trying to decipher the odd situation.

Rushing toward Mya, Paris asked, "Did he hit you? We heard a thud against the door."

"No," she replied curtly.

"Then what?" demanded Paris. "What did he do?"

"Paris," said Mya, "I know you're concerned, but it's none of your business. Let it go," she demanded.

"Whatever." Paris was disgusted. "You didn't speak to Molly," she added.

"Oh, shoot," replied Mya. "I'll call her this evening."

"I can throw in money from my bonus to buy her some clothing," said Paris.

"Are you sure you want to do that? If you do, it'd probably be best to purchase items beforehand and make it seem as if we're getting rid of clothing from my closet. That way she won't feel like a project, right?"

"Yeah. That's a great idea. This is exciting. I'm feeling a bit blasé regarding my current lifestyle," she laughed. "Helping someone else out for a change, would be refreshing."

· · · · · · · · · ·

Paris was thrilled to be back in her own office. How she had missed it so. Everything was as she'd left it, even though Mya had been running things while she was away. Mya knew how Paris worked and that she liked to maintain order.

Looking around her office and seeing it, for what felt like the first time in years, Paris noted that some updates and maintenance were warranted. The vacation photos were a bit dated, and the walls were faded from the sun. How had she not noticed the aging that had taken place? There were cracks in two corners of the room. Her desk lacked luster and either needed replacing or resurfacing, and there was a worn spot in the carpet where the chairs each sat. While she'd maintained her neat and orderly manner, she'd neglected the upkeep.

Paris picked up her phone and dialed Mya. "Hey," she said when she heard her friend's answer. "We need to makeover my office too. I can't believe you let me work in this."

"You weren't exactly easy to talk to, Paris," replied Mya. "Would you have listened to me if I'd brought the updating to your attention?"

"No. Probably not," she said quietly. "Anyway, I'm seeing it now. Do you think the board will give me money?"

"Call your dad and ask, though I doubt he'll be compliant. Not until you finish making improvements to yourself and proving you want to be here. Obviously, if you can win the board over, they'll let you do whatever you want with the office."

"I guess I can always try," she said optimistically.

"Okay, let me know how it goes," said Mya.

Paris hung up the phone and dialed her father.

"Hello?" answered Mikel. "Paris?"

"Yeah, Dad, it's me."

"To what do I owe this surprise call?" he asked cheerily.

"I'm wondering if you'd be willing to give me a stipend to update my office?" she asked.

"Ha," laughed her father. "You know that's not going to happen."

"But, Dad," she protested, "it'd help with my morale and performance."

"Honey, I'm one of your biggest fans, and I want you to succeed, but this here is tough love. It's what a parent has to do sometimes. Now, you prove yourself, and I'll personally give you the money, but right now you are; how should I say this in terms that fit your current temperament? Grounded until further notice." He laughed.

"Dad! I'm not a child!" she rebuked.

"Darling, your whining says otherwise. I don't want to treat you like a child, but this is the only way your mother and I felt we would be able to get through to you."

Straightening up in her chair, Paris replied, "I'm sorry. You're right. That came off a bit whiny, which was not my intention when I called. I want you to know that I'm serious about making changes. I need to prove myself to you and mom. I've got this," she stated confidently.

"That's my girl," he replied. "I believe in you. If you feel you need a small change with the office, why don't you take a little money out of the clothing fund you were allotted to clean up the walls and make some minor improvements. It'll be on your own time, though," he added.

"Okay," said Paris.

"Love you, honey," he said and hung up.

Paris looked around the room again. The walls were forest green, and she suddenly hated the color, but she had to let it go. She'd already agreed to put money from her bonus toward Molly, which left little for her own wardrobe updates. The modified office would be a treat and proof that she'd made it back to her old self, the one that existed before Alli's death, though in all honesty, the original Paris was gone. This Paris was a hybrid rising from the ashes of the past.

Despite the worn state of her office, she was happy to have it. She was no longer under Angela's thumb. No more coffee runs or working off of Angela's demands. They were equals, and what's more, Paris had a better rate of return than Angela could ever hope for.

"Hey, hotshot," said Tom.

Paris jumped at the sound of his voice. She hadn't expected anyone to stop by. She turned her chair around to face him. He looked good as always. His black hair was lightly slicked back and a bit disheveled. His normally controlled ringlets were spilling over into his eyes. He was dressed for the gym, and she could see the sweat glistening on his muscular, lean arms and forehead. Even after a workout, the man took her breath away. "What can I do for you?" she asked.

"I thought I'd check-in and see how you're feeling now that you're back in your own office again. I'm sure it's a relief."

Paris found herself mesmerized by his wide toothy grin and couldn't help but stare for a moment. Snapping herself back to reality, she said, "Yes, indeed. It's nice to be back in my own office. The last few weeks have been hellish."

"I'm sure," he replied, running his fingers over the silver apple paperweight that sat on her desk. "Say, would you like to grab an early lunch and discuss the division of clients? I know you want to step up and show the seniors what you're made of, right?"

Without a second thought, Paris replied, "I'd love to."

"Wonderful," said Tom. "Meet me at eleven in the café."

"Gladly," she said and watched him as he triumphantly walked away. *The day is off to a great start*, she thought.

In the office up the hall, Vic was off to a rough beginning. Walking into the building, he'd collided with one of the mail runners, which sent his coffee flying every which way. His shirt took the brunt of the overflow, and unfortunately, it was quite obvious from the looks of the coworkers he passed as he trudged onward to his office. When he opened the door, he found that Chase, while neat in appearance, was not neat when it came to small spaces. His desk was covered in files and stray papers. Grabbing his phone, he pounded in Chase's number.

"Howdy," replied Chase. "What's up?"

"What did you do to my desk?" growled Vic.

"What do you mean?"

Vic was shocked that Chase's response was so innocent. Was he truly oblivious to the way he was running the office? "There are papers and files everywhere. I don't know where to begin with cleaning this up. You need to get over here now and sort things out."

"You best watch your tone, and don't get your knickers in a twist. I'll be right over. It's really not that bad," he said and promptly hung up.

"Not that bad? Seriously? I wonder what his condo looks like?"

"Hey, Ettienne, you talking to yourself?" asked Angela.

"Please call me Vic. You know I don't care for my formal name," he replied irritably. He didn't care how hot she was. No one but his family could call him Ettienne, and even they avoided it unless they were angry.

"Vic, sorry," she corrected and then confidently marched into his office.

Turning his attention to her, he had to focus hard to keep his jaw from dropping. There she was in her black cage stilettos and a short green cotton skirt with a low-cut flowy blouse and her ample bosom nearly popping out. Surely there was a law against dressing so provocatively at work. To make the situation even more scandalous, she hopped up and sat herself down right in the middle of his messy desk. Crossing her legs, she smiled at him and licked her shiny pink lips.

"How's your day going so far?" she asked as if she had no idea.

"Chase's killing me. My desk's a mess. I don't know where to start. Some mail runner slammed into me on top of it all, and my coffee spilt all over my shirt. I didn't bring a spare, so you can guess how that makes me feel."

"Come over here," she said softly as she waved him toward her.

Moving slowly, he paused a couple of feet away. The woman had a devilish look in her eye, and he was certain she was trouble.

"Closer," she encouraged.

Vic took another hesitant step forward, and to his surprise, she wrapped her legs around him and grabbed onto his shirt, yanking him even closer. Starting at the top, she undid first one button and then another until his bare chest was exposed. He stared at her, unable to breathe for a moment.

"Take it off," she commanded.

"Um, don't you think we should at least shut the door?" he asked.

"Vic, stop screwing around. Take the shirt off. I'll get you a different one," she replied as she pushed him away and hopped down from his desk.

He removed the shirt and held it out to her, speechless. She grabbed it out of his hand and left him standing in silence with nothing to show but a raging boner.

"Hey, Vic," called Chase.

Oh shit, thought Vic. *Oh shit, shit, shit.* "Give me a minute," he replied awkwardly.

"Where's your shirt?" asked Chase.

"Seriously, Chase, I need a minute. Go outside, walk around the block of desks, and come back."

"But I thought you wanted me to sort your desk?" he asked cluelessly.

"For the love of God, please, go!" growled Vic. He was losing his temper, which also was helping him lose something else.

Chase disappeared from the room, and Vic walked over to take a seat in his desk chair. He immediately realized that his response was not helpful to his current life situation. He would have to apologize when Chase returned. Not a moment had passed, and Angela was back with a baby blue dress shirt. It wouldn't have been his first color choice, but it would have to do.

"Here," she said. "This should fit you."

"Thanks," he replied as he snatched the shirt out of her hand and hurried to button it up. She left the room without further conversation. Vic felt perplexed by her demeanor. He didn't want to know where the shirt had come from for fear that it was some ex-boyfriend's, or even worse, her own. His ego was bruised enough.

Chase popped his head back into the room. "Is it safe to come in now?"

"Yes," replied Vic. "Sorry about that. I didn't mean to snap at you. It's been a rough morning, and the situation was beyond awkward. Please don't ask. I don't want to go into any detail."

"I'll let it slide this time, but you really need to work on your temper. That's a huge part of what got you into this mess to begin with."

"Trust me. I know." He watched as Chase shuffled and sorted through the files. In only five minutes, he'd organized and put each file into its proper slot in the file cabinet. "I guess it wasn't so bad after all."

"No, it wasn't," said Chase sharply. "Geez, what do you take me for, some ignorant slob? Normally I don't leave files lying around, but Tom needed something at the last minute on Friday, and you all were waiting for me to head out. I didn't have time to put everything back."

"Again, I apologize. I've judged too quickly, and I'm sorry."

Chase paused to consider Vic's statement. "I don't want to pry, but have you looked into anger management, or maybe some grief counseling? There's no shame in talking to some-one."

Vic stared back at him. He knew he should go but he didn't want to.

"You know," said Chase, "attending counseling might help put you in good graces with the board."

Letting out a deep sigh, Vic said, "Set it up. Preferably for Friday, so I don't have to come back to work angry."

"Really?" asked Chase. He was excited that Vic was willing to take a chance and do something therapeutic for a change.

Vic nodded. "Really. I want to do everything the board has mentioned to get back to normal in my crazy life, so set it up, and I promise I'll go. If at all possible, find someone who specializes in grief and anger, that way, I can explore both scenarios," he said with a sarcastic wave of his hand. What harm could it do?

"Great," said Chase. "I'll see about a Friday, or perhaps Monday morning before the board meetings, because the counselor will help you sort how the prior week went," he thought out loud. "I'm so happy for you! This is a big step."

"You can be happy if it actually helps," he replied. "Oh, and don't tell anyone, except my father and mother, that I'm going."

"My lips are locked shut, and you can have the key," he laughed as he exited Vic's office.

What a funny dude, thought Vic, as he closed the door behind him.

· · · · •·•·• · · · ·

Paris arrived at ten to eleven and took a booth inside Alli's Tanzanite Fields Café, on the opposite side of Sense of Adventure from their coffee shop, Java Dough. She loved the quaint little café, which she helped design and decorate in memory of her sister, who loved Mediterranean cuisine. The endeavor had been rough, as it came around only six months after her sister's death, but she wanted to make her proud, so she pushed through and created something amazing as a memorial for her.

The café offered small plates ranging from cheeses and olives to fish, rice, and assorted fruits. All of the meals were simple yet satisfying. Alli had chosen the Mediterranean way of eating, and she had been quite healthy because of it. Paris wished she could commit to such a lifestyle, but her motivation had been derailed by the loss of her sister. Some days it took all of her energy to simply get out of bed.

"Ah, you are here," said Tom, breaking into Paris's thoughts. "What are we having?"

"I haven't ordered anything yet, but I'm thinking about some olives and cheese along with a salad. What do you normally order?"

"I'll probably go with a salad as well. Whatever today's special is." He swept into the seat across from her and pulled some papers out of his briefcase. "With all the changes taking place over the past few weeks, Angela and I have had to deal with most of your case files. I took yours, and she took Vic's. Chase and Mya helped, but we didn't feel comfortable letting them take the lead on anything.

Now that you're back, I've chosen a couple of files to get started. I'm sure you'd like to jump in full force, but I've been told to give you some smaller clients to see how you handle yourself."

"What? Seriously?" blurted Paris. "Who told you not to give me back my prior clients? I've been doing this for a few years. Why on Earth would anyone think I couldn't handle my usual caseload?"

"The entire board agreed. I tried to talk them into letting you resume the files you had previously, but they thought starting slowly was the best answer. Don't worry, I'm sure things will go back to normal in a week or two."

"This is crap," snapped Paris. "I mean seriously—a load of B.S. I should just leave and start over. No one is backing me." Paris knew she was pitying herself, but at that moment, she struggled to care. How could they do this to her? She worked her way back here, and now she couldn't even resume what she loved. How maddening.

Tom frowned. "Come on. Don't get so down on yourself. I believe in you. I know what will cheer you up. Let's go to dinner tomorrow night. We can hit that wine bar you like and let off some stress. What do you say? Join me?"

His eyes sparkled as he looked at her, waiting for the answer. Was he asking her out on a date? Rethinking the situation, she said, "Is this pity or something else?" She watched as one side of his mouth raised into a smirk.

"Do you doubt me?"

"Tell me," she urged. "Why?"

Leaning back in his chair, he stretched his arms out and said, "We'll call it something else. Just say you'll come." Leaning in, he arched his eyebrow and said, "If you come out with me, I'll give you a third client back."

Charming, thought Paris. Her lust for him, as well as for gaining back her clients and a little piece of normalcy, had her agreeing to his request. "Okay. You have a deal." In response, Tom handed her three files. Her heart fell. None of them were more than a couple of days of work.

At the end of the workday, Vic met Paris by the doors and walked with her toward home. "How'd your day go?" he asked with genuine interest.

"It's become clear that we're once again the babies of Sense of Adventure. I've never felt more rejected, and out of place as I did today with the piddly clients Tom gave me. None of them were previous files. They were all new and small beans. I knocked one of them out this afternoon. It was a themed birthday party for a six-year-old. A six-year-old! I can plan that in my sleep, for heaven's sake."

"I know how you feel. Angela told Chase which files to give me. Of the five, none were major accounts."

Paris stopped walking and stared at him. "Five? You got five cases? Tom was only going to give me two. He told me that the directive was straight from the board. I had to agree to go to dinner with him in order to get a third."

"I have no idea. Chase handed me the files and said he was instructed that these were the files I would work on this week. He said nothing about the board. Maybe we're being held to separate standards?"

"Maybe," she sighed. "This is frustrating."

"Or," said Vic as he reached out and grabbed her hand, "maybe he lied to you? Has he ever shown interest before this point? I mean, he basically bribed you, right?" He stared back at her with concern.

"No," she rejected, throwing his hand down. "He wouldn't lie to me about the files. What reason would he have? That's an idiotic assumption. And I wouldn't call it a bribe. He's just being nice and trying to cheer me up." Turning on her heel, she marched off, leaving him standing alone.

"It was simply a consideration. Maybe he doesn't want you to succeed." He called after her. He was hurt by Paris's reaction. He would never say so, but he didn't like how it felt to be rejected by her. How could she trust Tom more than him at this point?

By Tuesday's end, Paris was nearly finished planning all of her client's events. The only step left was to run the plan past her clients and then finalize and sign contracts with all the vendors. The process was quick, since Mya had already ironed out the main details, and Paris merely had to track down the specifics from each vendor. She wished she'd been given an adventure to plan, but Tom had commented about how that was more intense and wouldn't be suitable for her, as she had just gotten back in the saddle and adventure planning required a lot more time and focus.

Sitting down at her desk, she sipped on a cup of green tea with honey. She thought about her discussion with Vic the prior afternoon. Was he showing feelings for her? She couldn't see how it was beneficial to either of them. Paris knew his interest rarely lasted more than a week, and he often had up to four women on the hook at once. She could not allow herself to have feelings for someone as careless as he.

What's more, if she were to fall for him, and then he broke her heart, they would still have to work together on a daily basis. How unbelievably awkward would that be? On the upside, he would most likely lose interest by the week's end, so she wouldn't have to worry about it any longer. With that realization, she breathed a sigh of relief.

Looking up from her desk, she noticed Tom in the hall. He was carrying his briefcase, which meant he was going home to get ready for their dinner meeting. She'd have to abandon the remains of her tea and high-tail it on out of there to be ready when he arrived to pick her up.

Pushing away from her desk, she stretched deeply. Her body was not used to sitting so much as of late. Scanning her files, she looked to see if she'd left anything important unattended, but everything appeared to be in order. Her eyes moved over to the picture of Alli and Brody, and she stopped to admire her sister's beautiful smile. Brody was pushing Alli on a swing at the park, and you could see the love in their eyes. Gently touching her lips, Paris kissed her finger and then pressed it to Alli's cheek. "If you're out there somewhere, I could really use your guidance on how to get back to my old life. I miss you." Turning away, she headed out the door. She'd only taken a few steps when a friendly voice flagged her down.

"Hey, Paris," called Mya. "Are you done for the day?"

Paris turned to look at her friend, who was rushing up from behind her. "Yeah, are you heading out too?"

"Probably in an hour. I have something I need to take care of," replied Mya. "What's your evening looking like? Want to hang out later?"

"Tom asked me to dinner. Work stuff, I think."

"Or maybe more?" teased Mya. "Let me know how it goes."

"Okay, we'll catch up later," she said and turned toward the main exit.

Mya stood and watched Paris disappear. She was nervous and glad to keep her conversation with her friend short. She knew Paris could see right through her, and she couldn't handle any more questions. Marching over to the elevator, she pressed the button for the executive floor. The door opened, and she forced herself to get in. Cristo had requested she meet him after work in his office. He definitely had an agenda. She was not sure how she felt about it.

Over the past few months, Cristo had been pursuing Mya, and Mya had consistently rejected dating him. She had no desire to be in a serious relationship with someone as powerful as him. If things went south, she feared losing her job. She loved her job and the company. The executives were as much her family as they were Paris and Vic's, minus Cristo. Cristo was far from parental to her. Their relationship was becoming more intense as time went on. Something had to change, but she was unsure which direction it needed to go, which made her feel uneasy.

Exiting the elevator, Mya noted that the floor appeared to be desolate. It was six o'clock, and everyone seemed to have left for the evening, which increased the size of the knot in her stomach. Earlier in the day, Cristo had thrown a tantrum when she rejected his request to meet her this evening, which provoked him to pound his fist on the boardroom door. Out of fear of making an even larger scene, she agreed to continue the conversation later that evening, as he had requested from the start.

Approaching his office, she paused for a moment to gather her composure. She had no idea what to expect, but she'd put up a wall and remain strong. She was a lady, and she had clout. She couldn't give in to whatever he was looking for. Moving forward, she knocked on his door.

The door swung open, and Cristo met her with a grin. "I knew you'd come," he said.

Mya stared at him. He wreaked of Scotch. "How much have you had?" her tone overflowed with disgust. You know I don't like talking to you when you've drunk so much," she added, playing into the tone he had set.

"Only a few," he replied, "but that's the least of your concerns. Come inside." He motioned.

She hesitantly stepped forward, and he closed the door, locking it behind her. She noted that all the blinds were drawn.

"Sit down on the couch," he barked. "I have something to say." He stepped forward and nudged her toward the couch.

Mya took a seat. "What do you want?" she asked, hoping he'd get to the point quickly so they could move forward with their evening.

"Now, Mya," said Cristo, shaking his finger at her, "you've turned me down multiple times," he slurred. "I'm a rich and powerful man. Why do you hurt me like that? You know I can give you whatever you want, and you wouldn't even have to work anymore. Why do you want to hurt me? We both know you're more than interested."

"Cristo, you aren't my type," she replied flatly. "And you drink too much."

"Well, that's just mean," he replied slowly. "Isn't there anything I can do to get you to take me more seriously? I'll treat you well." Turning, he poured himself and her a drink. Sloshing Scotch over the sides of the glass, he handed it to Mya. "Whatta ya say? You want to change your mind and go on a couple of actual dates with me?" he urged. "Or do I need to show you how serious I am?"

"You couldn't pay me to change my mind," she replied coyly.

"Mya!" yelled Cristo as he threw his glass of Scotch to the floor. The crystal shattered, and pieces flew in every direction.

Always so dramatic, thought Mya as she watched him shuffle the pieces toward his metal garbage can. "Be careful. You don't want to cut yourself," she said with concern.

He turned to look at her. "See, there it is," he stated. "Those feelings you try to hide. You can't hide from me. I know you. Eventually, things will have to change."

Mya inched backward, trying to put more distance between herself and Cristo. She dared not let him get too close for fear of what the result would be.

"You're going to be my girl," he said more calmly. Walking over to his desk, he picked up a file and held it in the air. "Do you know what this is?" he asked, waving it back and forth. Not waiting for a response, he said, "This is the end."

"The end of what?" chirped Mya.

"The end of Paris and Vic's time at ADG and Sense of Adventure. This file holds information on them that, when given to the press, will force the board to remove them from the business, as well as the family, permanently."

Mya's face contorted into a look of horror. Licking her lips, she asked, "Why would you want to do that?" *He had to have come up with this scenario after he'd begun drinking,* she thought.

"Because, my dear, I have my agenda, which you need not know about. The question is, do you want to be a part of this or go down with a sinking ship?"

Mya shook her head. "I, I don't know," she replied innocently. "I don't understand. Why would you do this to your own family?"

Cristo shook his head again. "It's of no importance," he replied and then paused for a moment as if he was in deep thought. "There might be a way for you to help them," he replied. A smile crossed his lips. "Just give yourself to me, and I'll make this file disappear."

"What? No!" she yelled. "Absolutely not!"

"Well then, my dear, you'll go down with them. I know about that male prostitute you slept with last March. You've been such a naughty girl," he commented slyly.

"What? I don't know what you're talking about!" she replied, but in reality, she knew exactly what game he was playing. She watched as he turned away from her momentarily to address something on his desk. She rolled her eyes. This wasn't exactly how she'd envisioned the evening going.

"I have pictures," he said, "would you like to see?

"You've had me followed? You asshole!"

"So simple," he yawned. "I had to make sure you were staying out of trouble, but low and behold, you weren't. You really ought to be punished."

"What do you want, Cristo?"

"You. I only want you. Be with me, and all of this disappears. Show up with me to events. Look pretty and adore me. If you can do that, it all goes away. If not, I send it all to the media, and they do what they want with it. Most likely, it all comes out as a scandal within ADG, and the company takes a hit."

"You're a complete scoundrel. I can't believe I ever thought there was a good guy in there somewhere. What will your brother say? How could you hurt your own family?"

"Dom would probably be impressed. Anyway, I own you, baby, get used to it," he said with a lopsided grin. "Now, take the night to think about it, but I trust you'll make the right decision." Turning, he opened the door and held his hand out, motioning her to leave. He slapped her on the butt as she passed by him, and she jumped a little at the impact. "This will be fun. You'll see."

"I'm counting on it," she replied as she walked away. She couldn't help but grin. Definitely not the encounter she'd thought of in her head, but anything to avoid the inevitable a little longer. He was right. Something had to change.

• • • • • • • • • •

Across town, Paris and Tom had arrived at the Zen Omni Lotus, a Japanese fusion restaurant located in downtown Flores. Tom had opened her door upon entry and exit of the vehicle, as well as to the restaurant. He ordered a bottle of Pinot Noir, poured her a thoughtful amount, then toasted to a beautiful new start regarding her return to Sense of Adventure. Overall, it seemed he was trying to be a gentleman.

Paris felt overwhelmed, and his gestures were easily seducing her. If it was intentional, she couldn't say. She took a sip of wine and listened to him talk about climbing Mount Everest when he was in his twenties. She found the story interesting but unimpressive. To her, climbing Mount Everest was simply putting one's self in unwarranted danger. She believed anyone who did so had either a death wish or an inflated ego. As Vic had hinted, Tom had the latter, but she still found him unbelievably attractive. She hoped that if given a chance to know him better, she'd find he had more depth.

"Have you ever thought about climbing Everest?" he asked hopefully.

"Only every night when I dream," she lied and followed it with an invested laugh.

Changing the subject, Tom leaned forward and gently grabbed her hand. "You're gorgeous. Do you know that?" he asked.

"Tom, stop," blushed Paris. "You're making my face turn red, which is not attractive."

"No, you stop. You're amazing. From the moment I first saw you, I thought to myself, Tom, that girl is the most beautiful woman at Sense of Adventure. You would be crazy not to have her by your side."

Clearly, they were on a date, realized Paris. "So, why didn't you ask me out sooner?"

"Work got in the way. I didn't want you to think I was trying to gain ground within the company by asking you out. As time went by, I worried it would be a risky situation if things didn't work out."

"Why change your mind now?" she prodded.

"Life's too short. I figure we're at the top of the food chain, and we're two of the most beautiful people at work, so why not give it a shot?" He chortled.

"Sure, why not?" Paris couldn't believe he was showing genuine interest in her. She'd dreamt of this day for a very long time.

The evening continued on with Tom telling her all about his impressive travels and Paris volunteering information about herself and her education whenever she could get a word in. He loved to talk, but she didn't mind. It was nice to be out of her condo, having an adult conversation with someone other than Vic.

At the end of the night, when Tom opened the door to let her out of his car, he grabbed her waist and pulled her to him. Pressing their bodies firmly together, he kissed her gently on the lips. The kissing continued slowly and rhythmically for a minute until Paris pulled back for air. She saw stars and her knees felt uncharacteristically weak. He'd taken her breath away, and she had no memory of ever feeling such strong lust before.

"Goodnight, Paris. We should do this again soon," he said and nodded his head to her as he disappeared back into the car.

Turning away, she floated all the way up to her condo. She was in such a warm place in her mind that she didn't even notice Vic sitting on the sofa or that he called out her name as she passed by on her way to her room.

Vic shook his head. He was done. If she was going to ignore him, he was done. He wouldn't show her the soft side of himself any longer. He felt like an idiot. Only an idiot would be so easily forgotten.

Turning off the living room light, he got up and trudged down the hall to his room. Perhaps a good night's sleep would make him feel better, but somehow, he doubted it.

The next morning, Paris got up early and went for a run. Vic had made the same decision, though they had turned in opposite directions as they'd exited the building. At some point during their separate runs, the pair had turned off at the same street, and as Paris came around the corner, she and Vic nearly collided.

"Hi," he called out. "How's it going?"

"Fine," she replied as she tried to catch her breath. She'd been running at full speed, trying to burn off the excited energy from the previous night.

"What'd you do last night?" he asked, matching her stride.

"I went on a date with Tom."

"Oh, super," he replied. "That explains why you were so out of it when you came home."

Paris looked at him with confusion. "I wasn't out of it."

"Really? Tell me, Paris, where was I last night when you arrived home?"

"You were in bed," she shot back.

"Nope. I was sitting on the couch. I even called out your name, but you ignored me."

"Bull," she said. "I would've seen you."

"Apparently not. You're too absorbed in your own world once again."

"At least I'm happy, which is more than I can say for you. You just mope around all the time, and whenever someone doesn't do as you expect, you bite their head off."

"Maybe we should finish this run separately," he declared as he turned away from her in frustration. There it was again. He felt as if his emotions might boil over.

"Jerk," muttered Paris. She didn't understand what his problem was. It's not like they were in a relationship with each other. Her feet pounded the pavement as she retreated. By the time she had arrived back at the apartment, Vic had already showered and left for work. It was comforting to have the place to herself.

· · · · • · • · · · ·

"Hurry, Paris. She'll be here shortly," said Mya. She'd been on edge ever since her meeting with Cristo. He hadn't called on her yet, but she knew he would, and when he did, she didn't know what to expect. The waiting was causing irritability, which was not a normal Mya trait. They still hadn't discussed the matter at hand. His avoidance was giving her anxiety.

"Are you okay?" asked Paris. "I feel like there's something you're holding in. What is it?" she queried as she tapped her foot.

"It's nothing. There's nothing to tell," Mya snapped.

"I know this isn't you, but I'll let you talk when you're ready." She didn't know what had gotten into the girl, but she was pretty certain that it involved the situation with Cristo. She wished her friend would come clean.

"Great, thanks," she replied. "I just want everything in place before Molly arrives. I hope the clothes we picked will fit her properly.

Wednesday night, Paris and Mya had gone shopping to pick up some new items for Molly's wardrobe, along with makeup and a few other things. Paris spent four-hundred of the five-hundred dollars she'd been given on Molly. She then bought herself a couple of new but inexpensive items to add to her business attire. She was okay with holding back if it meant helping out a coworker and having someone else to watch her back.

Molly showed up for their girls' night, grinning wildly. She'd never been to Mya's condo before, and truth be told, she'd never had a makeover. The girls explained to her that, as Dom's personal assistant, she really needed to look professional and that her current clothing, which was much too big for her, made her look uninvested in her job. They convinced her the new clothing was secondhand, which helped ease any sense of charity.

Despite the desire to recruit Molly's eyes and ears within the company, Paris found that the girl actually had a great sense of humor. She fit right in with her and Mya. She could see making their get-togethers a more regular occurrence.

To help keep up the guise of being a makeover night, Paris gave Mya a facial, and Mya gave Paris a manicure while Molly tried on clothes. The clothing all fit well, and it was true, Molly was actually quite beautiful once they put her in properly fitted clothes and cleaned up her hair.

Mya took the time to explain different techniques for styling her hair to look more professional or seductive, depending on her need at any time. Paris dyed Molly's hair a deeper shade of brown, which made her eyes pop. She also taught her how to apply false lashes and to use her makeup more efficiently. Together with Paris, they discussed the idea of smaller glasses for her tiny face or investing in contacts, so she didn't have to hide behind her massive rims.

At the end of the makeover session, Paris asked Molly if she could request a favor, to which Molly was more than happy to help. She told them she felt great after the makeover, and wanted to repay them somehow.

"We need you to be our eyes and ears," said Mya. "Someone is trying to sabotage Vic and Paris. We think it's most likely to get them out of the company, but we don't know who's involved in the situation. Anything you hear or see; you report back to one of us."

"Sure thing," said Molly. "I'm glad to help."

"We appreciate it. Now, go home and get some sleep so you can get up and practice the techniques we taught you before work tomorrow. We want to see you wow everyone when you walk in," gushed Paris.

"Thanks. I'll keep you posted on anything I find," said Molly.

Mya walked Paris and Molly out, and then turning away, she locked the door behind both women. She felt the knot in her stomach again. Her conversation with Cristo was eating at the back of her mind. It was all the things they didn't say that were the problem.

CHAPTER TWELVE

The weekend came and went. Vic had played tennis with his family and ran each day with Chase, who was becoming one of his closest friends. He spent the afternoons at the office trying to avoid Paris while putting in extra effort at his job. In the evenings, he watched movies and drank a few beers. So that he wasn't drinking alone, he called Chase over to hang out in silence. Paris disappeared over to Mya's every night, which made things feel a little less hectic.

"Good morning," said Chase as Vic opened the door to his apartment. "I brought you an orange juice and a croissant. I thought you might want some food before your appointment. Today's meeting will be quick because the board has other things going on, so most likely they won't roll out the treats," he noted. Chase looked Vic up and down. "You aren't dressed. What have you been doing?"

Chase worried the previous night's drinks may have been a bad idea, and that he should have redirected Vic's actions to something more constructive. He was feeling invested in their budding friendship and Vic's future, which were unexpected feelings for him. He was a friendly person who kept to himself outside of work. Most of his friends were women, though he rarely allowed anyone to get too close. He had endured much discrimination in high school and college, which had led him to hours upon hours of therapy. He was stronger and more confident because of it.

"Sorry," he replied. "I woke up late." In reality, Vic had fallen asleep on the couch and never made it to his bed, so he was still wearing the shorts he'd worn the previous day and no shirt.

"Well, kudos on the abs," said Chase. "I can't seem to get myself to work on my core as much as I should." He followed Vic inside and took a seat while Vic located his clothes.

"It takes discipline," replied Vic from the hallway. He was wrestling his way into a polo shirt as he spoke. "What do you think will happen at the meeting today?" he asked.

"Nothing concerning. I don't think the board has any reason to be displeased." He was leafing through Paris's mail while Vic slid his feet into his shoes. "That girl gets a lot of junk mail," he commented.

"Put that down," barked Vic. "That's not yours. I don't need another reason for Paris to bite my head off," he added.

Chase released the envelopes and got to his feet. "Ready?"

"Yeah, let's go."

Chase dropped Vic at the main entrance to the clinic. "I'll be in one of the parking spots to the left of the door when you're done."

"Okay, see you in a bit." He pulled himself out of the car and trudged up to the doors. He hoped the board saw this as a genuine effort on his part.

Ninety minutes later, Vic returned to Chase's car, feeling slightly lighter than when he'd arrived.

"So, how'd it go?" asked Chase.

"We didn't get far, but I'm relieved to find that this guy is pretty easy to talk to. I spent a good chunk of time filling out paperwork, but of the conversation we had, I think this might prove helpful."

"That's great news," replied Chase. "See, not all counselors are quacks." He laughed.

"Yeah. I don't know what I was expecting, but it was fairly painless for a first session. I told him about Brody's death, the demotions, and how I'm trying to rectify my situation. He found it all quite amusing. I thought for sure he'd give me a load of shrink mumbo jumbo, but he had well thought out responses."

Chase felt as though a weight had lifted from his shoulders. "I'm glad to hear you're making progress. This is something positive that I can let your father know about. Your parents will be pleased. Anyway, let's get a move on. We need to make that meeting, and we're definitely cutting it close, though I doubt they'll fault us on our reason for being tardy."

......•.•....

In the boardroom, Paris was seated long before anyone else arrived. She enjoyed the quiet of the empty space and reveled in the idea that she could simply sit and be present in the solitude. Standing, she wandered to the window and opened the blinds to look out over the complex.

In front of the main ADG building sat a beautiful park, which accommodated several of the company's annual events. The park had a pond, several relaxation benches, and was home to hundreds of exotic-looking flowers, palm trees, colorful rocks, and strategically placed animal sculptures, which more than made up for the lack of grass in the vicinity. Around the perimeter of the park stood the rec center, a shopping center, and four sets of condos, each in different shades of blue and green.

The complex was home to many employees and their families. Paris had grown up in this place, and she felt a sense of pride as she surveyed her family's empire.

"The view still gets me too," said Nicola, walking over to stand next to her daughter. Reaching out, she brushed Paris's hair out of her eyes and tucked it behind her ear. "What's your favorite part?"

"I love the entire view, but if I had to pick one thing, it'd be the flowers."

"Ah, yes," replied her mother. "I especially love their fragrance on a warm summer night's breeze."

"Yes! A party in the park wouldn't be complete without that scent," said Paris.

Nicola eyed her tentatively. "Sweetheart, how are you doing?"

"When this whole situation began, I wasn't okay," she admitted. "I didn't think I'd ever be okay again, but somehow, amidst the craziness of the past few weeks, I feel as if I'm finding myself again. I think the biggest breakthrough for me was rekindling my relationship with Mya. I should have never taken my pain out on her. It felt like I was outside of my body, watching the destruction. I couldn't seem to stop. When I found out she'd been in the accident, it snapped me back to—" Paris couldn't continue.

Nicola put her arms around her daughter and gave her a gentle squeeze. She understood the pain Paris was in. "You're strong like your father and me both. Remember though, it's always okay to admit you need help. It broke my heart when you quit speaking to Mya, but I knew you'd eventually come around. Why don't we have brunch this weekend? You can bring Mya. It would be nice to spend time with you both outside of work."

"Sure," said Paris. She couldn't recall the last time she'd eaten a meal with her family, separate from work events.

"Morning, ladies," called Mikel as he and Dom walked into the room, followed closely by Jessamine, Cristo, and a not-so-happy-looking Mya.

Mya saw Paris by the window and immediately went to her. "How are you?" she asked, her eyes darting to Cristo. She'd received a call from him early that morning requesting her presence at a client dinner that evening. She had no desire to go but couldn't manage to say no.

"I'm well. The day's off to a decent start." Looking at her friend, she again saw the anxiety in her expression. "How about you?"

"Okay, I guess." Mya turned away, and Paris watched her take a seat. She placed herself at the opposite side of the room from Cristo, who was intently staring her friend down. She wanted to corner Cristo and demand he tell her what he'd done to her, but she knew that would only upset Mya further.

"Sorry, we're a little late," said Vic, breaking into Paris's thoughts. "We had an appointment prior to this one, and it ran longer than anticipated."

Dom looked at his son. "No harm, we're talking seconds, really." Chase had told him exactly where they would be that morning, and Dom had been quite pleased to hear that his son had finally taken a solid step forward in dealing with his anger and grief. Standing, he took a closer look at Vic and Paris. "We're pleased with your work this past week, and we'd like to offer you one of the Palm Condos as a reward, or if you like, each your own."

"I'll take my own," Paris chimed. Vic turned and looked at her in disbelief. He knew she was irritated with their last conversation, but he didn't think she'd cut him out of her life again. Vic stopped himself from shaking his head in disappointment. He didn't want the board to read into the situation, so he spoke up and spun her statement in a more positive direction. "Yeah, we could use a little extra space for spending time with friends and such."

Paris looked at Vic in return. His response surprised her, but it pleased her that he didn't make a scene.

"Okay, we can do that," said Mikel. Dom nodded in agreement. "We'll have your things moved today while you're at work. Mya and Chase, you may assist the movers in separating the items out and then show Vic and Paris to their new places this evening."

"Great job last week," said Jessamine. "Keep up the good work, and things will be back to normal before you know it."

"That's it for today," added Nicola. "Enjoy the week." She smiled warmly. Paris nodded at her and followed Mya out of the room. Vic and Chase paraded out behind them.

Fifteen minutes later, Paris stood in the entryway to Tom's office, watching him sort through client files. "You wanted to see me?"

"Yeah, come on in," he said, dazzling her with his smile. "Close the door." Paris stepped forward and swung the door shut behind her. Tom stood and met her halfway. Reaching out, he brushed back her hair and grabbed her chin lightly. "My God, Paris, you get lovelier and lovelier every day," he charmed.

Looking up at him, she froze in place. Her heartbeat quickened, and she realized she was holding her breath. "Thanks," she replied breathlessly.

"I called you over here to give you the files for this week. All new events, but with clients you've already worked with. The board still wants you to focus on a couple of files at a time, but in gratitude for our dinner the other night, here are three more, as before."

"Thanks," she replied, grabbing the files from his hand. She didn't know what to think. Why would the board only want her to have two clients at a time? She wanted to ask her father, but she didn't want to sound ungrateful.

"How about lunch at noon?" he suggested. "I hear they have your favorite chicken salad sandwich at the café today."

Paris never turned down the chicken salad. He was right. It was her favorite. "Definitely. I'll meet you there," she replied as she exited his office. She disguised her anger with a smile. How could she prove herself when she was receiving so little work?

Back in her own office, she picked up the phone and dialed Vic. She needed to talk to someone who would understand.

"Hi, Paris, what's up?" he asked with disinterest.

"Tom gave me three files again," she expelled. "I'm so frustrated. He says the board instructed him to only allow me to have a couple. How many did you get this week?"

"Angela gave me eight files. Like I said before, he's screwing with you," admonished Vic. "Ask your father. I bet you anything he says Tom's lying."

"Why would he lie? What good would it do for him to lie to me?" she demanded. "What kind of statement does that make about me if I have to run to my father for validation?"

"This is your career we're talking about. Clarity is essential in this situation. Tom probably wants you out of the way so he can have your clients. Or maybe he's using you for sex!" barked Vic. He was sure someone outside his office had heard him. He made a mental note to tone it down. Luckily, Angela and Tom's offices were further down the hall, and most of the people outside were interns.

"He wouldn't need to give me any files if that's all he wanted!" she spat back.

"Good, why don't you give in to him, then?" replied Vic through gritted teeth.

"Yeah, maybe I will," said Paris, slamming the phone down in Vic's ear. *Stupid man,* she thought.

Vic was still holding the phone in his hand. "Damn that woman!" he said as he set the phone back on its cradle. How naïve could she be? He realized Tom was after something, but whether it was Paris herself or something else, he couldn't say. He knew the concept would eat at his mind for the rest of the day.

At lunch, Paris sat and listened to Tom as he told stories about past clients and the crazy requests they made during event planning. The most ostentatious request was when one particular client decided he wanted to arrive at his event in a sleigh pulled by two polar bears. Tom spent two hours trying to explain how it would be wrong to bring polar bears to Nevada and that even if they could bring them to Nevada, they most likely couldn't train them to pull a sleigh in time for the event. There was also the possibility that the polar bears could act out and maim one, or several, of the guests. The client stormed out of the office, but Tom won him over with a secondary option.

Paris listened actively and laughed on cue. She found his stories to be interesting at the very least. She was amazed that he wanted to spend his free time with her. At the end of lunch, he leaned in toward her and said, "Your lips are the perfect shade of pink," and suddenly, grabbing her neck, he pulled her in for a mouth-devouring kiss. She was so stunned she didn't move. When he pulled away, she stared at him in awe. "That was nice," he said with a smile. "Now, shall we get back to work?" With that, he stood up and pulled her out of her seat. "You paying for lunch since I paid last time?" he asked casually and then walked away, leaving her speechless.

Paris dug out her wallet. Nothing was free at ADG. You had to earn it. The only people who ate for free were the board. At least she received a discount of fifty percent, being the owner's daughter and all. She threw down some cash and a tip, then headed back toward her office. Her mind was spinning from the day's developments.

Across the café, Molly had witnessed the kiss between Paris and Tom. Her head was swimming with excitement about the news she'd be able to bring to Mya. Like a fly on the wall, she observed their entire interaction. She wasn't out to hurt Paris, but she'd agreed to bring any pertinent information forward, and this, she felt, was pertinent information, even if it was about Paris. From what she knew of Tom, she didn't think his sudden interest in Paris was at all a coincidence, but she would let the others weigh in before she completed her condemnation.

Waiting until Paris was out of sight, Molly hurried down the hall toward Mya's office, but when she arrived, Mya was out attending to other business and not expected back until one or two that afternoon. Not able to contain the shiny new information she had obtained, she went straight to Vic, who was on a very heated call when she knocked.

"Just a moment," he said, covering the phone receiver.

"I'll wait outside until you're finished," replied Molly, to which Vic nodded.

Stepping around the corner, she tried not to listen, which was difficult. She heard him say, "I don't care if you have to hike a mountain to get them. They need to be at this event, so figure it out. You promised it wouldn't be an issue, and I'm holding you to your word." He slammed the phone down, causing Molly's heart to race.

"Molly," Vic called. "You may come in now."

Molly stepped forward. "Are you sure this is a good time?" she asked. She didn't want to be on his bad side. She'd heard many stories about Dom's son. His temper was legendary.

"Yeah, it's fine. What brings you to this part of the building?"

"I thought you should know; I saw Paris and Tom at lunch today in the café. They were kissing," she blurted. "Paris and

Mya wanted me to let them know if anything questionable was happening or if anyone was out to hurt you or Paris. Since this involves Paris, I thought I'd bring it to Mya, but she wasn't available, so I'm coming to you instead. Something feels off. Tom's all about business. I think he's trying to seduce Paris for a reason outside of caring for her. He's dated a couple of other women who work here and the only reason I know is because one was a friend of mine. He kept it quiet and outside of work. Why would he change that now?"

"I tried to warn her. She doesn't listen. Her rose-colored glasses are wearing on my last nerve." Pausing a moment, he exhaled. "Thanks for letting me know."

"Anytime," said Molly. "I need to get back upstairs. Let me know if you need anything else."

After she left, Vic picked up the phone again and dialed Paris.

"What do you want?" she hissed into the receiver, her cheeks reddening.

"I want you to know that I think you're being an idiot, and you should watch your back. You're playing right into what Tom wants."

"Are you spying on me now?" she demanded.

"No. Molly saw the two of you at lunch and was concerned. She said you were getting awfully close. She doesn't think Tom's feelings are genuine, either."

"Right. I'm sure Molly said that."

"In a matter of speaking, she did. I wouldn't lie to you. She said you were kissing."

"Whatever. You're just upset that someone is taking an interest in me," Paris replied, hanging up the phone.

"Why won't this nightmare end!" boomed Vic, causing the intern passing by his door to jump, then pick up her pace to move out of his line of sight.

· · · · **·** · **·** · · ·

At four-thirty, Mya called Paris to a brief meeting. Walking through the door, Paris's blood pressure spiked when she saw Vic and Chase.

"What's she doing here?" asked Vic. Everyone could see the contempt in his eyes.

"Shut your yaps and listen," said Chase. "We're dealing with a situation which, unfortunately, needs to be discussed." Turning his attention to Paris, he asked, "Are you seeing Tom?"

"We've shared a couple of meals. That's all," she hissed. "I don't know why this is anyone's business?"

"Paris, Vic and Molly might be right. Tom might be using you. You need to entertain the concept, even though you've had feelings for him for a long time," stated Mya.

Rolling her eyes, Paris asked, "What's his motive?"

"He may be trying to get you out of the way so he can go after the company," said Chase. "All we're saying is, be careful and watch your back," said Mya.

"And stop jabbing each other every chance you get," added Chase. "If you can't work together, the board will demote you again. Do you want that to happen?"

Paris felt as if she was being scolded by her father. "Fine. I'll watch my back, but I'm not talking to him unless I have to," she replied. Even she realized her response was juvenile. Her face reddened with embarrassment.

"Come on. What happened?" asked Mya. "Why are you at each other's throats? If this has to do with our weekend away, figure it out and deal with it. You're two major cogs in the ADG machine. If you can't work together, it could mean the downfall of ADG."

Nodding, Chase said, "I agree one-hundred percent. This is no time to fall apart."

Vic nodded as well. He knew Mya and Chase were right, but Paris had become oddly quiet. She shut down at some point during Mya's speech. What had happened? He had shown his interest. He knew they were playing with fire by getting into bed together, but he hadn't expected this outcome. Looking at her, he still felt drawn, despite his anger and resentment at how she was acting. Conceding, he said, "Paris, please. I know we're going through something, but please. We need to be careful. We need to back each other. Mya and Chase are right."

"I'm sorry," replied Paris. "I have to go. I can't do this right now." She felt deflated. She turned and exited the room. She couldn't stand to stay another moment under their scrutiny. She needed to walk away from the anger and embarrassment.

"Paris!" called Mya. Paris turned to look at her. She practically ran to keep up. "I haven't given you the keys to your new condo," she said, holding them out. "Your parents decided to put you in the Lotus building. Twelfth floor, unit 1. New condos."

"Where's Vic located?"

"He'll be in unit 3 at the opposite end and corner of the floor. I have even more exciting news. The board, as a bonus for Chase and me, moved us to the same floor. I'll be in unit 2 and Chase in unit 4. I know you're upset right now, but I think this will be a good thing. At least they put him in the farthest unit, away from you. Hopefully, that'll give you a little comfort."

"I'd be happier if he was on a different floor or in a separate building, but on a positive note, I'm excited to see the new units," she replied, grabbing the keys from Mya's outstretched hand.

Grinning, Mya said, "Let's go check them out!"

· · · • · • · · · ·

Mya knew Paris was going through a rough patch. She hoped her friend would figure things out sooner than later. For the moment, she'd let their conversation mellow. She knew her friend was at her threshold, and she didn't want to push her too far, too fast. It took a lot of strength for her to not ask Paris about whatever she had witnessed at the cabin. She didn't want to talk about Cristo, so she wouldn't press Paris about Vic.

The walk to the Lotus building was short. It was located two buildings over from corporate, compared to several blocks to her previous residence. Her old condo, from prior to the demotion, was located in the building between Lotus and corporate.

"Here we are," said Mya. "Are you ready?"

"I think so," replied Paris. She stepped forward and unlocked the door. Swinging it open, she paused, her jaw dropping. The unit was filled with her own furniture. It was also quite a bit larger than her old place, with a sprawling balcony.

Stepping onto the balcony, she saw a beautiful new wicker all-weather cushioned patio set arranged in an L around a table with lava rocks in the center. Jumping up and down, she pointed at the lava rocks. She'd always wanted a tabletop fireplace. Across from the patio set sat a large hot tub. The view she had was of the park below. She could smell the flowers on the warm evening breeze. She knew this was her mother's little touch.

"Your parents have been planning this move for quite some time. Do you love it?" asked Mya.

"It's perfect. Let's see the rest." Walking back inside, she inspected the living room, which was open to the kitchen and breakfast bar. Her kitchen now held a wine fridge and beautiful frosted glass front cabinets. It had bright, cheery white wood, black stainless-steel appliances, and black granite countertops, with a black, white, and steel backsplash. The black and white looked stunning together. The island in the center had four steel-looking bar stools on the far side and a gas cooktop on the inner. Paris ran her fingers over the granite countertop. She'd always wanted a black and white color scheme in her kitchen. Her parents had actually listened to her random ramblings from three years earlier.

Looking out over the living room, she had her beautiful white settee and a large black faux fur rug, which was new, along with her other furniture from her old place. There were new pillows on all the furniture, which brought a little color into the room. They were in shades of blue-green, grey, and black. Just a pop of color, as her mother would say.

"Let's look at the bathroom," said Mya. She was already halfway across the room. Paris followed her. Peering inside, they saw a white marble vanity, the usual stool, and a waterfall shower with dark gray marble tile, which also matched the floor. The walls were a light grey and decorated with a couple of large tropical flower prints, which Paris recognized immediately. Looking closer, she saw Brody's signature in the bottom right corner. Thick, black, ornate frames surrounded the photos. The rugs and towels were all blue-green, which looked great with the flower prints she knew Cristo had gifted. Paris couldn't stop smiling.

"I love it," said Mya. "You can really tell they went out of their way to make you feel at home."

"Yeah. I didn't think my parents were listening when I spoke of my dream condo."

"I didn't either," she laughed. "I guess we were both wrong."

Moving on to her new master suite, she found the room to be spacious. The entire condo, except for the bathrooms, had grey wood floors. Her new bedroom had a large white faux fur area rug. The bed had a beautiful down comforter with a pink duvet emblazoned with the Eiffel tower and other French-inspired images. The bed also contained four feather pillows. Two of which had shams matching her new bedspread.

Across the room, Paris threw open two slatted doors to reveal a large walk-in closet, which contained all her clothing and accessories, including built-in racks to show off her many pairs of shoes, and drawers to house her jewelry, watches, sunglasses, and any other item she needed to stow. Everything was hung neatly and easy to access. The closet's center held a large round bench with a purple plush tufted seat, which opened up to reveal several cozy blankets in blue-green, purple, and white and ranged from down to cashmere. Paris was thrilled. She loved her blankets.

Exiting the closet, she moved on to a second white-slatted door, which upon opening, revealed a large beautiful private bath with her own waterfall therapy shower and an oversized whirlpool tub with a window overlooking the park. The vanity was white and grey marble and held two sinks. The cabinet below the vanity was a beautiful grey wood, reminiscent of driftwood. The mirror above the vanity matched the cabinet. Paris immediately fell in love. There was even a built-in closet with plenty of shelves to hold towels and whatever else she wanted to store.

Exiting the bathroom, there was a second bedroom next door. This particular bedroom was decorated in Navy and white and had a large oak desk with a brand-new laptop and printer. There were even photos of her family, including Alli, hanging on the wall. "Wow, I didn't expect any of this."

"It's quite exceptional," said Mya. Looking over at Paris, she saw tears streaking her face.

"It's so perfect," she whispered.

Reaching for her friend, Mya pulled her into a hug. "You have made so much progress, and you are a huge asset to the company. You deserve this. Your parents want you to know that this is yours as long as you keep up the good work. This is their way of saying they believe in you. I believe in you too."

"I'm not sure I actually deserve any of this."

"Act like you do," Mya replied with the shake of her finger. "Anyway, I have to go. I'm heading to a dinner meeting this evening at Cristo's request."

"Why?" asked Paris. "That's not normal, is it?"

"I don't care to discuss it at this time," Mya replied. "Watch your own bobber," she said with a half smile.

"I know you think you're being cute, but that doesn't change my concern," said Paris. "Before you go, what are the other condos like?"

"Chase and I have smaller balconies with loungers and a table and chair set—no hot tub. My apartment is navy blue, tan, and brown. Chase's is in greys and blues. Our bathrooms are similar. So are the bedrooms. We have whirlpool tubs, but I'm sure a certain bestie will invite me over to sit in her hot tub. All of it's a similar style, but size and colors vary. Vic's place is just like yours, but his patio has a built-in grilling area and a small gas fire pit with Adirondack chairs surrounding it. The colors and décor, of course, are different as well. Oh, and his cabinets are solid mahogany without glass. Chase's are the same style, but mine are like yours."

"Cool," replied Paris. "Okay, you can go, I guess."

"We'll chat later," she said as she headed for the door. As Mya exited, she called over her shoulder. "Paris, I love you like a sister. Never forget."

Paris smiled at Mya's statement, then wandered back through her new home and flopped down on her settee. Her heart felt lighter because of the new apartment, but her brain reverted to thoughts about Vic and the situation with Tom. Feeling conflicted, she didn't know who to trust.

· · · · ● · · ● · · · ·

"Good evening, Mya. You look lovely," said Cristo. As requested, Mya presented herself

in a short black cocktail dress, short black gloves, black and white stiletto heels, and carried a black and white Gucci clutch, which Cristo had sent to her office as a gift earlier that day. She wore her straight red hair puffed and gathered at the back of her head with a silver floral clip.

Mya barely acknowledged Cristo as she climbed into the backseat of his long white stretch limo. Cristo climbed in behind her, and his driver closed them in. Scooting over, he situated himself across from her. "Would you like something to drink?"

"No. I'm good." She watched him tentatively. He was wearing a black tuxedo with a green vest. His short blonde hair was spiked as usual. He noticed her staring. "I chose the green to match your eyes," he admitted.

That particular bit of information made Mya feel slightly uncomfortable. What were they doing? "You know I don't want to be here, right?" she asked. "We haven't discussed things properly. I told you I wouldn't be joining you for these intimate meetings. This goes against who I am."

"Come on now," he said with a light air. "Of course, you don't mean that. We've worked together for many years and always without an issue. This is just a silly game between us." He grinned. "I'm the cat. You're the mouse. You say no, but you really mean yes. We do this all the time, you and I."

"No, Cristo, we don't. This is something entirely different. I can't be with you the way you want me to," she added and frowned back at him. "This is crossing a line."

"This is our thing," he replied adamantly. "Stop playing with me!" he snapped, and then more softly, "This is our thing." Mya thought his final statement was more to convince himself. She shook her head at him. "I need you to be on your best behavior," he stated. "I need you to present yourself like a debutante, and hang on my every word because I need this client to see me in an adoring relationship, or they'll leave the company. I assured them that I had an amazing partner and that she'd dazzle them. Please, just make me proud," he begged. "This is simply a different type of game, okay?"

Arriving at the restaurant, Cristo and Mya exited the car and proceeded inside. Her arm in his, he guided her to the table, and pulling out her chair, he helped her get settled. The client was not yet there but would arrive at any moment. Cristo ordered himself a glass of sparkling wine, and Mya a sparkling water with strawberries and lemon.

Theresa and Marco Perez arrived five minutes later. They were a beautiful couple who clearly adored one another. They'd chosen a dinner meeting to further plan a quinceañera for their daughter, Amrita, which is why they wanted someone family-oriented heading up their account. Cristo had conveniently told them that he and Mya were expecting their first child. Mrs. Perez was ecstatic, and much to Mya's dismay, the remainder of her evening was filled with all forms of 'baby talk' while the men discussed money and the different aspects of the party.

At the close of dinner, Mr. and Mrs. Perez thanked Cristo and Mya for a fantastic evening from the bottom of their hearts. Mrs. Perez added that she was pleased to have met Mya and that Mya would be an exceptional mother. Once the couple was out of sight, Mya could feel her face redden as she followed Cristo from the restaurant. She felt like a fraud.

"How could you do this to me?" she demanded. "How could you do this to them or the company? Lying to clients. You've stooped to a new low, Cristo."

"You were wonderful this evening," he replied, ignoring her angry outburst. "The evening went as anticipated."

"This is not a game I want to be a part of." It was possible she was angrier than warranted. But pretending they were together and with child? What was he thinking?

"You're being dramatic," he replied confidently. "There's no harm in a little white lie now and then."

"Cristo, this isn't a white lie. It's a major lie. Do you get that? It's straight-up a lie."

Cristo slid closer to her and reached for her hand. She yanked it away and scooted further from him. "Don't be like that," he said and moved closer. "I know you want this. I can feel that you do," he said with confidence.

Mya wondered if he'd suffered a recent brain trauma. "Don't you dare come any closer," she replied. They were not a couple. He had no right to put her in such a compromised position.

"Or what?" he asked coyly. Reaching out, he touched her face.

"Apples!" she declared and slapped his hand away.

Cristo's expression changed to shock. "You're serious? Fine. You win." He scooted away from her and said nothing the rest of the ride home, a distant look in his eyes and a frown creasing his lips.

Mya could see the hurt, but all she wanted was for him to leave her alone. The situation made her stomach churn. She'd made her feelings known, and he had applied extra pressure. Now the lines were blurred.

CHAPTER THIRTEEN

"Mya! Are you in there?" yelled Paris. She'd been banging on her friend's door for five minutes, with no answer. It was Sunday morning, and they were to meet her mother and father for brunch in half an hour. Giving up, she fished her phone out of her purse to dial Mya's number. As the phone rang, Paris heard her friend's ringtone coming from somewhere behind her. Turning around, she saw Mya walking down the hall with two coffees in hand.

"Hey!" called Mya. She looked cheerful as she approached Paris. "Here," she said, handing her a cup. "I thought you could use a mocha for the road."

"Geez, I thought something had happened to you," replied Paris.

"Nope, I'm all good. Sorry, I wasn't in there." She laughed. "You usually roll out of bed at the last minute, so I preemptively got us some coffees to make the transition smoother." Then, smiling at her, she said, "You're supposed to say, *Thanks, Mya.*"

Paris shook her head in agreement. "Thank you. I appreciate the thoughtful gesture. You know me too well."

"For many years, Paris, for many years. Anyway, I think the car is already waiting out front. I'm sure your parents have left church and are on their way as well. We should get a move on."

It took them the full thirty minutes to get to the restaurant, which was packed to capacity. Paris and Mya hurried to the booth her parents had acquired and took their seats opposite them.

"Good morning," said Mikel, a smile creasing his mustached face. "How are things?"

"Great," replied Mya.

"I concur," said Paris. "I'm enjoying my new place. Mya and I sat out on the balcony around the fire and drank mojitos last night. It was wonderful. Thanks for all of the thought you put into it."

"Sweetheart, you know we only want you to be happy," replied her mother. "We've had a rough year, but despite all that's happened, we're still on your side."

"Yes, darling, we'll always be on your side," added her father. "We love you."

"I love you too," replied Paris. "Since we're being open, may I ask you how I'm doing or what you'd like to see improvements on?"

"Sure," replied Nicola. "Personally, I feel you're doing well, though I've noticed a little distance between you and Vic. Is everything okay there?"

"It'll be fine. We're working through something," said Paris. "A minor disagreement, but I have every faith we'll get through it."

Mikel nodded solemnly. "Nothing wrong with that. It happens. I have to ask. Is this the why you requested your own place?"

Paris shook her head in response. "No. I need my space. It was more difficult living with him than I'd anticipated. We have some differences in how we want to keep our homes. We each have friends we want to invite over. It seemed like a good idea to go back to separate places." Her father seemed satisfied with her answer. He didn't push the issue any further.

The foursome ordered and ate their breakfast while chatting about the happenings in their daily lives. Paris felt, for once, like she had a complete family again, though there would always be a spot in her heart that felt empty without Alli. Having Mya back was like regaining a lost sister. The family agreed to plan more activities together for the future, beginning with regular Sunday brunches. Paris felt an unexpected relief at rekindling regular interactions with her parents.

• • • ◆ • ◆ • • • •

Vic and Paris were seated in the boardroom, waiting for the others to arrive. Thinking back to the weekend, Vic had partaken in his usual fitness and family routine, except for Saturday night, he changed things up. Bored while sitting at home, he walked over to the wine bar in the ADG complex. He knew there would be live music, and he was tired of beer.

Vic barely got through the door when he noticed Angela sitting alone at a table, a glass of red wine in hand. Moseying over, he asked, "Are you alone?" He hoped she'd say yes.

Looking up, a smile spread across her supple lips. "Completely," she replied. "I felt like listening to some music, so I wandered over to check this guy out," she motioned toward the performer, who was singing and playing an acoustic guitar.

Vic had to admit, he sounded great. "Do you mind if I join you?"

"Feel free," she said, motioning to the empty chair nearest him.

"Do you frequent this place?" he asked as he sat down. He wasted no time flagging down the server and ordering a glass of Syrah.

"Not really. Only when I'm dateless, feeling restless, and hard up for some live music."

"Do you date a lot?"

"That depends on your definition of a lot. I have a healthy appetite for meeting new people and trying new things," she replied. "What about you? I hear you like to *date* a lot."

"What you said before is my exact response." He gave her a lopsided grin. "By the way, you look nice."

Angela shook her head, "I know."

"It seems to me you have changed your wardrobe a bit as of late," he commented. "Why would that be?"

"I have?" she responded, batting her eyelashes. "What's different?"

Obviously, she was playing dumb. He was simply curious whether the change had to do with him.

Not responding fast enough, she asked again, "What's different?"

"I can't really say," he deflected. "But you look great." In reality, he knew it was the shorter, tighter skirts and the low-cut blouses along with the more prominent makeup, but he wouldn't be the one to point those details out.

Leaning forward, she beckoned him to lean in closer, which he did as though he had no control or choice in the matter. He could now see down her shirt, and the view made his temperature rise.

"It's the sexy clothing," she whispered. "I thought you'd enjoy it." Reaching out, she ran one manicured red nail lightly down his forearm, and he thought he might jump out of his skin. The woman was a flame, drawing him in. "Why don't we go back to my place?" she proposed.

Tossing back his nearly full glass of wine, he got to his feet. Angela started to get up, but he put his hand out to stop her. Reaching into his pocket, he grabbed a twenty and threw it on the table. He knew the situation might mean trouble, and he had no intentions of getting burned. "Enjoy your evening. Unfortunately, I have a previous engagement, which I should get to. It was lovely to see you," he said and turned to leave. Angela nodded in response and watched him walk away, stunned by the rejection.

Once outside, Vic paused to take a couple of deep breaths. Had he really rejected Angela Martini? What was wrong with him? Normally, he wouldn't have thought twice about getting involved with someone like her. Releasing a deep sigh, he headed for home. A cold shower would take care of everything. He was tired, he told himself. Any other night, he would have taken her up on her offer, but tonight, he was too tired. In the back of his mind, he knew he wasn't being completely honest with himself. There was a deeper reason for his change of heart.

Snapping back to the present moment, he noted that his father and Mikel had arrived. Their mothers, as well as Cristo, Mya, and Chase, would not be joining them on this occasion.

"We decided we would like to meet with you alone today," said Dom. "This is now the eighth week of your performance improvement plan, which means there are only four weeks left after this. You have these last weeks to prove, beyond a doubt, that you want what's best for ADG and to show us you're able to act like adults."

"Last week went well. We saw a glimpse of the old days in the work you performed. This week, as bonuses, you each are receiving a car of your choice, as well as $500 in fun money. In the next few weeks, we want to see you step up your game even further," stated Mikel.

"Wow, that's wonderful," replied Paris. "Thank you." She could use some of the money to update her office if she wanted, which was a nice thought. The car wasn't half bad either, though she preferred limo service to her own car.

"Yes, thank you," agreed Vic. He loved having his own vehicle and couldn't wait to get back in the driver's seat.

"You're welcome," replied Dom. "Make us proud. Mya and Chase have instructions on the purchase of the cars." Both men stood and exited the boardroom with no further comments. Paris looked at Vic.

"Is that it?" she questioned.

Vic shrugged his shoulders. "I guess so."

"Great. I have to get to a meeting," Paris replied, jumping up from her seat.

Before Paris could get away, Vic asked, "With who?"

"Tom. We need to go over my files."

"I can't believe you think this is normal. Why haven't you asked anyone to confirm the workload you're to be taking on?" he asked.

"Because I feel the board would have mentioned it if it was a problem," she replied. "There's nothing to look into, and it's none of your business." Turning away, she hastily left the room.

Vic wanted to pound his fist into the wall, but he refrained. Maddening. She was simply maddening. Getting up from his chair, he marched off down the hall toward the elevators. When he arrived, Paris was still waiting. He noted she had tears in her eyes.

"Don't look at me!" she hissed.

"Fine," he replied, "I'll take the stairs." His mind reeled. *Screw it,* he thought to himself. He had just the distraction needed to forget Paris and her idiocy.

Once he reached his office, he dialed Angela's line. She picked up on the second ring.

"Thursday night, seven o'clock, come to my place for dinner and wine. Give me a chance to make up for bailing on you this past weekend," he requested.

"Well, hello to you too," she replied. "What makes you think you deserve another chance?"

"You and I both know you'll be there," he said, and hung up the phone. He was satisfied with himself. If Paris wanted to pretend nothing had happened between them, he would too.

In the meantime, he needed to focus. He had a huge client coming in on Friday, and there were a lot of details he needed to iron out beforehand. The event was a surprise fiftieth wedding anniversary for the client's parents. He'd requested Vic specifically. The party would bring in one of the largest paydays of the year. He needed to locate and price out a horse-drawn carriage, pink peonies, a string quartet, and numerous other items on the list, which was so large they had broken the planning into two separate sessions. He'd start with the carriage and work his way up to the cake samples. Nothing he hadn't done hundreds of times before. Unlike Paris, he was now dealing with a full load of clients. It was thrilling to be back in the game.

Tuesday, Vic and Paris took ownership of their new cars. Mya and Chase had taken care of all the details. Paris chose a dark blue Lexus, fully loaded with sunroof, and Vic chose a silver fully loaded convertible Camaro. They drove off the lots and continued to go their separate ways. Mya with Paris and Chase with Vic. Neither Paris nor Vic had spoken a word to one another since Monday morning.

Vic's meticulous party planning had finished by Thursday afternoon, with the help of Chase. He felt he had earned a reason to relax and celebrate. As he left work, he saw Paris headed in his direction, so he picked up his pace to stay ahead of her. Anytime he saw her coming, he'd veer off into an office, or a separate hallway, or take the stairs to avoid another heated moment. All he wanted to do was get home so he could begin working on the meal he planned to serve Angela.

He prepared a simple menu. Cheeseburgers on his grill, with homemade garlic French fries. If the girl didn't like the food, she had no business being with him, was his motto. As an appetizer, he chose to serve bacon-wrapped goat cheese stuffed dates, which he'd heard were her favorite.

One of Vic's many charms was his professional cooking skills. Had he not joined up with Sense of Adventure, he could have been head chef at any of the group's restaurants, something he often toyed with in the back of his mind, even more so as of late.

Sometimes he dreamt of achieving a Michelin star. He'd trained at Le Cordon Bleu with some of the best chefs in the world. Now, most evenings, when he arrived home, he didn't feel like cooking. His love for cooking seemed to have died along with Brody until recently. His first inkling that the love was still alive was when the group had gone to the cabin, and he'd cooked most of their meals.

Angela arrived at seven, and Vic greeted her and showed her to the kitchen where he was removing the perfectly timed dates from the oven. He poured her a glass of pinot noir and said, "A toast to you showing up this evening."

She laughed. "But I thought you knew I'd show?"

"I assumed, but you know how that can sometimes go." He chuckled at his own comment.

They noshed on dates and sipped their wine while he cooked. She laughed at his jokes and complimented him in any way she could. She was an attentive guest who interacted well in the moment. He noted she was wearing the tightest, lowest-cut blue blouse he'd ever seen, along with a short flowing floral skirt and blue stilettos. She looked tastier than the food, but he pushed the thought aside for the time being.

After dinner, they retired with replenished wine glasses to the living room and took a seat on his couch. "The food was divine," complimented Angela. "Why don't you cook regularly? What made you take on the job at Sense of Adventure?"

"For many years, I thought I'd be a chef, but after shadowing my parents, I felt a new desire to join the family business. Vacation and party planning looked like fun, and it turned out I was right, even though I miss cooking at times."

"I can see the enjoyment you experience when you cook. Would you ever go back?"

"I don't know. Right now, no, but in the future, who can say?" Reaching out, he brushed her long blonde hair back and looked at her creamy alabaster skin. "You have beautiful eyes. I don't know if I've ever seen eyes so blue-green before."

"Thanks," she replied. "You're not so bad yourself. You should think about going back to cooking," she prodded. Then, reaching up, she undid the top button of her blouse, exposing her flesh further and giving him a view of her bright pink bra. He sucked in his breath and held it for a moment. He couldn't look away. As he watched, she undid yet another button and continued until her shirt hung open in front of him. He said nothing as he continued to gaze at her. Standing, she slid out of her skirt to reveal matching pink panties. Turning in a circle, she asked, "What do you think?"

Standing, he looked down at her and said, "I think tonight might be my lucky night." Taking a step toward her, he ripped off his shirt.

Angela grinned. "I think you might be right," she said, then reaching for him, she

unbuttoned his pants.

His passion for her grew with each touch. Pressing his lips to hers, he grabbed her hand,

leading her down the hall to his bedroom. *Paris who?* he thought as he closed the door behind them.

The following morning came with a jolt. Vic flew out of bed with the internal realization that something was not right. Angela was gone, his alarm turned off. It was eight-fifteen, and he was late meeting his client. His stomach soured at the realization. Had he turned the alarm off himself? He bolted to the bathroom to brush his teeth and splash water on his face, then returning to the bedroom, he threw on his best suit and rushed out of the apartment. As he was walking into Sense of Adventure, his phone rang.

"Where the hell are you?" demanded his father. "Why aren't you here? This is important, Vic! And where's Paris? I wanted to send her in, but she's not here either."

"I'm so sorry, pops, I don't know what happened. Somehow, my alarm got turned off. I'm on my way."

"Don't bother!" he boomed. "I told the client you were ill and sent your mother in to deal with it." Vic's heart sank. He knew this incident would come back to bite him. Thinking better of going into the office while the client was still there, he went back to his building and marched over to Paris's condo. He knocked, but there was no answer. Trying the door, he found it to be unlocked. Pushing it open, he instantly regretted his decision. Tom had Paris bent over the settee, giving it to her hard. Vic gaped at them.

Paris, realizing Vic was in the room, pushed Tom away and grabbed the nearest throw blanket to cover herself. "What are you doing? Get out!" she screamed. Vic backed himself out of the condo and slammed the door, stopping to lean against the wall while he forced himself to breathe. Before he could get away, Paris threw open the door and marched into the hallway.

"What are you doing? Why are you here, uninvited?"

"You're one to talk! I seem to recall you slipping into my apartment to steal my date's very expensive shoes out of the room we were screwing in. That was on purpose. This was an accident. Two different things, I'd say!" Vic cringed. He didn't want to rehash the situation with her. "I came over to tell you I screwed up, but we can discuss that later. I have to be somewhere," he said in a more controlled voice. Paris stood there staring at him. "You should get back in there, and for God's sake, put some clothes on!"

"What do you mean you screwed up?" asked Paris.

Vic shook his head and walked away.

"What do you mean?" she asked again, but he didn't answer. His words hurt more than Paris cared to admit. The knowledge that he'd seen her and Tom going at it, also hurt.

When she walked back into the condo, Tom was about to leave.

"Hey, it's been fun. I have a client at nine. I need to go prepare. See you later," he said and marched out the door. They'd been together all night, so obviously, he had to leave sometime. It wasn't as if he'd come and gone. They'd partaken in several lovemaking sessions over the past twelve hours. He'd devoted a good deal of time to her. She needed to go to work as well, but she couldn't get past the feeling that something was very wrong.

•••••••••••

"Dr. Morgan, I screwed up bad this week," said Vic. He was sitting in his therapist's office, telling the story of waking up late and seeing Paris with Tom.

"Why did you go over to Paris's condo in the first place?" asked Dr. Morgan.

"Honestly, I wanted to know why she wasn't at work yet and I wanted to see if she'd run some recon for me and find out how the meeting went for my mother. I'm pretty sure I can suture up the damage I created with the client, but the situation with the board is a whole other story. This was definitely me dropping the ball. It's a pretty big mess."

"Yes, indeed it is," replied Dr. Morgan. "I'm happy to see you've owned up to your mistake. That's progress."

"Thanks. It doesn't come easy for me."

"One step at a time," replied Dr. Morgan. "Tell me, Vic, how did it feel seeing Paris with Tom?"

"Horrible," he admitted. "It felt like I was being stabbed in the back, and I'm not even sure why."

"I'd encourage you to think about that some more. In order to mend the situation, you must first admit to yourself why you reacted in such a destructive way."

"Can things get any worse?" asked Vic. "The board will probably punish us both, considering Paris wasn't available to fill in."

"That is possible," said Dr. Morgan.

"The repercussions will be major; I fear."

The Dr. nodded. "Of that, my friend, I have no doubt. The question is: how will you react?"

Chapter Fourteen

"Honestly, Vic, where's your head?" asked Paris. It was Sunday morning, and Paris had finally calmed herself enough to agree to meet with him in person. Mya and Chase were also present as they discussed the mess they'd made and how to clean it up. "You have the nerve to talk to me about Tom, yet you run off and screw Angela?" They'd booked a meeting room at Sense of Adventure to stay on universal grounds. Vic was seated at the table, while Paris was standing just inside the door with her hands on her hips as she unleashed her disappointment on him.

Mya walked toward Paris and gave her a look to tell her to tone it down. Paris bit her lip and gave a brief, nearly imperceptible nod to her friend.

Chase stood, raising his palms in the air, and said, "We're not getting anywhere by pointing fingers. This isn't about Vic sleeping with Angela or Paris diddling Tom. This is about your future with the company. You need to look at this from the perspective that Vic overslept and missed an important appointment. The board doesn't know you're sleeping with Tom or Angela, and there's no need to mention it," he warned.

"I agree," stated Mya. "We need to get through tomorrow's meeting without further blowing up this situation. What the board doesn't know won't hurt you two, right?"

Paris nodded her head. "Yeah, but what if they know? What if someone informed them?"

In response, Mya replied, "Do you believe these relationships are genuine? If you do, then there's nothing to worry about. It isn't like you haven't dated others within the company before. ADG has never had a policy regarding interoffice relations, since obviously, the key players are married and best friends."

Nodding again, Paris agreed with her. Vic continued to stare at them and say nothing. He felt like an idiot on so many levels. He raked his fingers through the waves of his short, brown hair. Paris had every right to be angry, but at the same time, he was frustrated with her response. As he sat quietly seething, he realized her rejection was the driving force behind his behavior. With yet another epiphany, he recognized that no one had ever rejected him before.

Vic sat and stared back at Paris as she tried to keep calm. Something about her anger stirred further desire within him, but he had to find a way to let it go. He needed to back off and accept that she was not interested in him. He knew that for them to make it within the company; they had to find a way to level the playing field and diffuse their angry feelings.

Paris paced back and forth. Her anger was directed at the wrong situation. Vic had seen her with another man, and it wasn't something she took lightly. She knew he was not one to show up late, but his decision to sleep with Angela had gotten in the way of his work and then he had barged into her apartment unannounced, putting her in a highly uncomfortable and compromised position. "What do you think will happen in tomorrow's meeting?" she asked Chase and Mya.

Chase stepped forward. "I'm pretty sure we're looking at a major demotion. This isn't some small client. We're talking big bucks on the line."

"He's right. Prepare yourselves for the worst. If they don't demote you, I'll be shocked," said Mya. "I'd also wager a change in housing."

Vic's eyes dropped to the floor as he shook his head. "Paris, for what it's worth, I'm sorry. I wish I could take it back and erase it for both of us. Please forgive me." He hated asking for forgiveness, but he knew it was necessary.

"There's nothing we can do to change what's already done," she replied. At this point, she was more concerned about the consequences coming on Monday.

· · · · · · · · · ·

Monday morning, Vic and his peers arrived early to the boardroom. He wanted to show timeliness in light of his prior indiscretion. Try as he might, he couldn't wrap his head around how he'd missed his alarm. He wanted the board to arrive so they could be handed their punishment and move on from the humiliating events of the prior week. Looking at Paris, he ascertained her mutual feelings toward the matter. Lucky for them, the seniors arrived early as well.

"Good morning," said Jessamine. "We seem to have hit a little roadblock."

Cutting to the chase, Mikel said, "Vic, would you mind explaining why you were late for the meeting last Friday morning?"

"Sir," said Vic, "I have no excuse. I don't know if I forgot to set my alarm or what, but my actions were unacceptable. I'm ready to accept the consequences."

"You're always prompt," said Dom. "We raised you to be early. Knowing this isn't you, even at your worst, we've agreed on a suitable response to your misstep. We're moving you and Paris back into the first apartment you previously shared. Mya and Chase, you'll go with them to individual apartments on the same floor so you may maintain close contact while they reflect on what it means to be a professional working at ADG."

"Please, sir," appealed Vic, "don't punish everyone else for my mistake."

"Vic, dear," replied Jessamine, "you need to learn that in a company such as ADG, everyone must work together. Everyone has their part. Your success is their success and vice versa." True to her nature, Jessamine's voice was nothing short of empathetic. "The four of you are a team. I believe in you."

"Now, go on," said Nicola. "We know you have what it takes, but you need to find it within yourselves."

The board waited for them to leave. Paris led the foursome out into the hall and shut the door behind them.

Once the kids had gone, Nicola looked at her partners. "What's happened to them? Why have they stopped working together again?"

"I don't know," replied Dom. "Something's been off ever since they went to the cabin. At first, I thought they were in better spirits upon their return, but that's not the case at all. We've seen a steady decline."

"Should we have some other employees keep tabs on them?" asked Jessamine.

Mikel shook his head. "Let's wait it out. We already have their coworkers watching for improper conduct within Sense of Adventure. I think if something's going on, it'll come to light sooner than later."

"Has anyone else reported issues?" asked Cristo.

"No. The only reports we've been receiving are those that come from Chase and Mya directly. If they know something, they aren't letting on," stated Mikel.

"Do we need to sit Mya and Chase down to discuss this further?" asked Nicola.

"Look at it this way," said Mikel, "if they aren't telling us, that means they're maintaining at least some form of cohesion. They need to protect their own. We want them to protect each other. They'll work it out. Do we agree?" he asked the group.

Everyone nodded in response. Mikel was right. If Chase and Mya were still on their team, then at least something was going right.

"All we can do is wait and see what happens this week," said Dom. "I'm hoping there will be an improvement. I'd hate to have to send them back to the bottom again with so little time left. Either way, we've seen some positive changes thus far. They're at least halfway to where we want them."

"Sometimes, you need to take a couple of tumbles before your feet are firmly planted on the ground," replied Mikel.

•••••••••••

Walking into her office after the board meeting, Paris was greeted by a lovely scent. One dozen white roses were sitting in a vase on her desk. Snatching the envelope from its holder, she gently coaxed it open, being careful not to tear it. The note was simple and set her heart aflutter. *Thinking of you and the wonderful time we had. Yours, Tom.* Leaning in, she took a deep breath. How she loved the smell of roses. It seemed the man was smitten with her.

As the week progressed, Paris received several other reminders of Tom's affections. A voicemail saying how he was sorry about his last-minute meeting and having to pull out of lunch, but that he missed their alone time and would make it up to her. A quick note on her desk said how he was thinking of her. A box of chocolates sent to her condo with a note saying he would be out of town Friday night but would like her to come over Saturday when he returned. She couldn't stop thinking about him. Would he really make such gestures if he didn't like her?

Vic's week progressed smoothly, aside from him and Paris trying to stay out of each other's way within their not nearly large enough apartment. They were not mean to each other but still spoke few words. He could tell Paris was angry that they were once again stuck in the same place, but they both knew it was a mild price for Vic's mistake from the prior week. Most frustrating was that the construction still jolted them awake at six each morning.

Vic tried to quell his anger regarding Paris, still seeing Tom. Unlike Paris and Tom, who seemed to want to become even closer, Vic was doing his best to keep his distance from Angela. He nearly succeeded.

Thursday evening, as Vic returned to his office from a client meeting, he found the door unexpectedly closed. Swinging it open, he peered inside. Someone was sitting in his chair with their back to him.

"Hello?" he called out.

"Hello, yourself," replied the all too familiar silky feminine voice. Stepping inside, Vic shut the door behind him.

"What are you doing here, Angela?" She spun the chair around to face him, and his jaw dropped.

She was wearing only a black low-cut silk and lace slip. Her breasts were nearly busting out of the top. Vic instantly felt a tightening in his groin. Lord, how he wished his body wouldn't betray him.

"You aren't happy to see me?" she asked with a fake pout.

"I—"

"Be a lamb and lock the door, won't you?"

"I really don't think this is a good idea."

Standing, she let one strap slip from her shoulder, exposing more of her chest. "Oh, clumsy me," she purred and then slowly slipped the second strap off, allowing her negligée to slide to the floor. She stood in front of him in nothing but a lace thong, ready and waiting for him to make a move. In one quick motion, he locked the door and closed the space between them. Picking her up, he sat her on his desk and ripped her panties off. Unbuckling his belt, he yanked at the closure to his khakis, and let them drop to the floor.

"Commando? I love it!" squealed Angela.

Vic, reaching up, took one finger and placed it over her lips to tell her to keep quiet, and then grabbing her waist, he urgently pulled her toward him.

• • • ● • ● • • • •

It was nearly closing time when Mya arrived outside Vic's door. As she reached out her hand to knock, she heard the sound of a rhythmic thumping emitting from the room. Taking a step back, she paused. If she had any doubts as to what was going on, they were put to rest when she heard a woman's voice squeal, "Oh yes, Vic!" She knew the voice and instantly backed further away, but as the moment lengthened, so did the noise, and it became clear to the few employees nearby that something scandalous was happening.

No one would say that Vic and Angela had been bumping uglies at work because no one saw Angela leave his office. Everyone, including Mya, had cleared out by the time they emerged. Angela was safe and anyone who heard them would place complete blame on Vic. Vic, after all, was the one being scrutinized on his every move.

Mya was appalled by Vic's behavior, but at the same time, felt sorry for the idiot. She was certain Angela was out to sabotage him, though she really had no proof. All she knew was that Angela had never been the type to stick a single toe out of line at work. She never showed her sexuality, and she hadn't previously been the type to pursue her coworkers. To add to the situation, she recently had made drastic changes to her clothing style. Something was definitely off.

· · · · ·•·•· · · ·

Word quickly got around about the late afternoon rendezvous that happened inside Vic's office. It was midday Friday when his parents caught wind of his indiscretion. Any other company would have fired an employee for such misconduct, but ADG was not any other company. It took the board all weekend to decide how to handle the unfortunate event. Vic's parents were mortified and canceled all weekend plans with him. His morale took a massive hit. He sat in his apartment and drank whiskey on the rocks, trying not to think about the deep hole he'd dug himself into. If he thought he'd been at rock bottom previously, he was sadly mistaken.

Paris heard from Mya about Vic and Angela on Friday night. She was so angry; she had to force herself to leave the apartment so she wouldn't strangle him in his sleep. Saturday afternoon, she missed a call from Tom, who canceled their evening plans because of something that came up. The weekend felt like a bust.

·•·•·•·•·••··

Saturday night, Cristo asked Mya to go on a date. He had yet another client dinner, which she had no desire to attend, but she felt she had no choice due to his volatile state. At the end of the evening, he demanded he be allowed to walk her to her apartment and come in for a nightcap. She complied, though she felt it was completely unnecessary. Leaning in, he tried to kiss her, and she pushed him away.

"You will comply with my requests," he declared, "or I'll make sure your dirty little secret gets out." The game was on.

Mya nodded her understanding. She didn't want to give in to him, but she didn't want to make a scene either. He didn't press her further but instead swatted her on the butt and turned to walk away. She was left standing there feeling helpless. She knew the situation would be continued at a later date. She'd wait in anticipation, but her anxiety was piqued, still not knowing where they were headed.

CHAPTER FIFTEEN

Monday morning came with an early wake-up call. Dom boomed over the phone line, his complete and utter disgust at his son's recent in-office escapade. "How could you be so careless? Did you think someone wouldn't notice what you were doing? You should know better than anyone how well sound travels with those wood floors. You were there when we had them installed! I don't think I have to say how disappointed we all are. Furthermore, it hurts me to have to take action against both you and Paris for your stupidity!"

"Dad, I'm sorry. It won't happen again," assured Vic.

"You're damned right it won't happen again! If it does, you'll be cut off from the business, and this family! Keep your extracurriculars outside the office!" Quieting, Dom added, "There will be no board meeting today. I can't stand to look at you. Report back to maintenance, and take Paris with you." Before Vic had a chance to respond, Dom slammed the phone down in his ear.

"Shit," said Vic aloud, "shit, shit, shit!"

Paris, who had arrived home to change clothes in the middle of Vic's conversation, stood in the hallway listening. Vic stepped out of his room and jumped back, startled to see her standing there. "What's going on?" she asked, though she already had a good idea of his response.

"That was my father. No meeting this morning. He's sending us back to janitorial."

Paris threw her purse on the floor and stomped off to her bedroom. Stepping back into the hall, she pointed her finger at him. "I can't stand to look at you, let alone be in the same room as you! We're back at the bottom because you're an idiot, and you can't keep it in your pants!"

Turning, she marched back into her bedroom and slammed the door shut. Opening the door again, she popped her head out and yelled, "I actually felt something for you, but you're such a man-whore that I'd have to be an even bigger ignoramus to think you could be capable of showing genuine feelings for anyone, least of all me!" Turning away, she again slammed the door.

While Paris hadn't actually touched him, it felt as if he'd been slapped. He was an idiot. There was no question in his mind. She was right. How could she have possibly entertained the idea of being with him when he'd done nothing to prove he was capable of any form of commitment? He'd spent time and energy being angry at her for not wanting more when, in reality, it was his own fault she had shut down. He had played into exactly what she would've expected of him by sleeping with Angela.

Sitting down on the sofa, he lowered his head into his hands. What a mess he'd made. Paris was mad, his father was mad, and he definitely couldn't blame Chase and Mya if they felt angry as well, considering he had also gotten them thrown into smaller apartments because of his actions.

Paris lay face down on her bed in her room, sobbing into her pillow. She'd worked so hard to lift herself up, but she couldn't control Vic's actions. As she was lying there crying, it occurred to her she was part of the problem. She and Vic had stopped working together after the weekend at the cabin. They'd come so close to figuring things out and then turned their backs on one another because they let sex get in the way. How would they make it through the next several weeks if they couldn't handle speaking to each other or being in the same room? Sitting up, she wiped her face with a tissue. She knew the only way around their current roadblock would be for them to swallow their pride and talk things out.

Reaching out, Vic knocked on Paris's door. "Paris, I know you're angry with me, but I want you to know that I'm sorry for dragging you into this situation. I know I've been apologizing a lot lately. Let's go to work and give ourselves a day to think about things, and then, if you're ready, perhaps we can discuss what's happened, as well as our plan going forward?" He heard no response.

Paris listened until his footsteps disappeared, and then she got dressed for the day. She didn't exit her room until she was certain he had left for work. While she knew they'd eventually have to deal with all that had passed, she was going to give herself some time to think, as he had suggested. Feeling sorry for herself and humiliated, she was not ready to face him.

· · • • · • • • · ·

Chase was waiting at the elevator when Vic arrived. "I heard you've been demoted again," he commented. The look on his face was all business. "When will you grow up and realize your actions affect more than just you?" he asked. "You want your parents to treat you like an adult, but you're acting like a frat boy. You're twenty-nine. This behavior should have ended a long time ago."

Vic shook his head. "I'm scum," he replied. "None of you deserve to be stuck in the mud with me."

Chase looked at him and nodded in agreement. "What are you going to do about it?"

"Well, for starters, I plan to stay as far away from Angela as possible."

"Damn it, Vic! That goes without saying. What else will you do? You're running out of time, and I have to tell ya, I'm a little leery about where Mya and I are headed because of your actions."

Vic hung his head. "I'm realizing that. I know it's a little late, but I do understand. I want to fix this; I just don't completely know how."

"You have to be on your best behavior. You have to exhibit an executive attitude. You cannot afford to screw up anymore. This has turned into a bigger shit-show than I could have ever imagined. I'm coming over to your place tonight to discuss this further," he said as he exited the elevator. He didn't bother to wait for Vic to follow.

Vic headed out to maintenance, where he met his prior boss with a melancholy look.

"I hate to say it, but I knew you'd be back," said Burt.

"That makes one of us," replied Vic. "I really thought I was in the clear once I returned to my original position within the company."

"It can take time to make changes," he stated plainly. "This time, you better make it count. Suit up, and head to six. Got a broken toilet for ya. I've been advised to keep you and Paris separate for the day, so I'm sending her to work on some paperwork for the department. Your father seemed to think she might need some space to cool down after whatever it is you did to land the two of you back in my domain." He studied Vic, looking for an answer.

"I won't let you down, Burt. I know you don't want us here either," he replied.

"For a white-collar boy, you do alright with us, but no, I don't want you to stay here. You make people happy in other ways. It's your gift." He nodded with admiration.

Vic changed clothes and grabbed his tools. At least on the sixth floor, he wouldn't have to deal with seeing Angela or Tom. No one from Sense of Adventure had much reason to go up to six. His day would be quiet and provide plenty of time to reflect on how to fix the mess he'd made.

· · · · ● · ● · · · ·

When Paris checked in with Burt, she was happy to find she would be taking on some paperwork. She had no desire to clean bathrooms or fix broken toilets.

"You'll be alright, dear," said Burt. "I know you're a bit torqued off by Vic's actions, but I think he'll turn it around. Try to be patient," he said with kindness and understanding. Reaching out, he pulled her into a hug. "On a different note, try not to end up in medical this time around, will ya?" She'd earned a strong reputation as the clumsiest person to have ever worked in janitorial, because of her last stint there.

"I'll do my best," she replied, squeezing him harder. "Want to meet for lunch?"

"I'd love to," smiled Burt. "Anything to have some quality time with my girl."

"Okay, I'll come find you at noon," she replied, and headed for the office.

Paris hit her work hard. She sorted through and made sure each expense was recorded and filed properly. She updated the log for work completed throughout the building and even responded to work requests. Lunchtime arrived, and she was happy to take a break. She'd managed to focus all of her energy on work. Her mind never wandered to Vic, not even once.

"How'd it go?" asked her grandfather.

"Great," she replied. "I'm much better at the record-keeping end of maintenance than I am at the actual labor."

"Ain't that the truth," laughed Burt. "I think I prefer you in the office as well."

"Where are we going for lunch?" she asked.

"Remember that little café downtown, the Purple Turkey? I believe I took you there one other time."

"Yes, I recall it well," she mused. "The last time we went there was to celebrate my move to my current position at Sense of Adventure, or rather the position I previously held before I messed everything up." She shook her head in irritation at herself.

"Well, today we're celebrating your return to that position."

"How can you be so sure?" she asked.

"Sweetheart, if there is one thing I know about you, it's that you're extremely determined when you set your mind on a goal." He gently pat her shoulder. "I have faith, and so we're going to celebrate."

Paris wouldn't object. After all that she'd been through over the past two years, she was pleased that someone in the family was still cheering her on. Her grandfather had always been there for her when she needed someone to say the right words and mean them.

·····

After work, Vic trudged back to his and Paris's apartment. He hadn't seen her all day, but he remained unsurprised since he'd agreed to give her some space to think. Entering the apartment, he ripped off his clothing on the way to the bathroom, tossing the articles aside as he went. Turning the shower on, he paused a moment with his hand under the spray, waiting for it to warm. He needed to wash away the memory and feeling of the previous days.

Inside the shower, he silently broke down. It'd been years since he'd felt such emotion flow forth. He let go of the anger he felt toward himself, toward the company, toward Paris, and most of all, his cousin, for leaving him without his best friend. He stood under the hot water until he could no longer take the heat. Then, pulling himself together, he turned off the water and stepped out. Grabbing his towel from the hook at the back of the door, he wiped himself down and walked out of the bathroom, leaving the pain and sadness behind.

Dressed in blue jeans and a t-shirt, Vic sat on the couch waiting for Chase to arrive. He turned on some classical jazz music and let his mind mellow. He knew Chase was angry, but he felt better prepared to deal with him and set things right. He'd nearly fallen asleep when he heard a knock at the door.

"Come in," called Vic.

Chase opened the door and marched into the living room, taking a seat on the chair. "I like the music," he praised. "It's relaxing."

"Yeah," replied Vic. "I figured death metal wasn't the way to go tonight."

"From what I recall, you don't even like death metal," smirked Chase. "Here," he said, handing him a travel cup. "It's a Chai Latté. I thought you could use something with a little caffeine, but not quite as strong as a beer during our chat."

"Thanks, I think?" He wasn't much into tea, but he'd give it a whirl since Chase had done something nice.

Chase shook his head like a disappointed parent. "All I'm saying is we need to get serious about your situation. It's time to stick the landing, as they say in gymnastics. You're running out of time."

Vic nodded in agreement. "Oh, believe me, I get that."

"Do you, Vic? There was a point when I thought you did, but here we are again."

"I understand. I realize how serious things have gotten. This feels like rock-bottom, and I'm ready to move forward. I'm continuing to see my shrink. I'm committing to the company, and I realized something else."

Cocking his head, Chase asked, "What's that?"

"You, Paris, and Mya have become my closest friends. You don't deserve to be treated with such disrespect."

Chase beamed at him. "Man, you know, I've been waiting for you to recognize that for some time now."

"I've let the pain of losing Brody impede my life for much too long. He was family and my closest friend. I've told Paris several times we need to move forward and that they'd want us to, but I haven't done so myself."

"Sometimes, out of the ashes, new and beautiful things can be born. You need only be open to them," added Chase.

"Dude," said Vic. "This is sounding pretty sappy."

"Brother, get used to it. There's a new B.F.F. in town," laughed Chase.

Vic rolled his eyes. "Come on, I'm starved. Let's get some food and figure out what needs to happen in order for me to reach, and maintain, my proper place within the company."

· · · • · · • • · · ·

It was six o'clock when Molly dropped off the papers Dom requested she deliver to Tom's office. When she had arrived, the door was closed, so she knocked, but no one answered. Bending down, she shoved the file under the door. As she went to smooth her skirt and blouse, she heard a loud, high-pitched laugh come from within the office.

Moving over, she stood to the side and waited. The common area had emptied, aside from a couple of janitors running around sweeping and collecting trash bins. Her pause had been brief, but the wait began to payout.

"Thank God I'm done with her," she heard Tom's voice say. "She's a train wreck."

"What about him? Just pathetic," replied the female voice. "He's had so many chances."

"I don't think there's any way they can meet their deadline, do you?" asked Tom.

"I doubt it."

Molly scooted over to hear better, but as she did, her purse swung around and hit the wall.

"Did you hear that?" asked Tom.

Molly didn't wait to find out if they came looking for her. She darted for the elevators.

·· · • · • · · · ·

Tom opened the door to his office and stuck his head out. There was no one in sight. Bending down, he picked up the file folder lying on the floor. It was from Dom's office. "Dom's secretary," commented Tom. He didn't know Molly was friendly with Mya and Paris.

"Anyway, I think if we keep working at it, we could be running this company in a few years' time," said Angela.

"I hope you're right, and we aren't going through all this bullshit for a damn rumor."

"I'm telling you; I heard Mikel talking to Dom about retirement and naming their successors. We've got this in the bag."

....

Once Molly was safely out of sight, she pulled her cellphone from her purse and dialed Mya's number. Mya picked up after the first ring.

"Hi, Molly, what's up?"

"Oh, my gosh. I'm freaking out!" she erupted. "Dom had me deliver a file to Tom's office, and when I got there, his door was shut. There was a woman inside talking with him about two messed-up people. Anyway, my purse fell as I moved and hit the wall. They totally heard me outside. I didn't stick around to see if they would open the door. My heart is pounding out of my chest."

"Dang. How long were you listening for?" asked Mya.

"Not long. I heard a woman's laughter, which made me take pause. Who do you think the other person was?"

"Probably Angela. If I had to wager a guess, I'd say they were talking about Vic and Paris, but considering you weren't there long, you may have heard things out of context. Monitor them. Maybe you'll find an answer. It wouldn't be surprising if they turned out to be the saboteurs."

"I'll find some time to further monitor over the next week. Maybe we'll learn something else about the situation?" she said excitedly.

"Sounds good. Be careful."

"Careful is my middle name," replied Molly. "Though lately, I feel like it should be stalker." She laughed.

Mya hung up the phone and contemplated what Molly had said. She was certain it had to be Angela behind the door. Angela was sketchy, to say the least. She didn't understand how Vic could harp on Paris about Tom, then turn around and sleep with Angela. *Men,* she thought, tossing her phone back onto the counter.

Mya smiled. The day was over. She had made some popcorn and was just about to sit down when a knock sounded at her door. She wasn't expecting anyone and hoped it was Paris. Forgetting to check her peephole, she swung the door open and was surprised to find Cristo on the other side.

"Cristo? What brings you here tonight. We didn't have plans, did we?" she asked.

"You, of course, and no," he replied.

Looking him over, Mya realized he had once again been drinking. "Go home, Cristo. You're clearly inebriated. It's Monday night. All I want to do is eat my popcorn and watch a movie." She made a move to close the door on him, but he lurched forward and stuck his foot in the door jamb.

"I came all the way over here. Let me in!" he demanded.

"No! Go away!" she screeched.

Moving forward, Cristo shoved the door open with brute force, which made her step backward. Clearing the door, he slammed and bolted it behind him. "I want to continue our game," he replied softly. Reaching out, he grabbed her by the wrist and jerked her toward him. Mya slapped him across the face. He didn't even flinch but shoved her onto the sofa and stood before her. "You want it rough tonight?"

Mya looked up at him in anticipation, waiting for his next move.

"Every day, you walk into the office looking beautiful and flirting with me. This has gone on for years now, and I think it's time you admit your feelings. With no end in sight, I'm growing tired of this game. Don't you want to change things up?"

Mya stared back at him. She couldn't seem to find her words. Now he wanted to talk?

"Answer me!" he barked. Walking away, he went to the kitchen and began looking through the cupboards until he found a bottle of whiskey. Grabbing a glass, he poured out two fingers. Picking up the bottle, he took a large swig and then returned to the living room. "Here," he said, handing her the glass. "Drink that."

Continuing to stare at him, she shook her head no. She didn't want to drink it because she knew what would come after, and she was struggling with her composure. She didn't want to give in to his demands, but she felt like she was losing the battle.

"Just drink it!" he boomed. "Sometimes your games are simply maddening," he added. Getting up, he moved over and sat next to her on the couch. "I brought my friend with me," he replied as he patted the gun inside his coat. "Don't make me use it, okay? Unless it's a turn-on to you." He grinned. "Is it?"

"No," lied Mya. She knew the gun wasn't real.

"Okay, I didn't really think so." He laughed and then tipped the bottle back to his lips. Wiping his mouth with his coat sleeve, he said, "Now, this is how things are going to go down. You'll play nice and do as I say. We'll spend an enjoyable evening together. We're going to take our relationship to the next level because we've played enough games, don't you think?" Refilling her glass, he handed it to her.

Mya kept one eye on him as she downed the liquid. Her hands were now shaking so badly she dropped the glass on the floor, and it broke into two large pieces. She was anxious. She didn't want the game to change. She had no idea what would happen, which was a scary thought.

Cristo stood, kicking the glass pieces toward the kitchen. Reaching down, he grabbed her hand and pulled her off the sofa. Unzipping his pants, he let them drop to the floor and kicked them aside as well.

"Turn around," he requested. She didn't move. "Please, turn around," he said again. This time she turned away from him. "Take me to your bedroom so we can get more comfortable, okay, love?"

Mya led him out of the living room and down the hall. The whiskey was going to her head and making her feel numb. Once inside her room, she flipped on the bedside lamp and turned to look at him, but she didn't utter a word.

"Make love to me," he requested. "Let's enjoy this night."

"No," she replied firmly. Cristo didn't seem to notice the look of anger on her face.

"You don't really mean that, Mya. I know you. We know each other. Stop playing games." Walking toward her, he grabbed her blouse and began to unbutton it slowly. She trembled at his touch.

"I do mean it. No, I don't want to have sex with you!"

"Fine," he replied and took the gun out from under his coat. "If you really need the feel of fear to get excited, here you go," he said as he laid the gun on the bed next to her. "If you need further encouragement, well, your prior indiscretions should be plenty, wouldn't you say?" Pulling her blouse off, he dropped it next to the gun.

"You think this makes it okay?" she asked shakily.

"What makes it okay, Mya, is that we genuinely want each other. You can't get enough of me, so I'm giving it all to you." His voice held a sense of urgency.

"You're wrong, Cristo. I don't have the same feelings for you. This is sick and twisted!" she yelled.

"Damn it all, Mya," he shrieked. Grabbing her wrist, he jerked her around, so she faced away from him, then ripped her skirt at the seam. Tossing the shredded fabric aside, he grabbed the back of her neck and forced her down on the bed. With his other hand, he fumbled with her red silk panties, and ripped them away as well.

Mya's nerves continued to make her tremble.

"Knock it off. This is a ridiculous game you're playing," Cristo growled. Reaching around to her front, he snaked his fingers up into her bra and squeezed her breast. "You feel so good to me. Let me show you how good I can feel to you." Reaching down, he shoved his boxers aside. She could feel him pushed up against the back of her thigh. Mya attempted to move, but he firmly pressed her back down.

"Do whatever you want to me," she panted.

Leaning forward, he plunged himself into her. Moving his hand from her neck, he held both of her wrists onto the bed as he moved against her.

Mya said nothing. She was no longer shaking. He continued to move until he could take it no longer and cried out in ecstasy. Pulling away, he slapped her on the butt and flopped down beside her. Rolling over, she pressed her mouth to his and drank him in.

"There's my girl," he said cheerfully. Reaching down, he worked his fingers over her as she continued to kiss him and then gave in to the waves as she reached her climax. "Damn, girl, you really know how to make a man work for it, you little sicko." He laughed.

"Same time next week?" she requested.

"Hell, I've got nothing else going on," replied Cristo. "Want to watch that movie now?"

"Yes, let's," she said, then kissed him again. "The popcorn's probably cold but should be okay. Oh, I should probably clean up that broken glass, and I doubt I have to say this, but you owe me a new skirt and panties." Mya knew she hadn't escaped the conversation, but at least she'd bought herself a little more time to figure things out. The game would go on.

"Sure thing, kid, you know I'm good for it," he replied coolly.

· · · · ● · · ● · · · ·

As the week continued, Paris heard not a peep from Tom. She didn't understand how he could simply ignore her. She left voice messages, and he never returned the calls. It was becoming quite clear that she'd been ghosted. Perhaps Vic was right. Tom was playing her for some reason, but why, she couldn't say.

Feeling sorry for her, Burt let Paris continue with the office work for the remainder of the week, so she wouldn't have any more mishaps. Paris was grateful. She was certain that continuing on with maintenance would eventually kill her, with how clumsy she'd become.

Despite Vic's decision to let Paris have a day, one day turned into four. It was now Friday morning. Vic had slipped into the office and left a note on Paris's temporary desk, asking her to meet him at the apartment after work for dinner, wine, and a discussion. With the weekend coming, they needed to get themselves back on track before going up against the board again. Paris hoped that the current situation would improve. She, after all, had been on her best behavior. Her grandfather had commented that Vic was having a good week too, which was enough positivity for her to think things might be on the upswing.

At six o'clock, Paris marched into her and Vic's apartment and kicked off her heels. Vic was in the bathroom showering, but Paris was hungry and didn't want to wait for him to finish his evening routine. Creeping up to the door, she cracked it open. "Vic," she called out, "what do you want for dinner?"

"Oh, holy crap!" he yelped. Sliding around the shower, his wet feet squeaked as he tried to gain his footing. "Paris! You scared me half-to-death!"

"Sorry! I didn't mean to freak you out. Are you okay?"

"Yeah, I'll live," replied Vic, his heart pounding. "What was the question?"

"What do you want for dinner?" she asked again.

"Order a pizza. I'm not in the mood to cook tonight. Been a long week." He sighed.

"Okay, I'll order a Margherita, if that works for you?"

"Can we add sausage to it?"

"It's not really a Margherita then, but sure," she gave in and wandered off to place the order.

Vic turned off the water and climbed out of the shower. Reaching for his towel, he pulled it from the hook on the back of the door and ran it over his body. Brushing his fingers through his hair, he let the water spray off his fingertips. Paris hated it because he sprayed water everywhere, including the mirror, but it was the key to maintaining his short, wavy hairstyle. Well, that and the conditioner he used religiously. Towel drying had a tendency to cause frizz, and he hated frizz.

Turning toward the door, he cracked it to allow better airflow, then ran his towel across the mirror so he could see his reflection while shaving. After a week of fixing clogged and broken toilets, he wanted to feel clean and, as his mother would say, proper.

When he'd finished, he wiped the excess cream from his face and patted on some aftershave. Peering back at his reflection, he felt like himself again. "You're a handsome devil," he said with a grin. "Now, let's see if you can win over that hot-blooded woman in the other room."

In the living room, Paris was lying on the couch listening to the radio. She didn't want to feel or think about anything. She was tired. Tired of the craziness of her life. She wanted normal. She had to discuss normal with Vic, and she didn't know how to begin.

"Hey," said Vic. "Did you order food?" He had dressed in sweatpants and a black tank.

"Yeah, it should be here in about fifteen to twenty minutes, I think. You're looking comfortable," Paris mused.

"Hey, you aren't the only person who likes to be comfortable and relax on a Friday night. Should I have put on denim and a polo for you this evening?" he asked with an inquisitive look.

"No," laughed Paris. "It surprised me, that's all. You only wear sweats and a tank when you're going out for a run."

Vic headed into the kitchen and grabbed a bottle of wine and a corkscrew. Opening the bottle, he never took his eyes off her. She wore a pair of Mya's little black terry cloth shorts and a plain red tank. She looked beautiful, even when she dressed down. "Would you like some wine?" he asked.

"Yes, please," she replied. "How was your week?"

"I do believe it was what one would call 'uneventful,' in that nothing improper happened."

Straightening herself into a seated position, she nodded and said, "That's great. Do you think we'll be moving up this week?"

"Undoubtedly," he replied, handing her a glass of Zinfandel. Clanking the lip of her glass with his, he said, "To moving up and staying up."

"Yes!" she agreed. Paris could not handle any further let-downs. "Are you prepared to make permanent changes?"

Vic sat down next to her on the couch and took her in for a moment longer. "Yes."

She knew this might be a difficult subject for him, so she proceeded with caution. "I know we agreed to work together, but then things got a little complicated. We need to put our differences aside. I'm not sure what your goals are, but I intend to continue to stay away from pills and stealing. I want to take back my position as head of charity event planning. I'm willing to put the past to bed and move on with my life. Do you have a similar plan?"

"I hear ya. I've been seeing a shrink." He watched as Paris's eyes widened and her mouth parted. "I know, right? The big bad Vic isn't so big or bad after all."

Shaking her head, she said, "Seeing a shrink doesn't mean you're any less of a man."

"I know," he replied. "That was the first lesson I learned. Beyond the shrink, I too want

us to work together. I'm done sleeping with—how did you put it? Ah, yes. Anything that walks. I want to establish a meaningful relationship with a single woman at some point and also improve the relationships I have with family and coworkers. Apparently, I do have a bit of a hot temper. Something else I'm working on with my shrink. Also, no more sex in the office or walking into apartments uninvited. You should probably agree to that last one as well," he said, winking.

"Yes, yes, I agree to not enter anyone else's apartment without an invitation. By the way,

Tom has stopped speaking to me. I haven't heard from him all week, so you're probably right about him."

"That gives me no pleasure," Vic replied.

"It is what it is, I guess? What do you suggest we do to deal with our issues with each other?"

"That depends on how you answer the next question. Do you feel our problems stem completely from us sleeping together?"

"Yeah," she said, her eyes dropping to the floor. "We probably should have determined whether it was a one-time thing or something more. Do we have actual feelings for each other? Or are we using each other as a release because of our common situation? Questions that should be answered when two people as closely involved as us begin dabbling in extracurriculars."

"Dang, girl, you're making this into something bigger than it needs to be. This isn't a business transaction."

"Am I? Tell me, what did that night mean to you?"

"It was exciting." He grinned mischievously. "You're an attractive woman, and we connected. I never thought about the next step, obviously."

"Obviously," she retorted. Before she had a chance to say more, the buzzer for the main door sounded, letting them know their dinner had arrived. Paris downed the last two swigs of her wine. Vic's glass was already empty. "Here, give me your glass. I'll pour more wine if you go down to the lobby and retrieve our pizza."

"Deal," he replied. He needed a moment away from her to consider the questions she had posed, as well as her irritated response. What did Paris want? He contemplated the situation the entire walk down to the lobby and back. He knew he felt something more for her than what he felt toward previous casual partners, but neither of them had admitted what they were looking for. He struggled to put his feelings into words he could express out loud.

"Great timing," said Paris as he walked back into the apartment. "Mom called to say the board will meet with us at eight Monday morning instead of seven.

"Nice. Sounds like we can sleep in a little. That's probably good since it might take us all weekend to analyze our relationship," he joked.

"Let's just call it a simple one-night thing and move on," said Paris. "Don't you think?"

"Sure," replied Vic. He'd been caught off guard by her sudden interpretation of what the night had meant. She basically chalked it up to nothing, but were they really the type of people who could call it nothing when such a large history existed between them?

Taking his seat on the couch, he grabbed a slice of pizza and handed it to Paris, who in turn handed him a plate. He watched her as she daintily chewed her food. He couldn't help but feel something as he watched. He didn't think it was the type of feeling that one felt toward a one-night-stand. Grabbing her wrist, he moved her hand to release the pizza back onto her plate, and then pulling her to him, he planted a deep, urgent kiss on her lips. She kissed him back and, just like the night at the cabin, one thing led to another.

Chapter Sixteen

Saturday morning arrived with the embarrassing realization that Paris had once again fallen prey to the charming side of Vic's personality. He seemed to harbor some power over her that made her forget the reality of their relationship. His passionate kisses and impatient desire to have her had made him even more irresistible. He swept her into a fantasy world where she'd reverted to being the young girl who believed in princes, unicorns, and happy endings.

Pushing his arm off of her, she climbed out from underneath the covers. They'd ended up in her room, which was more suited toward a night of passion with its down comforter and lush pillows. Vic's room was quite sparse, and felt as if an inmate lived there. He'd chosen to go with the furnishings the condo had come equipped with. To say the least, it was drab with its white and grey color scheme.

As she crept into the kitchen to make some coffee, she noted Vic had not gone back to his own room in the middle of the night. She really didn't know what casual sex partner etiquette was when living in the same home, but surely it didn't require an all-night stay. Maybe he hadn't gotten up in the middle of the night?

Brushing her thoughts of Vic aside, she grabbed two coffee cups from the cupboard and placed them on the counter. Thinking better of her decision to make coffee, she put the cups back and decided to head over to Mya's instead. She brushed her teeth and her hair, and, still in her pajamas, she headed for Mya's.

Despite it being eight in the morning, Mya answered the door promptly. She was already dressed for a workout. She had always been an early riser. "Paris," she acknowledged swinging the door open. "Come on in. What brings you here so early? Did something happen?" she realized her friend was not dressed for the day.

"You could say something happened." She laughed nervously. "I had a discussion with Vic last night. We ate pizza and drank wine. One thing led to another, and we ended up sleeping together again. And then again," she added. "Four times, to be exact." She frowned as she waited for Mya's response.

Mya's jaw nearly hit the floor. "Wait, what? How? I mean, I'm perplexed by this. Do you hate each other or love each other?" She narrowed her eyes, trying to understand.

"I don't know that it's either of those things. I mean, I know we at least like each other enough to sleep together, but I think we might be friends with benefits."

"But you aren't sure?" Mya turned away and headed for the couch. "Get in here. This isn't a conversation suited for the hallway," she added.

"I don't know. If I put major thought into it, I'd say it's possible I care for him and am attracted to him on a cellular level, but the man is a bit of a whore, right?"

"Maybe he isn't when it comes to you?" she said hopefully.

"I'm not sure he's capable of more. Have we ever seen him in a long-lasting relationship?"

"Besides the odd dynamics of his relationship with Janel, no, but what if it's because he didn't have you?"

"Come on, Mya, he could tell me if that's how he feels, right?"

"Maybe it's not that easy," she said. "A lot of things have happened in the past two years that pushed you two apart. You didn't think he liked you to begin with, but maybe neither of you allowed the other to get close enough to find out."

Paris waved her off and headed for Mya's bedroom.

"Sure," Mya called after her, "help yourself to some of my clothing." She laughed.

When Paris returned, she wore a pair of Mya's yoga pants and a peach-colored workout tank. Most of Mya's clothing fit her well enough. Mya was shorter than Paris but had a tendency to buy pants that were slightly too long for her, which worked in Paris's favor. Their body builds, aside from height, were quite similar.

"You look comfortable. Outside of the Vic conundrum, what's on the docket for today?"

Paris flopped down on the opposite end of the couch. "Not much. I'd love to hang out with you and not think about last night."

"I still maintain that there could be something between you two. Anyway, let's go to the nine o'clock yoga session, then grab some brunch. That sounds like a good start to the day, don't you agree?"

"Yeah, I think that's a plan I can get on board with."

"Oh, and look," said Mya, "your yoga mat is already over here."

Paris laughed. The only reason her yoga mat was already there was that Paris only did yoga when she was with Mya. Mya had bought a secondary mat for those occasions when Paris might decide to join her.

· · · · · · · · · ·

Back at Paris and Vic's condo, Vic had been awoken by Paris's nine o'clock alarm. Feeling the bedsheets next to him, he ascertained Paris had left some time ago. Sitting, he stretched himself out, then climbed out of her bed. It surprised him to learn that she'd left the apartment altogether.

The prior night had been such a whirlwind that they hadn't even put the wine glasses or leftover wine away. He immediately set to tidying up. He couldn't stand the idea of leaving the living room in such disarray.

Once the condo was back in order, he called Chase, who picked up on the first ring. "Hey, man, I don't feel like playing tennis today. Want to meet me for a run?"

"What time is it?" asked Chase sleepily.

"Buddy, are you still in bed? It's almost ten-thirty."

Clicking his tongue, he said, "I didn't get to bed until four. When do you want to go?"

"Why were you up so late?"

"I had a date," he replied, "and before you ask, it went well."

"Good deal," replied Vic in amusement. "I didn't know you were seeing anyone. Scratch that. I didn't know you were back to dating after your breakup with Mitch."

"It's been two months. I'm not waiting around for him anymore. He doesn't deserve this," Chase replied.

"Too true," agreed Vic.

"What time?"

"Well, I meant now, but I suppose I can hold off a bit. Eleven works for you?"

"No," he said with a sigh, "but I'll be there."

"Wait, is your date still there?" asked Vic.

"Oh, no, he didn't stay. It's all good. I'll be over at eleven," he replied and hung up the phone.

• • • • • • • • • •

Chase arrived as he said he would, at eleven o'clock sharp. Vic was dressed and ready to go. He followed him out of the building, and they set out together at a nice brisk pace. Running was the other thing that helped Vic cope. Chase, luckily, shared a similar view, which is why they'd begun running together on a more regular basis.

Chase knew firsthand what it was like to struggle with life. As a thirty-year-old gay Native American, he was no stranger to prejudice. He'd grown a thick skin and worked hard to maintain his positive demeanor. Running and therapy had been his only saving graces as a young teenager; they helped remove him from the angry path he'd set out on and brought peace and calm back into his life. He hoped Vic would discover the same as he continued through his therapy.

"Hey, I want you to know, I think you and Paris did really well this week. Between you and me, there's a rumor that you'll be making a positive move next week. Possibly in more than one area," he relayed between breaths.

Vic glanced at him as he kept pace. "That sounds great. This situation is exhausting. I can't wait for it to end."

"Yeah," replied Chase, "let's hope it ends on a positive note."

After their run, they met Jack at the pool to get some sun and drink a couple of beers. Much to Vic's surprise, Mya and Paris were sprawled lazily on lounge chairs in their two-piece bathing suits when he and Chase arrived. Luckily, he had dark sunglasses on because he couldn't stop staring at Paris's nearly naked body. He had no desire to give himself away when she again was acting as if nothing had happened.

"How's it going?" he asked. Paris was lying on her stomach, her skin glistening in the sun. He noted she smelled like coconut and some exotic fruit he couldn't place.

Tipping her head back and sheltering her eyes, she looked up at him. "Oh, hey." Motioning toward Mya, she said, "We thought some sun was in order. Cool weather is going to be here before we know it. Supposedly we'll be getting some rough winds this fall."

"Isn't that the truth," replied Chase. "We were thinking the same thing."

"Have you seen Jack?" asked Vic. "He's supposed to meet us here."

Chase tapped Vic's shoulder and pointed across the pool at Jack, who was entering through the gate at that very moment. "It's uncanny how he materializes anytime someone is looking for him," laughed Chase.

"Yeah," agreed Mya. "He really does have that tendency, doesn't he?"

"So, what's the plan, boys?" asked Paris.

"We're going to enjoy some drinks and some splashes in the pool," replied Chase.

"After we've had enough of the pool, we plan to grill and have a fire in the park courtyard. Would you like to join us?" asked Vic.

Mya, nodded and said, "Yes! That sounds great."

"I guess that settles it," replied Paris. She felt hesitant due to last night's extracurriculars, but she was actually kind of excited about sitting around the fire and relaxing outdoors. It would be the perfect continuation of her day.

"Hey guys," said Jack. Grabbing another lounge chair, he pulled it over to the group and sat down on the edge. "What's happening?"

"We're discussing our plans for the day," replied Chase. "Are you up for grilling and a fire this evening?"

"I'm in! When was the last time we grilled and had a fire?"

"Aside from our little getaway to the cabin, we haven't had a fire out here once this summer, so, last year," replied Vic.

Jack smiled back at them. "Well then, that would be why I cannot recall the last time." Scooting closer to Paris, he tapped her on the shoulder. Tipping her head back, she looked up at him. "You need any sunscreen applied to that beautiful skin of yours?"

"Back off, junior. Mya's got me covered today."

"Bummer," he replied. "I aim to please."

Vic glared at Jack. It irritated the hell out of him that his little brother wanted to start something with Paris. It fueled an anger he didn't realize he had. Contemplating the situation further, he realized it wasn't just Jack. He didn't want anyone else to touch her. The idea made him see red.

"Hey, are you okay?" asked Mya.

Vic, pulling himself out of his own thoughts, realized he was noticeably balling his fists and clenching his teeth. "Oh, sorry.

I was thinking about something," he replied sheepishly. "Why don't I get us some drinks. Who wants what?"

The group shouted their orders at Vic, who mentally took them down and wandered off. He was glad to walk away, if even for a moment.

"Is he okay?" asked Mya to whoever was listening.

"I think so," replied Chase. "He's going through some stuff, but I think he's making progress."

"Aren't we all," replied Paris without so much as a glance.

The rest of the afternoon was filled with water games and lounging in the sun while drinking piña coladas, daiquiris, and for Vic and Jack, beers. Paris felt the most relaxed she had in months. There were no other awkward moments between her and Vic. Mya and Jack seemed to be having a great time. Chase always seemed to enjoy himself, so Paris was never concerned about him. All was peaceful and as it should be.

The evening brought further relaxation around the fire. The group reminisced over past trips and how fast time seemed to travel. Vic watched Paris from across the fire. The smile never left her face. Her beautiful black hair shimmered in the firelight. He found himself wishing he was sitting next to her, but he thought it better to keep his distance until they found time to discuss Friday night.

Paris's time was monopolized by Jack. He had to be next to her at all times. Anytime her drink was empty, he offered to refill it. If she had to use the restroom, he'd offer to walk her there. Vic felt a little sick watching the ridiculous display his brother was putting on, but he told himself to let it go. Paris would never fall for Jack. There was one thing Vic knew to be true, Jack was much too young in Paris's eyes.

·····•··•····

When Monday arrived, Paris found herself wishing it was still the weekend. Saturday had been the most fun she'd experienced in ages. Now it was time to again face their families and see what fate held in store.

"Good morning," sang Jessamine. "How are the two of you today?" she asked, her icy blue eyes sparkling.

Vic and Paris arrived together with smiles painted on. They discussed over the weekend how they planned to attack their meeting. They didn't want to give the board any further reasons to question their unity. They vowed to remain intact and work through any issues that presented together.

"They're great," chimed Chase as he scooted past Vic and Paris. "They were able to sleep in, so that helps," he laughed.

"Chase!" scolded Mya. She was already seated at the table. "Let them speak for themselves."

"We're feeling good," stated Vic. "He's right though, the extra sleep helped."

"How'd last week go?" asked Dom. "From the look of things, you appear to have mended whatever was in the way of your partnership." He nodded approvingly.

"We had a long discussion and did some team-building exercises," replied Vic, to which Paris kicked him under the table. Mya, who was in the know about Paris and Vic's weekend rendezvous, had to stifle a laugh. Chase was clueless and proceeded to pour himself a cup of coffee.

Mikel slapped his hand on the table. "That's great to hear!"

"Yes, I concur," said Cristo. "What type of team-building exercises did you partake in?"

"Mostly the conversational type," blurted Paris. "We discussed our issues and worked through them. We also agreed on how to handle any differences in the future. That sort of stuff."

"Well, at least you're in agreement," mused Nicola. "There was once a time when your fathers disagreed over business practices, and they refused to speak for a month. If only they could have fixed their issues the way you have."

Vic grinned. "Yeah, if only." Paris again kicked him under the table, and Mya, no longer able to hold it in, let out a small laugh.

"What's so funny, my dear?" asked Jessamine.

Mya straightened in her seat, and her face turned to a neutral look. "I apologize. My mind wandered to a funny cat meme I saw this morning," she lied.

"I see. I love a good cat meme as much as anyone else. You'll have to send it my way," said Jessamine.

"I sure will," replied Mya. Chase gave her an 'oh, please,' sort of look, then refocused on the pastry he'd swiped from the tray in the center of the table.

"I think we've fallen off track," said Dom. "You didn't answer my question. How'd last week go?"

"Oh," replied Paris, "I think we both agree that it went well, as long as they kept me away from the bathrooms," she laughed. "I'm proud to report that there were no mishaps." *Except for Friday night when I slept with Vic*, she thought to herself.

"I agree with Paris," Vic replied. "The week was productive, and there were no mishaps. We've come back to the boardroom with a sense of understanding between us, and we're ready to hit this week hard as well. I also want to take this time to apologize again for my prior indiscretions. I promise it will never happen again."

"Glad to hear that," replied Mikel, "because we're giving you back your upgraded apartments and your original jobs. As you know, there's little time left for you to prove you want to be a part of the company. We see you making progress, and we hope it continues. We're now down to the wire—no more mistakes. Like you said, Vic, we want you to hit it hard this week. Here are the keys to your apartments," he said, sliding them across the table.

"Now," said Jessamine, "make us proud." She stood, and the rest of the board stood as well. "Help yourselves to breakfast, and then you can move on with your day." She waved and followed the other partners out of the room.

"That went well," Chase commented cheerily.

"Geez, you couldn't wait to eat until they were done?" asked Mya. "I mean seriously."

"What? I'm starving. I can't think when I'm this hungry," said Chase.

"You two need to keep at this, and like they said, hit it hard this week. You cannot afford any more mistakes," said Mya.

• • • ● • ● • • • •

Back in her office, Paris looked over the scant few files Tom left her. She was once again feeling peeved when the devil himself knocked on her door. "I see you've made it back. I dropped those off this morning when I heard you'd be here. Mind if I come in?" he asked.

Glaring, she said, "I don't know. Are you still ignoring me?"

"Oh, come now, Paris. I haven't been ignoring you. I had a situation with my sister, which needed attending. I'm all yours now." He smiled suavely. "Let's get some dinner Wednesday night, my treat." He smoothed.

Paris shook her head. She didn't know what to think. "Yeah, I guess."

"You guess?" asked Tom. He was now standing next to her. Reaching down, he cupped her chin in his hand and tipped her head up to look at him. "Don't guess, darling. I only have eyes for you." Paris could feel her knees weaken. Tom let go of her chin and headed toward the door. Pausing, he said, "Pick a place. Whichever you prefer, and as expensive as you like. You deserve an enjoyable night out." Shutting the door behind him, Tom disappeared into the hall.

His ability to weasel his way back in amazed Paris. She took a deep breath and released it slowly to calm her racing heart and return to composure. Another knock sounded at the door. "Come in," she called.

"Hey," said Vic. "To celebrate moving back to normalcy, may I cook dinner for you this evening?"

Paris considered his proposal. "Sure, we can do that," she replied. "What time?"

"How about my place at six? I'll whip up some salad and tuna steaks."

"That sounds great. I could go for a nice salad. I think I ate a little too much junk food this past weekend. Marshmallows are not a part of my regular diet."

"Yes, but aren't they wonderful?" asked Vic. "You seemed to enjoy roasting them. I think you offered everyone who approached a marshmallow," he laughed.

"I did, didn't I?" she said, laughing.

"Okay, I'll see you after work," he said, then left the room.

Paris went back to skimming her client files. Snapping back to the present moment, she glowered at the low client load. Any peon off the street could have handled these files. She really needed to discuss it with Tom, but she wasn't in the mood to approach him yet. Perhaps she would work through them and ask for more once she had finished? With any luck, she would have them completed by Wednesday afternoon and could nicely bring up the idea of further work while at dinner.

· · · • · • · · ·

"Hey," said Paris. She was standing in the doorway to Vic's apartment as he feverishly chopped and prepared the dinner salads. "I knocked, but you didn't hear me."

"It's all good. You were actually invited this time." He laughed. "Come on in and pour yourself some wine," he motioned toward a bottle and some glasses.

"Okay, but I'm not planning on a repeat of Friday night," she said. "As a matter of fact, we should probably discuss that."

Vic nodded in agreement. "You found my ulterior motive for the dinner invitation."

"Oh?"

"We agreed to work through things, and this is one of those things we must face," he replied.

"Yeah. I'm with you."

"Let's wait until after dinner, though. I want to enjoy the food and company before we delve into such a serious matter."

Paris cocked her head at him. She wasn't sure why he wanted to wait. Was he planning on upsetting her? Did he think she wanted more? Did she want more? No, she knew she had to let it go. He didn't want more, and besides, Tom was still interested. She wanted Tom. Tom had always been the one to make her heart flutter. Her mind was spinning out of control. She needed to stop and take a breather.

Walking over to the island, Paris grabbed the bottle of Prosecco and poured them each a glass. "I didn't realize you like Prosecco," she mused. "Isn't it a little too sweet for you?"

"You know I picked it out for you, but it pairs well with fish. This particular Prosecco is less sweet than others."

"Thoughtful," she said as she further considered the bottle. "Why would you pick it for me?"

Finished searing the tuna, Vic placed it atop the salads he'd made and added tomatoes and fresh parmesan. As a final touch, he drizzled them with balsamic vinegar. "Here we are," he said, placing a plate in front of Paris. Walking around the island, he pulled out a chair to seat her at the table. Scooting her chair in, he then took the seat next to her. "To answer your question, it goes well with the meal, but since you're Italian, I figured it might be a nice gesture."

"A sweet consideration," she replied as she lifted her fork to take her first bite. The flavors erupted in her mouth. She closed her eyes and savored. "This is unbelievably good. I don't recall the last time I actually tasted such a perfect combination."

Vic smiled. "It's my job to know how to do that."

"Did you enjoy culinary school?"

"Very much. Honestly, there have been many days lately where I think maybe I would rather go off and run the restaurants. Food speaks to a person's soul. I enjoy making others feel good with my culinary creations."

"Wow, careful, Vic, people might think you have a soft side after all. I've never heard you speak like this before."

"Like what?" he asked.

"With passion and love. With heart," she replied.

"Well then, hold on to your knickers, cause it's about to get real in here."

"Oh, really? What will Vic say next?" she asked with amusement.

"Well, for starters, I want you to know that I have feelings for you."

"Sexual. I know," she stated.

"No, you don't know," he replied pointedly. "You don't. This is different, Paris." Reaching out, he caressed the top of her hand with his pointer finger. "I feel more for you than I've felt for anyone. Ever. This isn't about the sex. I think I'm falling for you."

Paris set her fork down and took a drink of her Prosecco. She needed a moment to think. She paused briefly. "You've never had a committed relationship," she replied. "Are you sure you know what it is to truly love someone?"

"Wow," he replied. "That's kind of harsh, don't you think?"

Raising her hand in defense, she said, "That may have come out wrong. I don't mean to offend, but I question the reality of those feelings. Is it because we've been through a life-changing ordeal together? Could it be because we've known each other forever, and now we feel safe with one another?"

"Why does it have to be any of that?" He could feel his face flushing. She was treating him like a teenager.

"I'm still seeing Tom."

Vic's nostrils flared at the sound of his name, but he silently vowed to keep his temper. "He's using you," he replied through clenched teeth. "Don't you see it? He wants to ruin you so he can take over your accounts!"

"Just stop," she said, jumping up from the table. "Enough. Tom likes me."

"No, Paris, not enough. I love you. Do you hear me? I tell you I have these deeper feelings for you, and you brush me off like some high school pup. It's difficult for me to say these things to you, or to see you making such a major mistake."

"I can't do this right now," she whispered. "I can't." Turning away, she headed for the door. She heard every word he'd said, and it set her mind to spinning once again.

"Where are you going?" called Vic. "We said we'd work through the tough stuff. This is the tough stuff!" Paris didn't respond.

Vic, frustrated with the awful turn of events, threw the dinner plates in the sink and headed out to the balcony to get some fresh air. As he stood watching, he saw Paris emerge from the shadows and walk out across the park. All he wanted was a chance with her. Was that too much to ask?

Thirty minutes after the blow-up with Paris, Vic heard a knock at the door. His heart quickened hoping she had returned. Springing up from the couch, he bounded across the living room and swung open the door. There she stood in a low-cut black dress that hung much too short. Angela Martini. Vic's heart fell.

"Hey, handsome, mind if I come in?"

Vic stared for a moment, unsure of what to say. Her tone, while sweet, was surely laced with venom. Before he composed a response, Paris turned the corner and nearly ran into Angela. Without a word, she shook her head and turned to leave. Angela didn't notice the near-collision.

"Well? Are you going to let me in?" she asked.

"No," he growled. "You need to leave. I'm not in the mood for visitors."

"Oh, come on now," she coaxed.

"No, Angela. Leave," he demanded and shut the door in her face. Waiting on the other side, he heard her swear, then walk away. He didn't know how he would fix things with Paris, but her return had to mean something.

• • • • • • • • • •

Wednesday evening, Dom again sent Molly to deliver urgent files to Tom. The door was closed, as it was the last time. She approached with caution. Surveying her surroundings, Molly noted only a couple of people were left in the open office, but they were far enough away that they most likely wouldn't notice her pausing outside Tom's door. Pulling out her phone, she hit record and listened. She could hear the same voices once again—an unknown woman and Tom.

"He rejected me when I went to his place last night," pouted the woman. "I don't know. Maybe we need to let this go? It was so easy at first. He played right into my seduction. I thought for sure he would figure me out when I shut off his alarm, but he didn't. Honestly, I was shocked I was able to coax him into submission in his office. If that didn't get him fired, I don't know what will? Now he's turned cold, and I fear he may know something's up."

"Angela, come on. You can't stop now. Where's your head? We're so close to getting what we want!" his voice raised an octave. "You want to run the company, don't you?"

"Of course I do," replied Angela. "Ever since those two idiots got themselves into trouble, I've been dreaming about it nightly."

"In order to get what we want, we need to continue derailing them in any way possible. You need to go over there after work and try again. I'm meeting Paris for dinner tonight. The deal is as good as done."

"I'm shocked she hasn't questioned the number of clients you keep giving her," said Angela. "Her parents will be pissed when they find out she's taking on so little."

"I know," laughed Tom. "I plan to tell them on Friday that she hasn't stepped up to the plate, and she's only doing the bare minimum."

"I don't think that'll be enough to get her ousted," replied Angela.

"It's all good. You see this?" he asked. "This is Jessamine's necklace. She won the bid for it at the charity auction and it was delivered this week. I swiped it from her office before she knew of its arrival. I plan to give it to Paris as a gift. When Jessamine sees it, she'll accuse Paris of theft, but for everything to come together, I need you to make it appear as though Vic is now sexually harassing you. We should plan a place to meet and I'll videotape the scene. We can send it straight to his ex, Janel. She'll be so mad, she'll take care of the rest for us. The board will have to let him go in order to save face. Our futures are in the bag."

Molly gasped and pulled away from the door. She prayed her phone recorder was as dedicated as she needed it to be. Clicking it off, she stowed it back in her purse. She didn't even bother to slide the files under the door. She would deliver them directly to Paris and Vic. They needed to know exactly what they were up against, and time was of the essence.

Chapter Seventeen

It was six-thirty, and Mya and Chase were seated on Mya's sofa discussing the week along with further improvements for Vic and Paris to work on. It was obvious something had, once again, gone awry between them. They put on a show for the board and their coworkers, but they couldn't fool Chase and Mya, which meant it would only be a matter of time before others began to notice.

"I didn't wanna bring this up, but Vic and Paris had a second sleepover this past weekend," said Mya. "I hoped they'd work through their issues, but here we go again."

Chase rolled his eyes and let out a sigh. "Oh, sister, what are we going to do about them? I think they have genuine feelings for one another. On more than one occasion, I've noticed how they look at each other when the other isn't paying attention. It's not with lust. Before this whole situation was put into action, I never would've guessed Vic was capable of such emotion, but I've seen some major changes in him over the passing weeks."

"Yeah, I feel the same about Paris. She's actually living her life again. For a long while, I worried she'd never make it back from the emotional scarring Alli's death created. I'm thankful she seems to be healing some, but this stuff with Vic is a setback for sure."

"You know you're a huge part of her return to normalcy, don't you? You've stood by her no matter how she acted. You loved her unconditionally, even though it hurt. I've seen first-hand the damaging blows that girl has dealt you, but you stayed through it all."

"I love her. She's my family," shrugged Mya. "Not to say there weren't times when I wanted to give up."

"Anyone would feel that way. The point is, you didn't give up. You helped her find her way back."

"I suppose. I felt in part like I owed it to Alli to stick it out. Anyway, it's a whole new ballgame now."

"I'm with you. We need to get those two to deal with each other, and then I think we'll be golden. The question is, how do we do that?"

Mya was about to answer when a knock sounded at the door. "Hold that thought," she replied. Hopping off the couch, she marched over to the door and checked the peephole. She was surprised to see Molly on the other side. Her brow furrowed as she chewed her bottom lip.

Opening the door, Mya said, "Hi, what's up?"

"Something major happened!" said Molly, as she shoved a stack of file folders into Mya's hands. "You need to take these and give them to Vic and Paris. I tried their apartments first, but no one answered.

"Okay?" Mya was confused. She didn't understand why the files had become a matter outside the office. She waited for Molly to proceed.

"Dom sent me to Tom's office to drop the files off. He wanted Tom to look them over and delegate them out, but I don't believe he will. When I approached his office, the door was closed and I heard the same voices as last time. No one was near me, so I took my phone out and recorded their conversation." Pulling her phone out of her purse, she fumbled with it momentarily, then played the recording. Chase and Mya listened attentively.

When the tape had finished, they exchanged glances while pausing a moment to digest the newly obtained information. Molly waited patiently for them to respond.

Chase shook his head in anger. "Holy crap. That's some major B.S.," he said.

"Thanks for bringing this to our attention. I understand Angela and Tom's desires for Paris and Vic to fail because it brings them more opportunities, but to stoop to such lows—"

Chase let out an exasperated sigh. "This is pretty bad. I hoped Vic was wrong about Tom using Paris, but this goes way beyond that."

"I can't believe they have that much malice. I knew there was some friction, but wow. They risked everything to gain something that could have potentially been theirs, anyway.

They could have been partners. I overheard Jessamine talking about exactly that. They would have been partners," said Mya.

"Well, now they'll be jobless," said Chase, "and possibly go to jail."

"Rightly so," added Molly.

"...and these files," said Mya as she waved the folders in the air. "You did the right thing by bringing them to us instead."

Molly nodded in acknowledgment. "Anything to protect the future of the company and

my friend."

"Will you send me that recording, please?" asked Mya.

"Yes," she replied. "It's on its way."

"Perfect," said Mya. "Once we have the voice recording, we can bring it to the board, but first, we need to contact Paris and Vic before any further damage is done."

"If there is nothing more, Molly, you may get on with your evening. We can handle it from here," said Chase.

"Sounds good," replied Molly. She looked relieved that she didn't have to stay. "Let me know how it goes," she called over her shoulder as she exited Mya's apartment.

Once Molly was out the door, Chase jumped up from his seat. "What in the actual frick?"

"I know, right? This is messed up." She couldn't believe anyone at Sense of Adventure could be so awful.

"We need to get Vic and Paris together, pronto."

"Call and tell them we need them here immediately," demanded Mya. "We can't waste another moment."

Chase had already punched in Vic's number. He listened as the phone rang. Vic was none too quick to answer. The voicemail picked up, and Chase clicked off the call. He had only gotten the words, "No answer," out when the phone rang back.

"Hey, what's up?" asked Vic.

"We need you to come over to Mya's as soon as possible."

"Is something wrong?"

"Just get here. We're calling an emergency meeting. I'm only filling you and Paris in on the situation once."

"Okay, fair enough. Let me throw on a shirt and I'll be right over," he said and hung up.

Mya was on her phone as well and had freshly hung up from speaking with Paris. "She's on her way."

"Lucky they were both home, I guess," said Chase. "Did you tell Paris that we called Vic over as well?"

"Yes. I didn't want to start the meeting off with any extra surprises. Hopefully, they'll be okay. Let's get everything out in the open right away so we can put a plan in place."

Fifteen minutes later, a knock sounded at the door. Mya hurried toward it. She found Paris and Vic both waiting on the other side.

"Good evening," said Vic as he stepped over the threshold. Paris followed him. They sat on opposite ends of the sofa.

"What's so urgent?" asked Paris. "I'm supposed to be on my way to a dinner date."

Vic's head whipped around to stare at her. The look in his eyes was contemptuous. "With whom?" he asked.

"None of your business," Paris responded.

"Get over yourselves," said Mya. She was tired of the bickering.

"Can Paris and I have a moment alone?" requested Vic. The tone of his voice suggested he wouldn't take no for an answer.

"Sure," said Chase. "We'll be in the hall. Knock on the door when you're ready for us to come in." He followed Mya out the door and shut it behind them.

"Listen, I don't know what you think happened Monday night, but literally, nothing happened. I didn't invite her over," he said calmly. "She showed up unannounced. I asked her to leave, and she did. I didn't even let her in the door."

"That's fine," Paris replied, her voice shaking.

"Please tell me you don't believe I turned around and called her after you left." The hurt could be seen in his eyes. "I know you're struggling to accept it, but I honestly care about you."

"I'm over it." Standing up, she walked to the door and knocked.

Mya opened the door a crack and peered inside. "Is everything okay?"

"Yes. We're fine," she snapped.

Chase and Mya marched back into the condo and took their seats. Mya looked at Vic and Paris in turn. "Why can't you two get it together?" she blurted.

"What do you mean?" asked Paris.

"Come on! This is ridiculous," vented Chase. "You guys are willing to screw up your entire future with the family and the company all because you screwed a couple of times? Get over yourselves and work it out. This company depends on you to be there to run it." Paris's eyes looked like they might pop out of her head, due to Chase's outburst.

"Which brings us back to why we called you over tonight," said Mya. Grabbing her phone from the coffee table, she waved it in the air. "Earlier this evening, Molly sent me a recording she made earlier today. You've got to hear this. It should clear up some of your problems."

"What kind of recording?" asked Vic.

"One that will prove you're being sabotaged," added Chase. He was thrilled that they had proof.

"By whom?" questioned Paris.

Mya gave Paris a look. "Just listen." Hitting play, she kept her eyes on Paris and Vic.

"Is that Tom and Angela?" asked Vic.

"Shh," snapped Mya. "Just wait." She let the sound clip play, and she could see from the expressions on both Paris and Vic's faces that they were sickened by what they were hearing. When the recording finished, she set her phone down and looked at her friends. "You were both being played," she said. Her tone was gentle but sincere.

"Oh, my God," replied Paris. She turned to look at Vic. "You were so busy looking at Tom that you failed to see what Angela was doing to you. This is exactly why you aren't relationship material. Because you're self-absorbed and you let your penis do the thinking." She was angry, and she felt dirty. She wanted to lock herself in Mya's bathroom and cry, but instead, she took it out on Vic.

Getting to his feet, Vic pointed a finger at her. "Seriously?" he asked. At least I try new things and experience life. You've had a crush on Tom for years and never even bothered to go after him. It took a crazy event such as your job and life hanging in the balance to make him come after you, and you thought it was legit? I guess the 'safe option' wasn't so safe after all. If that's how you want to live life, fine, but count me out. This self-absorbed man doesn't need a woman who is fearful and stuck in the past. No, thank you!"

"Whoa! Stop!" barked Chase. "That's enough out of you both. We need to deal with this situation before it gets worse, but with the way you're acting, I almost want to let Angela and Tom have the whole shebang. You're ridiculous. Mya and I can both see you're mad about one another."

"Whatever," Paris replied as she continued to glare at Vic. "I don't need to be buddies with him to run the company."

"Oh, now wait a minute," said Mya. "You think you can run this company without him? Think again."

"Why not? We've worked side by side for the past few years with no issues until now," she stated.

"Trust me, girlfriend," replied Chase. "You'll need each other. Running a company is a big messy deal, and you need people who understand the business as well as you do and who can help you make decisions and back you. You've got to be close, or this palace will crumble."

Mya held her hand up to tell Chase to pause. "Let's reign things in for a minute. It's clear work needs to be done regarding your relationship, but it'll have to wait until we secure your family's legacies. So, for now, please table your anger." Mya was not one to easily anger, but this situation made her want to pull her hair out.

"Okay," replied Vic. He sat back down on the sofa and looked at Paris, waiting for an agreement.

"I'm listening," she replied.

"Good, now let's get to it. We need to bring this situation to the board, but before we do, is there anyone else that could be working with them?" asked Chase.

"I doubt it. Angela and Tom probably wouldn't trust anyone with the knowledge of their plan," said Vic.

"I agree," replied Paris.

"Okay, then I suggest we call an emergency meeting with the board before anything else happens. Sorry Paris, you won't be going on that date tonight," said Mya.

Vic glared in Paris's direction. "I knew it. I knew it was him."

"Well, obviously!" screeched Paris. Mya reached out a hand and gently touched Paris's shoulder to calm her shakiness. "I'm fine," she said quietly. "I'll be fine."

"I know," whispered Mya. "Don't be so hard on him. You're both going through the same thing."

Whispering back, she replied, "I know, but why does it feel like everything is on me?"

"Because you blame yourself when things go wrong. It's a learning process. Don't be so hard on yourself either," said Mya.

Chase got to his feet. "Alrighty, who wants to make the call?"

"I will," replied Vic. "I think the board will appreciate the initiative."

Chase nodded. "Sounds good."

Picking up his phone, Vic dialed his father's number. The phone rang twice before Dom answered.

"Good evening, son. What's up?"

He sounded cheerful. Vic hated to ruin his mood. "Dad, do you think you can get the board together for an emergency meeting this evening?" he asked.

"Why? What's going on?" he asked.

"We have some information to share regarding a situation within the company."

"Okay, what kind of situation?"

"Scandal," he replied evenly. The kind that will require the entire board's presence." He looked at Paris, took a deep breath, then proceeded to say, "Paris and I might be involved in a lawsuit in the near future."

"Vic—" his father paused. "What have you done? Did you do something to Paris?"

"Dad! No!" he gasped. "Why would you think that?"

"I know something's going on between you two. I thought maybe this was part of it."

"No, Dad. Just—no. Paris and I are the victims, as well as ADG. Can we please get the board together to discuss it in person?"

"I'm sorry, son, that's not possible this evening. Mikel and Cristo are away on business. They won't be back until late morning tomorrow."

"Can you get them back sooner?" he asked.

"I wish I could, but this meeting is with a huge client."

"Fine," conceded Vic. "What time tomorrow can the board meet?"

"I'll put an urgent meeting on the schedule for one o'clock. I'm sure there'll be questions about what it's regarding."

"Tell them there's a lawsuit coming."

"Okay, kid, I hope you know what you're doing."

"I do, Dad. I'm standing up for our company."

"Okay, see you tomorrow," he said and hung up the phone.

Vic looked up to see three sets of eyes staring back at him.

"How'd he take it?" Paris asked.

"He was hesitant at first, but he understands the urgency, and of course, he's concerned about the company being a part of a lawsuit. I'm sure he'd like more details, but it's best we play him and the rest of the board the recording when they're all together."

"I agree," replied Paris. "What do you think?" She directed her question toward Mya and Chase.

"I think we have to keep Tom and Angela from finding out we know their game before we meet with the board tomorrow," said Chase.

"How so?" asked Paris.

"We don't want them disappearing or causing other issues before the board meets. That means, Paris, you need to get your butt to that date and act like nothing happened," said Chase.

Paris dropped her head into her hands. "How am I supposed to do that?" she moaned. "He'll know something's up." She felt sick to her stomach just thinking about dinner with Tom.

"Make an excuse. Something that will legitimately cover your agitated state," replied Vic.

"Like what?" she asked.

"Tell him your mom informed you your grandmother has fallen ill and is in the hospital. He'll believe that, won't he?"

Paris let out a loud sigh. "I suppose. He doesn't know much about my extended family, so he'll probably buy it."

"Okay then," said Mya. "Are you ready for dinner?" she asked Paris.

"No. I'm not dressed. I'm already late. I don't know how I'll pull this off?"

Mya held up a finger and said, "Hold that thought." She disappeared into her room. When she returned, she was holding a black cocktail dress. "Wear this. He won't even notice you were late."

"Thanks, Mya. You always know how to help."

"Okay, in the meantime, Vic, you keep up appearances with Angela as well. No more blowing her off. If she stops at your place tonight or calls and asks you to go out for a drink, you say yes," advised Chase.

Vic agreed, but hoped Angela wouldn't stop by. The thought of her made his blood boil.

· · · · · · · · · ·

Thirty minutes later Paris found herself seated across the table from Tom. "You look lovely," he said. "Now, do you want to tell me why you were late this evening? You seemed quite shaken on the phone," he added.

Paris was certain that she had sounded as if she were shaking because she was—in anger. "My grandmother has become ill and was admitted to the hospital this afternoon," she begrudgingly told him.

"Oh, that's too bad. Is there anything I can do?" he asked. Paris knew he was simply acting a part. He had no desire to do anything nice for her unless it meant helping himself.

"No, I don't think there's anything to be done," she said.

"This is Burt's ex-wife, correct?"

"Yeah. She's a tough old woman. Hopefully, she'll be fine."

Changing the subject, Tom said, "When I was younger, I volunteered for one of the park cleanups, and Burt was there. He told us stories all afternoon. It made the time fly by. He's a brilliant man. I've often wondered why he works in maintenance?"

"He doesn't need the money," replied Paris. "He likes fixing things, and he enjoys overseeing the cleanliness of ADG."

"Well, he does a fabulous job of it. I can't recall a day when the bathrooms were not in perfect order or that the floor didn't sparkle."

"Let me tell you, he keeps his crew on top of things. I hated working down there because I'm ridiculously clumsy, but I enjoyed being closer to my grandfather."

"I'm sure that was a bonus. Was he at the Gala this year?"

"No, he had a wedding to attend that weekend."

"Ah, that explains why I didn't see him. He loves any event where he can put on a tux, doesn't he?"

"Yes, he does." Nothing could keep her grandfather from showing people his clean-shaven debonaire side. "He needs a woman in his life," she sighed. "He isn't getting any younger."

"What exactly happened to your grandmother?" Tom asked. He sounded interested.

"Can we change the subject? I'm worried enough about my grandmother." Inside, Paris was seething. Her grandmother hadn't been heard from in years. She abandoned her family, but Tom didn't need to know that.

Raising a hand in the air, Paris flagged down the waiter. "Will you please get us a bottle of the house Chianti?" She needed some liquid courage to continue. The waiter disappeared, and Tom prattled on about his own family. Paris nodded and focused on the story as a way to keep herself from dwelling on the sick feeling in her stomach. She never would have guessed he was capable of such insubordination had she not heard the evidence played before her.

Returning to the table, the waiter poured them each a large glass of Chianti and took their orders. Paris tried to maintain a happy persona. Tom watched her every move.

"I've been thinking," said Tom. "Why don't you come over to my place after dinner? We can sit on the patio, drink some wine, and listen to music." Smiling, he reached into his coat pocket and pulled out a box. Handing the box to her, he said, "I saw this the other day and thought of you. It's a little something to show you how much I care."

All the red flags went up at once as she reached out and accepted the box from him. She had no desire to take the gift, but she also knew that not taking it would be suspicious. She pulled away the cover to reveal an ornate emerald necklace. Small white diamonds surrounded each emerald. Jessamine had excellent taste.

"It's breathtaking," she replied. "It must have cost you a fortune."

Tom smiled. "It will look beautiful with your dark hair and green eyes. Here," he said, standing up. "Let me put it on you."

Paris let him proceed. *Thank goodness for that recording*, she thought.

"Astounding," he said. "You look like royalty, my dear." Moving around the table, he took his seat.

"You're much too generous. Thank you," she said with a yawn. "It's been a long day. I hate to do this to you after such a beautiful surprise, but do you mind if I take my food to go? I'm exhausted and not in much of a social mood with my grandmother falling ill."

"I understand. Perhaps we can meet for lunch Monday afternoon instead?" asked Tom.

"Yes, that would be wonderful," replied Paris.

The food arrived, and Paris wasted no time in having the server package it up. She said one last thank you, and was out the door seven minutes later, which was not soon enough for her standards. Walking fast, she wanted to put as much space as possible between herself and Tom. She was glad she had told her driver to stay close.

As she approached the car, her stomach flipped, and her mouth watered. She knew things were about to turn ugly. Jack hopped out of the car and held the door for her. "Where'd you come from?" she asked, but before he could answer, she dropped her food container and ran for the bushes at the edge of the walk. Throwing herself to her knees, she lost the contents of her stomach all over the small patch of grass in front of the restaurant. Jack had run after her and was right there, holding her hair and rubbing her back.

"It's okay, I've got you. You're fine," he assured. When Paris finished, he helped her to her feet and handed her a handkerchief. "I keep it on me for situations like this," he shrugged. Paris let out a nervous laugh and accepted the cloth.

"Thanks," she replied after she'd blotted her face clean. "Do you also carry gum or mouthwash?" she asked.

"Actually, you're in luck," he replied, producing a package of gum from his coat pocket. Opening the pack, he handed her a piece. She took it from him, and unwrapping it, popped it into her mouth. "I'm sure there's some bottled water in the car," he said. "You'll feel a lot better after you've washed the taste out of your mouth."

"I'm sorry for sounding ungrateful, but why are you here?" she asked, as she watched Jack retrieve her leftovers from the sidewalk. Somehow, they managed not to spill.

"Vic called me when you were getting ready for dinner. He told me what happened with Tom and Angela and how you had to follow through with this awful date. I followed you in case you needed backup. Then I sent my driver home and asked the server to notify me if anything improper went down." He handed her the leftovers.

"Wow, Jack, that's going above and beyond," she replied. Paris admired the kid's tenacity, but she hated knowing she had to break his heart.

"I don't like the idea of anyone hurting you. Anyway, let's get out of here," he said, helping her into the car.

Upon settling into their seats, she leaned her head in and rested it on his shoulder. "I know you have feelings for me," she said.

"It's pretty obvious, huh?"

"You know I'm not Alli, right? She's irreplaceable."

"Yeah," said Jack.

"I couldn't be more different from her," she whispered. "I think your feelings for me are your way of holding on to her."

A tear rolled down Jack's cheek. Though Paris couldn't see it, she could feel his hurt. "I miss her like crazy," he replied.

"We all do, but you and I being together would never fix that, and it would never bring her back. You need to let me go. We can't be more than friends," she breathed.

"I know," he replied, "but there's a bigger reason than that for why we can never be more than friends, and I'm okay with it."

"What's that?" she asked as she turned to look at him.

"My brother's in love with you. You might not want to believe it, but it's true. I've never seen him act the way he does in your presence, toward any other woman."

Paris settled back in against Jack's shoulder, and though she said nothing, she squeezed his arm, and spent the rest of the car ride contemplating what he'd said.

When the car stopped, Jack gently nudged Paris, who had fallen asleep. She awoke to find that they had arrived back at ADG.

"Let me walk you to your door," requested Jack. "Are you feeling better?"

"Yeah, I'm okay now," said Paris. "I was so angry. The wine and my heightened state didn't mix well on an empty stomach."

"That's valid," he replied as he got out of the car and reached for her hand. They walked silently to her door. "I'm headed to Vic's. Do you need anything else?" he asked.

"Just for you to be okay with our friendship," she replied. "Oh, wait. There is something else." Reaching up, she removed the necklace Tom had given her. "Give this to your brother, please. He'll know what to do with it."

"Will do," he said. Leaning in, he wrapped her in a tight hug and held on for longer than normal. "I'm happy, Paris. I consider you family, and as long as you're in my life, I feel like part of Alli is still alive and well. Let me know if you need anything. I'll be right up the hall," he said as he turned and walked away.

"Goodnight, Jack!" she called after him. He gave her a brief wave without looking back, and she turned and disappeared into her condo.

Walking into the kitchen, she grabbed her favorite wine glass. All she wanted to do was eat her leftovers and curl up on her settee with a soft, cuddly blanket and her favorite Syrah, but she didn't want to do so alone. The events of the day had put her on edge, and she needed a security blanket to get her through the night. As she finished pouring the wine, her phone rang. It was Mya.

"Hey! I heard your date ended early. Are you okay? Did anything happen?"

"Somehow, I convinced him to let me take my food to go, and that I was not feeling well because of my grandmother's hospitalization," she replied. "But my nerves got the better of me as I was leaving the restaurant. I lost the minimal contents of my stomach in the bushes right outside the door."

"Classy," laughed Mya. "Sorry, I know it was a rough evening for you. I probably would have done the same."

"Will you come over?" Her voice shook. "I don't want to be alone."

"For sure. I'm packing a bag as we speak. Did you eat anything?"

"Not yet. I'll share my takeout with you if you want?"

"Sounds great. I'll bring popcorn and gummy bears."

Paris smiled at Mya's response. "You're the best. See you shortly."

Mya finished packing. She threw a bottle of sparkling wine in her bag, along with the snacks and Paris's favorite movie. She had her own situation to discuss, and she wanted the night to be comforting for both of them.

A few minutes later, Mya gave a quick knock on the outside of Paris's door and proceeded inside. Her friend was curled up on the settee with a full glass of red wine.

"Hey," said Paris with surprise. "That was record fast."

"I expected you'd want me here," she smiled. "Look, what I brought." She held up the movie, *Bottle Shock,* for Paris to see. "I also brought a bottle of sparkling wine. I thought we could celebrate your success."

"Thanks, but aren't we a little premature? We don't know what'll happen over the next week."

"Trust me, you'll be fine. You've made enough changes that the board will put the improvement plan to rest."

"Improvement plan," laughed Paris. "I guess this was an extreme form of an employee improvement plan, huh?"

"Definitely," replied Mya as she grabbed her favorite throw and got comfortable next to Paris on the couch. "There's something I need to tell you." Her voice wavered. "I want you to listen and keep an open mind about what I'm about to say. I have to tell someone, and you're the only person I can imagine who might understand."

Paris looked at her with curiosity. Immediately, her stomach tightened. She hated that reaction, but it was a defense mechanism she'd adopted ever since Alli's death. "Go on."

"Obviously, you've noticed something going on between me and Cristo."

"Yes. I've been quite concerned about you."

"Right, and you know the type of men I go for."

"Of course," replied Paris. She waited for Mya to continue.

"This is difficult for me to explain." She released a deep sigh.

"Girl, just tell me," Paris pressed. "I want to know if I need to go out and kick some ass for you."

"No, Paris, it's not like that at all. I'm safe, but you may not comprehend what's going on, so I'll explain it to the best of my abilities, and then you can ask me whatever questions you feel are relevant."

"Fair enough," she replied.

"So, Cristo's not my type. I've turned him down dozens of times over the years, which you know. He continued to pursue me, but over the past year, things changed. I don't know if it was because of the loneliness of being without you and Alli or if my taste has changed, but I felt something different toward him. While I still continued to turn him down, I entertained the idea of being with him to meet an unfulfilled sexual desire." Mya paused to see if Paris was following. Her friend nodded.

"Roughly six months ago, after one of our corporate schmoozing events, I lost the mental battle I was having with myself regarding the need to feel a human connection. The entire evening, Cristo stayed nearby. He brought me drinks, he danced with me, and he threw every compliment he could think of in my direction. I thought, why not?

"Maybe it was the alcohol, but I felt pretty bold that night. As he walked me to the car at the end of the event, I brushed the inside of his palm, placing a note there. He closed his hand, and I held up one finger to my lips to tell him not to speak. I got into the car, and the driver took me home. At one in the morning, a knock sounded at my door, and I knew exactly who it was."

"What did the note say?" demanded Paris.

Mya turned a light shade of red. "It said: *If you can keep a secret and tell no one of this incident ever, meet me at my place shortly, and I will entertain your desires.*"

"So? What happened?" Paris felt like a teenager waiting for Mya to spit out the details.

"I met him at the door with a glass of Scotch for each of us. I took him by the hand and sat him on my sofa, and then, as if I had turned into some sort of wild animal, I threw myself into his arms, spilling his drink and pressing my mouth to his. He tasted like Scotch and mints, but somehow it was what I was hungering for. With all the energy he'd stored during his pursuit of me, he nearly tore my clothes off. He couldn't wait to touch me, but it wasn't tender by any means. It was rough and dirty. We slammed into walls and fell over a table, breaking the legs. He threw me down on my bed and gave it to me hard. When we were done, I asked him to leave, which I could tell he found confusing. I think he thought I would want to cuddle or talk, but that was against the rules I'd determined in my head."

"So, he left?" Paris was waiting for the other shoe to drop.

"Yes, he left," Mya exhaled.

"Is that all?" asked Paris. There had to be more to the story.

"No. That's just the beginning. He began to text and call me, but I didn't take his messages. He felt frustrated and lost his temper. I didn't want to care, but something was gnawing at me and causing my brain to itch. For three months, I acted as if nothing had happened. I could tell the situation was driving him crazy. If I didn't acknowledge him, it was as if I was telling him he had made it up in his mind. The silence had become maddening."

"I'm sure it was," mused Paris. "So, what happened next?"

"One night, after another event, Cristo left a depressed message on my phone saying my reaction saddened him. He told me he was miserable and worried that he had hurt me. He didn't understand why I was acting like that evening never happened and that he, at the very least, deserved a reason for the turmoil I'd placed upon him."

Paris nodded. "Why'd you do it?"

"I'm getting there," replied Mya. "That night, I showed up at his place. When he opened the door, I told him this would have to be a secret if he wanted more. It would be a game between us, and no one else could be the wiser. I had my reputation to protect, and I didn't want the board snooping around. I also didn't want to allow myself to create anything serious. We were scratching an itch, and he had to agree to my terms, or I would turn around and leave."

Leaning forward, Paris asked, "Did he agree?"

"He more than agreed. This time, after we had ravaged one another, I told him that this couldn't progress into anything more than sex. To keep ourselves even further apart, we adopted different roles, and we played them well. Sometimes I was in charge, and he was my slave. Other times, he was the big bad wolf, and I was the innocent sheep."

"So, basically, you traded roles back and forth regarding who was the dominant and who was the submissive?"

"Yeah. I guess that's one way of putting it. Anyway, we always had a safe word, and until recently, no one ever used it, and we always enjoyed the game no matter how crazy the scenario."

"So, you have a crazy sex game going on with Cristo. Is that all? And who used the safe word?"

"Not entirely," she admitted. Pausing, her face turned red. "I used the safe word to push him away. I think I've fallen in love with him."

"What?" shrieked Paris, "Now, that, I didn't see coming. I always thought you might have a sick and twisted side somewhere within that perfectly composed package of yours, but in love with Cristo? How'd you let that happen?"

"It turns out he appears to be as sick and twisted as me."

"Well, as long as you have your safe word and you respect each other's boundaries, I say, have fun."

"Thanks," replied Mya. "So, what do I do about this? Do I end it with him, or do I pursue something more? How will the board react?"

"I think you do what makes you happy. The board loves you both. If you want to be with him, tell him. Maybe go on an actual date together?"

"But he's not my type, and he's nearly twice my age," complained Mya.

"Who says he's not your type? Maybe your type isn't what you perceived it to be?"

"He's nineteen years older than me, Paris."

"Mya, if you don't want to be with him, then don't, but if you care about him, age doesn't matter. Don't be an ageist," laughed Paris.

"Right, but if he were nineteen years in the other direction, I'd be a pedophile, so I don't know that ageist is a proper term in this type of situation."

"You know I was kidding, and clearly, I do not condone pedophilia," stated Paris. "All I'm saying is that if you care about him and he feels the same, why not try it?"

"What if it really is sex and nothing more?"

"Then your dates will be awkward, and you'll figure it out and move on."

Mya let out another deep sigh. "I guess you're right."

"I know I am, so why don't you shoot that man a message and tell him you need to talk?"

"Tonight?" asked Mya. Paris nodded. "I thought you didn't want to be alone?"

"I don't. He's out of town until tomorrow, remember?"

"Oh, yeah. I forgot about that. I'm a little nervous," replied Mya. "What if it ruins what we have?"

"I shouldn't be one to speak, but don't you know friends with benefits never work? Someone always falls in love. How can you not with the regular intimacy you're sharing?"

"Yeah. I thought I could keep it separate, but I'm quite positive I was wrong."

"Reach out to him!" pushed Paris.

"Fine," replied Mya in resignation. She retrieved her phone out of her purse and began typing up a message which read: *I think we need to talk. I thought I could do this, but something has changed for me. Let me know when you can meet.* When she finished, she pressed send. "Okay, it's done."

"Hey," Paris said as she gave Mya's shoulder a squeeze. "You have nothing to be anxious about. I'm pretty sure he has the same feelings for you."

Mya nodded. "I hope you're right and this isn't a mistake."

"You only live once, girlfriend. Now, what did you do with the movie?"

"It's already in the machine. You need only press play," she pointed out. Hopping up, Mya headed for the kitchen. "I'm heating the leftovers. With all this stress, we both need to eat something before we consume any more wine."

"I'm glad you're here. Don't worry, Mya, things are going to be fine.

Chapter Eighteen

Thursday morning was by far the most awkward morning Vic had experienced in a long time. Angela had made a point of walking into his office multiple times for next to no reason. She reached out and touched him twice. She smiled, laughed, and winked at him. As usual, she wore a low-cut top and short skirt to draw his attention. The display she was putting on repulsed him, but like Paris, he had to keep up appearances. He worried she'd notice he wasn't getting into it. To save himself from further interruptions, he asked her to dinner that evening and told her he needed to head out for a one o'clock meeting. She blew him a kiss and retreated to her desk. As soon as she was out of sight, he locked his office door and headed for the boardroom.

He stopped at Paris's office on the way. "Are you ready for this?" he asked.

"Not particularly, but what choice have we got? We need to make a stand for ourselves and the company, and I would love for nothing more than to see Angela and Tom go down in flames," she replied in a hushed tone.

Vic cocked an eyebrow at her as they headed down the hall. "Sounds like you're a little keyed up."

"Damn straight, I'm keyed up! No human being should ever treat another so cruelly."

"You mean like how you treated Mya?" asked Chase as he joined them.

"Yes. I agree, I treated Mya poorly, but I didn't sleep with Mya to work my way up in the company. I didn't throw myself at you to get an excellent report each week during this hellish ordeal," she stated angrily.

"Chase!" shouted Mya. She had shown up just in time to hear him scolding Paris. "I've forgiven her. What Tom and Angela have done to Vic and Paris isn't even close to the same level as what went on between Paris and me. Paris was hurting, and people often take their pain out on those who are closest to them. I don't need you to stand up for me when it's already done and over with," she said.

"Okay, guys," said Vic. "Let's all take it down a notch. I'm sure we're all feeling a little stressed right now," he said as he stepped into the elevator. The rest of the group followed him. The elevator was silent for the rest of the ride.

Outside the elevator, Paris stopped and turned to Mya. "You have the recording, right?" Mya held up her phone in response. "Great. I figured you did, but like Vic said, I'm a little stressed out right now, and I want this to go smoothly."

"It will," she said and patted Paris on the arm. "You've got this."

The board had already taken their seats when they entered the room. "Good morning," said Vic. He wasted no time getting down to business. "We've called you all here today for an important reason. Over the past weeks, Paris and I have made some major changes in our lives. We've done our best to overcome our grief from the loss of Brody and Alli and to get back to living our lives more purposefully. In the middle of everything we ran into, for lack of a better way to word it, temptations of the flesh."

"Oh, my God, Vic!" blurted Paris. Her face had turned crimson with embarrassment.

"Let him finish, my dear," rebuked her mother.

Vic took a deep breath and continued. "Amid everything, Paris and I became close with our counterparts, Tom and Angela, which hurt us both quite a bit. Mya is going to play a recording for you, and then we can discuss it if there are questions."

Mya pressed play on her phone. She placed it on the table in front of them so they could all hear. No one spoke a word while the recording played. As a matter of fact, no one spoke a word for at least two minutes once it had finished. Everyone appeared to be in shock, and then Nicola stood up. "Will you four please wait outside for a moment while we discuss something?" Silently, they filed out of the room and closed he door behind them.

"What do you suppose that's about?" asked Paris. "Aren't they angry? This isn't the response I expected."

"Me either," replied Mya. "I thought there'd be an angry outcry of rage toward the situation. I never could have dreamt they'd be so quiet and then ask us to wait outside."

"I'm sure they're discussing the details of the situation and what the appropriate response should be," said Chase.

"That's probably it," said Vic. "Who knows what's going on behind the scenes these days?"

Paris fidgeted nervously. "I hate waiting."

Chase paced back and forth. "Tell me about it. I'm too antsy for this sort of suspense."

Vic leaned back against the wall and let his body slide to the floor. "I've seen this before. You may as well get comfortable. This could take a while."

Paris joined him on the floor. "I don't understand. What are they discussing? Do they think we're to blame for this?"

"We did nothing illegal," replied Vic. "I don't see how they could blame us. They're probably discussing the best way to handle Tom and Angela, and they don't want us present while they figure out the legal aspects and what to do about the jobs they currently occupy. Who knows? There could be many factors we're unaware of."

"Like what?" asked Paris.

"The future they want for the company," said Chase.

Paris turned to Mya. "Is that what they're discussing? What do you know?"

"I'm not at liberty to discuss this," she replied. "I'm sorry, Paris. Chase shouldn't have said that."

"Mya! What aren't you telling us?" demanded Paris.

Vic placed his hand on Paris's chin and turned her to face him. "Listen, you need to let her be. She can't help it if the board asked her to maintain confidentiality regarding the company's future. We can wait this out. I'm sure everything will be revealed soon enough."

"Yeah, I suppose you're right, but I didn't think they'd give her and Chase that type of information and leave us in the dark."

Vic shook his head. "Can you blame them? They didn't know if we'd pull our shit together for this company or not."

"I know, but we have," Paris said.

The foursome waited for thirty-five minutes before the door finally opened again. Paris bounced up from the floor and hoisted Vic to his feet.

"You may come back in," said Dom. "Sorry that took so long."

The group filed back into the room and took their seats at the table.

"This whole situation comes as a shock to us," commented Nicola. Shaking her head, she continued, "We're deeply saddened by the realization that two of our own would stoop to such lows to hurt you. As you know, Angela and Tom have been with the company for many years. We're ashamed that such an incident has taken place under ADG's roof."

Pulling at the corner of his mustache, Mikel said, "We debated whether to give you the option to press charges, but in the end, we've decided ADG must move forward with the strictest of action. We can't let word get out that our company would allow such misconduct to go unpunished."

"Furthermore," said Cristo, "we'd like to extend our deepest apologies for what's happened here, and to offer you the next week off with pay, so that you may process. That said, take as much time as needed to deal with this terrible ordeal."

"We're also offering counseling to help you sort through the emotional strain Tom and Angela have put you through," added Jessamine. "I strongly suggest you explore how this may have affected you and your peer relationships."

"Thank you," replied Paris. "I think I speak for us both when I say the extra time won't be necessary." She turned to look at Vic, who nodded in response. "But we will take you up on the counseling, as we're both learning that it's better to get our feelings out, rather than to hold them in."

Turning her attention to the board, Jessamine's face contorted into a frown and she said, "On a similar subject, ADG has never had a rule that its employees couldn't date since two sets of couples formed the company. Do we need to explore this concept more thoroughly and create strict boundaries regarding deterring future misconduct within our company?"

"No," replied Cristo. "I don't think it's necessary. This is an isolated incident, and it's so heinous that I can't imagine it would ever happen again within company walls."

"Hold on," said Dom. "Maybe it's not a bad idea to set some boundaries to protect employee relationships. Our company is all about people and their lives. Living and loving. I think it makes sense to discuss things further at a later date."

"Agreed," said Nikola. "We'll table it until our next board meeting."

Turning back to the foursome, Dom said, "Thank you all for bringing the situation with Angela and Tom to our attention. We want you to know that we stand behind you one hundred percent. Regarding your positions within the company, we intend to give you further information at our meeting next Monday. Until then, please take care of yourselves, and reach out if you need to discuss anything further."

Getting up from his chair, Vic said, "Thank you." His friends nodded and followed him out of the room.

The door had barely closed behind them, and Chase let out a silent scream. "Does anyone else feel like they're about to freak out?" he asked.

"A little," said Mya. "I'm glad that's over."

"I can't even think about it. I'm still upset," said Paris. "I need to head back to my office to grab some files, but I wouldn't mind seeing Tom and Angela escorted from the building."

"Me too," replied Vic. He grinned like a jackal. He couldn't wait to see them ousted.

"I have another meeting up the hall," added Mya. "I'll catch up with you all later."

"I'm going to sort through some things in my office," said Chase. "Whoever wants to may come to my place this evening for a drink. We can let off some steam. Maybe discuss the future."

"Count me in," replied Paris.

"Yeah, me too," said Vic, but the tone in his voice wavered.

"And me!" called Mya as she wandered off toward her next meeting. "I'll be there!"

······

Mya was happy to be out of the boardroom but nervous for her next appointment, especially with Jessamine's mention about dating within the company. Breezing into the room, she came to an abrupt halt when she saw Cristo already seated at the conference room table.

"Come on in," he said. "You may shut the door behind you." His tone was all business.

Mya turned and closed the door. Stepping forward, she approached the table. She didn't want to sit. "I don't know if I can do this," she said, her voice squeaking.

"Do what?" asked Cristo. "End this? Walk away? Call it quits and move on?" He couldn't stop himself from putting words into her mouth. He feared what would come next. Normally, he was a strong and confident man, but today he was at her mercy. She was his only weakness.

"Stop! You need to listen."

"I don't want to listen if you're going to end what we have. I enjoy those moments with you, crazy as they are."

"That's the thing. So do I. I enjoy them very much, and that's why I'm afraid to say what I must, but the words are stuck."

"Tell me. What do you want?" Mya looked as if she might burst into tears at any moment. Cristo's heart felt like it might break. It took everything in him to sit there and wait for what was coming next. He didn't do waiting very well. He was a hot-blooded and impatient man.

"I—" she took a deep gulp of air. "I want more!" she blurted. "I need more than this."

"What?" Cristo was dumbfounded. He'd never expected her to say she wanted more. Every word out of her mouth regarding their situation had been about boundaries and not getting close. It was only sex. He stared at her in disbelief. Did she really say she wanted more?

"Say something," she prodded. "Anything."

"I'm speechless," he replied, then continued to stare at her for a moment. "You want more? What does that mean in Mya language?"

"It means that I'm falling for you. I never planned for this or wanted it. Lord knows you are not my usual type, but I want more. I want to go on dates and to cuddle and talk after sex. I want to hold your hand and experience life as a couple. I don't want to hide from your family. Cristo, I'm falling in love with you, and I need more."

"Wow, Mya. Are you sure?" It took every ounce of energy he had to contain himself and not burst from the excitement he felt.

"Of course, I'm sure! I've been battling it out in my mind for weeks. I finally told Paris last night. She said I needed to see this conversation through, so here I am. I'm telling you I love you, Cristo. I don't care about the games. I just want us to be together in whatever way possible."

"God, Mya, I've waited forever to hear you say those words. I never thought I'd see the day. I love you too," he replied. "Now get over here!".

Mya leaped up onto the table and crawled into his arms. He pulled her close and pressed his lips to hers. She kissed him back with the hunger of a thousand lifetimes.

"You have made me so happy," said Cristo.

"You don't know how much that pleases me," replied Mya.

"So, what's next?"

"Take me to dinner tonight? I want to get to know your interests outside of work and in the bedroom."

"It would be my pleasure," said Cristo as he squeezed her tight.

· · · · ·•·•· · · ·

Back at Paris's office, Vic and Paris waited impatiently, peering through the office window. Security hadn't shown up yet. They'd closed themselves in her office under the guise that they were in a meeting and wished not to be disturbed. Neither wanted to be approached by Angela or Tom.

"How long do you think this will take?" asked Vic. He paced the floor as they waited.

"It's been half an hour. I thought for sure they'd deal with the situation right away."

A knock sounded at the door, and they both jumped.

"Who do you think it is?" asked Vic.

"I don't know. More importantly, how did we miss someone approaching the door? What if it's one of them?"

"It's not," stated Vic. "It can't be. They'd have both passed by the windows to get to your door. Just answer it."

"Why don't you answer it?" she hissed.

"Because it's not my office, so whoever it is, is most likely here for you," he said.

"I suppose you've got me on that one," she replied. Grabbing the door handle, she cracked it open. Both Mya and Chase were waiting outside. "You two scared us half to death. Get in here before anyone else comes along." She grabbed Mya's wrist and pulled her inside.

"Geez, paranoid much?" asked Chase as he trailed behind her. "You don't need to hide. They're screwed either way.

"I don't want to create a scene," replied Paris.

"Those two are so wrapped up in themselves that they probably wouldn't even notice you're acting differently," said Chase.

Vic nodded in agreement. "He has a point. Perhaps we're being paranoid? They have no idea what's coming. Even if they knew, who cares? They deserve what they get."

"Amen to that!" Mya agreed.

The group sat and watched for another twenty minutes, and then it happened. Mikel and Dom marched past Paris's office with four security guards in tow. Their stonelike faces staring ahead as they walked. What Paris wouldn't give to be a fly on the wall of Tom's office when he was told his services would no longer be needed at Sense of Adventure. She wished she could give him a nice kick to the yarbles as well for the emotional pain and suffering he'd caused her. At some point, she knew this story would spread like wildfire. She didn't know if ADG could contain the situation or not.

"Well, shall we stay in here or go out and catch the show?" asked Chase, with a grin.

"Do we really want to witness this?" asked Mya.

"I think this is their shot to stand up for themselves and see this thing through to the end," replied Chase. "If you have something to say, now's your chance. Within reason, of course."

"Let's do it," said Vic. "Let's show them they can't hurt us. We're standing our ground."

"Okay," said Paris with hesitation in her voice. "If you think it won't make things worse."

"Don't say anything inflammatory, and you should be fine," said Chase.

Vic reached out and grabbed Paris's hand. "What do you say? I'll be right there beside you. We don't have to say anything if we don't want to."

"Okay," she said, "Let's do this." She pulled her hand out of Vic's and marched over to the door. Throwing it open, she proceeded into the hall, followed by the rest of the group. Angela and Tom were in a nearby meeting room with Mikel and his entourage. The door was closed, and she couldn't hear anything. "Let's take a seat in the common area and wait."

"Sounds good," replied Vic. They sat down at the closest table. "I wonder what he's saying to them?" Mikel's face was red, and he made several hand gestures as he spoke. Now and then, he'd look at Dom, and Dom would chip in with a few of his own words. At one point, Vic saw his father slam his fist down on the table. Angela and Tom sat on the opposite side, and both of them jumped. Mikel reached out and put a calming hand on Dom's shoulder, and Dom stepped back from the table.

"I don't think I've ever seen them so mad," said Mya.

"I'm not surprised," replied Chase. "Two of their top employees have done unspeakable things to not only their other employees but their children. This is personal for them on several levels."

Vic winced at Chase's statement. He hated being considered a victim and didn't want anyone's pity. He'd allowed himself to be played by Angela. Vic felt he should've been more vigilant. How stupid he was for falling for her bait. At the same time, he never intended for their relationship to be anything but sexual, though he preferred not to sleep with the enemy.

"Paris, are you okay?" asked Mya. Paris had a tear running down her cheek.

"I feel like an idiot. How could we have been so stupid?" she asked Vic.

"We were vulnerable, and they hit at the most opportune time. It is what it is," he replied. "Now we have to move beyond it and grow stronger, okay? You can do this," he encouraged. "You're tough, and you will not let this break you, right? Get mad. This is a point when anger is warranted."

"He's right," added Chase. "You should be pissed. Don't feel sorry for yourself. Feel angry toward them for taking advantage of your genuine feelings. No one deserves to be treated that way."

"You're right!" said Paris, jumping up from her seat and stomping her heel. "This is not my fault. They took advantage of me! I will not be the victim. I'm going to march up to them and tell them they deserve what they get and that I will see this trial through to the end to make sure they never hurt anyone again."

Paris had no more than made her statement when the door to the office opened, and Angela and Tom emerged flanked by security. Paris stepped forward, confronting them both.

"You thought you were clever, didn't you? I hope it was worth it. I'll see you in court. I guarantee you won't be getting a slap on the wrist, and I won't lose any sleep over you."

"I'm backing her one-hundred percent," added Vic. "What you did was despicable. When we're through with you, it'll be tough to find a job anywhere."

Angela had tears streaming down her face when she replied, "It was all his idea. He came up with the plan. I wanted nothing to do with it, but he pushed and pushed, and I gave in. It was all him!"

"Oh, well then, perhaps you should be pardoned? I mean, obviously, if Tom put you in that position, we can hardly blame you for it, right?" asked Chase. "He did put a gun to your head and force you to have unbridled sex with Vic in his office, correct?" Chase laughed. "No one forced you, honey. You did this to yourself. You make me sick. Playing with any-one's emotions simply to climb the corporate ladder is com-pletely twisted, and such indiscretions deserve the maximum punishment."

"Amen to that," said Mya. "Angela, you'll get what you deserve, as will Tom."

"This is bullshit!" expelled Tom. "There's no law against sleeping with people without having genuine feelings."

"No, there's not," stated Mikel, "but you signed your name on the line and broke your contract with Sense of Adventure when you manipulated your coworkers for corporate gain. Not to mention the other charges, which will come with re-playing the recording of what you intended to do to Paris and Vic. That's definitely illegal."

"Wow, you two are royally screwed," said Chase. "Good luck with that."

Mikel looked at Paris and Vic. "I think we've all said enough at this point." Turning to security, he said, "Please escort Tom and Angela off the property. As of now, they are no longer allowed access to anything on ADG grounds, including their apartments. We'll forward your belongings to a location of your choice tomorrow. You'll be hearing from our lawyers."

Mikel and Dom followed the guards to the elevator, then headed back to their offices. Vic and Paris watched them go. Paris felt a wave of relief but also a bit of panic, knowing they'd have to testify about what happened to them, and how much they'd be judged for it. She still felt stupid for allowing herself to let her guard down enough to believe that Tom had suddenly taken an interest in her.

"I can see the wheels in your head spinning," said Mya. She gently put her hand on Paris's shoulder. "You can't beat yourself up over this. You carried a torch for the man for years. Had I been in your situation, I would have done the same thing. Most anyone would have. He played your heartstrings. It was wrong, and he knew it was wrong. The only thing left to do is to work on healing. I'm here for you if you need to talk." She gave Paris a gentle smile. "You're okay. Like Vic said, you'll get past this."

"Thanks, Mya," she replied.

"Let's get out of here," said Vic. "I want to go home and forget this day ever happened."

"Yeah, me too," said Paris. "Chase, we'll see you at your place this evening for that drink."

"Okay, guys, take it easy," he smiled. "Later, we can toast to a brighter future."

"I hear you on that," said Vic.

·· • • 0· 0 • • ··

Late in the evening, Paris and Mya walked together over to Chase's apartment for the drink they'd agreed upon. The mood was much lighter than the past twenty-four hours. Paris felt as if a weight had lifted, and she could let her guard down some. Mya chattered away about the recent developments between her and Cristo. Paris was happy for her friend. She would have never guessed that genuine feelings would develop between them, but as long as they were happy, she was happy.

"I'm glad you two worked out your issues. How was your dinner date?"

"Awesome!" gushed Mya. "It was nice to get dressed up and go out in public without the guise of a business-related event. We have more in common than I could have imagined. I'm going over to his place after Chase's."

"That's great. I truly am happy for you."

"Thanks," she replied

When they arrived at Chase's, Paris was surprised to find that Vic was not there. Mya wasted no time in demanding to know where he was.

"He's not coming," said Chase. "He said he was tired and wanted to get a good night's sleep. Something about an interview."

"What interview?" asked Paris.

"I don't know," replied Chase. "He didn't elaborate."

"Is he leaving Sense of Adventure?" asked Paris.

Chase shook his head. "He hasn't told me a thing."

"You need to talk to him," said Mya. "Make sure he's not leaving because you're too stubborn to work through your issues."

"Me? I'm the stubborn one?" asked Paris.

"Yeah," said Chase. "He keeps trying to talk to you, and you keep shutting down."

"You should go over there and talk to him right now," said Mya. "Before it's too late."

"Fine," huffed Paris. "I'll call him in a bit. Now, where's that damn drink we came here for?"

CHAPTER NINETEEN

Monday morning, Mya rolled out of bed and headed for her closet, only to realize she wasn't in her apartment. The grogginess was still hanging over her when she heard Cristo stirring from his side of the bed.

"Morning," he said sleepily. "You're up early. What is it, five?"

Mya turned around and rubbed her eyes to try to adjust to the dim light. "I slept so well I forgot where I was," she replied.

Cristo propped himself up on one elbow so he could get a better look at her. "Is that good or bad?" He hoped it was good. It should mean she felt comfortable, but this whole sleepover thing was new to them both. He was still in shock that she wanted more, and he found himself silently praying that she wouldn't change her mind. Mya was an angel among humankind, and he never thought she'd choose him, but then again, he never thought he'd fall for someone so much younger than he. "Are you okay?" Mya hadn't responded, and the pause was beginning to fill his empty stomach with knots.

"Oh, I'm sorry," she said. "It's a good thing, I think. I feel safe with you." She smiled, then, walking over to the bed, she leaned in and planted a kiss on his lips. "I'm anxious to start this day. I need to know that Vic and Paris are going to be restored to their former glory. I can't take much more of this crazy rollercoaster ride."

"You know they'll be fine. Obviously, it comes down to what Mikel and Dom decide, but we all put in our two-cents."

"We should get moving. I could definitely use some food, and by the sound of your stomach, so could you." Cristo's stomach had been growling throughout their entire conversation.

"Yeah, I think you burnt up all my fuel last night." Winking, he said, "I'm open to another round if you like?"

"As wonderful as that sounds, I don't think I have the focus at this time. Let's allow the desire to build a little. Get your lazy butt out of bed. We need food, now!"

"Okay, okay." Cristo rolled out of bed and wandered to his closet, where he pulled on the first clean suit he found. Mya helped him put on his tie, though he didn't actually require any assistance. After, she wandered to the bathroom to freshen herself up and dress. She was surprised at how great it felt waking up in his bed. It felt as if she belonged there next to him. "I'm gonna grab a coffee and some toast to go," said Cristo. "With today's meeting, I should probably arrive early to discuss the final details with the rest of the board. You're welcome to stay here until you need to head over." He grabbed her hand and kissed it lightly. "This place feels more like a home with you in it."

•••••••••••

When Cristo arrived at the boardroom, Mikel was already there, staring out the window as he often did. "Hey, Mikel. How's it going?" he asked. The other board members filed in behind him.

Mikel turned toward Cristo with a contemplative look on his face. Shaking his head, he said, "For the life of me, I don't know how things got so out of control?"

"We own one of the largest companies in Nevada and we suffered a catastrophic loss that thoroughly shook our families. You need to give yourself a break," said Cristo.

Narrowing his eyes, Mikel said, "But how'd we miss the situation with Tom and Angela? How could we not realize our own children were being used?"

Nikola walked over to Mikel and hugged him. Pulling away, she looked into his eyes and said, "It makes me sick, too. Thankfully, Molly was in the right place at the right time, or this could have been much worse. When you've worked with people for as long as we have with Angela and Tom, you don't see the knife until it's being pulled from your back."

Jessamine took a seat at the table, tears flowing from her eyes. "I feel like a terrible mother," she sobbed. "Our children have been emotionally assaulted. We punished them instead of protecting them."

"Darling, you're a wonderful mother, but none of us saw this coming. We're human," said Dom, as he ran his fingers through his goatee.

Closing the distance between herself and Jessamine, Nicola placed a hand on her friend's shoulder. "Look at me," she said softly. Her voice full of compassion. "Our children needed tough love. It took a strong action to pull them out of the terrible grief they've been drowning in. Paris overdosed. They were both arrested. If we'd done nothing, they could have ended up doing serious time, or worse, dead." Grabbing a tissue, she handed it to Jessamine. "Dry your eyes, darling. Our children are alive, well, and thriving. Our family is finally beginning to feel whole again." She smiled.

Jessamine nodded. Moving on, she said, "It's getting late. We should probably take our seats."

"Okay," said Mikel, "Let's get down to business and discuss the future of ADG."

· · · · • · • · · · ·

Reaching for her phone, Paris let out a sigh as she dialed Vic's number. She'd been calling him all weekend, but he refused to pick up the phone. This time, it rang once and went to voicemail. He'd rejected her call, yet again. A tear ran down her cheek. What was wrong with her? Why didn't she talk to him when she had the chance?

She was lying upside-down with her feet propped up on top of her settee, passing time before her meeting, when she heard a knock at the door. The blood slowly flowed into her head. Part of her hoped she'd pass out and forget anything had ever happened between herself and Vic, but she knew that scenario would never see fruition. The knock sounded again, and Paris flipped herself around, nearly toppling over from the head-rush. "Just a second," she called out as she knocked into her coffee table.

Paris swung the door open to find Jack standing on the other side with Mya and Chase. Jack was holding a large bouquet of wildflowers, and Mya had a balloon that said 'Good Luck!' in large, brightly colored scrolling letters. "Wow," she said. "For me?"

"Of course, silly!" Mya handed Paris the balloon, and Jack and Chase followed her into the condo. "We couldn't let you go into that meeting without a positive sendoff," she replied excitedly.

"Do you have a vase for these?" asked Jack, as he waved the flowers in the air.

"Check under the kitchen sink," replied Paris, "and thank you. They're beautiful."

"Here," said Chase, "I brought you your favorite Syrah for later this evening." He handed the bottle to her, and she couldn't help but wrap him in a hug—something she'd never done before. Chase was taken by surprise but hugged her tightly in return.

"I have you all to thank for the support and for pushing me to be better. I couldn't have made changes without you. Honestly, looking back at how I acted, I don't blame the board for putting this plan into action. It made me realize how valuable my life really is and that I want to be surrounded by my friends and family.

"Where's Vic?" asked Chase. "I thought he might be here with you."

"Your guess is as good as mine," said Paris. "He isn't picking up my calls."

"He's embarrassed by what happened, and he feels like you rejected him. He needs a little time," said Jack. "I know my brother. He'll come around."

"I can try talking to him if you like?" added Chase. "He usually listens to me."

"Wow, man, my brother actually listens to someone? I thought he just pushed through the pain and buried it as deeply as possible."

"Nah, he's come a long way since his fall from grace," replied Chase. "We've gotten to be pretty close. I would go as far as to say we're *besties*," he said with a grin.

Jack raised an eyebrow. "I thought it seemed you two were hanging out quite a bit, but I wasn't sure if it was business or pleasure."

Chase smiled. "I enjoy his company, and we have similar interests. I'm as surprised as you are that this turned into a friendship. He was a bit of a jerk at first."

Jack nodded. "Like I said, bury the pain, which then comes out as anger and jerk behavior."

"True, that," added Mya. She turned to give Paris a pointed look.

"I know, I know," replied Paris. "I was a jerk."

Mya grabbed Paris's arm and hugged it. "But you're my B.F.F. again, so it doesn't matter anymore!"

"Okay, enough mushy stuff," said Paris. "Shall we get down to business?"

"Yeah," said Chase, "I think we should head out. Hopefully Vic's meeting us at the boardroom."

Paris's knees wobbled as she left her condo. She'd done everything the board asked of her, within her power. She couldn't help that Tom had deceived her. On the other side of her mind sat Vic. What was happening with him? Did he plan to stay with Sense of Adventure? Why was he avoiding her? The questions flowed through her mind like a never-ending river.

•••••••••••

Vic was already seated inside the boardroom, along with Cristo, his parents, and Paris's parents. He quietly watched the secondhand tick by as he awaited the arrival of Paris, Mya, and Chase.

Arriving at the boardroom, Jack turned to Paris, "This is where I leave you. I'll be at your condo tonight to celebrate. Good luck in there, though I don't think you'll need it," he said, giving her a quick hug.

"Thanks, Jack," she replied. Turning away, she stepped into the room, followed by Mya and Chase. She breathed a sigh of relief when she saw Vic at the table, but then her emotions took over and she had to look away. Thankfully, Mya and Chase sat in the chairs flanking Vic.

"Good morning," said Nicola, a smile on her face. "I see you're all here early. I like that. How's everyone feeling after the long weekend?"

"Wonderful," replied Vic. "How are you?"

"I'm glad we're coming to the end of this rehabilitative road you've been traveling over the past couple of months," she said. "I think Jessamine and I agree; this has been difficult for us as well. No one likes to see their children suffer."

Paris looked at her mother. "This hasn't been easy. I've spent a lot of time feeling angry at the board, angry at Mya, and frankly, hating myself. The day Alli died, we fought. I wasn't supportive of her and we didn't get a chance to makeup. When she died, I blamed myself."

"Sweetheart," said her mother. "Alli's death wasn't your fault."

Sniffling, Paris said, "I know, but it was hard to see that. I didn't think I deserved to be here when she wasn't. I never had a pill addiction, but there was a point when I wanted my life to end. I couldn't see the other side. Everything felt too heavy to carry, so I numbed the pain with the idea that maybe one day it would be over. I'd take one too many pills and never wake up. The day that happened, you all stepped in and brought me back."

Gasping, Nicola shook her head. "I wish you would have talked to us. We could have gotten you help."

"That's just it," said Paris. "I couldn't find the words to ask for help. I didn't think I deserved it." Pausing, she sniffled and wiped away her tears. "When you and the board forced us to start over, you saved my life." Unable to hold back, a loud sob escaped her throat. Mya leaned over and wrapped her in a hug. Breathing in through the watery snobbery mess, she said, "I wouldn't be here if you hadn't stepped in." Turning to Mya, she said, "that accident you and Chase were in, made me realize I want to be here. I want to be a part of this family, and I want to help Alli's legacy live on."

Walking over to her, Mikel bent down and wrapped his daughter in a hug. "I'm so glad to hear you say that. You mean the world to us, Paris. We love you more than you'll ever know."

On the other side of Mya, Vic wiped a tear from his cheek. "This whole experience has been eye-opening. I owe you all an apology for my terrible behavior. Some of you may not know this, but I've been seeing a therapist. He's helped me to find better outlets for my anger. I've also found a new friend in Chase." Turning toward Chase, he said, "You've been a blessing, man. Thanks for pushing me in the right direction."

Chase smiled back at Vic. "Anytime, brother."

"Well, hopefully not any time," said Vic. "I really don't want to go through this again," he said with a grin.

Chase rolled his eyes, but smiled. "Your timing is terrible."

"Yup. That's my son," said Dom, shaking his head. "Anyway, we're proud of the changes you've both made, which is why we've decided to permanently reinstate you to your original positions within the company."

Paris's whole body relaxed as she exhaled. "Thank you," she said. "You won't regret it."

"We're certain we won't," said Nikola, with a wink.

Straightening in her seat, Jessamine said, "With the removal of Angela and Tom, there will be two senior positions open at Sense of Adventure, and we feel it's only right to offer them to you, Mya and Chase. You don't have to decide right now, but we hope you'll say yes. The clients love you, and you've shown great strength over the past several months. Your addition will create a well-rounded team."

"Oh, My God," said Chase. "There's nothing to think about. I accept!"

"Me too!" replied Mya. "I always wanted to be an event planner," she said with a grin.

"Congratulations," said Paris. "This is great news!"

"Wonderful!" said Dom. "I think I speak for all of us here when I say we're pleased to have you as our newest planners."

Vic's eyes dropped to the table. "I have something I need to say." The room grew quiet as everyone's attention shifted to him. "After the alarm clock situation, I wasn't sure I'd be able to succeed in climbing out of the hole I'd dug. I started to look into other options and found out Le Hexagon is looking for a new Chef, so I put in an application. Last Friday I had an interview, and I've been offered the job."

Dom's eyes widened in surprise. "Did you take it?" he asked.

"I haven't decided," said Vic. "Living on a smaller budget forced me to rely more on my cooking skills. I'd forgotten how much I enjoy it. I have until Wednesday to let them know my decision."

"My dear," said Jessamine. "We love you, and we want you to be happy. If taking a new position as a Chef brings you joy, then you should do so, but know we will be sad to see you go."

Mikel pursed his lips and let out a low whistle. "This is un-expected, but whatever you decide, you'll always have a place within ADG."

"Thanks," said Vic. "I'll let you know as soon as I make a decision."

"That particular bit of information makes this next part a bit harder," said Dom.

Walking over to the dry erase board, Mikel wrote a single word in the center.

"Retirement?" asked Vic.

"Retirement," echoed Dom. "That's the word of the day."

"Please explain," requested Vic.

Mikel took the lead. "Well, kid, for the past couple of years, your father and I have been looking into the future of the company. We've discussed what else we want to achieve and where else we feel we should go. We've held the reins on ADG for many years now and, while we love our company, we've decided that we'd like to take a step back. We're retiring as CEO and COO of ADG, and we'd like the positions to be filled by you and Paris."

"This won't happen overnight," said Dom. "We're planning to retire in three years, which gives us plenty of time to transition.

Paris's jaw dropped when she realized what her father had said. She'd never imagined heading up ADG so soon. "What will you do with all your free time?" she asked.

"Well, sweetheart," replied Mikel, "I plan to work at one of our restaurants, and Dom plans to take one of your positions and go back to adventure planning for a while. We want young blood to lead ADG into an even brighter future, and while we won't be heading up the company any longer, we'll still be here to help you out when you need guidance."

"What do you think about that?" asked Dom.

"Wow," replied Vic. "I don't know what to say?"

Dom smiled warmly at his son. "Say you'll consider the job."

"I will," said Vic.

"Good. That's all I need to know at this time," said his father. "We'll table the rest of this discussion until after you've made your decision."

"Before we end this meeting, Vic and Paris, we've reinstated your trust funds," said Cristo. "And seeing as you've accepted the promotion, Mya and Chase, you'll be receiving company cars as well as a monthly living expense fund."

"After all we've been through together, you're a part of the family," said Jessamine. "We'll all be working closely together to design and execute the future plans of ADG."

Looking at the board, Chase said, "Thank you! I won't let you down."

"Now, if there are no questions, we can adjourn this meeting. We'll sign paperwork for the new positions next Monday," said Cristo. "Have a wonderful week."

The meeting ended, and the board exited the room. Paris was still in shock, as was Vic. She was about to say something to him when he got up from his chair and headed for the door. She wanted to call after him, but the words wouldn't come out. There was a slight twinge of pain in her chest as she watched him walk away.

"Hey," said Mya, "Go after him."

"I can't," replied Paris. "I just can't. He doesn't want to speak to me."

"Girl, you'd better step up, or he's gonna walk right out of your life," said Chase.

"I hear you both, but how am I supposed to talk to him when he won't look at me or take my calls?"

"Paris, if you let this go, you'll regret it," added Chase. "Run."

Nodding, Paris ran down the hall toward the elevators. "Vic! Wait!" When she turned the corner, no one was there and neither elevator had left the twelfth floor.

·· • • • • • • • • ··

The rest of the day was a blur of emotions for Paris. She'd cried, she'd laughed, she'd maniacally cleaned her office. She was doing anything she could to keep her mind from wandering to Vic, who was nowhere to be found.

At six-o-clock Paris began her trek home. The office was nearly empty, and she was happy to be alone. She wondered what Vic was up to and whether or not he was home. She thought back to the days spent living in the same apartment and then allowed her mind to wander to the night at the cabin when they first slept together, and then the night in their apartment when they once again lowered their walls and let one another in.

Could he be capable of more? No one had ever kissed her with such passion and desire. She'd never felt so at ease around another man, and she'd never caught herself thinking about someone as much as she did Vic. Jack said Vic loved her.

The walk back to her home was short, but it was enough time for Paris to roll everything from the past few months, and even years, around in her head. No matter how she stacked it, the positive aspects of being with Vic outweighed the negative. In reality, she didn't know if the negative even had legs for which to stand. She wanted him terribly, and by the time she reached the door to her condo, she'd made up her mind that if he'd have her, she was all in.

Picking up the phone, Paris dialed Vic's number. "Please don't let it go to voicemail," she said out loud, just before his voicemail clicked on. Sighing, she left him a frazzled message. "Vic, it's Paris. I need to talk to you, please. I'd prefer to speak in person, but you've been avoiding me and ignoring my calls. I'm sorry I judged you so harshly. Forgive me?" She paused for a moment and let out a sigh. "For what it's worth, I miss you, and I don't want you to leave the company."

Twenty minutes passed, and then a knock sounded at the door. Paris was sprawled out on the floor to her condo, ugly crying. The knock made her jump, as she hadn't been expecting it.

"Paris!" yelled Vic. "Are you in there?"

She was surprised that he hadn't heard the horrific caterwauling emitting from the condo. Wiping her face, she pushed herself off the floor and trudged over to the door. When she opened it, the look on Vic's face sobered and turned to concern.

"Paris, what's happening? Are you okay?" he asked.

Men, she thought to herself. How did he not know this was about him? "I'm fine," she sniffed.

"No, you're not," Vic replied adamantly. "Tell me, what's going on?"

"It's you. It's always you!" shrieked Paris as she burst into yet another round of tears.

"Oh, sweetie," he replied. Reaching out, he grabbed her shoulders and pulled her into a hug. "I'm here," he said softly as he buried his face in her silky black hair. "I'm right here."

"I know," she wailed, "but what does that mean?"

"It means," he replied deliberately, "that I'm here. I've decided to stay at ADG, and I want to give commitment a real go."

Pulling back from him, she wiped her nose and looked into his eyes. "You really mean that?"

"Yes, Paris, more than anything. I've never wanted to be with someone so badly in all my life. I've missed you too." Leaning in, he brushed back her damp hair and pressed his lips to hers. All his worries disappeared and were replaced by a comforting warmth. Kissing her felt right. Pulling away, he looked her over. She was smiling back at him in a slightly bashful way. "So, why don't we go inside and start working on being a couple?" As she looked back at him, she felt safe and she could once again see the possibilities of her future.

"I like that idea very much," she replied as she led him into her condo, pulling the door shut behind them.

Acknowledgements

This book has been in the works for five years. Thank you to my family and friends for your patience. Thank you to my wonderful beta readers for your great comments and suggestions. I appreciate all your hard work.

A special thanks to my editor, Kate Seger, who put up with my many edits, questions, and curiosities during the process of finalizing this story. Thank you. Thank you. Thank you. I never would have finished this book without your help. I probably owe you a giant plush spider.

T.K. Ambers lives in Wisconsin with her husband and two cats, Bellatrix and Kit. Her perfect day would be spent lakeside, where she would swim, play games, and then wind down with a bonfire, s'mores, and stories told by family and friends.

www.facebook.com/HappilyWriting
https://tkambers.wixsite.com/author
www.instagram.com/tk_loves_books

Always remember, the best gift you can give an author
is an honest review on Amazon.com and/or Goodreads.com.